British Story
A Romance

Michael Nath

route

First published by Route in 2014
PO Box 167, Pontefract, WF8 4WW
info@route-online.com
www.route-online.com

ISBN : 978-1901927-60-3

1st Edition

Michael Nath asserts his moral right to be
identified as the author of this book

Typeset in Bembo by Route

Printed and bound by CPI Group (UK) Ltd, Croydon, CR0 4YY

Contents

Part I: Kennedy

Part II: Arthur Mountain

Part III: Natalie's Tale

Part IV: Secretarial Version

Part V: To the Wars

To Sarah and my mother

I must succeed in giving up these ways, these awful fantasies.
[Dafydd ap Gwilym]

'Nay, sure, he's not in hell: he's in Arthur's bosom, if ever man went to Arthur's bosom.'
[Shakespeare]

'Who do you want to be?'
'A sorcerer. But I'll settle for an academic.'
[Alisdair Gray]

Part I: Kennedy

1. All the way to Essex.

Stories are cardinal. Life can't really do without them. On this we're generally agreed at the moment; which is sweet, so long as you can tell one …

Barbara appeared in the passage. Boo! Greenish light fell through the end door.

Kennedy attempted a double take. In grey sports jacket, he was making to leave.

'You're very smart, *cariño!*' Barbara called. 'Is that wine chilled?'

Shoving the Graves in a carrier bag, Kennedy said it was. The book he was trying to read was heavy for the plastic, so he slid that in his oxter like he was on the way to the khazi. In truth, the wine wasn't chilled at all.

Footballers were shouting in Ford Park; in filament shorts with orange trim, a young woman practised kick-boxing. They said you could tell the man from his shoes. Kennedy's were not the shoes of a kick-boxing man. Her foot whacked the pad like a drum machine. From Salon Shay a couple glimmered at him. Barbara texted not to forget flowers.

On the tube, he opened his book. A green Travelcard marked the page, journey forgotten, edge adorned with yellow triangles. Rolling a joint, a pale youth checked him. He read the page again. Given his profession, slow reading was a weakness, and Kennedy didn't conceal it from himself. Almost anything distracted him … Like, hey-pass! The youth was now a gent with flowers. Some people could read a hard book a day, and say something smart about it. He hauled himself to the next page, words waiting for him as at an open door. The gent with flowers opened the paper: *British fertility clinics near bottom of IVF league. Seventeenth out of twenty-three.* Obviously nothing to cheer about, if you were hankering for kids. Belgium was number one. Sod all else to do. Kennedy went back to his own reading.

At Liverpool Street he bought roses from a lady who called him geezer. Honoured. The info board was a splendid sight: places of his youth in gold on black. Two cops watched from on high.

*

Twice a year, kid Kennedy and his old man did Colchester Fair. On the Speedway or Cosmic 555, he wondered how such fun could be allowed. The men who took the money moved like sailors; on the PA, Mary Wells, Atomic Rooster, Blackfoot Sue.

As a youth, he went with mates. You had to try the Satellite. In the queue someone called it the Deathride. 'Blockbuster' was playing. As they took off to the siren, Kennedy felt cool. Harnessed, they spun like heroes, onions, oil, hot sugar in the snitch. The ride began its tilt to 90 degrees. Zoetropic trucks and lights passed the eyes.

Excitement changed. Someone spat their ring. His neck was breaking with the G's. Wasn't meant to go this fast. Whose hand was on the lever? Not meant to cripple you. Would the bastard never stop? Heard a mate laugh. Tried to laugh himself, but could not. Other people were screaming. This was fun? If he survived, he'd never wank or lie again, work much harder, learn to pray …

By twist of luck the music changed. Quick piano, lilting Cockney vocal. Could've spun now forever. Captain Kennedy, indestructible! But the Satellite reclined and slowed. It was over. Into the night stretched the cadence … 'I'm a believer'; a guitar went quietly wild. On the ramp, his legs were dough. Alive! Two girls from school were waiting for the next ride, and Rita James, she looked at him and smiled.

*

On the main line an infant was screaming. Kennedy did not blame it for the distraction, nor imagine wishing to fling it on the tracks. In other centuries, scholars endured the severest hardships, epidemics, bombardments, frostbite. The doors were centrally locked anyway. Let him change carriage if it was that bad. The kid rent the air;

12

maybe it wished not to exist. What are the words of Lear? As babies we cry, for we have entered a vale of tears. Cheer up, Your Majesty. Here came the inspector … *Hast seen The Faredodger's Tragedy? 'Tis a pretty play.*

Kennedy climbed back down a couple of pages; he'd not been taking much in and better start again. Sometimes he felt he'd already thought for himself whatever it was a book was saying, he was too soaked in the thought to absorb any more of it. But why trust your intuition?

A man and woman with flowers had the paper: *Scientists prove climate change will result from global warming.* Incontrovertibly. They'd reported to the UN, had the scientists. Obviously, this was something to cheer about, if the UN was going to roll its sleeves up now the scientists all agreed. On the other hand, it might have been nice if the scientists hadn't agreed at all. Nice if life could go on as it was without scientists indicating things about it, since their indications tended to gather into a hurricane once the politicians and the media got themselves involved, a hurricane being an eminently powerful force, and also a stupid one. Such thoughts, Kennedy kept to himself. The woman wore Italian boots and a short wool dress; her tights had a stripe in the nylon, and that was enough to distract him.

Here comes the Statue of Liberty! Presented ha-ha by his sister, Kennedy appeared in the kitchen, bearing flowers, carrier, book. Hair newly cut and styled, Mrs K was chopping mint. His old man tossed a pretzel in the air as his grandson looked on. Under the grey moustache, the little knot vanished.

How was his journey?

Oh it was fine really.

What could he say to entertain them? His brother-in-law, a compact and patient man, came in from the car with some forgotten items, shook his hand; they sent him back out for a melon. Perhaps he should make something up about the train.

'D'you want Classic?' said his old man. They were listening to a vintage show on Essex FM.

'What for?'

'Thought you'd prefer it.'

'I like this actually,' Kennedy told them. Procul Harum, 'Conquistador'. 'Haven't heard it for ages.'

'Where's Aunt Barbara?'

'She's gone to see her mum.' Kennedy picked up his nephew, who smelled of new wood, fresh plasters.

'Why didn't you both come here?'

'Because she had to see her own mother today. That's the tradition. Did you buy your mummy a present?'

'No.'

'He did!' Kennedy's sister said. 'A little one. Have you forgotten, darling?'

The child shook its head. Kennedy put him down, and he careered on the vinyl.

'"Ant music yeah!"' chanted Kennedy's sister. 'What year was this?'

'1980,' Kennedy told her.

'Knew you'd know!'

'He remembers everything don't you, babe?' Mrs K said. She made her way round them to check the oven, and they shuffled to give her room.

Kennedy's sister had introduced the custom of chatting in the kitchen. Where they'd actually spoken to each other before this innovation – well as a matter of fact, that was something Kennedy couldn't quite remember. They moved back into the space left by the chef, as she returned to her station. It's like looking for the corpses of garden birds, trying to remember how a thing used to be done. The old ways are picked clean so quick; then the bones disappear like magic.

'How's Barbara?'

'She met the Attorney General on Thursday,' Kennedy told them.

'Wow!'

'Yes,' Kennedy explained. 'He's been touring the firms. For some reason.' He should have made something up here as well, to keep it going. It was like a guillotine came down seconds after he began to tell people anything. On his face, he felt its killing wind. The other side of the blade, a few poor syllables twitched and died.

14

'You know Elsa?' his sister said. 'Her aunt volunteered at a centre for the impaired (in Glasgow – that's where her folks are from), where they could drop in for company. Just to chat, or play chess or use the Internet. Well sometimes, the volunteers buddy up with them, and Elsa's aunt, she made friends with this fella with no arms.'

'No arms?'

'He'd lost them in an industrial accident. He was working on the rigs. Poor lad.' Kennedy's sister nodded slightly. With her meaning glances, and mobile, spectacular mouth, she was accomplished in anecdotes.

'Why didn't he have prosthetics?'

'Well she didn't like to bring it up. She was so impressed by him, by his strength of character. He didn't even have a carer (who she could have asked). He made his own way over every day from Edinburgh.'

'Didn't they have a centre there? They must have,' Mrs K said.

'Of course they did! But he liked this one. That's why he came over by himself every day. He told her it was a drop-in centre nonpareil. And for why? Because they had volunteers like herself working there.'

By the radiator, returned from his quest, Kennedy's brother-in-law settled himself, hands in pockets.

'He told her he never knew the meaning of things before his injury. He did now. Big time. It was quite fusty in the centre, so she's like, Do you fancy an outing?, and they went for a walk in the park and he tells her all about himself and the times he's had. He's been an army officer, a thief, a film director, personal trainer, drug dealer – he's done it all. Then he made the fatal choice of working offshore, though it was like God wanted him to do it – so as to punish him, then help him see the light (but he had to be punished first obviously).'

Kennedy nodded … *Be grateful for thine arms. And mind you put them to good use.*

'Elsa's aunt, she hasn't ever heard anyone so honest. He's making her feel humble. Told her God forbid him prosthetics – like after the accident. That was his test, to get by with what he had left. And he does have a sort of charisma. His impairment, if anything it enhances him. By now they're proper pals. Been to the cinema together to see *Hellboy*, been to a tea dance (she had to steer him round), then he's talking about the pantomime.

'So they go to the pantomime and they have some mulled wine first for Christmas, then they have a drink before and one in the interval, and this geezer, he necks several bottles of Stella. Well he keeps fidgeting in the second part, and she says what's the matter and he asks if she can help him to the toilet. He doesn't mean just to the door,' Kennedy's sister lowered her voice, 'he means with his zip and everything – and the rest.'

'What's the rest, Mummy?'

'It's nothing, sweetheart. Go and check your dinosaur. He's hungry!'

'He isn't. He had a grape.'

Kennedy's sister held her hand to her mouth. 'So, Elsa's aunt, she had to … Ugh! … It took ages as well … D'you know what he said to her? "You're a real buddy. The Lord has told me!"'

'Oh my God!' cried Mrs K. 'Look at these two laughing! They're all as bad.'

'She cooks these things up with her mates!' winked the brother-in-law.

'I swear it's the truth. They couldn't talk to each other after the panto. He went off to the station on his tod. She needs a vodka to steady herself. Hold on! Day after next, she's at the centre and the duty manager's like, there's a call for you. Think it's your pal. Well she takes the call and it is him, and what d'you think he says?'

They were silent.

'"I got something to tell you. I had arms all the time. My wife tapes them for me every day before I get the coach." That's what he told her. And he couldn't lie to her any longer. That's what he said before she put the phone down.'

What a perv! Horrible man!

He did tell the truth. Eventually.

He rang her to gloat you fool!

You're missing something. The wife played her part.

Yeah? What did she get out of it?

She got the house to herself. While he's in Glasgow.

It was the aunt let it go too far.

She was being lied to!

There is nothing worse than being lied to.

By a friend. Supposed.

Did he actually commit a crime?

If anything, it was worse than lying. (And that's bad enough.) It was pretending something wasn't there when it was.

Impressed and troubled by what he heard, Kennedy was in a dream.

As the fine-scented steam rose from his plate, he considered what he was to them all: a figure who was after something that rose and broke in the air, like these silvery wraiths. He'd have something to show everyone, when they stopped chasing bucks and planning loft extensions, and he'd actually got hold of it. That was their idea of him. For something was missing from the world, as if a species of bird or the scent of a flower had left the garden; and though some said it had died out completely, they fancied Kennedy knew what it was, or where it had gone. Like many families, they interpreted consistent failure as rare ambition.

Yet Kennedy did believe in something – or to be precise, had got used to telling himself that he did. Even staked his professional reputation upon it. The problem was, it may never have been in the garden in the first place.

After the lamb, there was blackberry tart. The lunch gladdened Kennedy, who wasn't so metaphysical when it came to his meals – nor to brooding about women (unless that counted as a form of metaphysics). He'd missed a sight that morning. Mrs K saw Nancy (the grey cat who sat at point outside the house opposite) chase a fox down the close. She was a character, that Nancy. Mrs K found her upstairs once, sitting on the bed like she owned the place. Last week she was in hospital, after drinking Parson's Choice from a box in that skip outside the Hogans'. Now she was mixing it with foxes.

In another life she was a warrior.

Already is one!

Here came one about Kennedy, told for the benefit of brother-in-law.

'One day when he was five years old and I went to the school to collect him, there he was way behind the other kids, hobbling along. Here we go, I thought, he's had an accident. Well d'you know what he'd done? We'd just taught him his laces and when the teacher was telling them their story for home time (Miss Darling her name was) he was sat there tying his shoes together!'

They laughed and raised their glasses for Mother's Day.

2. The old man. Stride length and time.

'What "BST" means is less time, more light,' Kennedy was telling his nephew.

'Why?'

'Because the people in charge of things make all the clocks and watches jump forward and an hour gets left behind.' Kennedy showed his wristwatch.

'Where does the left hour go?'

'Well that's a good question. And d'you know what? We've been doing BST for ninety years now, which makes ninety hours. That's a lot of hours isn't it? I wonder where they've all gone?'

'I don't know.' Hands in the pockets of his new jeans, the little fellow watched his uncle's face. 'You know.'

'Well are they lying in the time-field like a pile of bricks? Or are they stored in a big gas tank that goes right up to the sky?'

'I think they're like jelly,' said the boy.

'That's an excellent idea. What flavour?'

'Man United!'

'Man United's not a flavour!'

The boy began to make faces.

Kennedy's old man laughed: 'You should write him a book!' On the stairs he was lacing walking boots the colour of Caramac − a symbolic purchase. Needing a bypass in the autumn of 2000, he sold his Telecom shares to go private. Post-op, Kennedy accompanied him to a leafy village to visit his consultant. Standing at a great desk of leather and dark wood, Barnaby Fall shouted,

'Two miles a day x 365! Rain or shine. Willy nilly. Keep those grafts pukkah! Shifty bugger sclerosis.' Here he began to murmur, seeming to point at a camouflaged enemy. 'Catch you napping.

Recumbency avoid. Pork pies ditto.' He passed them a 'Survival Sheet', handwritten, laminated. As Kennedy drove him home, his old man studied it.

Convalescing he went out to the drive one day, measured it with the brass-backed rule that Kennedy'd swished as a sword when he was small, then marched back and forth counting paces. Stride length calculated, he'd entered it in the black box which Kennedy now watched him clip to his belt. A blessing he'd been well enough to walk these past six years; yet it got Kennedy in his own heart, this little device for measuring distance.

Like the old man no longer trusted his own experience (unvaryingly he followed the same two-mile route – Kennedy knew because he'd checked with his mother). Then all these extra functions: 'CBDT' ('calories burned over distance travelled'); 'ASPM' ('average steps per minute'); 'GC:5' ('gradients compared in five most recent walks') – as if he were made from data!

But weren't we all suffering from this compulsion to meter our lives, to check against the units, stats and figures, what we used to manage on our own? Sex, drinking, breathing, eating. For Christ's sake, there was more text on the side of a sandwich carton than in the Lord's Prayer. Kennedy could have thrown the bloody box in the ditch and held his old man's hand, if only they were of a race where fathers and grown sons did such things. Still, it was science that saved his life when his heart went into fibrillation, not holding hands.

They'd reached the junction of the long lane, one mile exactly from the house. The old man asked Kennedy, face averted slightly, how it was going with his project. Two brown-feathered ducks appeared from a line of trees opposite and began to approach them on the asphalt, as if showing how it was done.

'I'm speaking at a conference on the first,' Kennedy said. 'In Swansea.' There was a pond beyond the trees. Over the high hedge to their right, a crop sent up green stems to knee height. You could see it through the gaps. In early summer, the field was chromate yellow with rapeseed.

The old man smiled. Conferences had their significance. 'Did they ask you?'

'No,' Kennedy said. 'I submitted a proposal.'

'How's Barbara?'

Kennedy told how she was. Out here beside the fields, he ought to have told his trouble.

The old man gazed at the church tower beyond. Time to turn back. His hair was a strong grey; to know his heart wasn't strong pained Kennedy.

He would have liked his boy to accompany him. It wasn't to be. Arms swinging, he made his retreat and Kennedy kept his eye on him till his figure became square and brown, diminishing in the afternoon light: the new hour lacked the brightness that ought to have been its property — as if it hadn't learned how to dress for the season. When he vanished from sight, Kennedy carried on.

At the top of the rape field the hedge fell away. Kennedy passed along on the lane, then round a sharp bend that brought him before the church. There was a broad gate of aluminium here beside an ancient kissing stile which led up a sloping track that passed between an open field on the right and high hedge on the left. Underfoot it was dry. Kennedy's shoes went with the territory. 'This is England,' he said to himself, and repeated the words. The clouds were banked and motionless, the air so still you could have been indoors. A white dog passed on the right and paused, cocking its head to watch him. Its owner caught up on a trail bike, urging it ahead of Kennedy, up the track in the still air. Above the high hedge a pylon was visible; Kennedy turned his gaze to the wood top right of the track, so he could imagine the land in another time. This was good. The ploughed field to his right was unfenced. The cyclist had gone.

Say it was 1600. Shakespeare was in London. The world was made of oak, linen, leather, iron. Ships creaked on the sea. For weeks there was no news. After dark you read, eyes close to the page, by smoky lamps or tapers. In the afternoon you watched a play, if you were a lad of the city, wondering at the language, the ladyboys and costumes. If you were out here, you watched the land, or the blossom. A stranger was an event. Maybe you had no news for years, unless a rumour of factions reached your ears. The Earl of Essex was your county's man. But what was he to you? You hardly knew the time of day, kept it by sky or shadows … *I'll meet thee when the sun's behind the church.*

The trees sucked an ashy vortex of birds. Kennedy continued till the track came abreast of the wood. A sign prohibited driving on bridleways. Sown with a thistly crop, the land dipped and rose like a model of space-time, while the track turned sharply to the right. The wood was to his side now; bluebells grew within among low banks and mounds; narrow paths wound about. Quiet as ever, and as empty; yet the stillness had today the barest buzz, like a buried generator.

What did we know of other centuries? There was more to the past than any history recorded. So much had been said that was never picked up. If only you could catch it now like starlight, what they uttered in these places … *I seen young Francis with my own eyes. Flying cross the long field. Then down he comes plup! and he's landed in the quag.* They saw what we don't see now. Lives short, days maybe longer. Did they live for each other as we do?

Where does the past go? What happens to its folk? Has time packed them away, or left them to their secrets? Are they all of them dust, or still romping? We can't know, for only characters stay around to speak to us – and of course, they weren't there in the first place.

The track curved about the undulating land. Above the thistly shoots shone a stony surface … *Here I am!* Visible now in a ray of sun which had broken through a gap in the western cloud, some two or three chains to his left; then gone; and as he reached the bottom of the track where a farm stood silent, it was back again. At the farm, Kennedy paused: stacks of timber were piled by a knackered vehicle; like a lance, a slender trunk was propped on it; rippling slightly in the still air, a George Cross hung from a post. When you see a quiet building, know what they're up to inside?

He kept his eye returning on the stony thing; it tricked the sight like a peeping child.

3. Rebecca. King Siren.

Before they came to this town, Kennedy's family lived further east in the county. The place here was left them by Kennedy's grandparents, savvy? In the holidays, Kennedy came to visit, lanky white youth with tidy hair. They asked if he had a girlfriend yet.

★

A Saturday in Colchester. 1980 by then. He's leaving the library in the rain. Under a neat umbrella, a young woman with black hair crossed the road. So what was he reading? He opened his carrier and she grinned like a cat. He'd seen Rebecca Sutton round Colchester, well out of his league. She invited him for a coffee in Woolworths. Made out he was in a rush, but he found himself walking beside her. She knew his name. When they passed the benches by BHS, a squaddie and a fat man shouted and she sneered. As they queued for their coffee, she told him the hassle she had from locals and yokels, like he knew something about it himself. Was she mistaking him? They sat down and talked about books, watching each other.

What did he think of *Ghost Story*?

Fairly frightening.

Really?

The characters were a joke though.

Was he really frightened?

Not the way he was about World War III ... Look! His cup could be a silo, with that plastic filter on it.

She told him he was imaginative.

Anyway, her dad said Mrs Thatcher'd stick it to the Russians. Seeing Kennedy was troubled, she made a joke about her dad. Her eyes were blue, with black mischief in the iris. A young man in a lace shirt sat by them, heavily made-up. She checked him and made a face. Kennedy sought a *bon mot*. When she laughed, her mouth spread like an American's.

On High Street she put up her umbrella. This was it then; he was dumb with anticipation of disappointment. The rain spotted his carrier bag. See you. Away he walked like a plank. A minute later she was at his shoulder, trying to conceal that she'd run. The soldier and pig were still sitting on the bench so she was coming this way.

Here was some kind of miracle! Kennedy came to life, chattering as if inspired. She walked with him to the station, then went off to buy a single. She was going to The Falstaff tonight. He could pick her up if he liked.

Man, he strode home like a giant! Flew like Faust on dragons! Rode in his imperial car! When he got in he laughed in his sister's face. Upstairs he tried on his best strides. In the kitchen, mum and sister were giggling. His old man brought him a sausage sandwich. Line your stomach if you're going on the town. How was he off for dosh? Kennedy said he was OK. The old man slipped him a couple of sheets. Buy her a drink. It's eight bob a pint now.

The Falstaff was one of the few places in town where new wave people didn't get shouted at or smacked. A lot of the guys wore make-up. Kennedy must have been the only one without dyed hair, a pierced ear, pointed shoes or second-hand clothes. As they talked of JP Sartre, Rebecca greeted people: Marc, Nik, Shep, Borax, Bitch. She asked about people at his school. Faces she meant. On each of them, she had something. She told him stories about Carew's Academy for girls. Her art teacher's finger was the shape of a cock. Mrs Rudge (English) looked like Quasimodo. The headmaster used a periscope to check if they were sniffing Zoff in the mini-maze. He liked dressing as a woman. Andrea True's big sister'd seen him in Soho. He asked her for a light. When Kennedy took a pause from laughing – two pints of Harp had gone to his head; people were looking – Rebecca said come home and I'll alter those trousers.

While she hacked at his turnups with an evil pair of scissors, he sat barelegged on her bed like a convalescing pasha. From a box at the bottom of her wardrobe, she'd pulled out for him a smoking jacket of purple silk. Her mother, aware an unknown youth was within, called up the stairs on the quarter hour. Rebecca yelled that she was sewing. She unstitched the seams, banged a Singer on her dressing table, then narrowed the trousers, feet curled like netted doves as she worked. Could he put on her new 45? The sleeve showed men in long raincoats and eyeliner.

Over she came with the trousers, hitched her skirt up and began to kiss his ear. Kennedy, desperate to prove himself, but apprehensive about such a concentration of fun, was almost relieved to hear her mother call time.

'Come tomorrow afternoon!' Rebecca told him in his ear. 'They're going to rally-cross.'

'Bloody hell! It's Rudolf Nureyev!' murmured his old man. 'What happened to your strides?' Kennedy sat with him to watch *Parkinson*. His head was full of lights.

★

Down there between Platforms 1 and 2 with six minutes to kill, Kennedy was back at the station. When his sister dropped him off she said something, but was looking at traffic so he missed it; then she was saying they should have another girls' night out, her and Barbara. This pleased Kennedy, who, as a sovereign might have hoped for affection in his court, or the governor of a colony for harmony between his subjects, really did desire that his people should get on; though he wondered if they'd love each other more without him – given their freedom, so to say; if he died or disappeared, or hadn't existed at all.

The lines ran on a high embankment at the town's end. Trains came in from eastern England and the sea. He looked about for himself 30 years ago, coming down the platform in three-stripe trainers; rare badge of his team sewn to his duffel bag. *Last seen on a visit to his grandparents: Good Friday 1976.* But he hadn't disappeared: he was here. Yet if back there once, there forever? Stitched into time …

Two stanchions supported a beam that carried power cables, yellow paintwork glowing hard in the extra light. Further back was a two-storey building: black steps leading up to an office; on the ground floor a door marked 'Entry Restricted'. Across the line from Platform 1 stood Portakabins, net-curtained. A PA crackled: 'For the security and safety of all our customers, this station is under 24-hour surveillance. Please report any suspicious activity to a police officer or a member of staff.'

With a trace of shame, Kennedy continued looking about. No doubt an eye was kept on the station from that office. They were watching him on screens. Other passengers examined their phones, or observed the air, bored beyond suspicion. Where the Portakabins ended, an empty cable drum had been turned for a table; an ashtray lay upon it and discarded golden packet, plastic office chair alongside. Stiffly, a fox came nosing, sliding out of sight beneath a windowless hut, slits of greenish glass on the front wall.

Late sun fell on a siding. In the cab of an azure diesel, an engineer sat smoking. A chart hid his face. There was a smooth thud and whistle and Kennedy said damn; behind him, his train was sliding westwards.

The diesel's cab was empty. The PA repeated its message. In order to look unsuspicious, you are advised not to miss your train. *He's proceeding further down platform. Perform identity search. Code November.* Why did Barbara make you jump this morning? On a piece of rolling stock by the siding's end, a dark figure stood, hand to eyes.

Kennedy went along; the figure disappeared. The vehicle was yellow, self-powered, cabs at either end called 'DYMAX'. Between the cabs was a beam with winch and hopper, the whole rig resembling a small boat. As Kennedy examined some text on the bodywork – *ENSURE SIRENS ARE WORKING BEFORE SERVICING OR OPERATING MACHINE* – the figure reappeared in the space between the cabs smoking a cigarette, the low-slung vehicle framing his dark shape. Trespasser well-dressed: lounge suit, waistcoat, flash of handkerchief. A third time, a fourth, the PA played its message: 'For the security and safety of all our customers, this station is under 24-hour surveillance. Please report any suspicious activity to a police officer or a member of staff.'

Since the events last summer, there was scarcely an activity more open to interpretation of malevolent intent among our watchers, than acting unconventionally at a station. Why should Kennedy hang around where another man was trespassing, instead of boarding an excellent train that had arrived on time and departed? Who'd believe him if he said he was looking for himself as a youth, with the badge of a Roman eagle?

You could do a lot of damage with a diesel, didn't he agree? Kennedy'd have to agree. Pale-blue diesel in the wrong hands was very probably a machine that could wreak havoc. What if you were to drive it the wrong way down the track? Carnage. You could make a godalmighty bomb with a sack of ballast (as stored on that yellow vehicle you was watching with the hopper) could you not? A sack of ballast and some fertiliser? Sweating, he would have to agree. Any imaginable charge against him, it was Kennedy's nature to entertain.

The figure drew itself up to listen – Christ but he was large! – and in doing so seemed to catch sight of Kennedy, who felt acknowledged by the glance which rose in the direction of the announcements. At once the suited figure withdrew from its position and a siren began to sound, filling the station with the song of war.

'Four-Minute Warning': time was, the phrase itself affected Kennedy with a fear that was primitive and total. They said eastern England would get it first. Would he reach 21, 35? ... He'd made both. Britain's bunkers were no longer even tourist attractions. Could have bought himself one as a study. Councils flogged them for the price of a car. But the sound of a siren still seized his heart.

Against the vortex of sound, the station PA emitted for a fifth, then sixth and seventh time its surveillance message, but the rising notes of the siren were penetrating the upper office and producing a riotous swooping feedback through the tannoy. Two staff were coming from Platform 2, towards the source. Kennedy remained where he stood. Mr Suit had let the bloody siren off. He had some brass neck. The figure reappeared chin raised, one hand in jacket pocket, a politician from another time, a maverick on the stump, a king performing his duty, and standing where the hell he wanted.

On Platform 2, an express from Norwich slid in, carriages brightly lit. The siren paused and the PA announced, 'Do not attempt to board this train! This service is for setting down only!', but Kennedy nipped across the path of the staff, and onto the express where he stood at the door. Towards the yellow vehicle, now silent, the staff made their way. At last they faced the dark figure. One of them asked him what he was doing up there, and he seemed to say, 'Looking for the wife, bud. Seen her around?'

The whistle blew, door slammed and Kennedy, he was out of there.

4. Famous thinker. Dr Frazer. Basil & Co.

You can get it up like an anti-aircraft gun at that age ... When their parents were out in the afternoons, he and Rebecca lay in bed at his house or hers, talking like a pair of sophisticates. Could this all be happening to him? Now and then he had a feeling she was practising; he didn't go into it. There were weird sunsets that year, from the Mount St Helens eruption. Rebecca's bedroom window faced west: one Saturday in October, her parents in town, the two of them saw a sky that seemed soaked in blood, almost all the way down the window. What if it was an omen! She mounted him and hid his face.

Maugre the trouser–altering incident, Kennedy was intractable to Rebecca's style ideas. In a dinner jacket with satin lapels (tried on in Oxfam), he resembled a bus driver auditioning for a Bond film. A raincoat that belted tightly with a big collar, just made him look like a Mormon. So she nagged him to order pointed boots with a zip, from Shelleys of London; Kennedy stuck to his black Balmorals, polished up like a flight-lieutenant's. He wouldn't dye his hair or wear make-up; he didn't care what he looked like. That became his attitude. There was a song about it. She bought him the single, and said you're like them. Actually, he was like himself. In her box of 45s were Wasted Youth, Fashion, Cuddly Toys, Bauhaus, Peter Perret, Soft Cell; men with faces like meringue and sharp stacks of hair. But she must have seen something in him. The months passed.

Would there be a riot in Colchester? Someone did the windows of the Indian restaurants, but it didn't catch on. Kennedy took his A-levels, marvelled at Botham's exploits, read a big book of philosophy; waited for Rebecca to call.

Late that year there was heavy snow. Returning to the station from The Falstaff, Rebecca slipped and went down. When Kennedy tried to help her she spoke sharply. What was up with her? On the bus, she said a lad called Frinton saw her fall on her bum. Which wouldn't do. Frinton was a hick who came to Colchester at weekends. Everyone ignored him in The Falstaff. He'd tell them all. They went back to Rebecca's. Her mum and dad were at a dance, so they did it on their bed. Hell, was she a practitioner! He stopped worrying about the parents. If they'd walked in, they'd have got an eyeful. In the event, they couldn't get home anyway. Rang to say they were snowed in at the dance. The snow was heavier than anyone could remember that year.

He stayed the night with her. They were the mum and dad now! She brought them toast, coleslaw, Scotch eggs. They had tea with her dad's Johnnie Walker in it. She asked if he'd heard of undines. He had not. She thought he knew everything! Well they were beings that had sex with humans, so they could get a soul. He read up on them years later, those so-called 'middle spirits'. She asked him to tell her everything he'd done. They had plenty of time. Where to start? She said 'start with the worst thing'. But he hadn't done any 'worst' thing. Wished to God he had.

She told him things she'd done. Some of them weren't honest. Actually a lot of them weren't. He couldn't believe she had; she couldn't believe he hadn't. On and on they talked, lying in the dark. He felt she was getting older, and he keeping up with her. She told him he'd be a famous thinker one day. In the morning he slid home tasting whisky in his throat; the sky so grey it was level with his head. It could have been his greatest moment.

★

Cy Frazer was working his desktop with heavy tups of his fingers, which was an extra distraction to Kennedy, since Frazer had no conference paper to prepare on this day yet there he was going at his admin like a hard-hat labourer. If only Kennedy could bring similar force to his own fascinating task! Sub specie aeternitatis, why was he at a computer anyway? Why not sit in a butt of Malmsey with his ink pen and a sheaf of onion skin, or compose it in Old High German while relaxing in a brothel? But everyone was at their computer nowadays, and Kennedy knew that to qualify as a 'maverick' you had better be pretty good at what you do, as opposed to somewhere below average ... *He who would not conform, let him first be sure he standeth above other men and not in a ditch or other low and nasty place.*

Say he couldn't write a conference paper because he forgot everything he meant, the whole map of his idea, and wandered into a dream when he tried to explain. Then he couldn't tell anyone a story because he remembered too much. The successful anecdote needs to leave plenty out and season the rest with the tricks of fiction. He was in a knot: dreamed when he should be thinking, remembered when he should be imagining. *Kunterbunt*, cack-brained, crinkum-crankum – that was Kennedy.

Meditations such as this were a habit; they seemed to light up the way and show where he was going wrong. Now and then, the fancy took him that he might collect his insights into a book of aphorisms in the manner of the fine thinkers, except that Kennedy wasn't a fine thinker, and besides, the mind-coaches and coffee-break philosophers of the media had cornered the market in failure-insight, and resolution of ethical puzzles (*Is it ever permissible to ...?*) – and good luck to them, though ...

'Hey, Kennedy!' Cy Frazer was swivelling in his chair. 'Here a sec!' Fine-featured was Cy Frazer, and he bore a princely tan. Flowering in delight at an exquisite offering, his face canted between his monitor and Kennedy, who coughed and said Jesus Christ! Thoroughly distracted, he returned to his desk.

'How's it going with your paper, my man?' asked Frazer presently.

'I don't know what the hell I'm doing,' Kennedy said, and Frazer grinned, not realising. He tupped another while and rose to visit the gym. For an aesthete, he was strong in body and arm. One Friday afternoon when they were bored, they had a sit-ups tournament. Frazer managed 360, cracking jokes like a coffin salesman. As Kennedy puffed his way to a respectable figure, modest Frazer took snuff at the window.

He patted Kennedy on the shoulder and Kennedy thought with some regret that he should try and talk things over with Cy, who'd offered him friendship over the years, suggesting they drink absinthe in dens he knew, persisting in this while others kept their distance; then he thought with more regret that he should have got into the way of talking things over with Frazer well before now. Now was too late; because at some point, Kennedy convinced himself he entirely lacked the company of like-minded people for conversation – which meant he had to imagine them; and was that healthy? Or possible.

Looking for Cy, two young women came to the door.

'He's just gone out,' Kennedy said.

'D'you know when he'll be back?'

'I'm not sure. I think he went to the Sportshall.'

One of the students was Chinese, an insouciant lass in red spectacles. They hung about outside for a while and Kennedy strained to hear what they were saying. There was laughter, which distracted him, then he saw the hall of mirrors in *The Lady from Shanghai*, where Michael O'Hara and his lover hunted each other, firing at reflections. The young women went away down the corridor and Kennedy logged off. Making his own departure, he wondered about Cy's visitors, both of them unknown to him. Well let the ignorance be mutual!

That he might be the object of complimentary knowledge was not conceivable to Kennedy, though as the opposite certainly wasn't, not to be known was desirable. He went downstairs without seeing anyone, said so long to the guys at reception and out onto the sloping road that passed the university.

In some degree, the sensitivity to what others may know of him was an effect of last autumn's trouble; though an earlier cause, Kennedy sometimes fancied, might lie half a lifetime away, when the reports of women cast a shadow over him. There he lingered, rather than finding daylight; which suggested that it wasn't being talked about in a certain way that was the problem, but partiality for the shadow itself, as if shame was his element, and experts might detect an original trauma, something encountered, or known, that should not have been, in the childhood of the man.

Screw the experts! Kennedy had no inclination to lay the blame there. He'd been a clever boy and if he'd known too much, then it was only of astronomy and gorgons, and the FA Cup. Indeed, after a parents' evening when Kennedy was starting Juniors, his old man asked him politely to cool it a little, instead of correcting Miss Everton about the size of the moon and the meaning of 'Pelagian', a word that'd he'd come across when reading about 'Pegasus' and could define without quite understanding – until he looked up 'Original Sin', and then was Kid Kennedy certain. But anyway, the old man said 'You ain't Magnus Magnusson yet, son!' and Kennedy felt ashamed of sticking up his hand so often and calling out. At night, he imagined what Miss Everton wore under her corduroy mini-skirt. Did he cool that too? If only we could remember the seasons of our fantasies, we might know ourselves better.

On the westbound tube, someone's paper said that population growth was more of a threat than climate change. The UN were going to roll their sleeves up. A threat to what exactly? Might it not be the case that newspapers were a bigger threat than climate change or population growth? Newspapers and the media generally, with their slick and sovereign authority? And you could say exactly what they were a threat to as well, though Kennedy kept this to himself.

Barbara said, 'Can you look at the fridge, darling? *No anda bien* – again!' The pack ice at the back had thawed, melting over the lower shelves and into the boxes at the bottom. His wife stood with hands on hips while Kennedy surveyed the scene, then moved off, the fridge being Kennedy's responsibility. Removing a lettuce that had suffered from the thaw, he dried it in kitchen towel, dried its bag and replaced it, then undertook a comprehensive removal of items and shelves, and began to lift puddling lumps of ice into the sink. It was rumoured in his schooldays that you could die from clutching a piece of ice, since the cold would be transmitted north to the heart. Kennedy dried the other items and he washed the fridge with a solution of bicarb. In the sink, the icy lumps melted, slowly becoming glass-clear, crystalline structure sliding, loosening. This was the death of ice, as Kennedy might have said to a boy beside him.

He cared for that fridge like an ageing monarch, whose passing might cause civil discord. When it started running a high temperature about a year ago (this being the fever of the fridge, as Kennedy said to himself), he took out a warranty for unlimited repairs. *All manner of thing shall be well, Your Majesty.* Whereupon an engineer called Basil visited to check its temperature, after such strenuous negotiation of dates and divisions of the day between Kennedy and a service centre whose relationship with the manufacturer was recherché (to put it politely), that Kennedy wondered how the hell complex events, such as the Olympic Games, orgies or the laying of cable systems, actually got themselves organised.

A toughish fellow in blue overalls was Basil, though not tough enough to get the fridge door off by himself. Tapping details of this visit and requirements for the next on a laptop in the black hard shell case that Kennedy had supposed would contain Basil's tools, Basil drank from the glass of mineral and lime with which Kennedy had supplied him. It can be disagreeable for a fellow working at home to have a man in, but less so if he isn't strong – and has no tools.

'Ides of March already.' Basil shook his head at his computer.

'Have you read it?' Kennedy enquired – *'Julius Caesar?'*

'Yeah. As a youth,' Basil said, with an air of having no more time for such things. 'It's when he got shanked.'

On the Kalends of April, Basil turned up with a strong colleague. Kennedy wondered if there'd be fresh quotations, but they were striving to remove the door from the fridge. On his right wrist Basil wore a thick bracelet of gold. Kennedy went and sat in his workroom while Basil and colleague grunted, wondering what the pair of them would be thinking of a man alone at home in the afternoon. He was thoroughly distracted, unable to do any more than re-read the same paragraph, until Basil called him, wishing to know the source of the power supply. Along went Kennedy to show. The door was now leaning against the wall, strong colleague sucking his teeth. Behind here. Kennedy pointed to a fitted cupboard.

Minutes later, Basil appeared at the door of Kennedy's workroom. Him and Pavel could not access the power supply unfortunately, since they weren't permitted to disassemble fitted units. On Kennedy's table was a photograph of Barbara which her mother'd had framed for Kennedy when he said her daughter looked like a countess in it. Kennedy was pleased to see that it had caught Basil's eye.

He'd had in mind an image of a carefree girl in a sports car with chestnut or mahogany hair streaming out behind her, in a European film it could have been or maybe an advert, which was certainly as close as Kennedy'd been to a countess; but to Barbara's mother, he'd become a connoisseur of the aristocracy. There was a lesson here about the things we say that may endear us most, namely, that we aren't absolutely required to have a clue what we're on about. Kennedy was quite taken aback to discover what an impression he'd made on his future mother-in-law. If he'd made more of the skill of speaking authoritatively of that which he knew nothing about, he could really have cut it in life – in a number of our modern professions. But that wasn't Kennedy's way, it was against his nature to pretend to know.

'It's all right,' Kennedy said, 'I authorise you.'

Like soothsayer or lawgiver of old, Basil raised his hand to explain protocol. The people that did the kitchen for Kennedy, let them first come back to the house to sequester the cupboard. Then would Basil and Pavel return. During this performance, Basil kept his eye on the penates, in the form of Barbara's photo, then away to his laptop, Kennedy bringing up the rear, to consider slots. Basil and Pavel having departed with their computer, Kennedy went back to his workroom to swear, and track down the original fitters.

What boots it to say that it was another three weeks before the latter, a Balkan outfit, arrived early one evening as Kennedy toiled at his project and, one of them prostrate, the other two crouching like a sniper's 'eye-men', instantly demonstrated a simple trick by which the cupboard could be unfastened and slid back and forth in its gap to reveal the plug that was the power source of the fridge? They refused payment so Kennedy gave them a tenner for a pint. As they thanked him, one of them asked after his wife (Barbara having supervised the original fitting).

Kennedy couldn't be at home for Basil's next, complexly-deferred visit, having to teach that day; so Barbara took an afternoon in May off as holiday. This time Basil brought the strongman, Pavel, and another man who was very strong and told jokes. They had the door off and fixed the condenser so quickly they all had time for tea and toast. How about that!

Toast! What was wrong with biscuits?

They hadn't charged anything for the visit.

Well that was the beauty of the warranty he'd paid for.

But listen, the funny man had invited Barbara to go and see football that night. At Stamford Bridge. If she was free. They could sit in the *extranjero* dugout. She'd told him of course she couldn't. He mustn't have known she was married must he? No, Kennedy said stiffly, picturing the four of them in the kitchen. Basil and Pavel obviously hadn't mentioned that there was fairly regularly a man in the house.

When the fridge began to play up again in the late summer of that year, Kennedy made a fresh appointment with Basil. A date was set for early autumn, the Ides of October. Kennedy'd had his part in this: the symmetry pleased him.

In the final minutes of the allotted period that day, Kennedy took a call from Basil, who'd been circling the flat for a while in his van. Boss was working at home again was he? Kennedy confirmed that he was. Did Basil wish to park outside? Basil muttered to his mate and laughed. They wouldn't bother boss at his desk! What he was going to do was order boss a new fridge yeah? To be fair, Basil was surprised the repairs had lasted. When they'd come in May, to tell boss the truth, Basil estimated six weeks max before the condenser went again. So he was arranging for boss (who'd now gone to the window in order to catch sight of Basil and co) to get the paperwork through the post. Then boss could plan when to have his new fridge delivered – totally free on the warranty. All right? Disheartened and unmanned, Kennedy said thanks. He did not *want* a new fridge.

On the evening where we began this report, Barbara appeared at the elbow of Kennedy, whose head was still in the appliance, to ask if he was daydreaming. Kennedy averred that he was not, and found a piece of ice to prove it. Barbara examined a bag of carrots: '*Pobritas zanahorias!*' When were they actually going to order the replacement though? She was just wondering. Because it was six months now since Basil sent the docs, and every two weeks this rigmarole with the ice – when he had his project to be getting on with. She stroked Kennedy's left hand: '*Congelada!*'

'I can't understand you!' she smiled. 'Why don't you just do the straightforward thing?'

'Because it's not as simple as it seems,' Kennedy said; and herein was wisdom. For Kennedy knew – and had indeed explained to his wife, who was admiring his endeavours as a visitor to a gallery might stand before a painting and wonder why it was thought of as a great example of whatever, scratching her left foot balletically with her right – Kennedy knew that arranging the delivery of the replacement appliance and at the same time the appearance of someone able to remove the old king and install the usurper (for the terms of the warranty did not extend, in 'normal circumstances', to the act of installation), was going to soak up more time in its parched dance of two variables than either of them had, practically or morally, to spare. It might cause them to fall out, such a complex, time-thirsty negotiation. And in an important sense, time was of the essence between Kennedy and his wife.

Since it was understood that Barbara should be allowed – or rather, that they were going – to have a baby, once Kennedy had brought to fruition his project. And you had to acknowledge Barbara's good nature in waiting around for Kennedy to finish, or succeed, or satisfy himself, or get the thing published – whatever his aim might be. Not that the understanding wasn't a complex, and not entirely stable, issue that had the potential to cause tensions between them. But it was nicely balanced, that was the thing – provided Kennedy didn't try and take advantage by spinning things out with this project of his (which Barbara'd had the grace not to warn him about frankly, unlike his sister). But to get back to the matter in hand, Kennedy's concern was that a new phase of negotiation might be the straw that broke the camel's back. This was how it seemed to Kennedy, in his wisdom ...

'Well I bet *I* could get them to install it!' Barbara was saying.

'Who?'

'The men who bring it.'

'The warranty says they won't in normal circumstances,' Kennedy explained, not for the first time. 'And besides, you'd have to keep taking days off because they never turn up when they say they will.'

'I bet they would,' she said to annoy him, as Kennedy went to the sink to see the dying ice.

God save the King.

5. Barbara. Kennedy's devil. Our lady of containers.

It was some time ago now, Halloween in fact, that Barbara suspended contraception. Kennedy could remember because a hooded kid in a devil mask came trick or treating to the front door and Kennedy gave him one fifty, just before she told him. The plan was to make the runway good and long before they started, and dump plenty of cowshit on the fields (an adage where she came from). OK. A rational proceeding: she wasn't getting any younger, and Kennedy wasn't either; but it did mean that Kennedy couldn't just come along and expect to lay his wife when he fancied.

How now! When had he ever just come along 'expecting' to lay his wife? Was that how she saw it? He hoped to God it wasn't; but what if? *Expecting*? Like a dog. Or worse ... Actually, the whole business soon became pretty flattering to your diffident petitioner, because when he did 'come along' in the following weeks, Barbara would say, finger wagging, 'What about your project, *cariño*? You have to see it through!' So, she made him a hero, breathing in his eye on one occasion till Kennedy, feeling his heart come, returned choking to his desk, like he had a task the size of Fitzcarraldo's.

But he was hooked on the way she'd said it, that magic (slightly-dated) phrase, putting herself just out of reach, like the masks, and bombs and phials of blood he'd stared at as a schoolboy with a few new pence in his pocket, through the Joke Shop window in old Colchester, the money seldom enough ... If only he could have laid her!

The way she chatted while undressing last night, way she pissed this morning, naked, clever, compact, pressing neatly with her toes on the bathroom floor, was in his mind now. She texted on her way to work, to hope he'd made his train. *Love*. Acton, Ealing, Southall passed. Can you text your love? On the table before him lay his conference paper.

*

The first time with her, 10 years this September, the look she gave him at the end was so complex, so obscure, Kennedy wasn't yet finished explaining it. Had she just found something that she'd set her heart on having? Or was it calculating, say she'd planned for someone more or less like him, and he would do? But he wondered then if it meant she'd lost something, and just accepted that it was gone for good, that look in which the brownness seemed to fill her eyes as if her soul would find a way out. Other times, he thought it had been as if one of them was drowning, the other watching, helpless, or not helping, because drowning was the penalty required by law, and if you offered a hand, the same would happen to you. Thus, his interpretations tended towards the melancholic; and this was at odds with the way they'd got it on in her room in Blackstock Road, when they came back from lunch in Camden.

During the lunch (at Blake's), Kennedy worried she'd have arranged to go shopping with friends at three, and could have kicked himself for not suggesting dinner. She was wearing red (which he certainly wasn't so superficial as to take for a promising sign) and was animated, telling him about the course she'd been doing, her mother, how exactly she'd got to be at the cricket the first time he saw her, films she'd just seen. *Besos en la Frente* she loved, *Casino* she found boring and horrible with a most horrible little man in it who attacked people with a ballpoint pen, *Lone Star* Kennedy had to see, *Twin Towns, Trainspotting* – well the accents were a problem with those; *Babe* – listen! Kennedy wasn't to tell anyone she loved *Babe* in case they thought she was uncool.

Hey! Now what was this? Chewing an apricot that had come with his lamb, hadn't Kennedy'd just heard (praise our Lord Jesus Christ, Zeus, Allah and co – not forgetting friend Satan, lest he cut up rough!) – had he not just heard her anticipate their future?

The first instalment was a visit to the flat in Blackstock Road to pick up her cardi in case it got chilly later. Kennedy was in heaven with the adverb of time, and became talkative the way he used to as a kid. This was on the Northern Line to King's Cross. She smiled, and the manner which had seemed so poised when they sat down to lunch, like *she'll go and talk to someone else soon*, was now for him. On the Victoria Line, she pressed her leg against him. He bent to tighten his shoelace, in case she wanted to free it, and looked at her feet. She was a flashing ensemble, red, white, brown. She kept her leg by him all the way. When he stopped talking, she was checking his face.

In a west-facing room, she entertained him with imitations of the roly-poly leg-spinner who'd tormented England that summer. Her perfume smelled of honey and thyme. Kennedy stood by the window with a glass of wine she'd poured him. Next to him was a laundry basket with a curious lid. Delighted, he watched her skipping to her mark. The sun fell on his shoulders and the basket, which was of dark-resinned cane culminating in a gull's head.

Come on! Where was her coach? In her red dress she reproached him, hands on hips, barefoot, absorbed in her game.

Look, he said. There was a cork-board on the wall above her dressing table, and pinned to its frame hung a golden apple by a little chain (above it he noticed a pink post-it which seemed to say something about him). He removed the wooden apple to show her the action by which a bowler imparts leg-spin to a cricket ball. You have to imagine turning a door handle anticlockwise then it sort of comes out of the back like this. He had to go behind her to show her how to do her arm, careful not to rub against her, wishing he could dance, she was so graceful, poised on the toes of her left foot. Her chestnut hair glowed. How precious is women's hair! A dog should guard it from men who come too close. She looked in his face to see how she was doing, so that was when he kissed her. They did more bowling and over they went; Kennedy being the larger, it was more likely that he'd tripped her, though there was something able in the way she fell with him, as if he was being judoed. At any rate, this was how it happened the first time, and the look she gave him ...

The printed copy of the paper was now so botched with carets, additions, proof-marks, curving arrows, re-explanations and bleachy scratches, that it was going to be impossible to read through smoothly, let alone deliver from memory with the style Kennedy would have liked to possess. The marks and annotations vandalised the text, defiled the margins, graffiti of a devil come by night to wreck his project. But the devil was his own.

He lacked confidence in his material, the setting of his thoughts to paper to be read out to a crowd whose approval he sort of cared about, since they sounded surer than him always, like they were people at a party who weren't invited last minute, and he a guest who hears his words click, rustle and fall and tastes them in his throat like filthy wax, when he's not even through the bloody door. Yeah, the *esprit de l'escalier* appears first as the Devil of Deference in your awkward guest, who behaves as if others were his betters, when he might know in his heart they're maybe no such thing; and this devil was one of several that made habit of tormenting Kennedy. In the present instance, it had probably been called up when Hester Pygg hinted pleasantly in an e-mail that opened with the words 'Hi there', that he was a last-moment choice to speak at 'Whatever Happened to Character?', a *sexy* professor having dropped out at short notice because SP had a better party to go to. Which meant Kennedy could come to the conference, as long as he was good, and did not say the wrong thing; for everyone would be watching him.

The problem with Kennedy's project was that his interest was in character. And when he said so, the academic world reacted like the PA at the station the other day. Told him what he must, could or mustn't mean, the assumption being that Kennedy conformed to its way of thinking – rather as the PA assumed that the passenger standing on the platform must agree with the 24-hour surveillance, safety and security announcement; for who would rationally say that they don't agree with safety and security? No one rational wants to be blown up, just as they don't actively want to inhale someone else's cigarette smoke. Though the question of what the rational *do* desire is its own puzzle …

Somehow he'd missed the lady over there, in a dress of white wool with navy-blue trim. Lustrous as the coal his grandparents burned, her hair was in a smooth, symmetrical cut, like an actress from the early days. Her mouth was a poppy, on a field of snow. From a silvery cellphone, she looked straight at the bard — like if he stared at her some more, he might be getting a slap. Eyes down he imagined what she saw.

A fellow with hair like a vicar; a brooder in a V-neck sweater; a man with more trouble than Hercules; an explorer who never got far because he was blown backwards by memory, sideways by dreams, God knows where by things said about him, and could hardly see what was just in front since he believed in something else; a weirdo in shoes of friendly-brown suede from an Italian shop where the 'Sale' sign was permanent; some kind of Englishman; nothing …

She was watching containers on the up-line. Smoke-blue, brown, pale-blue steel crates, *GE SEACO, TEX, CHINA SHIPPING*. What was her interest in this passing freight? *K LINE, DON FANG*, ink-blue, brick-red. As she twisted to look, a gap opened in her dress. Kennedy averted his head. There were secrets women kept in their clothing, for themselves alone.

In his own window, he caught the reflection of a waggon that was less hard-edged than the others, protected by some sort of tarpaulin, which appeared to be the end of the freight. He turned to look, but the woman covered the window as it passed. In her hand the silver phone was raised, compact as the stopwatch that timed races, when Kennedy was a youth and fair middle-distance runner.

He tried for the last time to concentrate on what lay before him. What he wished to say was simple really. Like he meant, he actually meant, when he said his interest was in character, that character is a person, right? This character in a play and that one in a novel, they are both of them *persons*. I, Kennedy, believe that character exists. But he couldn't say it the way he wanted to. The academic world was too clever for him, particularly at saying how what seemed to be so wasn't at all. And the truth of that world was powerful, even if it was negative; or perhaps it was powerful just, or only, because it was negative. Like the truth of the atheists:

So you're actually saying that 'miracles' do not obey the laws of physics?
I – I'm saying there may be breaches in those laws.
Believe in fairies do you?
But –
Do you or do you not believe in fairies?

Now Kennedy had a nice quotation in his notes from a venerable essay, 'On Seeming Wise', which said that people who want to seem clever always take the negative side, since it's much easier to shake your head and make a dismissive grin than it is to prove that a thing is so and where it belongs in the world. Yet he felt that academic negativity went both deeper than that, and nowhere at all. Which was what he was up against.

Then the woman spoke. Her voice was from the North and Kennedy didn't know if her words were to him or herself, but she seemed to say, 'This is your last chance to run.'

6. Worst time. Orson. The speakers.

At Swansea, Kennedy waited for her to step down. She blew cigarette smoke his way and was off, heels striking the platform. To their left were the hills of the city. As she moved towards the head of the line, she slung a Longchamp bag over her shoulder.

★

Just after Christmas '81, someone said they heard Kennedy'd had a fight with Rebecca Sutton, pushed her over on ice on High Street. Kennedy explained what actually happened. New Year's Eve, he found himself at a party Rebecca'd been nagging him to come to. The same person produced others to corroborate the story. Kennedy told the lot of them what actually happened. Rebecca's judgement of Frinton had been acute. Frinton it was who'd put these rumours about. The hick Frinton. When Rebecca arrived she could confirm it for herself. There was a row of them grinning at him in the hall, drinking cans. One of them said, 'You're evil you are!' and they cracked up. 'We're the good people!' He couldn't handle it. 'You're the worst!' He felt the heat in his face. Rebecca never did turn up. Leaning at the kitchen sink, a girl called Angie Thursday asked if he wanted to know who it was who'd been telling everyone he hit Rebecca; no one had heard of Frinton. He watched her head rise and fall as she threw up, then took his leave. Twice she called, 'Don't you want to know?' Outside the wind was raw, snow compacted like black glass. Would have been a blessing to break his neck. Could life actually get worse? Dante put liars and traitors at the bottom of hell; they'd taken Kennedy with them.

He discovered that Rebecca was actually at Dominos nightclub on the 31st of December with Marc and Borax. It was fancy dress. They all went as ghosts or vampires. When he mentioned it, Oh she would have asked him to come, but he'd have thought dressing up was trivial. Kennedy took the compliment.

Her mother called his house one night. Could he tell Rebecca she was to check the radiators when she came in, as they were going to bed early? But Rebecca wasn't here – she was not with him. In the hall where the telephone was, his old man patted his shoulder. Like a steel cord sinking through an iceblock, or a sword penetrating an angel, Kennedy felt the pressure of his hand.

Next day he's on a bench in his lunch break. The year he took out before university, he had a job clerking at the council. Rebecca walks past with a friend of hers, Betty Grey, peroxide-blonde. Over she comes, shameless as a cat. Why's he sitting there with a face like that? Is he coming to The Falstaff Wednesday? Isn't he cold? (He was wearing a denim jacket – no coat.) Did she know her mother'd called? Was she bothered? He couldn't handle her expression. Made him feel small for caring about honesty; so he shouted something at her, something terrible, and away she went up High Street with her nose in the air, she and Betty Grey like two viscountesses. She never looked back. It was finished.

Day after day, he lay on his bed. January was a bitter month, frozen hard. He'd lost heart for reading, taken to 'thinking'. So he called it, when his mother and old man asked what on earth he was up to in there. 'He's still thinking. Don't disturb him!' At evening when they set the table, sister Kate went stamping downstairs; that was her report.

When she told her mother she was with him, because she'd have been off doing something she shouldn't, what was she supposing? That he'd play along, pretend she was indeed at his house that Saturday evening, a make-believe slag? Maybe he'd got her in trouble. Kennedy would tell a lie for no one. Outside it was minus 6 and falling. In silver chords at twilight, a blackbird sang ... *Babe you couldn't lie to save your heart.*

Over the last year and a half, he'd spent so much time thinking of her that she was as vivid to him when she wasn't there as when he was inside her. Then why react so badly to her telling her mother she was at his place? If imagination made it true she was with him, image and soul, even when she wasn't, maybe her imagination worked the same way. He was with her in soul when he wasn't in fact. Maybe, she'd told her mother she was *with him*, rather than at his house? Ah, when he thought that, Kennedy beat at his temples with the heels of his hands! Was there anyone more stupid? What had he done? Expelled her soul from his. Shouted at her in the street, like the other scum. She must have thought him special; same as the rest, he abused her. Like a soul diva, the blackbird kept it coming, Minnie Ripperton, Jaibi, Mary Wells.

Never again was Rebecca to visit; yet as image, she remained. He rehearsed their time together. Incidents, occasions, conversations, actions. They all meant more now, with one exception. What he knew of her, her life and family, he started to see patterns in, compare with his own. Her dishonesty – why did it seem bigger than his honesty? A question that wouldn't leave him. Like an actor who's bought the theatre, he directed her in new scenes. He was in them too, or in the wings.

His old man was urging him to travel a bit. Had a bee in his bonnet about grape-picking. Perhaps Kennedy should have listened, gone to France; life might have turned out different. He stuck to Colchester like his feet were gummed. In his room, he watched TV. *Horace, Harvey Moon, A Kind of Loving.* Horace was a simple fellow. Lived with his mum in the Dales – he couldn't really take care of himself. Anything was an adventure: van with a puncture, tin of fruit rolling down the hill, cat in a coal bunker – such happenings fascinated Horace. Face shining under his cap, he took his time to look about. His mum wasn't always patient, so he told what he'd seen to a neighbour, a big old woman with a gnarled face. Everything was a kind of magic.

He caught an interview with Orson Welles. They'd draped him in black silk, to hide his bulk. This was it. Kennedy'd dreamed of hearing such a man. Genius. That deep brown voice, tobacco-rich, had a sort of liberal majesty. He played it like an organist. Ah – the lengths he'd gone, and enemies made, in the name of his art! He gave words his all. No wonder he was that size. He had a half ton of anecdotes in there. And this was only the interview. The films were to be shown as well.

In *Chimes at Midnight*, Welles played the fat knight Falstaff, and Kennedy, he adored him. Over the top? Well his capacity for love had developed since Rebecca Sutton went away over the ice; by now he could fall in love with images, as well as biophysics. Here, an old man with white hair, creased and rocky countenance, firkin chest, rumbling voice, a barrel of wit and melancholy. Against Falstaff, was there ever a comic who could hold his own? Words for everything, answer to anything. No one cleverer. In those days, 'wit' meant intelligence, wisdom; we mean less by it now. Christ could he talk! Outrageous. He made stuff up like we print newspapers; but what he made up, it lasted. His figures of speech were miracles. You couldn't catch him out either. When trouble loomed, he knew exactly what to say. What a gift! You're up to your neck in it, but you have the words. All that was the wit. The know-how.

But he was melancholy too, as if he knew something else – and wasn't telling. He was like a friend who would be yours if only he wasn't everyone's. He seemed to be for you, made for you, yet out of reach – that's how he was. Out of reach. And this was what made him so vivid. But another thing: he was a law unto himself. Like Rebecca.

He had a lover who sat upon his knee, and when he drove the swaggerer Pistol from the tavern, she covered his face with kisses. Doll Tearsheet was her name. Pistol calls her a whore and Falstaff draws, he sees him off. So she's perched on his knee like a blackbird on a boulder and she says, 'When wilt thou leave fighting a-days, and foining a-nights, and begin to patch up thine old body for heaven?' 'Foining' meant 'fucking'.

Falstaff's reply choked Kennedy: 'Peace, good Doll, do not speak like a death's-head, do not bid me remember mine end.' He could see from the beginning that Falstaff was worried by time. Doll was played by a French actress. He adored her too. On the instant. She was dark, as a Latin or Indian, with this wonderful earthy sharpness at the corners of her eyes. So, he wanted a wife like Doll, a friend like Sir John. Not much to ask, what? Doll may not have been honest, but she was faithful. When he's called to come to the wars, she weeps. At the tavern door, she begs him not to go; but Falstaff, he's on his way.

It got him reading again. The two parts of *Henry IV,* the whole of

Shakespeare. Maybe that was where his project started … Though in any account you give of your history, can you really say where something began?

★

'This is your last chance to run.'

Checking in at his hotel, Kennedy went over the words. Lyric, quotation, warning, threat? Past the Guildhall and along the seafront, a taxi took him to the university, where he registered in the Margam Suite. Oh it's you! said Hester Pygg in white peasant blouse. She handed Kennedy a badge with his name and institution, to clip on his jacket. Kennedy stuffed it in his pocket … *For the safety and security of all our delegates, name badges should be displayed at all times unless no one gives a fuck who you are anyway.* Hester Pygg smiled and gave him his pack: vouchers, map, names, timetable, postcard of a seventies' band. He was just in time for the Shakespeare 'parley'. Her necklace was of blue hearts, cut from thick stones.

The present speaker was Jack Cappello, a stout Canadian with toothbrush moustache. Kennedy, occupied in a fantasy calculus of the possibility, and desirability, of the black-haired lady's staying at his hotel, tried to organise his attention, for Cappello's paper was uncannily sympathetic …

'Let's face it. Our culture has lost its love of individuality. What's the consequence? I'll tell you now. We've spent half a century taking it out on character! We're like workmen sent into an old part of town by planners. Down comes that fine old building, then we slip off and never come back. Just leave a mountain of rubble!' And Cappello continued his warm-up with a survey of those specialists in negation who said character was no more than a poetic construction, a grammatical function, a rhetorical figure, a bourgeois mystification, an ideological bonbon, in fine, an illusion that must be abstained from now we were all in long trousers, with long faces to match. Which was so welcome to Kennedy, his attention took wing again, migrating in a dream of a fat private eye with a Cappello moustache; he watched him with his old man in the seventies, rolling round town in a silver Lincoln, slugging it out with liars, eating his meals alone …

People were clapping, looking round, laughing. 'We can't begin to love ourselves as individuals,' boomed Cappello, 'unless we take a lead from characters. And hear this! Shakespeare made these guys to last!' People clapped again, they laughed and looked around. Much encouraged, Kennedy wondered if he might introduce himself to the Canadian, but there were two more papers to hear.

The first was given by a boy professor, watched eagerly by two young women in the front row, one of them tapping his words into a black device. Kennedy thought he'd seen him on *Newsnight* recently talking about terrorism and the university. Striking a short line through the air, he said 7/7 had been a wake-up call – for anyone who needed it. As we all knew, Cultural Studies had been practising historically sensitive Shakespeare criticism for a quarter century at least; but all terrorism required was the excuse that some of us promoted Shakespeare like we were still holding the Festival of Britain. Yes, Globe Theatre, he meant you – but not only you. We had to stop looking for our national image in a proto-imperialist pantheon. When students of other faiths observed a Shakespearean king plan a bit of Middle-Eastern pagan bashing in order to distract everyone from a rebellion at home, what did they think? That's right!

He proceeded a while as if at a party conference. Was Cappello being got at? Or merely dismissed as irrelevant? Kennedy watched the Canadian, sitting with arms folded beside the speaker, who was now showing them on PowerPoint a 'Millennial Character Manifesto' to broker cultural difference. An admirable goal, no doubt, though the speaker's plans were so abstract, committing him neither to instances nor belief, that as the young women nodded and the redhead turned to check the audience, Kennedy became lost in contemplation.

Forking the air like a rapper, one eye half-closed in irony, the boy professor now called out, 'Wake up and smell the coffee!', which led to noisy applause and whooping. The redhead and her colleague rose and the redhead stuck her chest out. Applause continued. A big name stepped up and stood with left hand on hip, in high boots of champagne suede.

In a drawl that was persuasive and soft, Professor Winner said she wanted to begin, if she might, by revaluating Browning's theory of rhetorical character, which had done sterling service for a generation. As a matter of fact, it hadn't done Kennedy any kind of service, since the theory explained Elizabethan acting as a development of the ancient art of rhetoric. Your classical orator or politician produced his effect from action, of the eyes or hands. In the same way, *action* was the word for the performance of the Elizabethan actor who played Falstaff, Hamlet, et al – not 'acting', but 'action'. *I liked me well Master Burbage's action*, an apprentice on the Bankside might have said. He made no separation between rhetoric and acting. They were both means of giving character to an idea, or emotion, you wanted to communicate. *Sure, the player was most like to a murderous King*, they'd be thinking as they walked away through the mire of Southwark. They'd seen an action, and were satisfied. Didn't wonder what that King did, or where he went, between performances.

In a nutshell, that was Browning's theory. 'What you see is what you get' – character as communication. No suggestion of its outflanking its own performance because it has some kind of existence that's held back from action, or covered or concealed by it. That way of thinking about character (which happened to be Kennedy's) was silly because it wasn't historical. They didn't give any time to the thought that character was *deep* or private back in 1600, anymore than they believed in bacteria or democracy. When Hamlet says, 'I have that within which passes show', they waited for him to show it, nudging each other.

But how the hell could we be sure what everyone thought or didn't think in 1600, when our thoughts were so well hidden from each other in 2006? They would have had their secrets, as Kennedy had his. And as long as he didn't wave his hands or convey it with his eyes, no one was going to know it.

Brooding on his trouble, he became distracted. The speakers were now taking questions, then the chair led applause, and they were invited to a reception.

7. The clients. Starring Kennedy on Sir John Falstaff!

Holding his wine glass by the stem, Jack Cappello told a story to a man with a red beard. Since no one offered to introduce him, Kennedy spent the time with a group of people, to one or two of whom he was vaguely known, who were trying to name Badfinger's hit single. They asked Kennedy along to an Indian restaurant by the Guildhall and between the puppodums and starters, Cappello was denounced by a fellow from Worcester with a deep voice. The Canadian was such a notorious pest, he'd had to go into exile in Cracow for three years to give the freshwomen of Montreal a chance to graduate unmolested. No sooner was he back than he debauched two grad students in a hut by Lake Michigan and it was off to Ankara with Cappello for a much longer stretch. Incredible he retained tenure after these incidents – though he was of course an arch manipulator. Here someone said something Kennedy didn't pick up, and Worcester made a quick joke. The younger members of the group were narrowing their eyes, as Worcester advised them that Cappello deployed the concept *nature* like a fascist and talked about the individual like a kid stuffing himself with ice cream. What about Hegelian rationality? Everyone nodded, and narrowed or widened their eyes, except Kennedy, who was stuck on the wall side of the table and had to stay put and hear out the conversation, hot-faced, tasting nothing. At the end of the evening, the deep-voiced man went on somewhere else with two of the young women to discuss the law of the heart, and Kennedy returned to his hotel.

Next day he looked out for Cappello, but the latter was in a taxi to Bristol for an early flight home. Feeling like an agent in occupied land, Kennedy attended three more papers.

Lunch was in the Taliesin Theatre, where researchers and junior academics gathered about the speakers in something like the manner that clients were once drawn to the presence of wealthy Romans, or the hypothetical Higgs boson to larger subatomic particles. Their wish was to be known, or become memorable, though on the classical model, speakers like the boy professor had bullies to hand so that not everyone got through. As a matter of fact, the boy professor's bully was the cheer-leading redhead, now holding his plate of olives and flashing down the room the cold lights of her eyes.

If you did get through, the issue was, How to make someone remember you? Saying something brilliant was one way (though if it were too brilliant, the speaker might be inclined to forget you pretty quickly). Saying something complimentary was another, though this called for a degree of skill in flattery; and it was said by certain cynics that you weren't going to get anywhere without a willingness to back up the compliment with voluptuous favours like a good client; though others reckoned that sheer persistence or initiative would do, as in the Legend of Ralph Oliver.

All the way to Memphis went Childe Ralph, to an MLA conference of the early 90s, where he spent his days tracking Farrell Browning, whose theory had done sterling service, and who took with him wherever he went a living ring, a sort of *Fantasia* hedge, of fairly famous professors and clients. But Childe Ralph made observation of the times the hedge parted, and seized the chance to pursue that professor to a cubicle where he had gone. Oliver's detractors claimed he actually got inside, or over the top via the one next door. However he appeared, he gave his name and offered news. For Master Derrida had made right goodly tribute to Farrell Browning when Childe Ralph encountered him on a dune, down La Rochelle way in the summer. And though Oliver's detractors claimed the French titan called him *un quim Anglais*, rather than inviting him to lunch in Quimper, Ralph Oliver secured that afternoon a teaching fellowship at Farrell's department in Chicago and was now a famous professor himself in an excellent British university.

Professor Winner said excuse me and passed Kennedy to embrace a tall lady and then a tall man who were positioned in a dignified manner by some black curtains at the end of the room beside an unmanned bar. As he watched her go, wondering who that couple may have been, for he'd not noticed them at the conference (but now the gracious Professor was blocking his view), Kennedy discovered he had his own client. This was a young man who held the conference programme in Kennedy's face and said, indicating the afternoon's sessions, 'Is this you?' Kennedy confirmed that it was him, and the young man said he had a mind to attend Kennedy's paper. Kennedy enquired if the young man was working in the same area, perhaps for his PhD, and the young man made a face and said, 'You'll be lucky!', or something to that effect. Reasonably, Kennedy then asked what the young man's particular interests were, to which the latter retorted, 'Why do *you* want to know?' From a client, this was pretty insolent, though Kennedy himself, having neither influence nor reputation at his own university, was scarcely entitled to much deference. A rather beautiful young man he was, with hair like the angel who stretches out to Saint Matthew in Caravaggio's painting while the martyr toils at his gospel. 'See you later, alligator!' He turned away from Kennedy, strolling to the black curtains, where a large group had formed, the bar having apparently opened. In fact, Kennedy's part of the room was now virtually empty, apart from himself. He went outside for some fresh air and to phone Barbara. She was engaged, so he left a silly message as an April Fool's prank.

Another reason why his paper was such a mess (he'd come back in to practise), was that what he was trying to say just was not sayable academically. He'd still have to read the bloody thing, of course, for he lacked confidence to tell them, 'What I have to say is unsayable. There is no theory of character that can come close to explaining how it is that character exists. Goodbye. You won't be seeing me again.'

At four o'clock, Kennedy stood heavy-hearted at the door of the Cefn Bryn Salon with handouts, and Hester Pygg. He was scheduled for an abbreviated session, the speaker who was to precede him having fallen in the sea (albeit not fatally!) last night, and the speaker who was to follow having defaulted. 'So you're the last of the day (and the conference)!' called Ms Pygg. 'Good luck!' There was an audience of 14 for him. The beautiful young man was conspicuously not there, nor were any young women present, as the chairwoman introduced Kennedy and said that although yesterday was officially the Shakespeare session, he was going to tell us about 'Falstaff's Reserve'.

Kennedy began with a pleasantry about Falstaff and Wales. A middle-aged woman in a tweed cap grinned and the chairwoman laughed and showed bright teeth. It was the Welsh who'd been first to notice that Falstaff was a critical issue, as far back as 1772, when that energetic Welshman Maurice Morgann, who'd gone to America, governed New Jersey, and fought the slave-traders, published his *Essay on the Dramatic Character of Sir John Falstaff*. Now as was well known, Morgann had made a significant, if 'paradoxical', contribution to the study of character with his essay on Falstaff in the two parts of *Henry IV*, which was based in the principles of 'latency' and 'inference'.

What was meant by those terms? He noticed a man in a leather jacket that buttoned down the front. God help him. The listeners he'd imagined were not these tired people who'd paid him the respect of attending, but whose faces would do nothing. The listeners imagined were hostile, superior.

Kennedy skipped a paragraph. The woman in the tweed cap laughed at something.

What Morgann taught us was that there were latent aspects of Falstaff's character that we somehow had an impression of as existing alongside, or, to be precise, just behind the loud laughter and rascality. He also taught us that we made certain inferences about the background or previous life of Falstaff in something like the way we make inferences about a stranger we've just met, eg:

He's been around.

She's done this before.

He's smiling like he's going to rip me off.

I could spend the rest of my life with her.

'You're one bad pony and I ain't betting on you!'

Every joke he tells is a hiding place.

So, here was an instance of latency from the first part of *Henry IV* which was unlikely to be noticed on the stage … To spare his listeners, Kennedy skipped more material. A reckless, bridge-burning procedure when you're not extemporising. But the audience weren't enchanted; his tone was, of course, wrong for such an event. The inferences about strangers were too anecdotal. He should have used PowerPoint. Like menus before the nauseous, the paper handouts lay unexamined on the narrow lecterns that ran across each row of seats. He searched the devil's carnival of his own script. Alone, the woman in the tweed cap seemed to be enjoying something, though it probably wasn't Kennedy's argument, since he could see she was texting a message.

He found that he was now talking about early readers of the first part. A taboo subject in a way, because there was an academic shibboleth that *plays were for watching, not reading*; but unsupported by certain points from the skipped material about why the plays had never been only for the theatre (points admirable for an imaginary listener, but so potentially offensive in the circumstances, he wondered how he could have considered uttering them), he must sound as if he knew nothing whatsoever about the field. So he reminded them that quartos (little compact editions for reading only), were published in Watling Street at the Sign of the Star, 1599, 1604, 1613 – omitting the gag, 'something for the weekend, Sire?'

He began to flounder. Why on earth was he talking about early readers? ... Of course. That small instance of latency from the beginning of *Henry IV*, might have struck them (a handful perhaps), and they would ask themselves in the rooms where they read by daylight or candlelight and no one about them ceased from chattering, stitching, laughing, singing, belching, as they sat with quarto in hand, strange silent lumps of nature, *Why doth Falstaff ask the Prince the time?*

For in the opening lines of Act 1, Scene 2, when Falstaff and the Prince enter the world for the first time and the fat knight says, 'Now, Hal, what time of day is it lad?', the Prince doesn't answer the question. He tells Falstaff a man of his habits (eating, drinking, whoring, thieving, and so forth), doesn't need to know the time. Does Falstaff object?

As we all know, he plays along, as if the question about the time of day were utterly out of character. So, why *does* Falstaff ask the Prince the time?

Maybe he asks in irony, just because it isn't his kind of question; and thus he gets his first laugh. But a question asked in irony isn't necessarily a question that couldn't also have been meant, is it? Fair inference? What d'you think? Your faces are stone. Could I ever have imagined your nodding?

What's more, can't a question asked in irony imply a self that's keeping back from what everyone knows of you? You see with irony, you can split yourself in two, sending one out as your representative, while the other keeps behind in the shadows, on the side of the street that is out of the sun ... *Tune your lute you lyrical wanker!*

As to why that other self does keep back, we may infer a number of reasons why a person might act in public in a manner that is somehow contrary to, or different from, their private self. For one thing, it's almost a law of being a celebrity. In Falstaff, Shakespeare is giving us a very early instance of this, Falstaff's combination of charisma, drunkenness, wit and contempt for the law being a prototype of celebrity behaviour. And people who privately encounter a celebrity even to this day, when celebrities are as plentiful as cheap food, will insist that *they are not the same as they come across on TV.* For in the celebrity of 1597 as with the 2006 model, the general latency of human existence is magnified by the distance between private and public selves.

But Falstaff (for some minutes, Kennedy'd been letting himself go), Falstaff also keeps back the self that is concerned with the time because his relationship with the Prince is dangerous. Potentially fatal. All the time they're having fun together, death is there in the corner. It amuses the Prince to make jokes about the gallows to Falstaff, it being understood that the Prince has the power to protect this fat old thief from being hanged. Yet the question about the time would have reminded quiet readers of lessons they'd heard in church, in which the words of St Paul about 'redeeming the time' in which one has sinned, would have rung loud. A man who wasn't concerned with the time was damned. Falstaff, let's make the inference, wants God, but feels Him ever so far away. The Prince is closer, and the

Prince isn't having any of that. He wants Falstaff for fun; as a being with concern for his own soul, Falstaff is of no interest to the Prince. 'If you get serious on me, I'll let them hang thee, Jack!' – that's the threat implied. But since quiet readers were well-acquainted with the idea that their own monarchs were Supreme Governors of the Church of England, here they would have encountered the shocking suggestion that the Church itself was engineering the damnation of the fat old man.

Well once you start thinking that, the popular idea that Falstaff is the 'white-bearded old Satan' who tempts the Prince away from the straight and narrow, the source of such high spirits in Part 1 especially – that idea spills, it goes everywhere. What is temptation now? Who is tempting whom? Which of them called up the other? Did Falstaff appear one day before the Prince, to lead him astray? Or did the Prince seek out the old fat man, in his quest for a different sort of life from the one that starves him of experience? Was it from the corner of his eye that the one first spotted the other? Who needs whom? Who serves whom? What are they to each other? Which of them is it won't leave the other alone? ... *Dunno.*

This is my question. You see the Prince, he sticks to Falstaff, can't keep away, and this is because Falstaff has something in reserve, which the Prince fears and resents, even though he loves it. He resents Falstaff as any boss resents a worker with a secret, something of his own. And so he threatens Falstaff with death, because of this fearful resentment: 'Do not be yourself, on pain of death!' is his command. 'Just make me merry!'

This is clear enough isn't it? The audience looked on. The Prince fears Falstaff because he has something in reserve. He knows the fat knight has something in reserve because he denies him it in that very first instance. 'Don't ask the time!' What you deny, you acknowledge. Otherwise why deny? You see, the Prince is really a modern scholar, or a critic, who says character is character, and don't dare mistake it for a person. It does not *exist*! Character doesn't have anything behind its back. But the violence of the Prince, it's like the violence of us scholars, it doesn't want there to *be* more to a character than meets the ear or eye. But what it does not want there to *be* in Falstaff, it fears there *is*, it knows there *is*. In Falstaff there is soul … *Ha-lle-lujah! Hallelujah! Hallelujah!*

We know this for certain, because what does he do when he has a quiet moment, the Prince? Why, he says, 'I shall have a go at this *something in reserve* lark! I will carry on acting like a scoundrel but all the time I am really a diamond geezer inside, I promise. So when I give up acting like a scoundrel and take the throne, folk will be all the more amazed at what was there all along!' But this effort to get a second self, to exist apart from how he seems, well it's a fake. Like any of us saying, 'I have a soul.' We can't have it. We have science. We have 'rigour', don't we? We scholars. And you'll say, but the Prince, he doesn't have science, he's 409 years ago in play time; in historical time he's 600 years ago. He could have had a soul, for what it's worth.

No. He couldn't. Because although he doesn't have physical science or your critical science, he has the beginnings of it in the power he bears to do violence against whatever does not yield to him. That is his regal inheritance, a kind of first science. It kills souls!

Kennedy made an emphatic sign with his fist, as if to punch himself in the eye. Entering the Cefn Bryn Salon, a janitor began tidying up at the top. The chairwoman was saying something and showing Kennedy her wrist. Sincerely, relieved to be ending, Kennedy told the faces before him that his major project was an attempt to –

But the chairwoman was now rising and saying something pleasant in a rather tense manner, while the woman in the tweed cap was shaking her head as if she'd never heard the like of it. The audience smiled, rose and left clapping lightly and the janitor began to crush Kennedy's handouts. In a black bin bag they gathered, like baby ghosts.

8. Swansea Bay.

People were going on for drinks and farewell *swper* at the No Sign in Wind Street, but Kennedy slipped away from the white buildings of the university in the direction of the seafront. As he hurried across the carriageway and up an embankment, he imagined them discussing his paper.

He kept on until the urge to put distance between himself and his witnesses felt a pull from behind. He might be seen as a second Cappello. *Who the hell invited this pair of clowns? See how they both disappeared?* Perhaps he should rush into the bar they'd named like the man in Poe's story and confess, for Kennedy's habitual urge was to unconceal himself.

*

One summer, visiting his grandparents, he was taken by two boys to the fields. They were pissing about and trampling down the corn when Tony English yelled. Along the lane beside the little wood, a stout man, black dog and red-faced youth were advancing to a position at three o'clock from the boys where the sloping field levelled, now coming their way. Kennedy's pals took to their heels but Kennedy sank among the green shoots. Yet when the farmer passed at a distance, appraising damage, Kennedy rose from his green hiding place to give himself away. So he bore alone the farmer's anger, and a couple round the head from the red son. They let the dog chase him back to the wood, round the corner and down the track till his spit thickened.

Wasn't nobility made Kennedy rise from the corn, like he'd sacrificed himself to draw fire from the other boys; wasn't honesty either, like headmasters used to recommend. Long afterwards, he supposed he couldn't bear not to be known for his transgression. Something like that would have been his motive, as if there were nothing worse than guilt concealed – or perhaps, nothing worse than concealment itself. For how much damage had Kennedy and the boys who took him along that day been guilty of? Concealment was itself a kind of guilt, openness a form of contrition, even innocence.

He returned to his grandparents with a dirty face. They wanted to know if he'd been crying.

*

Drift on. He'd never find the bar; impetus was gone. Could have been home with Barbara by half eight easy, but he was stuck with the hotel room. What the hell had he imagined, when he booked two nights? So much for the 'otherworldliness'. Let him sit there by himself and pray ... for a couple of swingers with a skeleton key, a conscientious but filthy-minded cleaner who'd been in since late morning and still hadn't done the bathroom, a long-legged visitor in a Venetian mask, a lewd magician and his nephew. Yeah, sit alone and pray.

High on the water, a ferry came in. The bay curved, straightened. Way over there were orange fires. By the sea's edge a figure moved. The fires paled, dissolved: beneath them a blur of industrial plant. The bay was vast, a giant's bite. The fires returned. One, pale and hot, pulled tricks in evening air ... *Watch me, Kennedy! See what I can do, baby!* As the orange flare shimmied, his heart filled. Should be grateful anyone'd come to hear him at all. Distrust of the folk he'd thrown in his lot with, was becoming a vice with him.

A hooded youth passed and spat in a bin. There was a text incoming from Barbara, puzzled by the joke he'd left her, a message from his old man. On a small-wheeled bike passed another youth, smoking a joint. He came to an oblong enclosure of dark green water. At the far end, yachts were moored. Flats and bars lined three sides. From the decks of a rust-red lightship, parents called to kids. Kennedy went on along the esplanade, which was curiously ornamented: belvedere on slender legs, marked with cardinal points; green bullet, engorged, surmounted by vane; a sort of wheelless waggon, upper edges fitted with runners.

Whose hand was responsible? In a game whose players'd run away, all this might have signified. Perhaps they were hiding about here. Or these monstrous sculptures were dreamwork, hybrid shapes formed from thoughts that wouldn't go. Whose dream? In an etching of Goya's, a giant sits alone, the world his dream. Did such a giant dream this scene? They talked of an unconscious of cities. The sea breeze had stilled. Here a raised, boxy shape, with proboscis and curved blade.

A little further on, a convex slide, adorned with tools and sculpted junk like a pub with 'character'. As a child, he would have delighted in these objects. On the dark sand, a figure looked his way. The tide was rising. To the west, a little town glittered. As he went on, the figure seemed to turn.

At dusk he came to a domed tower. It appeared to be an observatory. Light fell upon lines engraved in the west wall:

TAN MWYN DDOE. NI DDIFLANNA DIM
ER ALLOSODIR OLL.
Y SAWL HEB SEL SYDD AR GOLL.

FOSSILIZED LIGHT. NOTHING DISAPPEARS
THOUGH ALL IS REARRANGED.
LOST ARE THEY WHO ARE UNAMAZED.

In spite of himself, the words affected him. Light from the stars was fossilized. Older than any time we knew, white as the bones of creatures long extinct. There was the promise of eternity, if only one knew how to recognise it; a threat of abandonment, to those who didn't. Through a tinted window, a large sheet of paper was visible, pinned to a board for an 'Astronomy Quiz', questions indecipherable. A lintel stone above the door bore the name 'Tower of the Ecliptic'.

Further on were flats, walls set with stones quoting Descartes, Wittgenstein, legible in the bracketed lamps with which they were fitted, and Newton's statement of the First Law of Motion:

Every body continues in its state of rest, or uniform motion in a straight line, unless it is compelled to change that state by forces impressed upon it.

Now Kennedy was no physicist, but knew enough as a reasonably-educated man to be aware of the mighty authority of this law, which was also known as the 'Principle of Inertia'. It meant that things stayed put if left alone, or proceeded in a straight line if fired by a rifle, a curved line if kicked by Captain Beckham, and a looping drifting line if bowled by Masters Mushtaq and Warne, until friction or gravity or whatever affected the straightness of their path. Certainly, in respect of free kicks, ballistics and leg-spin bowling, it was an excellent law. And when it came to setting your keys on the table at night so as to be able to leave the house punctually the next morning without concern that they'd slip off and hide in the bottom of the fridge; or placing a glass where it might be filled with red wine without peril to trousers or cornices, it could be relied on with full practical confidence. Yet Kennedy sometimes browsed in a fat blue book by a kindly man of science, who had a theory that things neither stayed put where they had been left, nor rolled along quite comfortably as they had been set to roll, when those things were very tiny and very quick.

Indeed, they might be in two places at once according to this theory, or spring from place to place in a capricious manner, according to a principle of the fundamental roguishness of energised matter. It was a theory, however, that was supposed to apply only to immature particles, knaves and nippers that could be allowed their sport, provided they upset no one, and got up to nothing, in the big world – of which, however, they seemed, paradoxically, to be ancient and very basic building blocks (and one or two mysterious things the kindly scientist said about 'entanglement' suggested the knavery might not be quite confined to the particle world).

Nonetheless, reality was pretty much as Newton said when he laid down the law – human reality was anyway; and it was a sin of the animal man, as Kennedy now reflected, to be ambivalent about this, taking reality for granted when it came, for example, to travelling by timetabled trains to attend academic conferences that occurred at a fixed date and place, on the one hand; and thinking it the more the pity that physical surprises just didn't happen in the big world, on the other. We wanted things just as they were, and also not at all as they were. When we were bored with rational arrangements, we wished the world mysterious again.

The orange fires burned. Twilight had acquired an old-metal lustre: the tide was in unnoticed. At the seawall water glugged; fell back swelling, levelled and came on. *Achtung*, Kennedy! In phase it swelled and levelled, like a cat's spine. Heavy now, carpet of silvery tons, it slid and smacked the wall. The Flood would have looked like this. When the giants copulated, so it sounded.

In the little town west of the bay, lights flashed like jewels. Under the sea wall were voices, hushed, adamant. Something should be taken to the north shore. A small boat must have come in on the tide; it was too dark now to see much. Kennedy heard laughter. Then a man called,

'The stoplines are still operational!'

9. As Kennedy told Barbara.

Know how Kennedy discovered Barbara? In action with strongman, 'Basil' and the Pole, telling them how to fucking go about it … For shame! Devil take you! She was standing with a flock of carrier bags at the kitchen door, so Kennedy was just in time to check his ageing monarch and help with the shopping. That's the truth of the matter. She grinned and said tell me how it went, the way married folk converse, not as professional people, or lovers, who sit to talk, but on the job like labourers.

'*Venga!* Those go in the freezer.' She was wearing jeans by 'Tribes of Time'. Beneath, her boots peeped out like moles. Handing over viands and cates, Kennedy fancied her a lady shepherd, himself a sort of looby.

'Aren't you going to tell me?'

Two days ago he wandered off on his own. There she was with her flock when he came in through the door from Wales-Land, wanting to know his adventures. And your dolt with hanging lip who loved the shepherdess, he would have much to impart, of tricks played on him, and wonderful sights. So where to start?

'Hm? *Cuéntame!*'

An event of that morning came sliding to mind.

The breakfast manager in the hotel, he looked like a toad, OK? A witch's pet. *Sapo de bruja.* He was hanging about behind Kennedy. There was a couple at the table there, a man in a suit whose back was to Kennedy and a lady opposite, who Kennedy couldn't really see either (in answer to Barbara's enquiry) because the manager's *culo gordo* was perpetually in the way. You might have thought the suited man was a sort of boss of the place or executive who turned up incognito to inspect the quality, but the toad was trying to check the room number – he was obviously suspicious this pair were freeloading; though the way the man in the suit was fobbing him off wasn't what you'd expect from someone who was trying to avoid being noticed.

'What was he saying?'

Well there'd been a string of silly answers and folderol, and some outrageous patter. The man was quoting Newton's First Law of Motion one minute, then he was singing 'Scarborough Fair' (an old English song), and rapping in Welsh, as far as Kennedy could make out, which sounded sort of funny and militant at the same time, and pretty cool as a matter of fact. He clapped his hands while he chanted like a teacher or playleader of kids, and Kennedy could see over his shoulder that the lady was waving a silver spoon in the air, a sort of second playleader.

'Did you want to go and play? Let's sit down. We can finish these later.' Barbara opened a bottle of Mendozan Cereza (not routine for a Sunday afternoon), bringing it to the little parlour that looked onto the front road and placing it on the low table beside the elephant. On the wall was a framed photograph they'd been saying they'd replace, in which a young woman who Kennedy once thought resembled Barbara was being applauded by men young and old at a street corner. She looked nervous – and small wonder: these *bufones* were acting out a pantomime of lechery ...

'Carry on!'

Ah – well Kennedy didn't really know the rules of the game, though all this clapping was going on. The breakfast manager, he was clapping too – though not in the same spirit. He was like a kid who doesn't know how to play. He was going to call the police – he wanted them to know; but he was drowned out cos it seemed like many more had joined the game. At other tables men (none of them from the conference, by the way) were singing and shouting. They must have been drinking all night, this crew; they really were the worse for wear, standing to chuck waffles at each other. Though in a way, they were kind of disciplined. He could hear them now: '12-inch incoming!'; 'Flak cluster 200 foot!'; 'Torpedo starboard bow! Hard to port, Jenks!'; 'Call in heavy mortar fire!'; 'Five-second Gatling burst, scrimshaw round, length ahead!'; 'Tone steady to rising, Pilot!'

Someone was making a siren sound that started off like a wah-wah pedal then soared round the room and filled it; Kennedy had the feeling this was done vocally, though it could be they'd brought an electronic device. A sausage hit his table, steaming like a squib or little bomb. Someone shouted sorry, bud. Must have meant he wasn't a target. Seemed to be the only one who wasn't joining in.

'What were you doing? Just eating?'

He'd been reading as well – trying to, anyway.

'What about?'

Props.

'What sort?' Her eyes were on him.

Well when a kid used a branch for a rifle, or said to his pals the bit under the drainpipe was a black hole and they'd get sucked in if they went near it, or the garage was a fort, the branch or the grating was a prop in his game.

'Was it a book about children?'

Like he'd been reading a fathering guide, while food flew about him.

No. It was about make-believe.

'But that is for children, darling. You know that!'

Well characters might also be props that made a game of make-believe possible. If you took a book, or play, as a kind of game. Nothing childish about that.

'But when we had that talk about your project, you said you "really believed" in character. This just sounds like *pretending*! Isn't that a waste of time?'

Ah, well the man said pretending was true first.

'The man in the suit with the lady with the spoon?' Barbara rose to straighten something on the table.

No! The man who wrote the book he was reading. You see, he said the orthodox view of pretence or fiction is that it depends on fact, like a shadow depends on whoever casts it, or a worm on the intestine it inhabits. But that's a mistake. Pretend truth might be the senior form; our ancestors knew it with their myths – and they could tell the difference.

'Which difference?' She'd returned to the settee.

Between fiction and fact. They just preferred fiction.

'Why did they?'

Ah, they may have had deep reasons!

'What sort?'

Too deep for us to know – or too high. Or maybe they saw things we don't anymore.

'And all this while you were eating your breakfast!'

Then a bean had actually hit his book.

'I don't understand how could you read with all this *escándalo*!'

It also hadn't actually hit his book.

'Hey?'

It was a quantum bean.

'*Tontito*! Now what happened to the lady and Mr Suit?'

Well the breakfast manager, he'd got some support because a couple of musclemen had come up from the spa but Mr Suit called out something about 'jurisdiction'. He still seemed to be playing, though the toad was shrieking now. Like he was the one with jurisdiction and he knew who the man was too. Knew his name.

At this point Kennedy tried the accent: 'Know my name! Everyone knows my name, fuck-o!' – that was what Mr Suit said. 'Where's that going to get you?' So far he'd been managing the anecdote with unaccustomed skill, but at this point it was as if, experimenting with a probang, that 'incomparable engine' for phlegm clearing, he'd gone down too far and brought up from the back of the throat a substance that coated the words of the Welshman in such a way as to thwart pronunciation (as Securicor vans spray a dye on stolen notes).

'Well I've never heard a voice like that.' Barbara's legs were upon him. 'You must be making it up.'

He averred that he was not. The voice had been rough, musical, brownish.

'A voice can't be brown.' Like the chopper in a children's game, her legs pressed.

It was the Welsh accent. That's what he meant. Mr Suit wasn't finished with Toad anyway because he knew they'd been here. The three of them. And Toad, he'd served them and he'd laughed with them. Telling them what they wanted to know. Time was, he would have been tarred and feathered. Today they were taking his ends!

'Who were?'

Mr Suit and his Jacks. That was how he referred to his crew.

'What does any of that mean? You made that up too!' Barbara decided. She poured them more wine, leaning out for the bottle as one in a boat.

No! He could still hear the words. She had to believe this – there was a big flash (he could feel the heat), and all these Jacks and Mr Suit, they were out of there! Like crows. They'd set the place on fire!

'But how did you escape?'

He just left.

'But had you checked out?'

He checked out on the way.

'The hotel's on fire and you stopped to check out!'

It wasn't as bad as it looked. They'd just set the cereal station ablaze. It might have been a sort of theatrical fire.

'You must have had one look at this pyromaniac!'

He had green eyes.

'Ugh!' Barbara hated green-eyed men.

Kennedy took note.

'But we've had nothing about you, Mister!' She wagged her finger. 'Perhaps he's covering something up about his trip!'

As a matter of fact, she trusted him as far as any reasonable woman might trust a man, which was a cause of double sadness to Kennedy. On the one hand, the trust was a fine affront to his maleness, taking it for granted he had no balls – a form of shearless castration (actually, that was overdoing it). On the other, her trust wasn't fully deserved, which made it beautiful beyond words, gentle, infinitely generous (and when Kennedy thought, as often he did now, like this, then the term 'fully' revolted him with its dishonesty). He played with her foot within her sock. He was covering nothing up about his trip, he protested.

'Now what about your talk?' Her curiosity was settling. 'You haven't said about it. Are you being modest?' Her socks were soft as any teenage girl's, pure cashmere, a Christmas gift from Kennedy.

The weather of Britain wasn't kind to her. 'Well?' For the talk had surely been the main thing. What he'd been on about for so long, given so much of his attention, at the expense of other matters. She drew her feet her way, gathering herself.

Oh it wasn't much good.

But he seemed jolly.

Actually he was.

But how about the project? Huh?

So he told her he was going to be more flexible.

She smiled.

Clothed La Barbara seemed such a neat figure; naked there was more of her, a sort of elemental density beneath the Western covering of denim and white cotton. Do clothes miniaturise women? Kennedy was wondering at her flesh and her hair, gold, black, wine red, compared to his own northern colour scheme, just standing there in his trance, when she said come on down, *caracol*. Get your things off!

Sometimes he imagined three of them. They were being watched. Then he was watching, waiting his turn. Or Barbara was sitting back in a chair (there by the window) leering and calling encouragement. Then Kennedy was leering back, or up or down, and who could tell who the mastery was with? When you gave it up it came right back; if you held on it betrayed you, in those pictures of his. Other times, they were alone, and then it wasn't images that drove Kennedy on but language.

On the final stretch of his journey this afternoon, on the tube, as he passed the park, he was entertaining a certain word, making phrases, dense, gorgeous, hot in the mouth, like meat roasted in the pot. It was a knack of Kennedy's, this building up a heat through words alone; though he kept them always to himself for shame, even though it was a kind of magic, subtler by far than the power of what you could look at online. Her eyes closed. That was good. They opened and seemed to read, as if there were a page between the two of them.

As the years passed, Kennedy wanted her to look at him the way she did the first time even though he hadn't known then if she was happy, satisfied or sad − so sad her soul would break out if only it could find a way; and he hadn't known if one was watching the other drown, without putting out a hand. Because obscure and complex as that look had been, it acquired a sort of simplicity, when repeated. You could compare it with certain artworks: they were pondered over, reflected on for so long, in pursuit of the question of their meaning that they became classics, universally recognised and a cause of wonder just because their meaning still hadn't been wholly explained. The most dedicated or well-funded research couldn't say *This is the meaning* of the classic.

Today, however, her look was not to be read, since it was she who was the reader. As he was finishing, she asked, 'Why did the green-eyed man burn up the hotel?'

Her leg twitched as Kennedy considered his answer. She was falling asleep; all of her. He watched their feet. Woman is classical; man grotesque. We ought to shove off back to the pit and leave them in peace. Who does she paint her nails for? Not for you. Don't worry, son. She does it because it's done – not for the traitor. A goddess instructs them.

Hey, Kennedy! Why not retrain, become a steelman? She could rub you down with Swarfega. Waiting with green gel. You'd need some work boots ...

Just hours ago his train passed mighty steelworks. Rolling plants, elevated walkways, pipelines, spread out for miles before the eyes. Port Talbot. He counted the furnaces, flues and chambers blackened. Orange fire hailed him, an old friend. Furnace No. 2 was the kit of an alchemist, ten times the height of a man. After Cardiff, the train passed meadows, and through these meadows, a broad stream meandered. The meadows rose up to a gentle hill, and upon that hill stood two men and a woman, beside a burned-out car.

10. Trudi Tower. The dons. Vanessa Lane.

It was getting on for six. 'I heard foxes last night,' Barbara told her husband. 'In the park.'

'Really?'

'Yes. They were fucking.'

'How long did it go on for?'

'An hour. At least. *Zorros de cojones!*' She rose and went from the bedroom, leaving Kennedy to reflect on these observations in the afterimage of her bum. One thing to be said in his favour was that he'd never really lacked for staying power, so she wasn't implying an animadversion along the lines *If only you could keep it up like a fox!* No. He was better than average and that was a fact, since Trudi Tower wrote only the other week, 'Basically, the average man can maintain thrusting for approximately 145 seconds before orgasm.' On the other hand (Kennedy managing to hurt his elbow as he reclined in thought), it rather sounded as if foxes were out of favour just now with Señora Barbara. Suppose *He takes as long to come as a fox!* was another family adage? The roots of her people were complex, Sicilian, West Country, South American. You never knew what she might come up with.

Seriously though, how long should you take? Kennedy lacked blokes to discuss this with. Of course, Trudi and other experts in these matters, would tell you that the person to discuss it with was not blokes anyway, but your wife or partner, *openness* being essential to a relationship – unless you were crucified with guilt about that affair you were having, when the experts often counselled tact, discretion, evasion, concealment or, to use a not nice word, *lies*.

But a broader concern that Kennedy lacked blokes to discuss with was the one of how often people did it who'd known each other a long time in the same house (i.e., people 'living as if married'). If he'd had a drinking friend (and been a drinker), this might have provided a topic for conversation. Actually, Cy Frazer had been hinting that he and Kennedy might have something to chat about on these lines, but Kennedy made excuses not to go along with Dr Frazer to the pub by their office. Cy had known a handsome lady called Angharad Register for a long time in the same house, but seemed to be on splendid terms with a number of ladies (Parsley, Leila, Moon-girl) in other houses as well. He was a bit of a player, Cy, and oddly (as he hinted) he thought Kennedy was a player too, but Kennedy was not eager for a conversation about that, so his broader concern went undiscussed (which shouldn't be taken to mean that it gathered dust).

As it happened, this was a topic the experts had no expertise in, because, to quote for a second time Trudi Tower, 'the frequency of sex in couples who are in long-term relationships is dramatically under-researched'. Accordingly, Trudi was 'about to embark on a three-year research project' to put this right. Kennedy remembered these words, from a paper in which he took a critical interest. They'd provoked him. *Why* should sex be 'researched'? Who benefited? Leave long-term couples alone, for Christ's sake! Why should research poke its nose in? Maybe long-term couples didn't want to know how *their* frequency compared with anyone else's, or the public average. Maybe they wanted a mystery of their own.

But another thing that occurred to Kennedy just after that little outburst was that since the sex expert should *be* in a long-term relationship if worth their salt, then they ought to start by researching themself ... Except why bother with research? Surely they'd just *know* how often they did it? On the other hand, maybe the sex expert was a dead loss at arithmetic, long-term relationships — or copulating. One for the book of aphorisms!

Anyway, he knew the frequency of sex in his long-term relationship, particularly since Halloween, when Barbara made her announcement coming from the little corridor between the kitchen and the cupboard with an orange folder in her hand, and Kennedy merely said 'Ah', because he had that image of the kid in the mask still before him. He knew. And now, Kennedy rose from the marriage bed and went to see what his wife was up to.

He found her on the phone, irregularly dressed. She waved at him and he went away, thinking of a time when they marked their heights on a door frame in pencil. Barbara stood on a chair to do him; she was smaller by a full half cubit or ell.

On the theme of 'frequency over a lifetime', which probably bothered people on their deathbed more than a lot of other stuff, words from an obituary had stuck in Kennedy's mind: 'No Johnco, if I don't get it three times a day I feel physically ill, I really do.' *Three*? Jesus. This lad (a showbiz lawyer) must have had enough girlfriends. Kennedy hadn't, and any amount of scanning statistical breakdowns about British Sexual Behaviour was not going to put his mind at rest about it. If 5% of men had had 150 partners or more, then a number in single figures was, in fact, the norm: '35% reported between 7 and 8 partners'. *Report*? When did they 'report'? And who to? (The sex researchers, stupid!) Yet by no stretch of the imagination did Kennedy make 'between 7 and 8' either – or perhaps that should be rephrased as 'by no effort of interpretation', since Kennedy *in* imagination could probably report about 15,000 partners (if not 150,000, or even one and a half million, considering his years). But the girls he passed on the high street, who made his heart flinch because they were living art and a vindication of all created things, the professional ladies and matrons at restaurants, talks or galleries, whose shoes and outfits distracted him from the paintings (over time, he'd become a connoisseur of women's style) – with not one of these could he interpret fantasy as reportable fact (though the shame felt real enough). In between the two women he'd loved, his record was a disappointment that kept him rummaging in the past like one of those geniuses of the charity shop, or car boot sale.

*

So off he went to university, to learn from the dons about character. With money from his old man, he bought notebooks and new shoes for the adventure. He was on a full grant.

Now at that time, 'Essex' wasn't yet used as an attributive adjective to poke fun at young men and women with a lot of money in their pocket or handbag who made a noise in wine bars. This was a few years before Baroness Thatcher opened the City to wideboys and noised up all the Julians, the Henrys and the Sebs; but the Southern middle classes of the early 1980s must already have associated Essex with common vulgarity before they used the word for the nouveau-riche kind, because Kennedy didn't feel at home those first weeks. Certainly, the university was not a grand one, but every time he tried to be sociable, the others made him feel as if he was knocking their door. They were all freshers together together; why should he feel he'd come late, that they were all there before him? Why did he have to keep saying his name? They all seemed to know each other's. And where did this assurance they had come from? He was *alone*.

He soon found out that all the other freshers from comprehensive schools had been keeping their heads down during the first fortnight, sitting behind their doors with their reading lists, writing to their mothers, making casseroles with carrots and cheap cuts of meat. They invited him to the bar with them. His new chums spent the night sniping at the privately-educated kids with their luxuriant hair and unpitted faces. Their own faces were frightened or sharp, their eyes wouldn't stay still. He decided not to be their friend. More alone.

It was cool. No one could better him intellectually, so he told himself, public school or pleb. In his own thinking, he was secure. Another thing: whatever the kids with money thought, he was from the oldest town in Britain. Didn't need to be admitted. His town was there at the beginning. Observing a crematorium from the window of his room, he engaged in imaginary conversations.

To study character, that's what he was here for. Loneliness was no concern, with this before him. Actually, wasn't loneliness at all, but a kind of solitariness, like Zarathustra when he went up into the mountain, with only the birds and hedgehogs for company, far from the babble of men. Had his notebooks ready, buff-covered: 'Character I, II, III ...' Each week, his sister wrote, with news now and then of Rebecca Sutton. Until he reminded himself that the actual person is a shadow of the image we keep, he found the news hard to bear.

His mother sent a cake, to share with his new friends. The old man sent him a tenner, to buy a round of drinks. He walked about the grounds of the crematorium. It lay above a soft green vale, planted with yews and dark conifers. A cortège arrived, two cars as black as her hair had been.

Sister Kate wrote to say Rebecca'd been given a conditional discharge for shoplifting. But he was here to look for characters, not speculate on Rebecca Sutton's latest sin. The lecturers, however, weren't helping much. In fact, they were as arrant a pack of traitors to the cause as a young man could encounter (and he knew something about betrayal). In the first class, a little man with a black beard told them that 'literature' was a 'contested' term. Anything could be literature. He showed them a magazine. Had he become a don by studying magazines? Condescending wanker! In the second class, a man in dungarees told them literature didn't exist in a vacuum. It was inextricably linked with the politics of the time in which it was produced. Kennedy raised his hand. He thought that was journalism, not literature. The man in dungarees laughed. In the third class, a little dry man told them he didn't want to hear the word 'character' from any of them, OK? That was A-level stuff. They were at university now. Which happened to be the first lecture on Shakespearean Drama. Kennedy felt like the night Rebecca's mother phoned about the radiators. As the words sliced through him, he froze. The other students nodded their heads. The little dry man was telling everyone about Shakespearean comedy. They had to focus on gender, and identity, and class, and the way they were constructed (he made a spooling motion with his hands) through *discourse*. Now what was discourse? Here, for the first time, Kennedy heard the names of the French titans of thought or (as the little man put it in his conclusion) *theory*, who became his bugbear … *Utterly alone.*

The motto of the Kennedys! As he read and daydreamed, one world joined the other. The people about him were transformed.

There was a rich lad at his hall called Thayers. When he began to figure him as Gratiano, the redneck from *The Merchant of Venice*, rather than Oliver Thayers of St Grarl's College for the Sons of Clystermen, he detested him less. A surprise. Perhaps he even began to enjoy Thayer's practical jokes and wantonly-offensive comments in their little windowless bar, now he had the secret of him. Which worried him, but he couldn't deny it. Began to enjoy Dave Day too. At first, he'd recoiled from Day's furtive and virulent diatribes against the public-school kids, particularly his way of talking about the young women and what they needed. Then he read *Troilus and Cressida*. Instantly he saw Day as Thersites, the 'deformed and scurrilous Greek' who tells such bitter and venereal truths about the war at Troy that he regularly gets the crap kicked out of him by the Greek generals for damaging morale. He had a way of putting Kennedy's feelings about the lecturers who were betraying his dreams into memorable expression. He was funny, he was foul; he told the truth. And with time, Kennedy came to see the lecturers themselves as character types who could scarcely help the way they were or the forces that drove them. Perhaps they were like Malvolio, or the little academy of scholars in *Love's Labours Lost* … He thought it over; maybe they were more like characters of Ben Jonson, because the spirit of the time spoke through them, and the life of the mind has its fashions, so that what everyone agrees is cool this season, everyone ridicules in the next. Though there are always a handful of people who don't believe in fashion, and find the going hard in every season. He was twenty years of age and saw this.

In time, he sussed out someone like Shakespeare's Beatrice, a warm Venetian blonde who spoke as if wit were still in fashion. Vanessa Lane drank with blokes and held her own; she wore a black beret. Expelled from her school in Sussex, she was re-admitted when the girls marched through the village with burning torches. Their parents arrived to support the protest. Among them were friends of Michael Foot, Alan Clark, and the fella who wrote *Rumpole of the Bailey*. As Kennedy variously gathered, she'd brewed pilsner in an attic that was out of bounds, brought women's porn to the library on a Scandlines ferry, invited the IRA to speech day. After a night on the beer, she wrote her essays, light never out, the window of her ground-floor room always open. As Kennedy returned to his floor, he heard her talking to people, smelled the smoke from her

Marlboro Reds. Once she called his name. At her window, she asked what he'd thought of the lecture on *Doctor Faustus* that morning. Kennedy made like Dr Fry, conjuring the name 'Marcel Foucault' with his hands. She laughed and offered him a cup of wine, and as he stood there at her window, he was a wandering poet. Would she ask him in? There was a knock at her door and Thayers appeared along with a romantic-looking fellow called Hythe carrying a volume of Schopenhauer. Kennedy tapped his cup on the tavern sill and away like Villon or Rimbaud. Next morning she left early on her bike. Did she never sleep?

He wasn't so alone. His Number 1 don was Edgar Knight, a delicate malcontent from New South Wales with the head of a lion, bearded, golden, ever watching his back. He made an art of it in corridors, glancing wildly over shoulder at a footfall. Discovered ear to door, he wrestled air like Eric Morecambe. Kennedy, a connoisseur of his antics, knew Knight was no sneak. He wanted to be caught.

On his office wall he had a rococo print and an aboriginal mask. He began the tutorial in a murmur: 'What have they been telling you this week?' He meant the lectures given by Black-Beard, Dungaree and Dr Fry. As Day and Kennedy gave him the low-down, Knight rolled his eyes. Kennedy watched him closely. Why wouldn't he level with them, tell how *he* saw things? A stolid lad from Preston (a sort of Enobarbus) reported that Mr Hampton had told them tragedy was the legitimation of hierarchy. Kennedy added that Mr Hampton had swapped his dungarees for leg warmers this week. Edgar Knight put hand to mouth.

Kennedy's dedication to character piqued him: 'Are you saying …? Do you mean …? Are you now saying …?' Remembering what Kennedy'd come out with the week before, he confronted him with it; for at first, Kennedy thought it clever to contribute what he fancied were uncanny or provocative observations, or offer opinions that startled with their common sense, without caring too much about the implications of one contribution for the next. At Knight's concern for his thinking, he felt himself flush, recollecting with shame ideas he'd uttered; and began to understand that he was being trained not to give away his best thoughts until – perhaps until he could live by them. Or Knight may have meant they weren't for everyone. He was working out what Kennedy believed in.

At the end of the tutorial, he'd remark something to Kennedy as the others left; once he lent him a book. Kennedy had to think a while to find his character. Then fancied him as Richard II, delicate, exquisite, scrupulous, so much more intelligent than the thugs, traitors and temporisers who surround him. In his imaginary conversations, Edgar Knight was a partner.

'People say things about you two,' Vanessa Lane told him. He'd bumped into her in the crematorium grounds, where she went to read *The Faerie Queen*. Kennedy didn't ask what they said. He'd been told lies about before. Vanessa lit a Marlboro Red. Which bit was she reading?

It was where Prince Arthur came to help the Knight of Temperance. The Knight of Temperance was scared of ladies, in case they turned him on. Was that not virtuous?

Wasn't he a bit of a creep?

Oh! Did Kennedy think so? He didn't like wine either. Babes and booze were out of order for the Knight of Temperance. When the lady Acrasia showed him her paps, he smashed up her bower. She was wearing a see-through nightdress. It maddened him utterly.

Without saying goodbye, she rose and left.

One night in February, to celebrate receiving a first from Edgar Knight, Kennedy got canned. Drunkenness was a novel sensation … from room to room of a party, along the corridors, asking women if they were Doll Tearsheet, repeating himself.

What the hell was he on? One or two laughed; others called him arsehole.

In near darkness on a carpet he came round. Room wasn't too steady, but he felt OK. Had the height. Tying his shoe he went down again, sticky round the mouth. Everything he'd drunk, sherry in his room, quarter bottle of Bells someone passed him, all the other stuff, he rehearsed. After bumping round, after wandering by traffic, he got back to his room. A blackout. You have to experience these things …

'You're a card!' If he'd been closer to the end, he would have toppled off the bench where they sat next afternoon as Vanessa (who hadn't been at the party, but had her spies) recounted his exploits. How come he'd gotten spifflicated, bushwhacked, shikker? Wasn't like him at all, to be press-ganged by the demon distiller! She nudged him again; he turned to appeal. In the still air, her smoke mixed and cleared. Getting cock-eyed wasn't the foremost concern just now; what he wished to discover was what had happened in the dark on the ill-smelling carpet – with a young woman named Louise Dyer.

'Oh she's always making out guys jump her!' Vanessa called gaily. 'D'you think you're the first who jumped Louise Dyer?'

But he hadn't, he protested, not liking the sound of this. For what had he been doing on the floor? Mustn't there have been somebody down with him?

'Dyer the Liar, we call her!' Vanessa shouted, as if seeing off phantom supporters of the former.

Kennedy wasn't sure he knew her (which was obviously no defence).

'Oh you wouldn't! She's a nonentity, a jim-jam!'

But had she told Vanessa that he did that?

'Oh it gets around!' Vanessa assured him. 'Your exploits have been well-bruited, bwana. It was a veritable tournament of lewdness. My lady was undelighted by the spectacle of your cock – only rhetorically mind!'

His?

'Ethical genitive!'

Perhaps he should go straight round and apologise.

'What the hell for!'

Everything.

'Oh don't be so pathetic! Please! She's a mendacious owl!'

But he must have done something.

'Well good on you, mate!' Vanessa cried. 'Everyone thought you were Edgar Knight's battyman!'

Was that what they'd been saying? He'd supposed the rumours were just about favouritism, or sucking up.

'*I* knew it wasn't true!' Vanessa shoved him. 'I knew you had *cojones*! – We've been laughing like laughing-gas manufacturers who've had a toot at Dyer! Whingeing cow! Her daddy's branch secretary in the Deptford NF.'

Kennedy sat as if encased in an iceblock such as Victorians had delivered for refrigeration. These announcements, intended to cheer him, seemed to have been bred in a nest of two-headed snakes, the only relief being that the latest bite momentarily anaesthetised the previous; but memory, as he knew, would bring back each variation of pain. He would not lack time to brood on the harm he may have done the reputation of Edgar Knight, as well as the general sniggering about himself. Just now, though, he was suffering from a division of attention between the pronoun 'We' (how many of them already knew about all this, for Christ's sake?), and the report that he'd jumped Louise Dyer. This bite introduced several poisons. One of them was the possibility that Dyer the Liar was in fact no liar at all. Furthermore (here was a venom that chilled the heart), what if the story Rebecca Sutton told about his pushing her on ice was no untruth either? The past dissolved; his being was not his own; truth was whatever others told of him …

'Cheer up, big ears!' Vanessa called through his block. 'Avaunt, paranoia! I'm only pulling your leg. Let's go back to mine. I've got a bottle of wine!' Anxious, he trailed along. At the crematorium gates, Vanessa Lane took him by the hand. He fancied he smelled candyfloss. It was only her hair, sweet pink amid the gold.

'Now what did make you get so deliquescent, honey?' Like a long infant, he lay with her; the golden scrub in her armpit was abrasive, pleasantly so. 'Isn't really your thing, is it?'

He agreed it was not (he'd thawed somewhat). Well, to celebrate the grade he received Friday, he'd bought a bottle of Harveys Bristol Cream on the way home (with the tenner his old man sent him – he'd saved it long enough). Vanessa was amused by the choice of tipple; fiddled with his ear and called him 'Vicar'. He explained that 'sherris-sack' was Falstaff's favourite drink.

She stroked his face. So what had he written on for his essay?

On Shakespeare's female characters.

Lady Macbeth? No. Cordelia? No. Beatrice? Not her. Those

bobbins in *Midsummer Night's Dream*? Not them either. Who then? Doll Tearsheet actually.

Who?

He was explaining about Doll, hand on her below the sheet, when there was a rap on the door. 'Come in!' called Vanessa Lane.

Jesus Christ must she always be the hostess? As Kennedy complained to himself, a muddy Thayers appeared over the bed, with a carrier of cans and the *News of the World*. He'd brought a chum.

'Yo! Kennedy my man!' Thayers bawled, bending to high-five as Kennedy tried to cover himself. 'Kennedy's my main man!' Thayers insisted, standing back to roll his paper.

'You boys can join us!' Vanessa told them. 'Long as you take your shoes off.' She swigged from her wine bottle.

'No way, Ness!' yelled Thayers. 'Your man there might rape us all up the arse!' He nudged his chum, who snorted. Under white sheets sat Kennedy, lonely as a king, while Thayers watched him through his telescope.

11. Oval Test. Sunday evening with Clive.

Barbara was calling him to help her in the kitchen, and as he shoved that shameful episode back under the pile, Kennedy wondered he'd ever found a wife at all, after swearing to confine his dealings with women to the imagination (and never ever be drunk again): Affidavit, nineteenth day of February 1983.

'What are you thinking about?' Barbara was stabbing at leaves with her fork, in the modern manner.

'How we met.' Kennedy had finished his food.

'Ah!'

She smiled as one about to leave church might have smiled, her stock of reverence having comfortably lasted the service in which miracles had been spoken of, but who was now inclining to thoughts on other matters.

In the beginning, they'd often talked of how miraculous it was, their coming together, like tireless children. Later, the wonder was reserved, kept specially for accounts to friends, who might have asked, or find themselves being told anyway, at Barbara's discretion. In time, Kennedy noticed, his wife had grown up about the matter; she had the future, their future, to think about. To him it was unfathomably marvellous, a mystery of the heart. He imagined scenes in which he held forth about it, to famous strangers and friends yet unknown, who nodded and shared his wonder; then they offered him some form of ultimate accolade, these listening phantoms.

★

Ten years ago, towards end of summer, Oval Test. David Day had looked him up. By then it was already more than ten years since they'd graduated. The decades run on don't they? Like a forgotten tap. When the sink's full, that's your time. He remembered Kennedy liked the game. He had a spare ticket.

Kennedy was indeed fond of cricket. Comparing sport and art, cricket was obviously the novel. The players were characters – or used to be. God knew how much time he'd lost to test matches, standing at the TV solo. The England team of that period was fragile, rich in disappointments and ways of failing. He accepted Day's invitation. Ungrateful not to. Besides, he had some curiosity to see what the old Thersites had made of himself.

They met outside the underground. 'Still can't believe you got a first!' was Day's greeting. 'Spent as much time taking the piss as I did!' He'd put on weight, taken a job in an investment bank. Couldn't believe Kennedy was a don himself now. Kennedy explained he was nothing more than a wandering tutor on ten quid an hour, but Day wasn't having any of that and addressed him with snatches of verse and prose from the plays he remembered, adapting them for the present. He'd developed a comic's patter. As a matter of fact, he'd been doing a bit of stand-up in a pub in Belsize Park, if Kennedy fancied going along next Wednesday; then he was spooling away *a là* Dr Fry while they waited for drinks in the beer tent.

Was Kennedy married? They were waiting for play to start. Kennedy wasn't. Wise geezer. Married twice himself. Second time he fucked up quicker than a cardinal in a boys' home. Couldn't hack it. Kennedy asked why? (Wondering when he could get something to eat to go with the lager.) Because having wasn't half as sweet as chasing (Day adapting a line from *The Merchant of Venice*). Wasn't good for conversation either, marriage. You got more chat at Bank Holiday in a morgue. He'd acquired a way of laughing his words, lending syllables a tremolo effect.

That babe Kennedy used to knock about with, one with hair the colour of custard powder (Vanessa Lane he meant), he'd seen her on TV last week. On a travel programme. Mounted on an elephant. Well forward she was – riding his neck, legs round the ears. Lager wobbled in Day's plastic mug. Kennedy'd been there before the elephant! From Prudent Kennedy, this had drawn no response. How much did Day remember? Eyes black-brown in the iris, shiny as a dog's. Would Kennedy have to be on guard all day? No doubt Day would bring up other stuff, once he'd got him bragging about Vanessa Lane. Scurrilous bastard would have him believing any old rumour, given the opening. Kennedy explained he never really saw much of Vanessa after first year, which was the truth, and off trotted Day for more beer.

Kennedy was feeling the lack of his TV. The Pakistani leg-spinner was beginning to torment England, but his tricks were invisible from the stand. Hell, was he raising some dust out there! Oh for replays of those hissing deliveries, and quiet explanations from Mr Benaud! But here came Day with a tray and five pints, to save them having to get up and down, and observations on the G-string of the barmaid. What a volume on the bastard! Kennedy wished he'd go somewhere else – back into his kennel in the past ideally. There was a young woman in the row below them, with mahogany hair and a summer dress of red and white gingham. He'd been keeping an eye on her, trying to see who she was with. She could obviously hear everything that Day called out, furnished with the sort of details women hate, not wanting to know what it is men dedicate such effort to in imagination; as much effort, indeed, as the Jesuit to his prayer, which has to animate all the senses before it can connect him with God.

Well she was turning round now to investigate Day's output, and what he beheld was the image of the actress who played Doll. It wasn't her quite as she'd appeared in the film; it was her as the image from the film had lodged in him during the years since he watched it, and in this time it had changed from its initial and particular sharpness into a type, though in the first place it may have made him love it, that image, as a type, since that word may also signify essence or perfection ... God was he appalled. There she was! Why appear now of all times, like a deity to a man with unbrushed teeth? He wasn't ready for her. Would he ever be? *Imagination, thou art a runt, the very truant of practice.* 'Lord Jim Syndrome'. Yet ready he might have been, if it weren't for the bubbling pervert beside him. She obviously took Kennedy for his sidekick – he knew because she didn't check him out for a second when she turned to look at Day.

Soon after, she left. A short-haired man in a Euro '96 T-shirt who'd been sitting by her stayed; so they weren't together.

They watched England go down then Kennedy took Day to a curry house in Kennington. He had one and one quarter gallons of lager in him, along with pints Kennedy hadn't finished. Needed something to soak it up. It was going to be the last they saw of each other. Upon that Kennedy decided, as he worked his way through the little steel bowls and Day called out for Cobra. But his invitation turned out to be a blessing.

★

For the rest of the evening, Kennedy sat on the settee with the Sunday paper in which he took a critical interest, instead of going off to his workroom, wishing that Barbara might join him. Who knew but that her willingness for a repeat performance of the afternoon hadn't been piqued by his reverie at the dinner table? As a matter of fact, Kennedy himself knew: she'd be planning her wardrobe for Monday, in between fixing appointments and making calls to friends. When Kennedy overheard these calls, he wondered at the tenderness and repetition with which women check their love for each other. Like wine on the tongue, he could still taste her. Would they hear foxes tonight?

In the area of the paper beyond the news, lay the opinion pages. It was a curious thing to Kennedy, that the journalists who supplied the news were faceless, while the opinion columns were headed with a photograph of someone looking clever, or cross, often with slightly-narrowed eyes or even holding their chin in the attitude of thought. Perhaps this was because the opinion-columnists (or 'writers' as they'd started to be known) were more famous than the news reporters, and as opinions were subjective things, whereas the news was objective, this suggested our culture, while very properly respecting objectivity, idolised subjectivity, particularly when it expressed itself with the cruel élan, murderous rationality, superb and radical disregard for tact, the superfine hatred and excellent humour, of these columnists of right and left, whose furious and thoughtful photos introduced what they had to say with (to the sensitive soul) such naughty eloquence.

Watching you from the page as if you were just arriving at a barbecue in his garden was Clive Shaw. Now Clive fixed his attention mainly on districts of British culture where he was sure to be hearing cant, such as the BBC, the liberal press, the front bench of the present Labour Government, the CRE, the Arts Council, academia, the Turner Prize and single-issues activism. Yet, in spite of being an enemy of cant, he was no admirer of its opposite, namely frank and virulent racism, misogyny, homophobia, anti-Semitism; in other words, Clive enjoyed an exceptionally sure sense of where his feet were, could pick the rocks from the marsh while looking the reader in the eye – and would never invite a fascist to his barbecue.

Today Clive was having a row with the proposed reform of the law relating to sexual consent when a woman was intoxicated. Hadn't human beings been getting themselves dick-wiped and dundered since the origin of fermentation in pursuit of a leg-over (not to put too fine a point on it)? Historically, this was the primary purpose of intoxication, in anyone under the age of forty. If only sober women were able in law to give consent, you had to suspect a plot by the Greens to reduce the population of Great Britain to mediaeval levels (exaggeration was Clive's stock in trade). How was it to be ascertained that a woman was sober? Did it require the presence of medical personnel in the bedroom, or would a breathalyser kit do the trick? Perhaps a tongue-twister could be applied (twisting reason in the direction of silliness was another of Clive's rhetorical engines).

But you had to wonder what would happen to desire during the moratorium in which sobriety was being established. And it was goodbye to seduction, an art that depended on at least one party being susceptible, if sex was from now on to be the consequence of a rational decision. For where was the rationality of two naked people? Did it come off with the clothes or continue to shine, like a warden's torch in a dogging spot? Did we rationally decide to get naked with another person, or was it the animal's call? If we were irrational enough to participate in a game of penalty Sardines or Strip-Pontoon, how were we going to recover our rationality in time to be competent to judge the legality of that activity into which such games tended sadly to degenerate?

How indeed was the non-sober man to think rationally? Did the proposed change in the law assume that drunk men could still judge the rights or wrongs of a course of action, while drunk women were not legally capable of thinking at all? Was it actually assuming that in the mainstream carnal tradition in Britain, stone-cold sober men regularly had sex with trashed women? Was drunkenness itself now culpable, as a dereliction of the rationality, judgement and memory required for sexual navigation? Think about it, gentlemen!

Kennedy thought, and read the column again, and as he rehearsed a recent episode of drunkenness, opinion began to shimmer with truth. Before bed, he got round to checking his e-mail. On the path outside his workroom, a fox loped and vanished. There was a little message waiting. Sweet dreams, Dr K!

Part II: Arthur Mountain

12. Screen. King Lludd. Concerning shadows.

For once, Kennedy was easily persuaded to The Inventors' Arms. You're coming and I'm not hearing no, Frazer said. It's nearly the vac, geezer.

A drink might help take his mind off the problem riding him since last night. He'd even toyed with the idea of confiding in Frazer about the e-mail, hoping that Cy would help him laugh it off, and have something like that of his own to share ... You could actually say (Kennedy imagined declaring), that the whole business was Cy's fault, for going off and leaving him that time. At the quiz. Remember?

But what if Cy not only remembered, but knew more than him? There'd been months for the story to get round. On the principle of the 'Darwinism of words', the latest version was bound to be more vigorous and plausible than Kennedy's account. Luckily, they ran into Hannah Raider on the first floor, who decided to come with them, so Kennedy was saved from a conversation for which he lacked the nerve. As Hannah and Cy talked shop, Kennedy examined a misted screen between their table and the next.

Its white surface was etched with frosty decorations, ferns and feathers, swirls and waves, a sword, an anchor, an animal's head. A man was behind it talking; now and then another person murmured. Strange how audible the voice was, absorbing Kennedy's attention from Hannah's question about the conference, for the Welshman was not speaking loudly ...

'I have heard say it was quieter in the past and certainly you didn't have the variety of noises that drive us up the wall nowadays, electronic announcements for example: *Unattended luggage presents a security threat and may be removed and destroyed.* What with exactly? An ICBM? A pin? Where the fuck are they proposing to destroy it if we may ask? *In* the station? Or these BBC reporters who sound like they've got pie all over their teeth, not to mention you imps with your hands-free phones telling the world about your hangover or bum problems. (Don't sulk! I spoke inclusively – you aren't particularly discreet on that thing anyway, if you want the truth … I tell you because I love you. Yeah … God knows why I do bother, but there it is.) Anyhow, these fucking noises – and anyone could add to the list if we asked around – there's nothing new about them. Put it down. What they are is shadows of the original noise, but that noise was one thing, and these are all broken up like splinters. Where there was one, now are many. Hm. Down, Johnny boy, put it down … Original noise?

'Well in the time of King Lludd (two ells two dees), a plague hit the land and do you know what sort of plague it was? No. Not Bubonic. Sonic, as it happens. The plague was a scream. Audible everywhere, upon the eve of the first of May. Like a siren. You couldn't hide. Cast the British into a great despondency. The women miscarried their babies, the men lost heart and lived in fear, kids went mad, cattle died. Must have been the worse because they knew it was coming. Each spring, fear mounting. Imagine how they felt as April passed. Like waiting for war. Worse even – a war might not happen: the scream will. Well Lludd, he cured the land of the scream in the end. He discovered the cause … What was it? Dragons kicking off. And he did some magic, which we won't go into here as I see you are grinning with your technologically-enhanced teeth, Johnny bach, but the point is that the multitude of noises that piss in our ears are shadows of the scream. Like the modern world's trying to get back to the one terror, from a million nuisances. And we see this sort of thing again and again. If we know how to look …

'I'll ho ho you! Only one way you know how to look. Like a fucking Corinthian, amigo. How much that haircut cost you? Come on! Fifty quid plus wasn't it? Seventy-five I'll warrant. Paul and Tall Saul. Chapo Guapo. Where d'you go? I know you Corinthians. Haven't spent seventy-five quid in my life on hairdos. Style my own fucking hair I do. Look. Feel it. Won't bite.

'Fact we don't have to look any further than King Lludd for

another instance because around the time of Plague No. 1, they also had trouble with a tribe called the Corranieid. (Give me that I'll spell it – you haven't filled this properly now have you? Your life's a simcard, Jonathan. The requirements of penmanship are quite beyond you, lovely boy.) They could hear anything that was said, one corner of Britain to the other. Imagine the power this gave them. Lludd's people were dismayed. How can you resist a tribe who hear your business, plans, tactics, secrets, the lot, even when you whisper? Soon, they began to fear this tribe could hear their thoughts too. Which made them sick with self-consciousness. This was the second plague of Lludd's reign. Anyone who can't see how today shadows it has no more wit than a pickled turd, a wiping, a columnist. Know what I mean, Johnny?'

I do! Kennedy wanted to say.

'Someone's no doubt listening to all we say this minute. Bugging, surveillance, closed circuit, wire taps and so on are now among the main forms of English activity. For every supposed terrorist you've got at least one and a half dozen intelligence operatives, Special Branch, monitors, nose pickers, fake landlords who are really disgraced opera singers that have been blackmailed into playing a part in counter-terrorism and staining their face to look Asian, midgets who can fit in holdalls, handy Andies, shite-stirrers, werewolves and mechanics. They end up listening in to everyone, because since the communicating ability and potential connections of a suspect are unlimited, everywhere he wanders with his tiny phone is buggable, ditto his connections. (Don't put this there, put it in the middle. I'm improvising – obviously.) And as we all know, there's a camera on every corner with an overweight lad keeping one eye on your movements in a control centre while he does the *Daily Star* puzzle page, even when you are just going down the road and if you try anything unorthodox, he's going to flag it. The eavesdropping and surveillance methods of today are shadows of the second plague of King Lludd. Got me?

'Which he cured by means of insects. Believe it or not … It's a legend, Sire. You may shake your head. The Spanish Fly among them, a capital vesicant. Make a spy's face swell like a puppodum. Lovely green beetle, till you powder him. *Lenocinium Linnaeus*. Employed in the original Chinese stink bomb, Pong Dynasty. Latterly as an aphrodisiac. Bet you look it up when I'm gone! ... You'll ask Natalie? That's what you think, scout. I forbid you on pain of you know what.

'Well thank you. Sincerely. I'm glad you don't mind if I've married her. Means a lot to me. Really it does. I do feel my time's coming to an end. Soon he'll be among us. Let him come! ... She's waited by me. At death's door, she waited by me. Put it down. We've been beating round the bush for a while, Johnny bach. I know I haven't been keeping it tight but you've got to get your lovely head down now, butt, and fill your notebook. Our last year will determine how the world understands us, on the principle that ends are causes of understanding ... Put that down. Verbatim, butty. Someone's going to start listening soon. Need our story in order ...

'Natalie, she's been through what I have. Been through her own stuff too, years ago. Which is for her to tell. As she will, before the summer's out. I want you to try and be friends with her. Lift your bitch-shield, bach! She loves you as much as I do. Don't make faces. Recognise your kin. Set your page in three columns to allow for digressions, and all the other stuff I come up with. Three-way column, Johnny boy. Tonight could be the night ...'

Frazer's jacket was of bright brown tweed. Hannah was asking him to roll her a cigarette. She had a silvery sheen, pale, as if moon-born and educated, jewellery of fine and hard silver. Knowing who had to be behind the screen, Kennedy'd been distracted for some minutes by the Welshman, while taking part in his colleagues' conversation like the second-in-command of a pleasure vessel that's hit waters he never experienced but knows to be hazardous. As Hannah badgered Kennedy about Swansea, the voice of the Welshman stilled.

'He's being modest!' Cy suggested kindly, and Kennedy excused himself to visit the Gents', for he had to look behind the screen, let them know he was there, as a kid at hide-and-seek will suddenly reveal himself before he's found. When he stepped past the little booth, however, Kennedy was changed from such a kid to the seeker himself, for the smoke in that enclosure hid its occupants.

Carrying on down narrow stairs to the Gents', he got a flash of a chemistry lesson. In thick tubes that made the girls smirk, they heated ammonium chloride until the white crystals turned to inspissated smoke. When the smoke reached the neck of the tube and you took away the Bunsen burner, the crystals reformed on the glass: crystal, smoke, crystal without melting. Sublimation. The compound returned to exactly the same state higher up. Psychologists like Nietzsche and Freud thought human behaviour worked in a similar way: older forms of behaviour and attitudes came back in higher forms, and kept doing so. The old would return in disguise, essence unchanged.

On the way back, Kennedy surely saw a flash of green through the smoke in the booth, in which the leathery tang of a cigar was now discernible. Then the smoke seemed to clear like foam from a rock, and Kennedy hurried to his place. Cy'd bought him another beer, which he didn't really fancy, but he needed to give some account of the conference to his colleagues. Yet all the time he spoke, he could hear the voice to his left, which had now resumed, as if they were two batsmen practising in the nets and the other were the master.

The Welshman was speaking of his wife. Trouble she'd had obtaining a timetable. He was quick, adamant, an attacking speaker, turning out his words like a rapper. Fucker was online only now. She was trying to get hold of 1980s copies. Check its authority against what she knew. See if it told the whole truth. Put it down. Put it all down. The authority of the timetable, what was it really? What was it worth? At one time, they called it the Bible ... Indeed they did.

For that matter, what was the authority of the Bible itself? How exclusive was its authority? You had the Jewish books going back to 900BC. You had the Christian books 1K later. Who knew who wrote the Gospels? No one was sure. Paul wrote his. But who was behind Matthew, Mark and co? A man with no name who wasn't born till forty years after Christ died. He hadn't witnessed Christ on the Cross. Hadn't heard Him, hadn't seen Him. Q he was going by. Q. Not the mag for seventy-five year old blokes who liked making lists of the greatest bass players of all time. The source for the first four Gospels – that Q. The Germans hypothesised it. Meant 'fountainhead': Q – *Quelle*. And of course you had the Apocryphal Books ... Hm?

Books the Church couldn't make up its mind about, they were. *Secrets of Enoch. Bel and the Dragon. Book of the Ecliptic. Third Book of Hell. Ship Captain's Medical Guide. Dudley's Miscellany,* to name a few. *The Nebuchadnezzarion. Song of the Three. Caldicott's Holiday Annual.* Catholics accepted them, Protestants did not. How could you not accept *Bel and the Dragon?* Serialised on French TV. Gerard Depardieu guest-starred ... What as? As a fucking hill in the Ardennes, that's what as.

Then you had the Gnostic texts. Texts and revelations. The secret ones they were. In the early days, the Christians regarded them as heresies. Ha ha! You could see why. Gnostics thought the God of the Old Testament was Satan. The Demiurge they called him. To the Gnostic, the World Creator was evil itself. For why? Because he trapped the bright spirit in dark matter, that was why, like someone who catches a drifting spark from a campfire and buries it in a modern shopping centre. Put the wind up your mainstream Christian the Gnostics did. What if the knowledge they professed was the truth? The Devil was Christ's dad! Bloody hell what if ... ? *Sorry everybody – there's a hitch. The Devil made the whole shooting match! From hydrogen to Facebook.* What was more, they were secretive. Secret wisdom was their thing. Always gets people. What do they know that we don't? Why won't they let on? Why do they meet in the shadows, turn their backs on us? Why don't they want us to join? Persecuted they were. Keep putting it down! Stoned, massacred, burned alive.

The Christians made out it was because of their sexual code, which did on the surface you had to concede bear some resemblance to the excellent modern hobby known as dogging. Two or three of them hanging out by some rocks, in the shadow, a wife, a couple of fellows, fellow, a couple of wives. Soon you had a gathering ... over by there, look! Syrian scene: red rock, shadow growing, every manjack sliding or sucking. The expressions on their faces, the sounds of them – what d'you see? What do you hear? There were hints in the *Apocryphon of Basil.* These orgies touched the sublime, they touched the pit. What wouldn't you give to travel back there, Syria circa

135? Maybe you'd wish you hadn't. Would they pull you down, or throw you out? Or just look through you like the ghost you were? But they were not in it for pleasure. So if it wasn't for pleasure, what was it? Guess! ...

When he was by himself, Kennedy was going to guess. He fancied more of this. Meanwhile, he seemed to be entertaining them about the conference. As an anecdote-man, he was improving. Cy listened grinning, shrewd, fine-featured; Hannah (with whom he'd had some difficulty last year) watched his face as if till now she hadn't known him.

Anyway, to come back to the point, announced the voice behind the screen, whose decorations shone from a slant of light like Hannah's necklaces and rings – to come back to the point, though they were persecuted, they stuck to their doctrine, the Gnostics. They would not recognise the authority of the Church in the early centuries. Did Johnny boy get that? *Not to recognise the authority of whoever tells you, 'This is the way it is, friend! Obey, or perish!'* That was the fundamental Gnostic stance. Not to recognise the official line. Ever ... But mark this. Mark this well. The official line didn't even get going until the Gnostics announced *their* beliefs, *their* principles. It was the secret order that actually gave rise to the official order: *first* Gnosticism; then *orthodox* Christianity. Christianity couldn't establish its own doctrines, till it reacted against the Gnostic consciousness. Like if you saw a shadow going along the pavement in your neighbourhood, day in, day out, for quite some time; and then one day a man was attached to it. He's come along and found a shadow to dominate. From now on it can't get away from him, this striding git with his mobile phone; but it was there first, the shadow was, and don't be too sure it won't be dancing on the stones when *Graham* is long gone!

Now Johnny boy was looking at him as if he'd lost the point completely. *Tout à fait.* Come on, Mr Secretary! Well watch the point return. So so so ... Now what were they talking of before the Bible? Natalie and her timetables. Particularly her quest for early 1980s copies. Now had he not explained that the BR Standard Timetable was known at one time by the railbuffs as the 'Bible'? Indeed he had.

And had he not explained that the authority of the Christian Bible was a doubtful thing? One because no one knew who wrote it. Two because it took its authority, in *some measure*, from the secret teachings of the Gnostics. But if that was the case with the Bible, was it not also the case with the Standard Timetable? That the official info was a latecomer, with respect to the shadow order?

Indeed, was it not generally the case? Behind the screen there was hacking laughter.

13. Some legal terms. An introduction.

In the morning there was another e-mail. The tone was unthreatening, which, if not worse, was no safer than hostility; this subtle soul could see danger in mild or harmless spots, as well as where snakes lay coiled. The message said, 'Me again! Don't be a stranger ...' Plaintive in a way; though what was that ellipsis intimating? Seized by an impulse to make a clean breast of it to Barbara, Kennedy held it down. But at times like this, you really could wish your partner had trouble as bad (at least) as your own: for a moment he heard them swapping secrets over a glass of wine ... *Is that all you've been worrying about? You should hear what I get up to!*

Were they bugged in here? Kennedy watched the heads of his students. In little groups they compared passages: Acrasia in her bower with the Knight of Temperance; the Duchess of Malfi in her bedroom, new husband and maid beside her. They could be reporting what he made them read ... *Dutty man!* Elsie Begum, who wore a headscarf, glanced at him, grinned, put her phone away. Perhaps he should broaden the discussion. 'She totally ain't making O-face!' Elsie told her neighbour. 'The knight's still got his armoured suit on.'

At the end of the class, Elsie B and Cindy Formula said thanks for the year and his heart lifted. Some colleagues received cards and gifts, when teaching was over. Outside a cafe where students sat, he said hello and passed on quickly. How much did they know? Before him lay the afternoon.

In a way, an agreeable thing about his job was that you didn't have to account for your presence, from one day to the next. No doubt Bram Shoddy, Faculty 'Skyreader', who'd set up a Research Vane to register the productivity of the various Departments, was on the case; but as things were, Kennedy could have left for home now teaching was done, taken a walk round the capital or gone to the cinema. Indeed, he could have spent the afternoon in the brothel in Stevedore Street, for all anyone would have been the wiser. But he went back to the office, where he sat brooding at the computer. More attentively than any institution, some of us bug ourselves. Our souls see to it. At intervals he checked his mail.

Would have helped to have a church to go to. For all his otherworldliness, when did he? Led his life like a standard modern atheist ... *Isn't that your type, Kennedy? Fend for yourself in matters of conscience. But can you? Aren't you all at sea really, whole faithless crew of you?*

For once Kennedy invited Cy Frazer for a drink, but Cy had a date in Harlesden so Kennedy went alone. The voice behind the screen was louder tonight, yet bar staff and punters seemed to notice it no more than the smoke of the previous evening.

'So much for church and shadow. Let's crack on with the law ... Now if someone threatens me, or wrongs me, and I think you may have got wind of this, Jonathan bach, I pays him back according to my rules, my code. Never go to law I don't. Never have. An offence against me isn't criminal, and it isn't civil and it isn't a tort. It's *sarhad*. *Sarhad* alone, savvy? S-A-R-H-A-D. An offence against *you* may be criminal. Say someone holds you up for your mobile phone – which you insist on carrying. Down to the cophouse you go and you tell em you've been mugged at toothpick point. While they were at it, they got a bit carried away, slashed your jacket with their weapon. You've incurred a flesh wound. Sergeant asks the doctor to examine it so as to grade the offence, AB, GB, whatever.

'Or someone's been lying about you, you take out a grievance against him according to the procedures where you work, if it was at work; or if it was in print, in a newspaper or a contemporary novel – excuse me while I have a sip of this to clear my mouth of those nouns: PAH! – if it was in print, you'll speak to a solicitor and see if you can reasonably produce a case of libel against your detractor. Hm! That is what you will do, you and many other modern boys bach. Not *me*. I don't have the cops deciding on my status as a victim. I don't have institutions or workplaces regulating it. I don't have professionals representing it. Someone commits an offence against me, I know who they've done it to, and I know what they've done it to. Because I know what I am. Don't need anyone going on patrol for me with a description of a hooded youth with a toothpick behind his ear, don't need disciplinary panels, mediation boards, tribunals, courts or letters of injunction functioning on my behalf, for my sake. Don't need anyone acting for me, and I don't need anyone speaking for me. For why, J boy? Because I speaks for myself, right?

'According to the principle of *braint*. That's how I speak for myself. *Braint*. B-R-A-I-N-T. That's our old word for status. Means my status as a freeman, you'll find if you consult Dai Dumville, the pseudo-Nennius – are you getting all these? – Glanville Jones or indeed the *Dream of Rhonabwy* – R-H-O-N-A-B-W-Y. Now my status as a freeman, my *braint*, what does it do? Here's what it do. Tells me the nature of the *sarhad* committed against me. Tells me how to feel the offence, tells me the scale of the dishonour or injury I've encountered from the perpetrator. It's my status tells me the value of the offence. And d'you know what else it tells me, lovely boy? Hey? Well it tells me what the fuck to do about it as well. And when. Got that? Don't forget *when*. – Let me look a minute. Sure you're not getting half this … When I respond to an offence, I do it my way. According to the principles – put it down just like this, bach – according to the principles of *braint* and *sarhad*. These are old terms. But with me, they are still operational. How many men or women can say that? – Can you wave her to bring me a pint? …

'An offence against me,' the voice continued, after a short dispute, 'I judge too according to the perpetrator's standing with regard to me when he did it, and certain considerations of substance. How did his status, or hers, acknowledge mine? For example, were we full on to each other? Full and half? Half and half? Thick and thin? Craven and tremendous? *Folie à deux*? Eternal and ephemeral. And so forth. That's what I want to know. In general terms. In terms exact. Like her just now. Wouldn't bring me a drink over but I didn't take it amiss. And why not? Cos I likes her glasses. Like her face. Like her *braint*. Took some pluck to tell me off. Probably a student she is. You'll find she's got her book for tomorrow's tutorial behind the bar. *Ulysses* by J.A.A.

Joyce. Sovereign insolence. See that tattoo on her shoulder, brown one? You'll find that goes all the way down her back if you have a look. An owl it is. Her familiar. Wouldn't be at all surprised to find she's got some Welsh in her. Woe betide any lecturer who tries it on with her. Ride him round the islands she will. Won't let him go till it suits her. Serves him right for trying. Should have worked out his status – his true status – before he came on to her. Cos she will turn him into something he didn't know he was and there he'll stay till his hair's grey and his lips crack and the weeds grow through his house … Where was I?'

Whispering.

Kennedy held on to his pint.

'OK. Status. Standing of the perpetrator with regard to me. Good. And we all know nowadays, the young fellas talk about "respect" … "You disrespected me. I is gonna shank you, man. I is gonna smak you widda equaliser!" … blah blah blah. In a way, they are outside the law – certainly outside the law of fucking grammar. But they aren't freemen for all that. *Au contraire.* Too concerned with what their team thinks of them they are. Cellular existence. Disgusting. Like insects. "Respect". I'll give em respect! How much respect are you going to get with a hedgehog rammed sideways up your arsehole, pantyboy? – *Braint* is what I am concerned with, Jonathan.

'Means that an act of *sarhad* against me is special to me, special to the offender. Occurs in its own way. Time and place don't count. I could spend half a lifetime deliberating on it. That wouldn't be time as you know it. When I make my response, it's like the offence happened yesterday. Got that? There once was an offence against me, J boy. Or it was yesterday? Waverley … Before your time, but you're going to know. Note in your book. Attaboy! Then it'll be like yesterday. Meanwhile,' there was a slurp from behind the screen, 'I'm gathering my kin!

'Hey? How are my kin different from a gang? If you are asking that in a spirit of genuine enquiry – as I believe you are – and not just to be a provocative twat, then my answer is as follows. The difference between kin and gang – how many zips you got on that jacket by the way? Look like fucking Houdini, if you don't mind my saying so. Why d'you mam let you out in it? – the difference is one of relatedness. What I have in mind here is the quality of status. How is a gang related? They all come from the same neighbourhood, "ends" they call it – E-N-D-Z – and they all worship violence. Furthermore, they're all bonsdmen to each other. Which was why I was using words such as "cellular", "insect", "pismire" and so forth when I touched on this previously. They all do what each other's doing and they all do the same thing, ad infinitum. They're on the street, they spy a cop, they spit and go, "Boydem!". Have to. No choice. The quality of relatedness in the gang is a matter of repetition, matter of inertia. Do you think they ever vary? Say we got a gang called "G Block". Do you suppose any of the soldiers or whatever they call themselves say "I ain't suckin today, blud. I is going to the library to see if I can't crack the phenomenological reduction"? Your bwoy might fancy it. He might fancy going down to the cliffs to gather samphire. He's not going to though. Why not? Because he's not free to. Who says he isn't free? What is it stops him being a freeman? What compels him to hang round in stairwells, talk shit and stab bus passengers? What fear is it keeps you a slave to your gang? Is it because you're scared of being lonely? Is it because that's all you know, and there aren't enough fucking facilities in the area, as the sociologists tell us? Is it because you're afraid of dying? Or because you lack character? …

    'Kin? Haven't defined it yet? … Between the lines of all I've just told you, bach! And not just between either. Kin's got status, kin's got character, and I've got a bladder full of Montrachet or the excuse for tiff they sell in this place. Hold on a momento, Johnny boy.'

    Compelled to show himself, Kennedy rattled downstairs to the Gents'. Behind him someone cursed the towel dispenser:

    'Like trying to milk a wooden tit!'

    Zipped up, Kennedy turned to grin. The speaker wore a suit like an impresario's, fine stripe of purple in the dark cloth. But the look he gave Kennedy, head held back, mingled haughtiness, approval, good will, like a master waiting at the gates for a late-arriving boy, amused by the spectacle of snail-like progress; perhaps he even knew how the boy, owing to certain handicaps, had done well to get to school at all. His hair was full and strangely textured, like the rolling tobacco favoured by Cy Frazer, a sort of shaggy, glinting goldenness darkening into brown. Kennedy was reminded of an autumn god, costumed like a mortal, who'd overshot the period he intended to check out (unless his dresser had a vintage fetish). As he lit a cigarette he hummed to himself, appraising Kennedy still as he smoked, one eye slightly closed in parody of fierceness, the other shining greenly, a bottle-glass prosthetic. Now he waved his cigarette like a little wand, causing smoke to fold and eddy about his face. It was Kennedy to speak.

'What are the stoplines?' Kennedy asked, to show he remembered.

'I'll give you stoplines! Who d'you think you are?'

Kennedy's impulse was to leap forward in obeisance; his fate was fastened to this stagey growler.

'My name's Kennedy,' he explained, adding foolishly, 'pleased to meet you!'

'Well my name's Cunt!' bawled the other, 'and I'm not at all pleased to meet you!', almost elbowing Kennedy into the urinal on his way out.

Not long after, Kennedy went resolutely up the stairs to collect his briefcase, which meant he had to walk directly in front of the booth behind the screen. This time, he kept his eyes on the floor. To his surprise, a fresh pint was waiting in his place.

'We're in by here, mun!' a voice called. 'Come on, Kid Kennedy! We won't bite!'

Kennedy made his way round to the other side of the frosted screen where two men stirred to give him room. One was the green-eyed figure, smoking a thick cigar from a white Davidoff carton. He had a second cigar burning in the ashtray, where a short untipped cigarette also smouldered; charred pieces of coloured cardboard ripped from a beer mat, and blackened flowers of notepaper on which handwriting was still visible in negative, filled the ashtray. The other figure at the table, Kennedy felt sure he knew as well, a rather beautiful young man, smaller than the other, hair cut like a celebrity. He wore a blouson of soft leather adorned with zips.

'Sorry about that fuss in the khazi,' Cunt confided to Kennedy. 'Took me by surprise you did in there!'

Puzzled, grateful, Kennedy sat in silence.

'Your timing – how d'you do it? Never seen it managed like that before! You are something else, sir. That very moment, and there you were!'

'I'm sorry,' Kennedy said.

'No, no! My fault!' insisted the green-eyed Welshman, now putting out his hand: 'Arthur Mountain. – Sorry about the smoke in here by the way. We put some out when we're dictating. Don't want every manjack sticking his nose in!'

14. A talk with Arthur Mountain. Prince of Terror.

One eye cocked against the smoke from his cigar, which was down to the stub, Arthur Mountain examined Kennedy. The young man, introduced as Johnny boy, was evidently a secretary. On the table lay a large notebook, where he'd been writing in columns. The paper was specked with ash from cigars and unfiltered cigarettes, maculated with alcohol. Twisting a broad gold ring engraved with black waves, the Welshman hummed, while the secretary diddled a nice black fountain pen. At last, he looked at Kennedy too, as his governor grinned. Hadn't they met before? It was risking a put-down from the young man to say so – his manner was bloody frosty. But they were waiting for him to speak, the ring twisting some kind of cue ...

'Congratulations!' Kennedy called out, raising his pint. 'On your marriage! – You got married lately!' Arthur Mountain looked on. 'To Natalie!' Kennedy explained.

'What page is that on?' Arthur Mountain desired to know.

Back there. Johnny boy turned corners with his thumb. Day ago at least. 'Feels more like a fortnight,' he added, 'way you've been going on.'

'I'll give you look!' Flicking the ear of his insolent scribe, the Welshman gazed dully at Kennedy. 'Have you been snitching in here?' He indicated the broad notebook with his thumb.

'Certainly I haven't,' Kennedy replied. 'Not at all.'

'Ha!' cried Arthur Mountain. 'You must have been listening in then. Eavesdropping. Thought as much I did. When I laid eyes on you. What else did you hear while you were listening in? Should have showed yourself. Sitting there brooding like a mildewed tonk! Where did you position yourself for these eavesdropping orgies, if you don't mind my asking you a direct question, *man to man*?'

'Next door!' replied Kennedy, flustered and cross.

'What? Did you drill holes?'

'No, no,' Kennedy said. 'I mean behind this screen. And with respect, if you didn't talk so bloody loudly, I wouldn't have heard a thing.' He was emboldened to this by an impression he had that Mountain was winking behind the pint glass he was now swigging, which appeared to contain white wine.

'Don't be thinking I'm messing when I'm angry!' the Welshman advised him, leaning forward reasonably.

'OK,' Kennedy agreed.

'And don't think I'm angry when I'm messing either,' Arthur Mountain added, in a less friendly but still reasonable tone.

Kennedy said nothing.

'What's her name?' the Welshman enquired, from behind his hand.

'Whose?'

'My wife.'

'Natalie,' Kennedy said. 'Like I told you.'

'Told me? When?'

'He told you above,' Johnny boy offered his notebook. 'It's just up here.'

'Pretty handy with names aren't you?' Mountain said. Was he messing now, or angry? He wasn't easy to keep track of, with these caprices of his. 'That's twice you've had my wife's name in your mouth. Whose name is it, I'd like to know?'

'Hers – obviously!' Kennedy replied, a bit too smart.

'Well if it's hers, what are you doing with it in that mouth of yours?'

'I'm sorry!' said Kennedy prudently.

'How much of my wife have you had in your mouth altogether, kiddo?'

'None. Obviously!' Kennedy tried to grin.

'Her name's her isn't it? Or is it not? What do you say? Think before you answer. Her name is her like her eyes are, or her big toe. What do you say? Bird in the mouth's worth two in the bush. What's her name taste like?'

'Nothing,' Kennedy said.

'What!'

'Well, I mean names aren't flavoursome ...' Kennedy explained. Why wouldn't this glowering, winking character give him time to answer? Telling him to think first, then continually forcing him to say the first thing that came to mind. Putting him on the spot.

'Are you telling me my wife's name is not flavoursome?' Arthur Mountain enquired fiercely. 'Think before you answer!'

'Not to me, obviously,' Kennedy said carefully. 'It probably is to you – I'm sure it is.'

'You saying she hasn't got universal appeal?'

'No one has,' Kennedy said bravely enough.

The Welshman looked upward along his nose, as if a plane were passing with engine trouble. 'Are you sure?'

'Maybe not anymore,' Kennedy said.

'Ah.' Arthur Mountain shook his head. 'Seriously though, do you really think names don't have flavours. Example, when I come across "Nigel", I has a flavour like the taste of infused string – know what I mean? Like you get on a joint of lamb. Toothsome. Do you like lamb, Dr Kennedy?'

'Yes,' Kennedy said. How had this character discovered his title?

'The name of my wife, now this tastes to me like Christmas, dark icing (made with molasses, hard in the mouth as cinder toffee), and red melon glacé con vodka, OK? Whereas "Kennedy"' – Arthur Mountain sniffed and whirled the wine in his pint – 'now that name tastes to me like a boy at the back of the room. Reminds me of schooldays. "Kennedy. Fourth form."'

'But that's not a flavour,' Kennedy pointed out.

'We're moving on. Mind your columns, Jonathan! – Don't you think that the name is the essence? A little drop of the self, pure as Absolut? Have I just told you the essence of yourself or have I not? Could a name tell us how bad a person was? Or how great?' While Kennedy was considering the name "Arthur Mountain" according to these guidelines, the latter demanded, 'What's your wife's name?'

'Barbara,' Kennedy told him, and Johnny boy took it down.

Arthur Mountain hummed and with licked finger mended his cigar. 'What d'you tell me for?'

'You asked!' Kennedy replied.

'Would you give me anything I asked?'

'No,' Kennedy said. 'Not *anything*.'

'But a name's OK. Toss a name in the pot any time, is it? Doesn't mean anything, to give a name away. The name's not the person, person's not the name. Only a savage would think different. Only a primitive fellow would think them the same thing.'

'I know what you mean,' Kennedy said, who didn't want a lesson in anthropology. 'Obviously there is such a thing as name magic. But no one believes in it anymore.'

'Oho! Don't be so sure of that. We're not all as modern as you are,' Arthur Mountain advised him. 'Not what I'm on about at the moment though, magic. What I'm thinking of is what the person who asks the name is after. Why do they want to know? What's their game? If they want the name, don't they want the person? As a friend, enemy, possession, victim, opponent, for example? Who ever asked a name that didn't want any of those things? You ask a person's name, you want to arrest them, give them a hiding, take them to your bed, give them a present, sack them, recruit them, send them up the main-mast off Cape Horn, borrow their recipe, return them their lost purse, find out about their family, contacts, friends, track them down.'

'What about when you read a book?' asked Kennedy, as diversion from sorting through this list.

'What about it?'

'You want the names of people, the characters. But it's not so you can *do* anything with them!'

'Isn't it now?' the Welshman asked.

'No. It's so they can have individuality, so they can exist. Imagine a book where it just kept saying "He" or "She"!'

'But is it you who's making them exist?'

'Interesting question,' Kennedy said, glad to be off the subject of his wife, and the Welshman's. 'In a way it is. It's a sort of collaboration. Between you and the author, you and the writing.'

'Collaboration,' Arthur Mountain said to himself, and to Johnny boy, 'Put that down. "Existence depends on collaboration." – That's dicey, Dr Kennedy, cos collaboration is a heinous thing.'

White smoke (he now had two stubby cigarettes lit) came off the Welshman in columns and jets, hazing Kennedy's eyes.

'I didn't mean it that way,' Kennedy said.

'Which way?'

'Like collaboration in wartime.'

'Meant books didn't you?'

'Yes.'

'Where the people don't count in reality?'

'Oh they do though!' Kennedy protested.

'Well for six years in Europe, you gave someone's name to any fucker in a suit like mine who asked for it, chances are they'll be murdered or taken away, their family too, and their pals. Yet there you sit and tell me, "Existence depends on collaboration!"'

'But we aren't under occupation now!' Kennedy said, as a smoke slanted his way.

'Were we then?'

'Well no. Not in these Isles,' Kennedy said. 'Not in Britain.'

'"Britons never ever shall be slaves!" Were we freer then? Or now?'

'Well the standard line is we're a lot freer now,' Kennedy said.

'What sort of freedom is it?'

'Well, negative freedom to a large extent.' Where was this going? Did Mountain genuinely want them to think something through together?

'And what is negative freedom? – Not badgering you, Doc', the Welshman added a little uncannily. 'Want to hear your view. Here to learn I am!'

'Freedom to do what you want. – Sexually for example.'

'Yeah. Just about having fun really, isn't it? That's all.'

'I suppose it is,' said Kennedy.

'So if we aren't free in a true sense, what's going on? Who are we under?'

'Maybe we're under ourselves,' Kennedy said.

'Ourselves?'

'Some of us.'

Arthur Mountain hummed and made a chewing face. 'Now if you were just about to be occupied – say it was two days off – how would you rate your freedom exactly then? Just that afternoon, when your street's being strafed, you're trying to get the family away, it's the last of everything: last train out, last bread loaf, last bottle of brandy. Maximum or minimum – how's your freedom? Does a thing grow biggest just before the death, or is it hardly there at all? – Or are you really freer once the invasion begins? If we don't know what our freedom is, how do we know if we're occupied or not? How do we know when it starts? How do we know if it starts? How do we know when it ended? – If it did at all. Fill me, Johnson!

'If we aren't free,' Arthur Mountain continued, Johnny boy having returned from his errand to fetch the governor a pint of white wine along with a smaller quantity of white in a conventional wine glass, which the Welshman poured in the ashtray to produce a glistening black mass – 'if we aren't free, we must be under occupation. That's one way of looking at it. The occupiers have taken our freedom – whoever they are.

'If we aren't free, it's because we're living in peace. That's another way of looking at it. Peace makes us comfortable. You can't be comfortable and free, except in that negative way you were telling us about, Ken. PinkWorld unlimited on your PC, dozen syrups to liven up your cappuccino with, inalienable right to wear a baseball cap. – Hold on.' A hooded youth came to the table with a note for Arthur Mountain, who handed some kind of tip to the messenger and waved him away. Kennedy was rather impressed by this, the Welshman reading the message up against the light in a theatrical manner then seeming to dispose of it between his fingers, before dropping it in a sheet of yellow to join the burned mass in the ashtray.

'So we're only free on the verge of invasion,' Arthur Mountain continued. 'Ten to midnight. That's when we know ourselves. Who we really are. That's when we know what we've got to lose. That's when we reckon our past. Have we been slacking all along, taking

111

it easy? Or have we been ready for this moment? Because this is the point where we know what we have to do as well. Can we do it? We'll see. See if we can. We know we have to. This cuts us loose. Sets us free. At last, something counts! Five to midnight. They're nearly here. See them on the horizon. Hear them coming. Maybe we'll be betrayed. Maybe we'll die in a trap. Will we do what we have to? – What do you think?' Arthur Mountain took some wine, sucking it oldly through his teeth.

'Do you mean it metaphorically?' Kennedy suggested. 'This talking about war?'

'No I don't! Totally I mean it. No metaphors. Totally – for me and my kin. Ever heard of the Battle of Waverley?'

'Rings a bell,' said Kennedy, wondering if he shouldn't be thinking of getting home.

'Good battle that was. Four and twenty years ago. Outnumbered approximately 15 to one we were. Still here look!' Kennedy said nothing. 'Don't you want to come to the wars?' Arthur Mountain enquired, sitting back so far on his stool that his face fell into shadow.

'I don't think so.'

'Why d'you come round here then?'

'You asked me to. You invited me.'

'I take it this public house is your local?' Kennedy demurred. 'Well it's just by your work isn't it? You know it?'

'Yes,' Kennedy said.

'Who's inviting who then? You or me? – Your place and I'm here or my place and you are? If I ask you round to have a drink with me, aren't I just showing you respect in your place? Isn't it you who's making me do the asking? Haven't I appeared in your manor? But if you aren't aggrieved to have me here, I must have your permission. Therefore, in effect you must have asked me. You got the power, butty! According to the latest sociological research.'

'But it's not like that!' Kennedy protested.

'How is it then?'

'Just happenstance.'

'Just bumped into each other have we?' A chef preparing a sinister reduction, Arthur Mountain began to stir the slick mass of black in the ashtray with a matchstick. 'Nothing to each other? A casual encounter?'

'In a way,' Kennedy said, meaning to avoid committing himself to some sort of compact, which seemed to be hinted at by the Welshman.

'War or peace? Where are we?'

'Peace,' replied Kennedy. 'Of course.'

'So that's why you came round – because you reckon it's peacetime? Which is why you gave me your wife's name? A peacetime gesture. Supposing we're both on the same side – and bent on mutual safety, support and whatnot?'

'But you asked me!' Kennedy protested, uneasy again. What was this character up to? What did he want?

'Better had be peacetime, kiddo. You're a traitor otherwise. Giving names to God knows who. – But as I outlined in the theses above, if we're at peace, our freedom suffers from it. – Hm. There we are then … What d'you say, John boy?'

Johnny boy was in a huff. If Arthur would keep going on to him (meaning Kennedy) about wives, how was he meant to keep his columns? Or decide what was important? If anything was. Sorry and correct him if he was making a scandalous error, but he'd heard nothing but flim-flam since *he* came to sit with them (your secretary was certainly not being free with Kennedy's name). If Arthur would insist on chatting to strangers from beginning to end of the session, Johnny boy was off to see his friends at the Soho Theatre. What about the stoplines? The secretary held out his notebook where there was a blank column between the other two, headed in black ink, neatly underlined.

'Think we haven't been on it, bach?' Arthur Mountain patted his scribe and winked at Kennedy, who was brooding about the word 'traitor'. 'Aren't we always on it, even when we seem far off? – "Nothing disappears though all is rearranged. Lost are they who are unamazed!"' With a little banging of the heart, Kennedy heard the lines from the Tower. 'Well here's something for your notebook, Jonathan Sir. Bit of Ladybird history. – Ready? Fire One!'

Now Kennedy'd have to hear this out. Would he ever get home?

It was nearly eight. Barbara would be noticing his absence. He'd have called her, but the production of a phone would be noticed by Arthur Mountain, who'd probably have something to say about such equipment.

'Now in twelve seventy-six we were invaded by the English. King Edward the First couldn't stick the fact we were a sovereign principality under Llywelyn, which Johnny boy has been practising spelling I fancy!' Arthur beamed at his secretary. 'Cos he's going to have his bollocks clipped for stew by an albino alewife, if he gets it wrong. I bet Dr Kennedy can spell it. We don't want to look like fools.

'So they came in, as they have been prone to do here, there and everywhere. This was ancient colonialism and this is an ancient Welsh grouse. Any boy from the valleys will tell you this, but he won't tell it like me. Now Llywelyn was a figurehead, a charismatic fellow – and he was unifying Wales, after his own fashion. It wasn't easy. What you have got to understand is in Wales, the smaller lords would fight their princes at the slightest opportunity. Accordingly, you might well have to employ both terror and largesse to bring them into line, and create allies. This Llywelyn did. Terror and largesse. Can you picture it? Seven hundred and thirty years ago. Can you picture a prince of terror and largesse? Has he got a brown paper bag on his head, "Santa" written on one side in black marker pen, and on the other "Satan"?' Arthur Mountain looked closely at Johnny boy, to see if this was what he was imagining. 'Or is he like Peter Mandelson coming to your door with a hamper?' He looked at Kennedy, who shook his head. 'What do you see? Anything? What quantity of wet blood, and fire?

'And how much laughter, by the way? These pictures of the past, you can never hear the laughter in them can you? Have you noticed that, Dr K?'

'I have thought about it,' Kennedy said.

'Did they laugh when they brought gifts, Prince Llywelyn's boys? Or only when they torched a hamlet? Was he good at impressions? A natural wit? … By the way – put this separate J boy – what was the funniest year in history? Which year did people laugh most, per caput? Important isn't it?' Arthur Mountain put his hand to his ear, against the background roar and chime of The Inventors' Arms. 'And not a manjack to research it. – Maybe it's better that way.' He stared at Kennedy in a manner Kennedy now understood as checking, rather than hostile. 'Don't want the academics in on our laughter, do we?'

A wonderful thought. The funniest year … Heaven on earth?

'Very interesting it is how global Llywelyn was in his strategy, over seven hundred years ago,' Arthur Mountain continued. Kennedy wondered if he wore his hair after the fashion of mediaeval Wales, caulked with some sort of resin to see him through the winter, which he wouldn't wash out till Easter. When would a prince of terror and largesse have time to wash his hair – or even go home?

'Conducting operations against Edward from foreign bases Llywelyn was, in France and Palestine as well. Terror on a continental scale. And who says the English didn't deserve it? Edward held his court in Bordeaux didn't he? What the fuck was an English king doing down there? Westminster should have been enough; but no, he has to have Bordeaux as well. His brother's already been given Sicily as a present. Most of us get socks, or some fucking DVD we don't want. He gets Sicily. This is how English royalty gorges itself on foreign lands with no authority except that obtained from its own use of force – or threat to use it. Well Llywelyn made it his business to pick the English off by remote control, in these selfsame foreign fields. This was his rebellion by terror and influence from afar against English power. Soon the poets were calling him "King of the Welsh".'

Arthur Mountain swigged from his wine pint till it was empty, and Kennedy went along to the bar to negotiate another drink for him. While he waited on the process of aliquots and aliquants, for the barmaid with the spectacles (who Kennedy did indeed recognise as a literature student) could not serve wine by the pint measure, Kennedy wondered if Johnny boy might not be, by analogy, a sort of poet in the set-up into which Kennedy himself was apparently being introduced. Here was the wine.

'Now Edward, he does not care for this appellation, "King of the Welsh". Only one king in circulation, and it's himself. So he gives Llywelyn a chance to come up to London and show him some respect. Homage, obeisance, so forth. – Would Llywelyn go up and bend the knee? Not he!' Arthur Mountain cried. In his large right hand the glass lodged snug. 'Edward Longshanks could come down to Carmarthen and kiss the hole in the shadow of the valley of his arse, for all Llywelyn was concerned. The valley royal, fringed with firs, lofty pines, crooked beeches and stately planes where the cattle graze and the lonely goat chews and ponders his lot. – Now are you starting to see what kind of man Llywelyn was? Have you met his kind?

'People took strongly to him, one way or the other. His brother Dafydd, he fucking ratted him. What d'you think he had against his brother? Was it his charisma he resented? What was it he envied? – Envied so much he'd turn his back on his own kin for an English king?'

'Is that kin like you mean it?' Kennedy enquired, remembering what he'd overheard the night before in the talk of *braint*.

Arthur Mountain watched him, then said, 'I choose my kin, Dr Kennedy. – In revenge, Llywelyn declared war against the English. That way round it was. What sense of danger do you think this man had? What did danger mean to him? Do you hear me? – Has this question yet been answered? What does danger mean to you? What's it there for? Why does the world allow it? – Do you know anything of that?'

Kennedy looked down from the Welshman's eyes. He should be on his way home.

'Now you saw the American fleet sailing for Iraq in the springtime three years ago?' With large hands, Arthur Mountain made a gesture of magnitude. 'Such a force did Edward send against the Welsh. Attacked by sea, attacked by land, up in the mountains. Counter-insurgency this was. Seven hundred and thirty years ago. Cleared the Welsh forests, Edward did; built forts, built castles. Recruited Welsh auxiliaries, against their own. And this is what the imperial powers are still doing of course. – But every so often,' Arthur Mountain dropped his voice and looked about, came back to Kennedy with eyes dead green – 'every so often, Edward's men ran into the most

terrible resistance. Left their skin on the rocks. And this is where …'
A hooded youth, stockier than the previous messenger, came to the table smoking a spliff and handed Arthur a little roll of paper who opened it, tutted, rose and said, 'Back in a minute.'

'Is he going to say about the stoplines?' Kennedy asked Johnny boy.

'When?' Johnny boy asked Kennedy. 'Do you have a particular slot in mind?'

'Well when he gets back,' Kennedy said a little impatiently.

'You'll be lucky!' Johnny boy announced with a mouth that implied 'What-have-we-here?' – as if Kennedy had just presented a moody passport at a border checkpoint.

'Isn't he coming back?' Kennedy asked, with a mixture of disappointment and relief.

'How do I know?' Johnny boy complained. 'Do you think I keep his diary? – He could be back in a flash. It may be a month. I don't know. He could have run off with the Muffin Man for all I care. I've got plenty to do.' He and Kennedy sat in silence, Johnny boy checking his texts; Kennedy produced his phone too, thinking to tell Barbara he was on his way. He replaced it in his pocket. Arthur Mountain might indeed be back in a flash.

Where had he gone though? Kennedy felt punctured, a little wound of neglect. He and Johnny boy sat on a while.

'What is it you're writing?' Kennedy asked. It intrigued him that this snooty but put-upon young man should subject himself as notary to the desultory Mountain. 'Is it some sort of study you're working on?' Kennedy continued, in gentle tones. If it was field-work, the method was pretty old-fashioned. What did Arthur Mountain represent for Johnny boy? He was quite a character obviously; but who took such careful notes on the pronouncements of eccentrics nowadays?

'His life,' said Johnny boy and made a face. 'It's a nightmare keeping this tally. Why d'you think I've got all these columns? Look! Page after page after bloody page!'

'Because he keeps changing the subject?' Kennedy ventured.

'It's not changing the subject,' Johnny boy explained in a tone of irritable recitation. 'I wouldn't bother if it was only that. No one would. – Didn't you hear him say, we're always on it even when we seem far off? To him, everything's related.'

'But why do you keep it up?' Kennedy asked. 'Why d'you do it for him?'

Johnny boy mouthed the words like a gossip: Don't you know he's killed a man!

15. Murderer. Cell 3. Green beret.

The vacation came just in time. Kennedy could keep clear of the office and The Inventors' Arms, where Arthur Mountain might be waiting for him to look in. After learning the Welshman was a killer, Kennedy went home like he'd finally heard the Four-Minute Warning. By the park he composed his face for Barbara, but she came in late that evening.

In truth, it wasn't peace that was over, but innocence threatened. Kennedy's duty now was to steer clear of the Welshman. The attraction was diabolic. To doubt the words of Johnny boy was not an option. In Kennedy's ethic, a thing was the more likely to be true for being unpleasant. As one who has tasted less unpleasant fare than that upon which he presently dines, he began to wish his earlier trouble would return; it was this that had taken him into The Inventors' Arms in the first place. In vain, he checked his Inbox.

Yet his project was advancing. Working with unusual absorption, he felt he'd obtained something coveted by scholars, a sort of guarantee of meaning. Barbara, meanwhile, appeared to have decided upon a period of silence, where their agreement was concerned. She was busier than usual at Hill and Mynor, the legal firm where she was Director of Promotions and Entertainment.

About the apparent, or possible, cause of his scholarly renaissance, namely, Arthur Mountain, Kennedy added nothing to what he'd told about the breakfast riot. Like a kid with a mad pal at the end of the street, he should keep the Welshman secret.

The main reason for doing so, obviously, was that his new (and former) friend was a murderer. Could he in honesty mention Arthur without saying that he had killed a man? Moreover, Barbara worked for a legal outfit. Mustn't be compromised. Her husband's socialising with a killer, arsonist and trespasser on the railways, would end her career if it got out. So Kennedy never spoke of the green-eyed Welshman. Then he received another mail.

And wished to see Arthur Mountain immediately. Having wanted Mountain to take his mind off his trouble, he wished his old trouble back when he heard he'd killed a man; well now that it had indeed come back, he would have the greater of two evils reappear to drive it away. Was there a wish left? There'd been something conclusive about the Welshman's departure from The Inventors' Arms some nights ago, promising to return in a minute when the hooded youth brought his message. You had to suppose he'd gone for good. What was there to keep him? Kennedy had no illusions about his own claims on that character.

So he went up to the office, on pretext of checking his pigeon-hole. Truth was, he yearned to bump into certain colleagues and be responded to normally by them, particularly his Head of Department. Now and then, he wondered what might be written in his file. That she had her eye on him as a potential wrong un was a worry Clown Kennedy had converted into probability one autumn morning in Cell 3, the small, windowless room that housed the photocopier.

Hearing a class beginning with cheerful sounds in 357 (which backed onto the cell), Kennedy left the copier producing handouts and stooped to the connecting door (aware that William Bow, a strangely-popular humgruffin, taught in 357 at that hour). A white sack for recycling was fastened to the handle, so he swung it aside to look through the keyhole, but could make out nothing except Bow's torso at the white board and heads of female students. Something set him off; he stifled it, but had to linger at the keyhole to check no one in the class had heard, by some freak of acoustics – like *I can hear snorting, Sir William, I swear!* Then he got cramp in his thigh, and was stuck there holding the sack like a net curtain; which sets him off again, so he has to re-check he hasn't been heard. When the photocopier stopped shuttling and he clocked his boss in the main door of the cell holding a certificate, he was still beside himself.

The end of the third-floor corridor was darker than normal, few staff being around. Here, Kennedy did indeed encounter his boss, who came through a double swing-door at some pace, seemed to rear up at him to his right, muttered then set off down a side corridor by the Polar Suite. She might just have been surprised to see him in the dark, might even have been in a hurry – in the objective world. Kennedy, however, had form. From the Cell 3 incident, she'd walked away without comment, leaving Kennedy to it; but such spectacles whet the appetite of suspicion, which appreciates them fully with the appearance of second or third courses. Who knew what she'd heard of him lately? No wonder she'd recoiled. Could have died for a kind word from her; though in the objective world, Jane Hall did not waste words.

Holding the sides of the pigeon-hole, Kennedy imagined whispering. At the end of the corridor were voices. A door shut. Outside the building the wind blew. In his slot there was nothing, bar a book catalogue and leaflet from the student counselling service.

The other motive for dropping by the office was that it made it necessary to pass on the way to the underground The Inventors' Arms, into which he now looked and, since someone was just behind him, entered. The booth with the white frosted screen in which Arthur Mountain and Johnny boy once sat was empty so Kennedy ordered himself a pint of black stout and took his place there. Magic had gone from the furnishings. Perhaps they'd never been here at all. The barmaid with spectacles and, according to Mountain's augury, an owl on her back did not acknowledge him. Surely she'd recall the fuss about wine in pint glasses, the smoke that swirled? The ashtray was empty, bright, the stout had a trousery bouquet. She could have made a joke about his being on his own tonight. In dejection Kennedy took the catalogue from his briefcase. It advertised books on Social History, Ghosts, Tea and the Tea-table, Witchcraft, Public Drinking in the Early Modern World.

'According to the latest sociological research on public drinking ...' As Kennedy considered the words, the door banged. Round the side of the screen, Kennedy beheld Arthur Mountain passing from the west door down the side of the pub. How many miles to Babylon?

Let him get to the south door unobserved, he'd be gone forever. Behind him came shopping bags, a lady wearing fur. In dumbshow they inceded. Kennedy almost cried out. Like a boy in a tale, perhaps he did, for Mountain and the lady had come to a halt far side of the horseshoe bar, facing the booth directly.

The Welshman wore a beret in a fresh shade of green. Coldly he looked on. Had he been chatting to Kennedy's boss? Staring, he asked the time of day.

The lady replied, the barmaid added something, Mountain sang, like a disordered child,

Have you seen the muffin man?
Muffin man, muffin man,
Oh *have* you ever seen the boog?
NO I FUCKING HAVEN'T!

Kennedy felt himself the object of a ceremony of disapproval. The three of them were now eyeballing him. He wished to God there were a way out the back of the booth, transfixed by the stare of this haughty murderer, now uttering a short word to his lady, her mouth the red of a chilled fruit. No doubt a comment regarding Kennedy's presence. Not to have been in for a week might be an injury to the majesty of the Welshman; to be there now, worse still. The etiquette of court was palpable, as if the centuries were but a modern dream.

Arthur Mountain adjusted his beret for the lady's approval, tilting his big chin as she removed her coat. Placing her finger under the collar, she hung the fur over her shoulder, manly, white throat dazzling. Kennedy looked at his pint for distraction; his glass was empty. Maybe Arthur Mountain killed a man for not knowing how to look when he brought his lady in a pub. There were such men. And those old Welsh terms would no doubt OK it. Now he was staring him down again. So the man across the bar could outstare nature itself, emit his green light for eternity.

16. Natalie. The free wife.

'You're a one!' Arthur Mountain was now saying to Kennedy. 'Had me going over there you did!' Choking slightly, Kennedy swigged his new drink. How he was meant to have prevailed in the staring session, he was none too clear, though your merry-andrew here'd been on about it for several minutes, soliciting endorsements from the woman called Natalie he'd introduced as his wife when they came to visit Kennedy with a pint for him, Mountain pulling a black trolley of solid construction, some three foot in length (this it was that had given the appearance of spontaneous motion to the shopping bags Kennedy saw them enter with). Natalie's eyes were on Kennedy. The Welshman concluded expatiation on his unfriendly performance with apology and excuse: the way Dr Kennedy'd been staring at his new beret made him self-conscious.

'What d'you think though, honestly?' The Welshman patted his cap, which was the green of a dainty elm Kennedy loved to see in Ford Park in Maytime.

'He probably thinks it's ridiculous,' the woman called Natalie said, lighting a Benson and Hedges, lips sealed about the filter. As when through height or time sky darkens, her eyes were the ultimate phase of blue.

'Let him say for himself, love!' the Welshman cried merrily. The woman crossed her right leg over her left and smiled. She was wearing tall heels. Her shoes looked expensive to Kennedy, who of course had seen her before.

'What else did you buy?' Kennedy asked ingeniously. What was he meant to say? It wasn't the colour was the problem. The problem was the man. The combination. Tilted on the tobacco mass of Mountain's hair, big face below, the beret gave him the look of a rococo simpleton, 'humorist' in a joke tam, almost horrifically silly. Had this woman, whose right foot was chummily close to Kennedy (he spied an ankle chain beneath her tights, which were sheer), given him a tip? If he agreed it was ridiculous and said why, would he get laughs and more pats on the shoulder? Mountain did seem in the mood for sport, positively demanding the piss-take …

On the other hand, he might react very badly indeed to an insult. What if this was some sort of trap, and Natalie the setter? Say the Welshman was a psychopath. Say the pair of them were. Kennedy foresaw a lengthening series of such horrid tests as their friendship developed. Sooner or later, he'd get it wrong, whereupon Arthur Mountain would smash a glass in his face or paralyse him from the neck down. All very well for him to sit there grinning and winking, with his pint of wine …

'Oh ho!' the Welshman was now laughing. 'Dr K is prevaricating, if I'm not mistaken.' The bastard was evidently a mind-reader as well. Kennedy's way out was blocked by the black trolley, standing there like a hound. It was a trap. Mind-readers the pair of them. She knew what he'd been thinking on the train (and after). Made the Welshman murder anyone who fantasised about her, when they'd been given a last chance to run.

Having moistened his mouth with his stout, Kennedy was going to settle the thing one way or another by saying, 'Is it true that you've killed a man?', but in fact came out with a joke about Mountain's beret. Natalie bit her lip.

It wasn't boldness or recklessness that had roused him to mock the Welshman; it was a desire to have done with whatever the latter might have in store for him. His joke was really a substitute for the question about killing, and more likely to provoke the truth, at least if Mountain was uncontrollably violent. Such a person when laughed at may find it hard to hide the truth he could keep from a straight question. And why endure future tests, one of which you must sooner or later fail, when you might know the worst, and feel it on your neck, without the ordeal of waiting? As when he rose from the corn for punishment, what he feared was time …

'How d'you like that?' the Welshman shouted, banging glasses on the table. A minute or two earlier, he'd been at the southern door of The Inventors' Arms with a handful of fire, as if Goya's giant had found a stray sun. The beret, soaked in vodka, burned blue, blazed yellow. 'At your word, Dr K, I will destroy my new hat! What does that teach you?' Natalie stubbed out a cigarette and uncrossed her legs.

A lot was what it taught (pertaining to the ethnology of friendship, for example), so much indeed that the prudent man would do well to answer with extreme care. Quivering with meaning, the Welshman looked haughtily about while Kennedy arranged his ideas. Luckily, however, the question seemed to have been rhetorical.

Since in the manner that a countryman might whistle for his dog, Arthur Mountain was now beginning to note the absence of Johnny boy. Meanwhile Natalie was showing Kennedy her wedding ring, which appeared to be one of a pair with Arthur's, though a little more delicate, a band of gold engraved with black snakes. He wondered who'd chosen them. Should he kiss her hand? Close to his face she held it, licking a flake of lipstick from an incisor with the tip of her tongue, as if Kennedy were a mirror. It is beautiful, Kennedy said, majestic. She held it there a while longer, then withdrew her hand. Did she merely want to show it off, or was he regarded as some kind of connoisseur?

'Doesn't your wife go around with you?' Natalie said.

'Not so much,' Kennedy explained.

'As when you were first married?'

'Oh we go out for dinner sometimes.' Kennedy paused. 'Or walks. Or see friends of hers.'

'Don't you let her?'

'How d'you mean?'

'Let her come to the pub with you.'

'Oh I hardly ever go to the pub myself.'

'Well you were in here when we came in.' While Kennedy organised an answer, Natalie admonished him: 'Arthur says you're always in here. It's your local. You've even got your own patch.' She indicated the booth they sat in.

'I swear, I've been in here more times in the last couple of weeks than ever before!' Kennedy laughed. Had he conceded the point?

'The barmaid, she said you're a face in here too!' Kennedy was about to protest, but Natalie was teasing. 'So you don't let her after all do you!'

'Come to the pub? Of course I would – if she wanted to.'

'You let her do what she wants?' Her accent was stony, northern, direct.

'Yes,' Kennedy said. 'Of course I do.'

'Absolutely anything?'

'Well – I suppose so.' What did Barbara want? A child. Was that all she wanted? He didn't know. He tried to make, or keep, her happy. But her desires – what did he know of them?

'So she's free?'

'We were talking about this before, Arthur and I,' Kennedy said, with a view to getting the former into the conversation. Head down, the Welshman was rummaging among the shopping bags.

'Whether your wives were free or not? I see! Good job I came along this time, what? I wonder what you both had to say!' She was having fun with him.

'We were actually talking about freedom in general,' Kennedy explained.

'In Welsh law,' Arthur had risen to the table, red in the face, 'you'll find that a freeman's wife may give away her tunic and her mantle and her kerchief and her shoes, and her flour and cheese and butter and milk, without her husband's permission, and may lend all the household utensils.'

'Here!' Placing her right ankle on her knee, Natalie took off her shoe and then the other one, and put them on the table before Kennedy. They were night-sky platforms, round-toed, that seemed to sparkle as if deeply inset with feint stars. The heels were close to five inch. The maker's name (no surprise this to Kennedy) was printed in black on a white label on the sole, where her foot went. 'You were looking at them so you can have them! Sniff them if you like!'

'But I don't want them!' Kennedy protested. Wasn't this even heavier than the beret burning? An awful gift. And now for Christ's sake she had two fingers at the throat of her blouse, flashing her eyes, wife of a freeman …

'I was of course referring to 12th-century Welsh law,' Arthur explained, 'though since our time is the bright past's shadow, Natalie's actions occur within the original illumination of the law. And it's a great compliment to me, to my status, that she is giving you her things like this. *Braint* we call it, the status of a man before his kin. Have you got your kerchief, your flour or your cheese, sweetheart?' Natalie shook her head.

What happened next was that Arthur rose and stood at the end of the table blocking the view from the bar while Natalie unbuttoned her blouse and passed it to Kennedy who sat with the shoes before him on the table, the blouse on his arm, sightless as Master Po; her perfume was trouble enough: the more he kept his eyes ahead, the more it ravished him – as if the smell, sharp, heady, peppery, a salad of ginger and lilies, had teeth and fingers. This was where you could die. As if cloaked, Mountain seemed to cast a shadow on them. What in God's name did they want of him, this pair?

'What can your wife give?' the Welshman asked. 'Reflects on your status. If you're a freeman, all this stuff (cheeses included – sure we've got some in one of these bags). If you're a villein, all your wife can give without your permission is her riddle. See how it plays out? Wife of a freeman is free of him; she can do what she likes. Wife of a villein isn't free because he isn't – he's got a lord over him. Accordingly, the more your wife gives, the freer yourself are. If she gives everything, then you are sovereign. Thanks to her power. Which isn't the conventional way of looking at things, but is an improvement to the world and also *radically* feminist, which we tend to be in Wales. Have you thought yet – about your wife?'

As Kennedy went over all this, mumchance, Arthur pointed at Natalie's shoes: 'That heel there (or one like it) did stout service at the Battle of Waverley. Trepanned a tattooed and bare-chested nyaff, didn't you love?'

'Ay, our Arthur – years ago,' Natalie said.

'Never sat by the fire at mammy's knee with his porridge cowl, after that bloody day.'

Christ. Another killer.

Arthur watched a while then began to shake with laughter: 'We haven't done you there have we, Doc? Haven't kippered you? Only joking we were! Natalie just wants to try her new things on.' And with this, Mountain produced a shoe-box from the bags on the trolley and an item which must be a blouse, wrapped in lilac paper. 'Don't think we're serious when we're messing!' Arthur laughed, as Natalie put on new sandals from the same designer, and a silk top of bluish grey with a snaky design, which Kennedy could now look at. 'Lesson to you,' Arthur said. 'Don't confuse life with a lecture – even when it sounds like it.'

'Right,' Kennedy said, who was, however, interested in what had just been said – and in his academic manner, was now comparing the elements of Welsh law he'd heard when he was the other side of the screen with the latest gear. Was it all a spoof? If it were, he'd made a fresh fool of himself by sitting here so solemn. He was brooding on this when Natalie touched him on the arm and asked if he liked her new things. She stood to model them, placing one foot where he could see it on the chair beside him. Behind her, Arthur was at the bar again, seeming to be offering the shoes in which Natalie'd entered an hour ago to the barmaid, who took them, bent below the jump to try them on, and reappeared with a smile such as Kennedy would have loved to cause.

'Don't mind Arthur,' Natalie said looking down at him like a cabaret star picking a fellow from the audience. 'He's just trying to impress you.'

'Oh!' Kennedy said. Hadn't she been party to it? She smiled at him and sat as Arthur returned with more drinks. Maybe she had just been trying on her new things. Where did their money come from?

'I think you're great,' Natalie murmured, and then with an air of imparting something rare, 'You've got soul.'

Indeed. It was the rest he lacked.

'What's your favourite food?'

'Chips,' Kennedy said, which happened to be the truth.

'You can't live on chips, young man,' Natalie told him. 'You'll be the size of a house.'

Kennedy tried to laugh. Her eyes were enchanting him. Arthur's voice appeared from below (he was down among the bags again), to tell them his favourite.

'They're not good for you either,' Natalie said, taking a power puff on her B&H, an action that emphasised the wonderful lines of her face. 'Is that why your wife takes you walking – to burn the chips off?'

'I dunno,' Kennedy said. 'I suppose it could be. Not the only reason though.'

'Now what d'you talk about?' Natalie asked, smiling as if Kennedy were ever so important.

'Oh,' Kennedy said, lost for words before her eyes. Barbara actually spent a good part of their walks by the river chatting to friends on her mobile phone. He complained now and then, but as she pointed out, it gave him time to think about his project.

'Husband and wife things?' Natalie smiled to help him.

'Yes,' Kennedy said.

'I know how it is.'

'You got married recently?' Kennedy said, knowing what women liked to talk about, even if he could provide nothing himself.

She smiled and it was as if he'd switched her on. Her being blazed at him. 'Yes!' she told Kennedy. 'It's so exciting. I feel I've known him forever. I'd love to get married every day!' While Kennedy weighed these words, Natalie said to Arthur, 'Are you digging for the cellar?', which made Kennedy think of *Hamlet*, and got the Welshman back up at the table. He'd lost one of the bags, the one with the thing he'd been wanting to show Kennedy.

'Oh that!' Natalie said. 'Well you should be more careful. Somebody probably nicked it off the trolley!'

'Christ! D'you think so!' Arthur cried.

'Yes I do think so,' his wife advised him. 'If you will trail it round with all those flash bags on, you're asking for it aren't you? Some ragamuffin's whipped it. That's what's happened.'

'I'll go and look for it!' Arthur Mountain decided. 'I'll hunt high and low for the fucking thing and I shan't rest till I've recovered it either. I want Dr K to have it in his hand. Got it specially for him. – Don't try and stop me!'

'No one was trying to,' Natalie told him.

'Really,' Kennedy begged to differ, 'if it's something you got me, please don't put yourself out going to look for it. It could be anywhere!'

'I know where it dropped,' Arthur averred. 'Heard it. By Green Park it was.'

'But that's a mile away, at least,' Kennedy protested. 'And someone's bound to have picked it up – or pinched it, like Natalie said.'

'So you aren't bothered about your present? There's gratitude for you. "Just leave it on the pavement, Arthur!" Like that hey?'

'It's the thought that counts,' Kennedy said. 'That's all I meant.' He was troubled by this talk of a present for him, which played on his anxieties about the largesse of the unpredictable friend over there. How much did Arthur want to give him? And how much (the question was like a siren) was he expected to give in return? What had he to give?

'Well I'll be off,' Arthur was now saying, examining his cuffs. 'Don't let Dr K vamoose, sweetheart. I'll be back with his gift. He'll be glad when he sees it.'

'I really must be off myself soon,' Kennedy protested.

'His wife will be waiting,' Natalie declared. 'We mustn't keep him. He should be home for his tea.'

'Why don't you ring her?' Arthur proposed. 'Get her to come along here.'

'I think she'd need a bit more notice,' Kennedy said.

'Come on!' Arthur winked. 'Be spontaneous! Tell her to come along and meet your new pals!' He continued checking his cuffs: 'Told them I wanted five buttons on the sleeve. They've put four. That's no fucking use is it?'

'He's just had a suit made,' Natalie explained to Kennedy.

'Yes,' Arthur looked down at Kennedy. 'What d'you reckon?'

'It's a beautiful suit,' he told Arthur, who beamed with pleasure. 'Extremely elegant.'

'Sure now?' Arthur cleared his throat. The barmaid gazed at their little group, Kennedy and Natalie seated, Arthur standing above them preparing his departure.

'Of course.'

'You aren't ashamed of us though?'

'Why? Of course not!' Kennedy protested.

'Well if I had some new friends and I respected them, I'd make haste to introduce my wife to them,' Arthur declared, head back, gazing down his nose.

Wives again … Were they trying to madden him? Was that what they were up to? 'Maybe next time,' Kennedy said, hoping Natalie would stick up for him.

'Give over, Arthur,' Natalie said. 'You can't have it your own way every time.'

'But I could drop in and bring her along,' Arthur said, 'when I go hunting.'

'Hunting?'

'Yes. Hunting. For the miscreant who made off with Dr K's gift.'

'But we don't live anywhere near Green Park,' Kennedy protested. 'It'd take you ages.'

'Oh I can send a messenger,' Arthur assured him.

'I'll try and bring her next time,' Kennedy said. 'I will.' Was he ever going to be able to leave here? He felt like the victim of kidnappers who, discovering they have the wrong man, are carrying through their plan nevertheless, but with the obligation now to be as nice as possible. Perhaps, as observed in case studies, they were even forming a bond with their captive. But of course, he was free to go. All he had to do was stand and say 'See you later'. They'd even suggested he ring Barbara – invited him to make contact with the outside world … which was how such people operated.

'What if there isn't a next time?' Arthur asked, staring down upon them.

'There will be!' Kennedy hastened to tell this green-eyed figure of fate who had killed a man, as one might assure one's abductors that one will be 'straight back' after popping out for a paper/ breath of fresh air – in the direction of the nearest taxi firm.

'You misunderstand me,' Arthur said. 'We'll always be together now. Friends are friends. What I meant was the war may have started by then. We won't have time to sit around like this. *Carpe diem!*

Adiós!' He bent to murmur to Natalie so Kennedy could hear, 'Now don't let him go, love! I can tell he's dying to rush off, but all will be well. – I'll be back in a tick.' As Arthur marched to the door, Natalie raised her eyebrows at Kennedy, in gesture of understanding.

'I know you think he's up to something,' she told him. 'But you've got to trust Arthur. Just relax.'

While Kennedy was considering these statements, which seemed directed at himself in particular but also at some more general law, Arthur Mountain reappeared at the side of his wife: 'I forgot. If Johnny boy turns up, tell the little whore we're doing the stoplines tonight!'

'Don't be foul!' Natalie cried. 'How dare you call him that? Bastard!'

'Well Dr K can't wait forever. He's been good enough to attend on us for the past two hours as it is!' With that, he was gone, leaving Kennedy a little easier.

'Tell me how you met your wife,' Natalie ordered Kennedy kindly. 'Ring her to let her know you'll be a while, then tell me all about it. Go on! – Look at that!' She was bending round Arthur's side of the table, to gather some items that lay there, which in fact was the suit Arthur had entered in. He must have been changing into his new one while out of sight below the table. 'He's like a kid!' she told Kennedy happily.

17. How he met her. Bampa. The Jacks.

It was easy when his listeners were phantoms. Natalie's gaze, tube of smoke in her hand, how her red mouth waited on his words, and snaky top adorned the occasion, Kennedy experienced now as a mixture of stage fright, and the tension of long races his school put him in for. Over came the barmaid with a tray ... *You can do it, kiddo!*

Now along with handicaps mentioned in passing, Kennedy had the following weakness as a storyteller: in the parlance of the experts, he 'lacked narrative drive'. But what he lacked in that department, nature had compensated with the gift of 'rummaging stamina', so Natalie hears about Dave Day, and here's Kennedy at university, then out the pile comes *Chimes at Midnight*, Falstaff, Orson, Doll, Shakespeare, Jeanne Moreau, a blackbird, an ancient girlfriend, and certain matters and moments of questionable relevance. Natalie, however, was a skilful listener, unfazed by dust and old smells; so on he goes, crinkum-crankum ...

Was the barmaid spiking the drinks? There was a kind of gelling of the air where they sat that caused him to see with a lapse between the image and its identity. When Rebecca Sutton listened to him, like that time the sky was a bloody flag, she watched as Natalie watched now, absorbing what she could, with the twist that in the quarter of a century between now and then, the present scene seemed to have seniority, so that he and Natalie had been sitting here all that time, and perhaps for longer, while the first time was just another version, a modification or postscript.

'So who was it you met at the cricket?' Natalie said at last. 'A girl in a gingham dress, a hooker in a play you read or an actress in a film you watched? You're welding stuff!'

Uncomfortably, Kennedy felt Barbara wasn't appearing clearly, which he did not want at all. Wasn't he whoring her, for the amusement of his audience? Wasn't that the gist of his story, that she looked like a whore from a Shakespeare film, in her neat dress of red and white checks, knowing nothing of the sport, having gone along to a test match in the hope of meeting someone nice?

'Barbara.' There was a tremor in his voice. 'The others were just images.'

'Well what did you say to her?' demanded Natalie. Someone was bending over them to clear the ashtray and see if they needed anything, her shadow covering the wall to Kennedy's left. She wore a short-sleeved blouse and a red and green creature on her bicep seemed to be looking at him, like the demon in the Cardinal's fishpond. 'I like your tat!' Natalie said.

'It's by Tamora Vine.' She whispered something to Natalie and they giggled. 'Can I really have these shoes?'

'Of course, dear,' Natalie said. 'D'you know this man?'

'He's a lecturer.'

Natalie murmured something and the barmaid agreed.

'I didn't say anything,' admitted Kennedy, 'that day.'

'Oh you're a right one, you are!' cried Natalie. 'Deceitful get! What a tease! What a dreamer! So it wasn't how you met her! You could have asked her out there and then. Should have! Been dreaming of her since you were a youth. How many chances do you think you get, Dr Kennedy?'

'There was a man beside her,' Kennedy remembered.

'Bet you're just saying that!'

'He had a Euro '96 shirt on. I thought he might be her boyfriend. I remember now. I was worried he might start a fight with Dave Day. Kept looking round.'

'So she was going with a hooligan?' Natalie opened her eyes wide.

'No. She left on her own.'

'Didn't you follow her out?' The ice in Natalie's drink flashed and rang. Her cigarette was long, crossed legs professional. 'You could have chased her and taken her for a treat!'

'Ah – Dave and I stayed till the end. Then went for a curry.' Played,

Kennedy! Bravo! Solid anti-climax. Natalie, however, wasn't there yet.

'So how was it you did hook up with her then?' The featureless face of a bank robber, her knee communed with his. Obviously he wouldn't touch it, but if he did would it develop a mouth and bite his finger off at the knuckle, blow his belly out with a sawn-off? Or just let itself be stroked? 'Not been making her up have you, Dr K? Have you really got nowt for me?'

So to please the lady beside him, Kennedy completed the account, which he had to admit really wasn't much of a story. As he finished, a hooded youth came to the table with a note, for which she paid him with cigarettes and glittering coins.

'So can't you see,' Natalie said as they strode down Regent Street then across to Bond Street, her voice ringing huskily in the April evening, heels clattering – 'can't you see, that is a story!' She was stunning, strong, a lieutenant in drag. But Kennedy – well, he wasn't convinced he'd made it with her. Surely, she couldn't be that easily pleased? Still, he'd told the truth – or at least made nothing up. They marched on. She was a particularly fast walker. But had he managed to make the story sound a blessing? As of course it had been. Had he betrayed his heart? Or handed Barbara over, just by speaking of her? 'That's magic, is that,' Natalie cried, still rating Kennedy's performance. 'Like you went into a special cave and found her!' In a dark court they swooped upon a takeaway.

'Where's she from though, Barbara?' Natalie enquired, and the sound of his wife's name in the mouth of this glamorous lieutenant, it troubled Kennedy. She was dealing with the grill-man, a hot-eyed fella in a crimson scarf. Could he guarantee the lamb on his spit was Welsh? 'Someone'll know if it isn't,' she explained as the man called for invoices from the back, 'and there'll be hell to pay. Don't worry, sir!' she added, indicating Kennedy, who wasn't comfortable with these demands. 'Isn't this one who's fussy!' She'd ordered a shawarma for him with the sauces he liked, Kennedy noted, and a bundle of chips, marking the wrappings 'K'.

They marched on. Kennedy, supposing his account must have

caused a vivid impression, explained his wife was from Argentina. A grandfather had emigrated from Sicily to the Cono Sur, but there'd already been some English great-grandparents in the background who'd gone out there as engineers. Anyway, when she was 12 or so, Barbara's family came to Britain. It was time to return to the old country was the feeling; there were still cousins here and so on. It was one of them who'd given her a ticket for the Oval incidentally (she liked trying new things). She went to school in Gloucestershire. It hadn't been easy for her, Kennedy added warmly: she'd been picked on and it wasn't the best time to have a Spanish accent either, the early 1980s. Still, she'd got to university and then …

'And then she met you!' Natalie said. They seemed now to be crossing Piccadilly, though the angle at which they'd issued from the streets east of Mayfair made the appearance of the main road unfamiliar.

'Well, yes, though she did other things as well,' Kennedy explained. 'I came later really.'

'It was magic though!' Natalie took Kennedy's hand to lead him across. 'Who gives a stuff about the interim!'

'True,' Kennedy said. 'Where are we going now? To see Arthur?' The darker air of the park lay ahead. On a bench, Arthur Mountain was waiting for them, singing to himself:

She said, 'Take it easy!
Don't be afraid!
You've got nothing to lose,
You're in a penny arcade!'

'Look who I've brought!' Natalie cried.

'Good!' Arthur laughed, legs stretched out before him. 'High time we had some fresh air. Can't spend all your life in the boozer you know, Ken.' Natalie removed her new shoes and ran up and down on the grass opposite before passing Arthur his bundle like a stand-off to her Number 11. Kennedy received his too and sat down to the feast with Arthur while Natalie crouched on the grass. 'I can tell this is Welsh,' Mountain hummed. 'North Gower if I'm not mistaken. Marsh lamb! Quite excellent, darling.' Like a child, Kennedy filled himself with chips, covering his fingers in sauce. There was a can of Coke apiece, and Natalie had wipes for them all, then the Welshman began to call for fruit and she produced three oranges from her handbag, a roomy item of the softest white leather, about 600 quid's worth to Kennedy's eye. He was gladdened to the heart by the specificity of the dinner, its 'just rightness'.

'Like this I has my oranges!' Arthur demonstrated a method of peeling. Now what's so special about that? Kennedy thought, as Mountain dug at his fruit with his thumbs. 'Bampa used to eat them like this, he did. Every day he ate an orange, without fail, between four and five pm. Come hell or high water. Lived to 90 years old. Thinks I'm going to say he smoked 30 cigs a day too don't you?'

'Yes,' Kennedy said. Arthur was now eyeing him naughtily, like an elephant Kennedy had stopped to watch on honeymoon.

'Damn right, mun! Age of fifteen, he started smoking. Smoked three quarters of a million cigs in his span, he did. And remembered every one of them. Every single cig. What sort of memory d'you think that took, Ken? What sort of mnemonic? Think of the discipline! Nowadays they can't even remember their last text message. Never mind last! By the time they get to the end of the one they're reading, they've forgotten that too!' As if trying to filter something locked within its fibres, Arthur Mountain sucked toothily at his orange then chanted, 'Bamps, you were my kinsman!' To Natalie, who was sitting on the grass with her hands behind her, smoking a cigarette freestyle, he called, 'He would have loved you, darling!'

'Are the jacks kin, by the way?' Kennedy asked, who'd been meaning to get round to this.

'Hark at him!' Arthur laughed, turning to show how he'd made a sort of boxer's mouthguard with a section of orange peel, which gave him a synthetic and alarming appearance in the dark. Towards Kennedy, he put out his arms, zombie fashion: 'Who are the jacks?' he asked spookily. 'Who exactly are they?'

'Well,' Kennedy said carefully, thinking it prudent not to show too much familiarity with the hotel-burning incident, 'I think they're a kind of friends of yours.'

'Indeed they are,' Arthur conceded, tossing his mouthguard into the air. 'Doesn't make em kin though, I can tell you. – A Jack is just a Swansea boy. Capital "J" by the way. Got you something.' He handed Kennedy a black carrier bag that contained a book. This must be the lost present. 'Meant to buy you a bumper annual of erotica,' he murmured to Kennedy, 'but Natalie was watching.'

'Ah!' Kennedy said, and pulled out his present. It was, by coincidence, a book called *Swansea Jacks*, consisting of photographic plates and reminiscences of hooligans from Swansea City's firm. Kennedy'd seen shelves of such books in Waterstone's, each with its town (Shrewsbury, Portsmouth, Leicester, Lincoln) and its crew. The Swansea Jacks were snapped in a variety of places (car parks, pubs, stations, Ibiza, that area by the bay that Kennedy had walked along) and they seemed to like dressing up: in this one they were sporting seventies skinhead gear, braces, check-shirts, and so forth, while in this they appeared rather dandified in cravats and silk jackets, though they were all bloody strong in the arm, no doubt from weight training. In the text, they recalled violent battles with Chelsea, Leeds, Stoke, knifings, cracked heads, and fatalities. But they seemed to have had fun too.

'I've used these boys in my projects now and then,' Arthur said. 'From my own town they are, after all. Say I need to settle something, I'll put em on a retainer if it's a local matter. Wouldn't use em strategically though. Wouldn't be right. Only the kin will do, for strategic matters. Different status.'

'There's one of you here!' Kennedy said, browsing. In a pub car park, a group of characters grinning hard flanked Arthur Mountain in a suit. Beneath the photo, the text named the Jacks present ('Barry, Roy, Jenks, Nutter, Pilot') as being in the company of 'a friendly stranger'.

Arthur Mountain hummed and said he didn't like having his photograph taken (an assertion Kennedy found fairly implausible). He must have weakened on that occasion. 'No idea I was in here! Really no idea.' He shouted to Natalie to come and see. Kennedy gazed at his present. Had the Welshman appeared in other books?

'What have you two been talking about, love?' Arthur asked, his arm round Natalie, who sat now between the pair of them. 'Thanks for the food by the way. Lovely that was.'

'Don't mention it,' Natalie said, kissing her husband. Kennedy clutched his book of Jacks. If only this bench were the one place life went on, if the world were here and nowhere else, he'd be happy. 'Ken was telling me how he met his wife.'

'Ah, why do ladies always want to know about that stuff? Was she pestering you, Dr K?'

'Not at all,' Kennedy replied. 'I'm afraid I wasn't particularly interesting but Natalie was very polite.'

'Don't be daft, you!' Natalie said. 'It was a brahma!' She murmured something to Arthur. Kennedy wondered if she'd set eyes on the annual Arthur'd meant to buy him.

Humming, Arthur lit a cigarette from a broad box. 'There we are then.' His smoke curled and fled. The box was decorated with the face of a sailor. 'So what's the trouble?'

At length, Kennedy asked what trouble?

'The trouble that brings you in The Inventors' Arms. You look like a haunted man, Dr K. What really is the matter?'

18. Kennedy's trouble I. Quiz and dive.

There was a bandstand over the way. Italians passed them in a group, soft booted, laughing as one of their number ascended to perform.

'Bet he doesn't know "The Bristol Road Leads to Dachau",' murmured Arthur Mountain. 'Now a blessing's a blessing, Doc, and Natalie seems to have heard a nice account of one this evening, but that wasn't everything you have to say, was it? Something left over I fancy.'

'But am I meant to tell you everything?' asked Kennedy.

'We'll know when you're finished – as you will yourself. That'll be everything.'

'But I have to get home.'

'Off you go then!'

Kennedy made no sign of leaving.

'What are you scared of?'

'I'm no good at anecdotes,' Kennedy said. 'And this isn't something to be proud of.'

'Get it off your chest, mun! Before you go. Shouldn't take trouble home with you. Leave it in the park. Pass it on like the backs. See when Natalie was practising her rugby over by there? Yeah? Well that's what you've got to do with trouble, Ken. Pull it out the scrum, pass it down the centres, out to your winger, let him run! Go through the phases. Reprocess. Thus ends my metaphor. A rugby ball is made for passing!'

'But it'll take so long …'

'Not if we walk,' Arthur said. 'Let us come a way with you and you can start. Next time we meet you can tell us more. I can see you're inclined! Come on, Ken! Attaboy! Let's start our walk. I won't butt in.'

He readied his trolley for departure, then they made south through the park andante, Natalie's heels keeping up a military rhythm. It was twenty past eleven. The tubes would be running for a while yet.

Last autumn, they had a quiz in their department. Boss Hall decided it would cheer everyone up. Arthur Mountain hummed. Behind him slid his trolley. The teams were mixed, staff and students; there was wine, alas; Kennedy excelled. The students couldn't have thought him the brightest of their lecturers, way they went on about his score.

'What d'you get?'

Nine out of nine.

Arthur Mountain wished to know each of the questions.

You can't keep shtumm for two minutes, you! Natalie told him.

Well not being a university man himself, he had to see how he'd have done.

Kennedy recited the questions – there was good reason not to have forgotten the agreeable part of the evening. Arthur lit a short cigarette, stalled his trolley and said arri. Six his score was, possibly seven. No more than that.

Three more like, Natalie said, and they resumed their march, crossing The Mall into St James's Park.

Well Kennedy's team won and he was awarded the individual prize, a bottle of wine (non-drinkers could have a book voucher). Some students were hanging around. They got him to open his prize. His colleagues were highly complimentary, though most of them didn't rate general knowledge. Arthur Mountain wished to know why; Natalie told him cool it.

He was here to learn.

He was here to listen.

The students were digging Kennedy anyway. Together they drank the prize. They brought a couple more bottles of red. Kept topping him up. He began to feel he had something in common with them. They wanted his opinion on things. Why did he never tell them about his personal life in class? Other lecturers did! This surprised him. He took another glass of red. Could have been his sixth, maybe seventh; he'd lost count. Wasn't much of a drinker. Soon began to feel he had more in common with them. Most of his colleagues had left by now. Cy Frazer, a pal of his, and Hannah Raider were still with a group of students, other side of the room; Hannah went.

Kennedy carried on with his gang. What it was he had in common with them, he became fuddled about. They were extremely frank. Made him feel like a child – an aged one. The things they got up to while travelling, stuff they did in each other's flats – they implied he knew all about, though the funny thing was, they seemed concerned he wouldn't approve. They were talking about some dives by the university. Cy Frazer was grinning, making signs. Kennedy could see him by the door. The students wanted to take him to a dive. He wouldn't go. They wanted to know about other staff. Was it true Cy Frazer had a gun? Were Caspar Fine and Helen Harley married, like wife and husband? Did Dr Bow do stand-up comedy? (That was a surprise.) Why did Dr Forth try so hard to make people warm to him? (Another surprise.) Had he seen how Hannah Raider writhed at guys (guys standing by grinned hard) and put her bitch shield down like this when any girl answered a question in class? He told them that was unfair. They seemed to have another bottle. He had to have first glass. Hadn't felt so drunk since a student himself.

'You drank your wine in pint glasses, you wouldn't run into this sort of problem.'

A dark-haired girl – she'd been in Kennedy's team – was still there. They had a league table for the lecturers who taught them, but he was the mysterious one. Other students poured him more wine. None of them knew what he really thought. Did he believe the stuff he taught them? Other lecturers seemed to have faith in what they said, whereas Kennedy – well he seemed to believe in something else really, like he had some secret. Which he wouldn't tell them. The dark-haired student was Dorothy. On everyone's behalf, she told him off for keeping a secret; wagging her finger.

Kennedy enjoyed this, he was afraid to say, fearing students'd thought him a pretty cross fellow. He did try and explain his secret (which was about character). Wasn't too coherent. For truth's sake, he tried to explain he was an academic failure. Which was why he kept things secret. Totally unable to explain them – that's all it was. His secret was just an idea he was rubbish at explaining. The students would not hear of this. Dark Dorothy asked if he liked her tits. Obviously couldn't say no; mustn't say *Yes* either. Sure sign he shouldn't be there any longer, now they were asking questions he couldn't safely answer. Yeah. He ought to have been out of there; but their attention made it difficult. He tried to leave.

Then did leave but found himself with a handful of students at the door to a dive. The street lights – he could see them and the tube was over there, but the world had shrunk. Shrunk and opened up. Imagine an explorer who's found some sort of shrine; the steamer's signalling but the natives of the place are all over him, chattering, poking, showing. That was how it was at that doorway.

God was it loud in the dive. They gave him a sticky shot. The sticky shot tasted of aniseed. Two or three of these. Kept repeating himself. Had to shout in Dorothy's ear. Sometimes forgot her name but she stuck by him. How to get home, he couldn't remember. He did like her tits – that he confirmed. She insisted. His attention was full of her. Couldn't see anything either side. Moving round him, she was a solid shadow. Like on a roundabout or fairground ride. You know when it goes so fast, you can see only one thing? He was brilliant, had all the secrets. She believed him.

Next thing he was in a dark room, but just before, he thought they'd been dancing. Who else was there altogether (or had been) he couldn't be clear. Impression of a party going on, voice calling, 'Tutor in the hole!' There were faces above him, like planning a rescue. Someone was whistling. Might have been him, show he was OK. There was music, an electro-version of a big band, frenzied, stupid song with dogs barking, a strange thing, a kind of Irish disco track with a wailing voice and banjo that he felt he must know from somewhere, people laughing, someone undoing his shoelaces. Where was his secret? She wanted to know.

Arthur and Natalie marched on as if there was a steppe to cover. Natalie's heels rattled; now and then on broad streets, the trolley jolted. A woman passed them grinning. Speak up mun, said Arthur Mountain. So Kennedy went on rotating his trouble, like a connoisseur in poor light.

'You're hard on yourself, you,' Natalie told him, Arthur having entered a 24-hour store, where he was bargaining over licensing time. Her eyes showed they'd been listening.

He was sorry. The whole bloody thing was so abject. Never told anyone.

'Don't be sorry.'

It was his conscience. Never left him alone.

'You like women don't you?' She touched his arm.

Arthur appeared with a bottle of whisky and some chocolate for their journey. They'd passed Victoria a while ago and Kennedy was now heading them along rich streets towards South Kensington, where he might still pick up a late tube westbound. Where did his friends plan to spend the night? Top hotel, you'd imagine, from the bags on the trolley. He was a flash fellow, this green-eyed Welshman, now swigging in bliss. Who was it they came to visit? Many people perhaps, depending on the extent of the 'kin'. The Welshman handed him the bottle of Whyte and Mackay, from which he took a burning sip. Then they might stay only among the kin, according to some *braint* principle of lodging.

'Where are you staying, by the way?' Kennedy enquired. Natalie, having hitched a ride on Arthur's trolley, was holding her shoes like a figurehead in tow.

'We'll decide on that when we've heard you out, mun,' Arthur decreed. 'Your trouble's not over yet.'

This was no doubt very generous (and true as well), yet posed serious problems for Kennedy, who had a lot more to say, but wished to get home now, and was apprehensive that his friends would expect to come in and hear out his story … and why shouldn't they? Had we become so bourgeois that we no longer took in people to complete stories we'd inflicted on them, after a certain hour? Indeed we had – if Kennedy was anything to go by.

'Don't worry,' Arthur was declaring, 'we'll stick by you till the end of this. Have to hear the lot. Want to as well. We'll come home with you if necessary.'

There it was! Bloody hell. Barbara just had no experience of Kennedy's bringing stray friends home at night. None at all. Never once tried his hand as Mr Bloom (odd, come to think of it, in years of marriage); certainly no couples. Maybe that was less odd ... but why should it be? Didn't many people keep open house, for strays, old friends who'd come down, bedless intellectuals – or husbands and wives? Of course they did. Kennedy didn't. Perhaps Barbara would have been agreeable to it before now, if he'd taken the lead. On the other hand, to bring people into the home of a woman when that woman was unprepared – particularly for a visitor like Natalie to cast her eyes at the design and the bathroom – was a sure cause of a row; though Barbara was just unpredictable enough to be excited by such irregularity. Then what? She'd join them in the kitchen in her black pyjamas, Arthur insisting that Kennedy continue the account of his trouble ...

19. Kennedy's trouble II. 4x4. Tribunal.

So as they approached the underground, Kennedy needed a stratagem, and needed it fast. The Welshman must have no cause to enter his house: imperative now to keep his friends outside till the story was done, then arrange a hotel in the neighbourhood. But Kennedy was no Ulysses. The trains were still running, and Arthur was keen for Natalie to put her feet up: where better than a comfortable carriage heading the way of the Kennedy household?

Spying a cocktail bar on Old Brompton Road, he suggested a 'late taste'. No dice. Arthur was pleased with his whisky, and they were now at the entrance, when someone called out to Natalie, who stepped from the trolley and over to see him. Kennedy, wishing for an asthma attack, a District Line ASBO, a memory-deleting stroke, a life-or-death text (*Come to Harwich immediately! Don't bring anyone.*), a total power blackout, an Al Qaeda threat, an asteroid impact or some form of Quantum miracle, was reprieved for a while. The Welshman had lit a cigarette and Natalie was in conversation with a man who stood just right of the entrance. There was laughter; Natalie hugged the man and called Arthur over. Kennedy felt there was something familiar about the figure against the ox-blood tiling of the station, but he was keeping well back. In fact, the encounter worked to his advantage, because by the time the conversation had ended, with hugs all round, a barred gate had banged shut this end of the arcade and the underground was closed. They'd have to walk then (unless the bloody trolley folded to fit in a black cab).

'No problem!' Arthur laughed. 'And if we have to spend the night at Dr Kennedy's, and meet his wife at long last, we got togs for tomorrow' – here indicating their shopping. 'Bought enough to stay a week, as it happens!' He rubbed his hands, patted Kennedy on the shoulder and winked, a gesture from which Kennedy, resigning himself to his fate (in its latest aspect, instant divorce) drew an atom of hope. So they set off, Natalie on foot again, and Kennedy resumed his tale.

Last September there was a meeting to go over the reports from the external examiners (who checked students' work was being marked fairly and accurately). These meetings worried Kennedy, in case he was singled out for grading too leniently. Samples were being circulated; he couldn't take his eyes off an essay by Lydia Lightman, which had a mark of 78 – and a written commendation from Orla Gree (Lead Examiner). He'd taught Ms Lightman the year before and warned her about stealing other people's work in her essays – plagiarism as it's known in the trade. The university had procedures for dealing with plagiarism – a whole code of practice. But he didn't really like to give the individual up to the system even if they had been naughty – felt like a betrayal. Particularly if they'd stolen only a few words. Dr Kennedy preferred a quiet warning it must not happen again, because they would be found out, and next time would be outside his jurisdiction. On a second offence, you might be sent down. That was you finished in higher education. Try explaining to an employer how it was you went to university and left without a degree. An act of dishonesty could taint your life. In other words, the naughty student was bloody lucky to have run into the merciful arms of Dr Kennedy on this occasion, who was going to deduct a mere five marks from the essay and say no more about it.

'Like the principle, Doctor K. Dealt with cheats my own way when I was a clerk.'

Kennedy wasn't so sure now. Let certain people off, they'd take the whole institution for a sucker. Looking over Lightman's work that morning, he saw the little thief had stolen far more this time, great blocks of it. The style just wasn't her own.

Hannah Raider was swanking to herself in lunar jewellery about the acclaimed essay. She it was who'd set it and marked it before it was sent to the externals. She hadn't sussed. Nor had Orla Gree.

But all work submitted by students was checked for Internet theft or copying by an electronic surveillance system called HORSEY, since there were websites you could copy an essay from – or just get someone to write it for you for thirty quid and download it. So if a piece of work had been HORSEYed and returned a low reading in terms of recognised content, the marker often regarded it as a fair attempt and didn't look into it further. The temptation was for markers to put their trust in HORSEY.

As if secreting acid in some chamber of his jaw, Arthur Mountain emitted a thick hissing sound.

But when it came down to theft from hardbacked books in the library (most of which weren't on the Web), the technology wasn't so effective. The marker had to go by experience, or taste. In this instance, the suspect style was ironic, jeering, prone to the use of qualifying adverbs. Kennedy could identify the voice: an English theorist who'd bugged him since his own student days.

Which his colleagues applauded with a hint of nostalgia – like he'd just come out with the words from a song no one could name, though it was in the charts when they were kids. The crime, however, couldn't be confirmed until after the meeting, when Jane Hall sent him down to the library to search for the book, mark the stolen passages and report back to her in camera.

Arthur Mountain, who'd stopped to look around at the territory they were crossing at the moment, said that surveillance was now nine tenths of the law. What wasn't caught electronically hadn't happened, crime or no – though of course, it *had* happened; or had it?

'But in a way,' the Welshman seemed to be sniffing the air, 'we've always had this. The worst stuff gets away again and again. Can't catch it with science, or techniques. Maybe there's no technique can match the Devil. And if he made the world – you might be familiar with the idea Dr K – then who's the biggest technocrat there's been? The Devil himself. Which means surveillance is rigged his way. He's making sure it's only small fry show up on it. We need old eyes to catch the Devil, old ears.

'Can you imagine what goes on if you just look for yourself, like you did with this cheat, Ken? 99% settle with the latest equipment –

always they do: any given time. And in equipment, I include history, as well as gadgetry. What is history after all? Technique! We'll have you for the Plebs' League yet, Dr K!'

Kennedy was wondering what sort of compliment this may be when Arthur Mountain went, 'Tchah!' like a man driving a cat from his garden. On the left-hand side of the road, a dark 4x4 passed them at cruising speed and a hand was raised within. They'd come to a stadium, accoutred with shops and flash restaurants, giant club badge on the wall.

'Combat 18 territory this used to be,' Arthur said. 'Still smell em. Gone elsewhere they have now, but I can smell em on the air. – Why d'you bring us this way, Ken? For a good sniff was it?' The 4x4 passed again, now on the near side. Within, a large man and a woman Kennedy felt he recognised, looked their way and seemed to laugh. A third figure, observing them from the back, shook a shaved head. Arthur Mountain suddenly stooped to his trolley and flung with great power at the 4x4 a dark missile which hit the bodywork with a crack, bouncing off into the road. Slowing its speed, as if in momentary deliberation over returning, the vehicle carried on into the night, eastward down the Fulham Road. Arthur walked over to recover his missile, which Kennedy saw was a combination lock of black steel, around half the size of the Welshman's fist. 'All scratched it is now look!' he said to Natalie. 'What did I tell you, love?'

'So I see,' Natalie said. 'Dr Kennedy's done well to bring us this way.'

Kennedy, whose plan for a good long walk had certainly not been so pointed as to include an encounter such as that just witnessed, made to protest that throwing sharp objects at this time of night at expensive cars with large men and their friends sitting in them was bloody risky, even if this was West London as opposed to South Wales; but Natalie was watching and Arthur handed him the whisky: valour got the better of discretion.

Mouth burning, he asked who those people were.

'D'you want to know?' Arthur said. 'That may be a commitment, I have to advise you, Ken.'

OK said Kennedy. From the south-west the wind blew at them

and into the stadium behind. He imagined it taking shape there, forming teams, a chanting crowd …

'Cos when I asked you if you wanted to come to the wars once, you said you didn't know,' Arthur continued, clenching his raised fist round the black missile.

Kennedy nodded, wondering how 'once' went with *last week*, for it was only then that Arthur had asked him. Natalie smiled, like he hadn't to say Yes, if he really didn't want to; as a lady of a certain age might smile at a boy in her bed.

'Well,' Arthur said, rolling his trolley, 'if you come with me all the way, you shall see for yourself. But when we last heard from you, you were on your way down to the library to search for the book.' From Stamford Bridge, they now looped north, as Kennedy continued his tale.

He was standing in the lane where he'd just found the plagiarised book when someone said, 'Now what are you up to, Dr Kennedy?', in a tone that might have been used to a three-year-old on a stool with his nose in the cupboard, or trying the remote control for the adult channel. But Kennedy was old enough to be the father of Lydia Lightman, so there was no need for him to respond like a child caught red-handed, as she faced him down the lane between the shelves of books.

Some of the students were women already; Lydia Lightman was a child. No make-up or hairstyle to speak of – like she defied the world of adornment. Stood there grinning in an obstinate way she had, you could take her for a paragon of sincerity, if you didn't know already she was a thief.

He showed her what he was looking at. Held it up in his right hand at the lane's blind end, authority leaking. Couldn't get out to his left and she was in his way to the right. What if she charged him? Could he resist her if she snatched it? He doubted himself. Went towards her with the book in front, like a shield of faith. She seemed to get the wrong idea: gulped, turned, vanished. But on his way back to the department, he asked himself why he was worried about her gulping like that. Bang to rights, was she not?

He took the book to the office of Boss Hall, who didn't offer him a coffee from her espresso machine, evidently unthrilled by Kennedy's forensic enterprise. Made the external examiners look bloody silly for one thing. That was irritating her, the silliness of the examiners, but the irritation had room for his interference with the institutional apple-cart – as he now saw of course. Meanwhile, Hannah Raider had taken the rest of the day off sick, deeply anxious about the knock-on effect of this incident on her professional reputation. Well done, Kennedy! Nice work. Only a 24-carat schlemiel could have brought this one off.

'Why did you let Lady Jane Hall make you feel like that?' Natalie paused to ask. 'You'd done the right thing!'

The three of them were now on North End Road. Wind banged the shutters of the stores and calmed.

Ah, Kennedy said, she'd caught him doing something once. Ever since, he'd felt she was on to him.

'Can we ask what it was?'

She'd caught him looking through a keyhole. Didn't give a good impression really.

'What were you looking at?

He didn't know. It was just a whim. Couldn't really see anything anyway. But she'd come in and found him – in the photocopying room.

Leaning at a deserted market stall, Arthur Mountain laughed: 'You're a one, Dr K! Naked honesty. Die of it if you're not careful!'

'I daresay!' Kennedy shouted, above the wind. They all took a drink from Arthur's bottle, there at the stall. Scraps and cartons ran along, stopped for breath, rattled on.

So he was trying to show Jane Hall the plagiarised passages and where they were lifted from, suspect essay on his left knee, book on his right, and since he'd not had time to mark them in red on the essay itself, or check the book for the exact pages (on account of the incident in the lane), he was getting nowhere as the boss sat waiting for results. Her office chair was higher than his. Felt her riding him down, a mounted policewoman. Frazer said she was trained in a martial art devised for taking people out very quickly. He was nervous Hannah Raider would appear and scream, 'He's just the sort who used to burn witches!' They'd be thinking between them it was typical of Kennedy to single out female students. Be a sight slower to notice a male plagiarist – on that you could bet. Why not conduct a rigorous back-search of all the essays Witchfinder Kennedy had marked in his time, and see how many male students got away with the dark art?

How could he press on, when there were so many truths competing with his? Jane Hall propelled herself backwards in her office chair like a Bond girl, to kick him in the face with those long boots she wore. Could he back out now, as if he'd just been dabbling? How was that going to look? Hot-faced, he went on with his work as she searched her PC for student records. On her filing cabinet stood a dusty Cointreau bottle.

'Well well! There we are,' Jane said as he showed the passages; 'and there's another. OK. I see it now. This is pretty bad. Bloody well should have been picked up immediately. Out-and-out larceny. Sure you want to go through with this?'

He said of course. He knew the process. But she asked again if he was sure and when he said he was, she said something like, 'You don't know how they can be these days,' then she was talking about the tribunal. There'd have to be a tribunal, since Lightman was now a final-year student. Which meant the cheating offence at this stage, if proved, meant the death penalty. A tribunal at which Lightman would be entitled to defend herself, as formally as necessary – which might include bringing counter-charges against particular academics. Jane Hall sighed. If only Lydia Lightman could have been spotted as a potential plagiarist earlier in her university career – spotted and warned, officially warned – it would have been possible to nip all this in the bud. But it was too late now.

See what Kennedy had sown by doing it his way? He sat there with cold fire in his face. Last bloody thing he wanted for Lydia was the death penalty. God knew how much rotten fruit would come of this …

She was afraid he'd have to appear at the tribunal, Jane was saying. He'd be advised of the date. Good work. She'd turned back to her desk before he was out of there.

20. Kennedy's trouble III. The rides. Maida Vale.

So they could probably see why it was one hell of a shock, Kennedy now explained, when he was with Dorothy (she's still on about his secret), and, needing the khazi, he bumped into Lydia coming out of her bedroom in white pyjamas. She might have gulped like when she ran away in the library, though since she seemed to grin, it might have been him who did. Couldn't be sure. Or maybe one of them screamed. She might have said, 'Now what are you looking for, Dr Kennedy?' He was not certain. Either time was a dream. Might have called him gonk or gonzo. He was presenting a clear view of himself ...

'Bollock naked?'

Kennedy said yeah and on the corner of North End Road, Mountain laughed for a spell in great cracks, and at first they seemed arrested in his lungs then broke free as if to take out the windows of the record company opposite. From a passing Maria, three fuzz checked them out, grouped about the trolley. Hands in pockets, Kennedy watched the Welshman roar like a dying warrior, hilarious at the spectacle of his own leaking life.

'Fuck me what a coincidence! Who'd have thought it, mun?' he cried at last. 'Who would have thought! So she's in the house! All the time! The Plagiaristic Ghost! What a fucking surprise! Schmeitasapeyel! Steak-knife! Sublime!' He paused to splash whisky on the pavement. 'The horror, the horror! Like a ghost,' he watched Kennedy, 'and you at your most physical hour!' They resumed their walk, westward down Kensington High Street, Mountain humming in approval.

'Must have been the last person you wanted to run into, I should think,' Natalie observed. 'But what time did you get home?' Kennedy felt the quick and marvellous tact of this question, which got him clothed and out of Dorothy and Lydia's shared flat. They had been playing rugby with his trouble. He felt like a sick man pulled out for exercise – though his disease was waiting faithfully.

Believe it or not, he'd been in North West London. Walking down a long road, he came to Maida Vale. On the Bakerloo Line, the first trains were running. A tube journey was going to take time, but he couldn't see a taxi anywhere. Besides, he'd mislaid his cash card. About Barbara, God, was he in a panic, a rattling dry panic. Have to tell her the whole thing of course – that was the only way he could imagine dealing with this night of disaster; and invite her to pour petrol over him out on the back lawn. They could siphon some from the car. He deserved nothing less than a thorough immolation. Let her set him alight with a kitchen match, stepping well back while her husband spun, a vortex of yellow flame. How could he lie? Dissimulate? She trusted him completely. To lie would be wicked as abusing a child. Had to give himself up immediately, the second he got in.

She was lying in silence, saying nothing, betrayed. He lay beside her, unwashed. Let her smell the evidence. Still she said nothing. Torment. He wanted his punishment fast. She didn't stir. What if she'd poisoned herself? He checked her face. Believe it or not, she was sleeping soundly. More than he'd hoped for – or expected. He was coming home for his punishment: on that he was dead set. And she was asleep; she hadn't left one of her post-its, nothing on voice-mail. The rattling panic left him. There he lay. Free. Scot-free at any rate … The relief didn't last. It was a hellish fairground. You came off one ride, another waited.

What to say in the morning? She was bound to ask. He couldn't just hide where he'd been till 5am; how the hell to explain what he was doing in Maida Vale? His drinks were spiked? He'd been kidnapped? When he woke he was being checked out by the captain of the women's boxing team?

'Did she ask?'

God he wished she had. Might have saved him from the next terror-ride.

'Being?'

Regulations. What were the rules about staff and students? Everyone agreed they shouldn't associate. The regulations were now concerned with staff exploiting their power in relationships, with the whole issue of trust, not to mention integrity when it came to marking work (all very proper, no doubt), along with the bringing of legal actions by students and their fathers; the institution aspiring to that modern ideal of 'transparency', in the form of a liberal purdah or apartheid separating two groups of people whose contact might steam up the windows.

But what was to stop the student? Twenty years old – that's all they were; and not here for regulations. What they were here for was adventure – that was the idea. The lecturers indicated the territory, imparted their knowledge, told them what to read, how to read it; then sent them off alone like explorers, to write their essays. If they wanted more, who was to say *No*? On the one hand their teachers were getting them to use their initiative, question what was taken for granted at every level – rules included. On the other, they were saying, Oh it was only a mental adventure after all! A virtual one. There was a limit you couldn't cross: the physical existence of your lecturer was out of bounds. Some adventure!

'And I know you two may think me a dull fellow,' Kennedy now declared, 'but the truth is, I'm for adventure rather than regulations. You can't have both though, and life's been opting for regulations for a long time now.'

Here Arthur Mountain stalled his trolley to ask Kennedy about one or two matters.

So the next ride he was dragged on as he lay by Barbara was the plagiarism tribunal, a kind of star chamber, where it might be established that the witness in the case had behaved improperly (to put it mildly) with the flatmate of the accused (which counted against the integrity of the witness, because he had not reported the adventure to his line manager). Then cross-examination would reveal that the flatmate complied with the witness solely because he had already demonstrated his power by persecuting her flatmate with a charge of Plagiarism in the First Degree, after abusing his professional responsibility by waiving a first offence (in the manner of a tyrant offering strawberries to his victim). Oh God, and those heads looking down at him (he still couldn't be sure when they'd left) might testify he'd ordered everyone to join in a Shakespearean-brothel reconstruction relating to his frankly-noxious research project, like, *He said we all had to be whores and he was Justice Shallow!*, before prancing down the hall, indecently exposed, to taunt Ms Lightman who was innocently trying to visit the bathroom in her own property having retired to bed at a decent time. If only he could remember clearly what he'd done!

'Now hold on a minute!' cried Arthur Mountain. 'What the fuck is all this? Getting yourself in a right state, bach! Who's the one doesn't like regulations? Dr Kennedy? Sounds like he can't get enough of em. Well how's this for a regulation?

'If an adult woman complain she has been caused to tarry beside a naked man in a wood or thicket (that's a way of saying Maida Vale) or a house known to her for as long as the moon has shown itself twelve times at the full (that's a way of saying student flat), let a bull of three winters be taken and its tail shaved and smeared with tallow and let the tail be thrust through a hurdle. And now let the man take the tail in his hands while the woman and her friend stir up the bull with goads or sharp and tickling feathers, and if the man can hold the bull, then is he innocent of the complaint; and if not, let the woman's family exact their penalty according to the principles of *sarhad* and *braint*. Welsh Law, twelfth century, with my own redaction.'

It was no joke!

'Are you sure? Do you expect us to take this seriously? Sure you didn't buy a life ticket for this particular funfair?'

They walked in silence a while crossing Hammersmith, twenty minutes from home.

Well if he did, he could never leave.

'Madness that is, Doc!'

Not mad. There had to be something, a meaning in it. His friends looking on, Kennedy paused. Now bumping into Lydia Lightman in the hall – how could that just be coincidence? Didn't it suggest a plot?

'But just now,' Arthur Mountain laughed, 'just now, right, you were giving us all this baloney how you're a threat to students!'

Forget all that!

'So you've been framed?'

He was seeing it now.

'That's exactly how it looks to me, fella,' Natalie said. 'I was wondering when you'd realise. Come across some maddening tricks in my time.'

Couldn't be coincidence he'd ended up at Lydia Lightman's flat could it? Had no idea she and Dorothy shared. Whatsoever.

'Right on. That's your honeytrap. They ruin a bloke by setting him up with a young lass he shouldn't be fraternising with.'

Take Orson Welles, Natalie! They put a twelve-year-old in his bed. In the wardrobe, you've got a cameraman. When Welles comes in, she's going to jump him and out the wardrobe pops the cameraman. Orson ruined. That was what they did to you if you defied them. It was Randolph Hearst (the Murdoch of his day) who had the child planted in the bed. He hated how Welles played him in *Kane*. As a consequence …

'Easy now, the pair of you!' Arthur Mountain decreed. 'This is how you spoil it. The coincidence *is* the story. And a fine story it is too, as I said when the fuzz were passing. Cos you've got a great surprise in there, unbeatable. Now what are you doing? You aren't letting it be. You're adding yourself to it, like a conjuror telling the audience about his arse problems. The problem with you, sir, is your imagination heads for hell like a homing pigeon. The coincidence will do nicely, on its own. The tale of your trouble concludes there, does it not! I take it your wife never did find out? Half a year ago, and she's none the wiser about our adventures in Maida Vale!' Greenly, Arthur Mountain stared at Kennedy.

He knew what Arthur meant. And maybe it would all be over, if only they hadn't started mailing him.

'Who? The students?'

Yes. Since the beginning of the month, they'd e-mailed – a couple of times.

'What to say?'

Oh – nothing really. It might be they were just messing around, Kennedy explained hurriedly. It was Dorothy really, but he could feel

Lydia there as well. Nothing threatening – the opposite if anything. But it'd been playing on him. And the tribunal hadn't been held yet. It was meant to be in January, but they had to postpone it till the end of this month.

'This is your house isn't it?' Arthur said, pointing across the wall and small front garden.

How did he know?

'Because we've finally had the whole story, haven't we? Though I do have to say, you rushed that last bit about the e-mails and the tribunal. Timing is all, butt. Anyhow, we needn't come in now and bother you!'

Kennedy said nothing.

'So that was your trouble?' Arthur continued, leaning on his trolley. 'Is it finished now? Off your chest? – Or are we on a war footing? Your call, Dr K. What's it to be?'

But while Kennedy was brooding on this, Arthur and Natalie began to move away up the street. When they were some way from him, they began a sort of dance, Natalie backing off from Arthur then advancing slowly while he walked on, trolley in tow, till they bumped. So they performed it as they went and at each collision, Natalie raised her hands ecstatically. At last they disappeared.

They'd been re-enacting what happened with Lydia. No doubt Dorothy was just teasing him with these messages. Maybe she and her flatmate were in awe. He had big friends, people like Arthur Mountain. And with this foolish thought Kennedy fell asleep, holding his wife's cool fingers.

21. Oxbridge v Plebs' League. Practical critique of the mobile phone.

Westerly gusting through the trees: Kennedy not at home.

Temperature fell when the wind howled. Under four hours' sleep and rain in the air. With a dull crack and shout, white figures ran. Kennedy sat tight and figures crossed. Puddle on the step before him. Moved his legs to keep his shoes out of it. Wind dropped, air cracked.

Say a spell! Go on!

Wind moderate!

Air crack!

Let me go home …

Manqué! Pathetic.

At 8am a knock at the front door had been answered by Kennedy half-dressed. A hooded youth was there with a request from Arthur Mountain (verbal, not written) saying please to join the latter and his secretary to watch cricket today in Oxfordshire, if Dr Kennedy wasn't too busy. Kennedy said thanks very much, found a two pound coin in his trousers for a tip, and closed the door before Barbara had time to witness the messenger.

He didn't even enjoy this form of the game. Like many cricket followers, Dr Kennedy was interested only in international contests. The attraction of watching Oxford University playing Glamorgan CCC in weather like this was so weak, you had to wonder what he was doing here at all.

Maybe he felt obliged because Arthur Mountain now had something of a hold on him, knowing the story of his trouble. But wasn't Mountain far too noble even to consider exploiting this knowledge? Indeed, he'd come along with some hope that the Welshman might continue putting his mind at rest about the Maida

Vale incident. Perhaps Natalie'd be there too and she and Arthur would do that dance again (last night's performance had given Kennedy sweeter dreams than he was used to). He was falling for this character, who showed new sides at each encounter. Must be why he'd come. He was being charmed. Something else as well: the promise of the company of Arthur's secretary. Kennedy was curious about these 'stoplines' which Johnny boy'd been meant to be taking notes on last night, when he failed to show up. Perhaps he'd get the full story today was Kennedy's thinking, as he sat on the train.

'Oh, played!' Ever so politely, Arthur Mountain clapped his hands. He was wearing a black coat of thick leather that reminded Kennedy of a war film his old man took him to on his fourteenth, and a white panama trilby. Not for the first time, the ensemble was daring you to challenge it. Kennedy hadn't received the warmest welcome when he arrived by taxi at The Parks. Seated on his own (without Natalie, Kennedy was saddened to notice) in front of the pavilion of red brick, Arthur merely said, 'Oh there you are!', as if Kennedy lived somewhere in the ground, rather than having travelled 70 miles or whatever it was at his beck and call – and then began nagging him to say spells. The cause of the guvnor's displeasure this morning was, as a matter of fact, Johnny boy, who, it now turned out, had been at a dinner at his old college the night before and was still AWOL.

'But you were expecting him in The Inventors' Arms,' Kennedy recalled.

'Natalie forgot to tell me where he was.'

Bothered by a feeling of coincidence that would not unfold into accident, Kennedy looked at his shoes.

'Is he an Oxford graduate then?'

'Yes,' Arthur replied shortly, adding after a while, 'His old man's a cheesemaker. That's how they got the brass to send him, like. Invented a new strength cheddar.'

'What strength?' Kennedy was interested.

'Strength *18* for all I fucking know!' Arthur suggested rudely. 'Only took him on in the first place I did because he was at the Welsh college.'

'Is that Jesus?' Kennedy said.

'Yes. Jesus College. Daresay he's hungover, little tramp. Tchah!'

A fielder turned, Arthur Mountain waved. 'Hungover or he's romping – sorry, butt!'

'Is he Welsh then, Johnny boy?' Kennedy asked.

'*Welsh*!' roared Mountain. 'I'll give you Welsh! He's not anything! A *hole*, that's what he is! A fucking Corinthian.'

'OK,' Kennedy said. No doubt Arthur'd have been cursing *him*, if he hadn't turned up.

'Call it a university! You'd get more education from a ten-minute conversation with a hot cross bun than you'll have in three years at this twatheap!' Arthur Mountain exclaimed.

'Well I wasn't at Oxford myself,' Kennedy said crossly.

'You went to a modern university didn't you? Marks you for life it does, mun. Academic catalogue I happened to be looking at while Natalie was shopping, you've got an advert for a five-volume study of "public drinking in the early modern world." *Five volume*? Full fathom five you pippins lie! What do you know? Tell me!

'What does your academic know about drinkers? Tell me! What d'you know about the hours they put in? The imagination, the self-deception, the acid-stomach – what d'you know about it? Hey? The practical drinkers – what do you know of em? The wise talk and tall talk, the lies and false friendship; the laughter, jokes, late nights; the torn-up marriages and fucked-up livers, the knifings, phantoms, DTs – what do you know? What about the experience? What does your academic know about the experience? Tell me! You've never had the experience. That's why you are what you are. That's why you are where you are. "So far public drinking has only been represented anecdotally and has not figured in the academic consciousness." That's a quote, right? Now why's your bourgeois academic so fucking down on anecdotes, hey? Why d'you get so bloody excited about studies and stats and methodology and discourses? Anything remotely to do with the fact your bourgeois academic couldn't tell an anecdote if you gave him a silver sixpence and a two-inch dick extension? Why do you need *theory*? Why do you love fucking theory? What's the big deal with *conceptualisation*?

What are you scared of? Shit on your fingers? Bite on the nose? Bum-boils? Death?'

'I may be no good at anecdotes,' admitted Kennedy, wondering what happened to Mountain's nocturnal enthusiasm for his tale of trouble; 'but I don't like theory! That's the truth. And I'm a laughing stock professionally because of it.'

'Who says I was talking about you?' Arthur Mountain suggested. 'But like it or not, you went to university. And if you don't mind my saying so, it has made you timid, made you bourgeois. Isn't that really your trouble, Ken?'

'I was timid before I ever went to university,' Kennedy said. 'And that's the truth.' But when had Mountain read that catalogue? Had he been going through Kennedy's pigeon-hole? Checking his mail? Yet it had been sealed in its plastic wrapper, only yesterday afternoon when Kennedy found it ...

The Welshman hummed and lit a cigarette in the wind, mood changing. 'But you had a big idea once. I can see you did. Probably just a boy you were. And you've let a life at the university persuade you it's just one idea among many and not even a very clever one. Am I right?' Here Arthur called out a joke to a skinny red-haired fielder, murmuring to Kennedy, 'Biggest shagger in the side he is! Wouldn't think it to look at him would you? – What I mean is, Ken, has the university been the right sort of place for a man like yourself?'

'I don't know,' Kennedy said. 'Maybe not.'

'Then why the hell have you given it the best years of your life, mun? Tell me. You're almost finished – by your own reckoning. And all you've done is hang round in universities.'

Sad and rather impressed, Kennedy thought about this while Arthur filled him in on the whole of the Glamorgan fielding side: shagger, tightwad, alky, psycho; and the one who wrote poetry, who looked as unlike a poet as the red-haired whippet a stud. Arthur Mountain knew them all, knew their stats as well. Knew all about them.

'I couldn't see another way,' Kennedy said at last. 'And I don't think I had the nerve.'

'Who's Justice Shallow? You said last night you were recreating him in Maida Vale.'

'Shallow's an old fool who boasts about his adventures with Falstaff in a brothel.'

'What's it called?'

'The Windmill. Falstaff tells the audience the whores laughed themselves silly when Shallow stripped off.'

'You should do more classes like that, mun.'

'And ruin myself professionally? Once is bad enough!'

'C'mon!' Arthur urged. 'Set up you're own university and do nude Shakespeare sketches. I'll pay for it! I'll help too. Always fancied the academic life myself.'

'You?' Kennedy was astounded. Would this character ever show some constancy damn him?

'The Plebs' League was the thing you see.' Arthur pointed at Kennedy. 'Might have suited a man like you.'

'What was it?' Kennedy asked.

'Oh it was big in Wales, last century. Education for workers, sort of anti-university, university in reverse. They wouldn't have it with bourgeoisification in the Plebs' League, I can tell you. Wouldn't have it with "academic consciousness" either. Any of that, you'll have your academic bollocks up for auction at the offal butcher; what's more, you'll be bambasted, intellectually humiliated. They could do that to you in the PL, if you were so unwise as to theorise about what the students knew bloody well in practice. What you have to remember, Dr K, is how much the Plebs' League student knew already. And this is because they were in industry. So you are careful how you theorise about what they know already. Cos when the miner puts his tools on the bar and goes home for a wash-down prior to attending his lecture, he's not just a cog or a operative. He's a craftsman. Swears by his tools. Locks em down when his shift's done. No one else better touch those tools. He is a craftsman, he is a geologist. Architect as well, with the judgement of a sculptor. So if you're a tutor, better think twice before you tell him he's alienated. Better be on your mettle if you're teaching him he's sold his soul to the company store. What's the matter?'

'Nothing,' Kennedy said.

'Yes there is! Saw doubt in your soul, like a pond in the instant it begins to freeze – or a woman pulling the curtain.'

Christ! Did this green-eyed bastard miss nothing? Better tell – he's killed a man.

'Well the miner doesn't sell the coal he's dug does he?'

'You're quite right to object!' Arthur called out. The spectators were applauding. 'Respect you for that. My point here is about manners, tact. If the academic dun't recognise the skill of the miner, then it's the academic who's doing the alienating the exact moment he tells him he's alienated. It's like your wife telling you you dunno how to make it with her when you've been doing it very well for the last ten years – or whatever. Get me?'

Kennedy nodded.

'Cos you can alienate a man by not knowing his skill – as well as pinching his surplus value. Take the tinmen. Bampa was a tinman. There was no micrometer invented could gauge a layer of plate like he could with his thumb. He could see numbers, and he could see ratios. Studied applied maths and pure in the League, Bamps did. The world to him was figures, metal and figures. Figures were his dreams. He had thumbs like this from where they were smashed by steel bar. Look, Ken! No wonder he could peel an orange in two turns. But figures were his freedom.

'So if you're a Plebs' League tutor you're on your fucking manners when these men and women – and don't forget how many young women you had in the tinworks – when they come down the co-op or church hall to listen to you talk. You think to yourself, Maybe it's them who should be doing the talking. Maybe I should shut up and listen. Cos it is possible that in a practical manner, they know more about Karl Marx, Engels, Michelson, Morley, Einstein, Caldecott, Shaddock, McTaggart, Freud, Niedrich Frietzsche, Shaximilian Meler, Harry Bhattacharya, Jan Van Derpant ...'

'Who's that?' Kennedy enquired.

'Never heard of Jan Van Derpant?'

'Can't say I have.'

'Meant to be learned, aren't you?' While Kennedy was considering his answer to this taunt, Arthur shouted, 'Excellent!

'Made him up. You avoided the bourgeois gesture of nodding like you knew all the big names because it was part of your cultural

164

inheritance, regardless of whether you have fucking read em or not! All at it aren't they? Waving their hands on the *Culture Show*. Why can't they fucking sit still? Cos they're pretending they've read books. What mortal twats they are, what scabs, what berks! Not you. We'll have you for the Plebs' League yet. I loves you!' With this he kissed Kennedy on the cheek, who sat in the wind feeling flustered and proud, hoping to God no one's seen that. 'Wipe it off if you like!' Arthur murmured, making with his elephant look.

'The tutors in the Plebs' League, they were not of this world,' he continued, with a smoky pass of his right hand. 'Only trace of this world about them was that they were Welsh, right? That apart, they were a crew of intellectual demons. Compared to the Plebs' League tutors, your average academic (present company excepted) is a box of dried peas, a twenty-five per center, an early-to-bed man, a cowardy custard, a pimp with no whores.' From such a list, Kennedy was pretty glad to be excluded, even if Arthur was only being kind. 'Noah Ablett! Mark Starr! Pwll Du Parry! J Joseph Jones!' bawled the Welshman: 'Cadwallader Wilson, Dai Iawn, Nun Nicholas! These were the demons!'

Was Kennedy now expected to protest that some of these names were made up, as proof he wasn't bourgeois? That supposed that he knew at least some of them to be genuine, which he did not. Yet if he indicated familiarity with not one of these 'demon tutors', that could be as fatal as pretending to have heard of them all. Either way, you were spitting on the plebs and Bampa Mountain's memory, weren't you? Passionately the Welshman stared at him; the law recognises passion in mitigation of murder. So this was how you died ...

'Nun Nicholas,' Kennedy murmured like a wine taster. 'What a name!'

'D'you reckon it's a nun?' Arthur Mountain asked shrewdly.

'In my mind's eye, I sort of do,' Kennedy said. 'But I think it was probably a man.'

'You're absolutely right of course! It was a man. Had the shape of a man, at least, but this is a trick among the demons. By the way, I don't mean "demon" in the wicked way, Ken. Don't need to tell you that I'm sure. Mean it in the Greek way I do. They had a lot of *character* these tutors, that's what I mean.'

'That's cool,' Kennedy said, who was now enjoying himself.

'Nun Nicholas, he was a fantastic scholar of history and philosophy, he was a magnificent, magnetic lecturer and terrifying too, like a stand-up and a peripatetic rolled into one, Aristotle crossed with Jerry Sadowitz – yeah? He had the manners of a pig, a wolf – your *Piggenwolf*, put it that way. Wouldn't lecture till he had a pint of black rum under his belt. "The value of sobriety is a deception imposed by the bourgeoisie upon all opportunity for ecstasy among the plebs!" – that was one of his aphorisms. Say he needed a slash, he'd do it right there on the stage, over in the corner so as not to break his flow. Does your *Piggenwolf* care where he pisseth? Neither did Nun Nicholas. He's got his first and second helpers when he's lecturing. A girl called Jane Morgan and a girl from Bilbao. Jane, she has these leather gloves with strips of lead fastened to em and the Spanish girl has a hanger. He invited questions, Nun, but anyone asks a bourgeois question, down come the helpers and give him a tap. Jane was a tinworker herself. He needed protection too, Nun Nicholas, cos he provoked people wherever he went and he didn't give a damn. Cops, politicians, heavies, bullies, athletes, dogs – he fucking wound them all up. He needed a Spanish swordswoman from time to time, when he was outnumbered and he'd bitten off more than he could chew.

'And in nothing was he less bourgeois, mark you, than this, Dr K. We should all hold ourselves in common, men and women, husbands and wives. That was the belief of Nun Nicholas. Fuck who you fancy – provided they're agreeable. Don't observe the sanctity of marriage or family. These things are our torment, our profoundest torment. And which man or woman is not tormented by these things, even unto the good year 2006, Dr Kennedy? Didn't your story last night prove that?' Arthur Mountain reminded Kennedy, with a green glance. 'But of course, the way of the Plebs' League in sexual matters isn't for everyone. Indeed, I have some doubts about it myself. Smacks of the 1960s. A *Dumkopf* decade.'

Kennedy was about to suggest that Nun Nicholas had enough theories when it suited him, did he not, when his phone began to ring and Arthur was suddenly fussing at his breast pocket: 'Quick, Ken! Answer it!'

The caller was called Clifford, but Arthur'd by now snatched the phone from Kennedy and was roaring into it. Meanwhile, Kennedy looked to his left, where a woman observed them. The Welshman seemed happy. Maybe Clifford was one of the *kin*. The woman smiled in Kennedy's direction. Under a flat cap, her hair was dyed a colour fashionable in Kennedy's youth; in keeping with the tweed, she wore a waxed jacket. Say she was a style-conscious student of the university early 1980s, reverting to class as she got older (you might expect to see a copy of *The Spectator* at her side, or some sort of horse mag). The insignia of the upper-middle classes were a little hectic in her, designed to annoy your sight. Kennedy imagined her part of a tweedy family with a nasty streak. Elder brother would really put an elbow in your eye. Daddy'd have the country constabulary in his pocket. As she turned from Kennedy's gaze, she laughed to herself, as one who can't believe what she's hearing. He shuddered with déjà vu. Beside him, Arthur was roaring to Clifford about Natalie and the shark. Kennedy fancied her heels clicking as she passed tanks of blue fish and fish with tiger stripes, on her way to the Reef Encounter. Arthur handed him his phone and said, 'Ta.'

'You don't have your own?' Kennedy asked.

'Course not! Be the death of me that would.'

'Why would it?'

'Because I like to keep the older channels open,' Arthur Mountain replied, green as a cat. 'Have to. To the modern man the mobile phone is now indispensable. He'd rather leave the house without trousers than his phone. My argument isn't with him really; I'm aware of the way capitalism tricks people into needing equipment; everyone's aware, yet they keep falling for it. Can't tell *I want* from *I need*. Fills my heart with sadness, it does, to see people hunched over these things. And what are they waiting for? Another fucking voice, a few words of message. Pathetic really. And extra pathetic because the more you fiddle with that little box, the less you hear what's also there to be heard.'

'What's that?' Kennedy asked.

Arthur Mountain made a sign, and said, 'Everything that comes down the older channels. Spirits and whatnot.'

'What about Clifford?' Kennedy said cheekily. 'Can't he come down the older channels?'

'He can when he wants to,' Arthur grinned. 'But you've got to go the way the world goes for the most part, play it the world's way. People think you're *twp* otherwise. That's why I unaffectedly enjoy worldly things, wine, tobacco, women. My disguise it is, know what I mean?' Arthur Mountain winked. 'Anyway, I haven't got a theoretical opposition to the mobile phone; just makes me sad, that's all – as I explained a minute ago. My attitude above all is practical – in all things. If my friend is carrying a mobile phone, that's enough for me, do nicely that will. I'll use it if necessary. On another occasion, I'll send a message by hand, or imagination – or I'll just go without.'

As Kennedy tried to work out the logic of this, he became distracted by the question of how Arthur had obtained his number to pass on to his chums, since he'd definitely never given it to him – though it would've been natural to. Better not ask; the Welshman'd already taken pains to send a messenger to Kennedy's house this morning, a difficulty he'd have been saved if Kennedy had been a bit freer with his personal details.

'You've met my wife?' Arthur was saying.

'Of course I have!' Kennedy answered, though he must have misheard the stress, because Arthur now demanded to know where *Kennedy's* was today.

'She's at work,' Kennedy explained, a piece of information the Welshman received with a twitching of the nose, as if this were quaint news indeed.

'Should have brought her, mun!' he admonished Kennedy. 'She'll be feeling neglected.'

'Well if there'd been more notice,' Kennedy said politely, trying not to be overheard by the countrywoman, 'I would have.' It was their special game after all, the cause of their being together; though what she'd have made of Arthur Mountain was another matter. He was hardly the sort of fella she was used to (if Kennedy was any kind of yardstick in the matter).

'Natalie told me how you met,' Arthur said now. 'Classic I call that! Pure chance, after you'd set your heart on her at the cricket that time. That's why I thought she might like to come along with you today, as a remembrance.' He sucked his teeth and hummed. 'She only gave me the bare bones of it though – we were trying to get off to sleep, but we always tell each other a story first. I'd love to hear it from the horse's mouth, Ken.'

'It was ridiculous really,' Kennedy said by way of apology, adding that it was wonderful too, obviously, since Arthur was now watching him with delight.

So he was passing a small gallery in Camden that had caught his eye once or twice. Well on this occasion, a late-summer afternoon ten years ago, as he'd explained to Natalie, he decided to try it because he wanted a gift for his father (he had some idea of obtaining a technical drawing – an idea that excited the Welshman's approval). But though he pulled at the door, it was locked. As Kennedy turned away, however, the door flew open and a young woman called to him to come in if he wanted, but could he hurry? Fearing he might look like a burglar, forcibly trying doors then walking off, he entered, and the door was slammed behind him. The whole place was blacked out because some sort of UV exhibition was in progress, so you had no idea who else was in there. As for the exhibited pieces, well they were rather puerile, in fluorescent, Opal-Fruit colours, hanging from the ceiling or arranged on shelves.

'Were they skeletons?' Arthur Mountain enquired eagerly. 'Where is this place exactly? Must have a look for myself!'

Kennedy explained the location. Why was the Welshman so excited? The artworks weren't skeletons, but bits of bric-a-brac, quaint items, birdcages, and the like (attempting to recall them brought to Kennedy's mind those dream pieces on the promenade at Swansea). It was all kitsch stuff really, and other people seemed to be giggling or going wooh! in the dark. Anyway, someone opened the door at last and Kennedy slipped out just behind some young women (hoping not to be asked his opinion of the pieces). One of them called to him as he departed, 'Did we help you escape?'

Well when Kennedy turned to the young woman who'd spoken

to him, there was a girl beside her who was surely the one who'd sat in the row in front of him a few weeks ago at the Oval. Surely she was! He had to ask her. She said, 'Oh! You were the one with the funny friend!' Kennedy apologised. The young woman who first spoke to him invited him to come and have a drink with them. They wandered for a bit; some wanted coffee, others wine. In the end they went somewhere that served both. The young women (there were three of them besides the cricket lass) were making a fuss of the coincidence (praise be) and decided it would be bad luck if Kennedy and Barbara didn't have a date. The place happened to serve food, so they must have lunch exactly there the following Saturday. Which they did. She became his wife.

'Fantastic!' Arthur Mountain seemed as excited as Natalie, though Kennedy'd told the tale with no more dazzle than last night, and in a good rough voice the Welshman sung,

> Baby, now that I've found you
> I won't let you go!
> I'll build my world around you
> I need you so …

'That's good!' Kennedy's heart rose to his throat.

'British soul, Ken! Can you see her here now? Down in front of you? Like you did years ago? Look, now! Look! Look for her!'

But as Kennedy was looking for the small brown figure in the gingham dress, Arthur cried,

'Here's Clifford!' Lankily along the perimeter, a long-haired figure approached the gate.

'Attaboy, Cliff!' Arthur Mountain yelled. 'We're in by here, mun! – Thank you for your patience, Dr Kennedy!'

22. Curious technician. Worst man there is.

'I see you brought lunch, Cliff!' Arthur said, making introductions. Kennedy wondered what might be in the pale orange carriers.

'Now this man I know already!' Dark sweater sparkling with drizzle, Clifford grinned pleasantly at Kennedy, who felt he'd seen him before, though since he had the look of an ageing roadie, it could have been on the *Whistle Test* 30 years ago rearranging the set after a John Otway freak-out, or a Polaroid of a free festival. But Clifford explained he worked afternoons at the university, and Kennedy was embarrassed not to have recognised him at once.

That was cool. Clifford was no academic. Just a technician.

But the IT office was in Kennedy's building, as Kennedy pointed out (feeling ruder still, for he really liked this guy's face), which would make them close neighbours.

Ah, Clifford wasn't that kind of technician. Didn't deal with computers, if he could avoid it. From the carrier on the right he drew two black cans. Would they have a cider? On an empty stomach Kennedy drank cider, as Clifford explained where his office was.

Perhaps Dr Kennedy knew the mews behind the main building? Kennedy did, though he had no idea the university owned property there.

It didn't really. Dr Kennedy was not wrong. Clifford cracked a black can for himself. But at the end of the mews were some bushes. Dr Kennedy might have noticed them? Well if you passed through the bushes, you'd find the mews wasn't quite a dead end since there were some steps that led up to a yard backing on to Stevedore Street and the rear of Hotel Belvedere. At the end of the yard was a staircase that led into a basement. There were a couple of stone sheds with low eaves down there, which had been used for storing anti-aircraft ordnance in the war. The Belvedere actually stood on the site of the North Soho flak battery. Anyhow, that was Clifford's 'office', the sheds having come into the university's possession by default at some point.

Fancying he might go and check out Clifford's office for himself one of these days, Kennedy enquired what sort of technical work it was that Clifford did, and the latter murmured something about curating the university's reel-to-reel collection, and older video stuff, repairing mics, bits of audio equipment, and what have you.

Ah, Kennedy said, wondering if this amiable fellow was in truth some kind of university spy.

Offering more cider, Clifford pulled a vine of heavy, dullish-red tomatoes from his other carrier. Kennedy raised one to his nose. It had a deep, rather sour, leathery aroma. They consumed a tomato each, and another. This, it appeared, *was* lunch. They talked of tomatoes, Horticultural Mountain hefting one in the palm of his hand. Bampa grew his own in a greenhouse.

They talked of cannabis. In a greenhouse Clifford once grew his own. Now he grew only tomatoes. Did Dr Kennedy smoke much pot? Truthfully, Kennedy said he didn't, and Clifford assured him he'd given up hallucinogenics. At one time, he'd been a real head, but he'd drawn the line. Kennedy nodded and sipped his cider.

Supposing he was concentrating on the match, Arthur Mountain and Clifford spoke among themselves. He heard Clifford say, 'Did she come today?', Arthur replying he hadn't really noticed – too busy chatting to Dr Kennedy. Maybe she did – he couldn't say either way. Kennedy glanced to his left. The countrywoman was no longer there. She couldn't have left without passing in front of him, so must be inside the pavilion. What were they on about? Was he to be party to it? Arthur would keep asking if he was coming to the wars. He'd killed a man. Would Johnny boy have invented that? But if it was true, wasn't Johnny boy taking a serious risk by not turning up? He must have a lot of trust in his governor, that tyke. What were the wars? Once Johnny boy came with his notebooks, he might understand Arthur's meaning. From the dry cider he felt a cold glow. Perhaps the wars were just a game. Beside him, Clifford and Arthur were laughing at an *Evening Standard*, two years out of date he noticed, which Clifford had brought along.

They were reading about the conviction of some football thugs, illustrated with rows of mug-shots, some of them shaven-headed older men, others the age of Kennedy's students. Arthur Mountain pointed out one head and another, inventing responses to their jail terms. He and Clifford seemed well amused with this pastime. A scrawny fellow, sharp-eyed, was a victim of mistaken identity: *I be a simple poacher of the New Forest. Never been near a football ground, your Honour!* A youth like a putto, or milkmaid of truculent mien, had an alibi: *Swear I been on the Solent on a brig o' five sail at the time of the incident, your Honour! Serving as captain's nipper.*

'Check him, Cliff! Austin English. Austin hails from Dartford, Kent. English by name, English by nature! Austin has received two years' bird. Chin up, English cunt! You will be happy in the English sector of prison, where you can drape yourself in the George Cross at recreation time to play pool, as is your right under European law.'

They turned to the text, which told of a planned fight between firms from Charlton and Southampton at a railway station in Greenwich. Members of the public were forced to flee because of the mass of chanting men with shaven heads running to meet the Southampton fans alighting on the eastbound platform. In the booking hall they cowered in terror, as the two groups of men fought and hurled bottles.

'"Cowering in terror" my arse!' Arthur roared. 'Stock phrase that is. For all the journalists know, they were having a cup of tea and a Tunnock and laughing their fucking heads off at the running men with shaved heads. – Here's another! Here's a plum: *Many of the Charlton mob were huge, real shaven-headed pork-pie eaters*, said one detective. Fuck me. Have the public cowering in the booking hall that will, when the pork-pie eaters are on the rampage. – What do these pompoms in the press know of fear? Honestly? Tell me, Cliff, what do they know?'

'Fear's how they project it,' Kennedy said abruptly.

'What's that, Ken?'

'Fear is the media's projection. They don't describe it. It isn't there till they report it as having been there, with words like "cowering in terror". Then it becomes part of the official record of an event. The media project the world they report on,' Dr Kennedy added. 'Like a false film.'

'Am I hearing you suggest that leaves something out, Ken?' Arthur leaned back in his chair to examine Kennedy's face from behind Clifford. 'Like the pork-pie crumbs? Who writes about the crumbs, hey? The trail of crumbs left by these huge shaven-headed men?'

'It has to – has to leave something out,' Kennedy said, thinking of his work on Falstaff, and all that was left out in the official accounts. Kennedy knew better. And Arthur Mountain and this curious technician, did they know better as well? If they did, what was it they knew? Perhaps he would discover by listening. To his left, the countrywoman had returned to her seat, where she was laughing into her phone.

'Yes,' Arthur Mountain was deciding. 'Has to. Something gets left out. Something's always overlooked … May even be the big thing – not just the pie crumbs. We know of one instance at least. And the one suggests the many.'

Kennedy sat in silence, while his friends returned to their game.

'These aren't his teams though, Charlton and The Saints.' Arthur examined a blurred photo in which men seemed to be dancing. 'Was he there? Hasn't switched to Charlton has he?'

'I imagine he might get involved in something like this just to slip the CCTV. In, out, never there,' Clifford suggested.

Arthur Mountain paused, and lit an untipped cigarette. 'D'you really think so, Cliff? – Getting subtle that is, isn't it?'

'Sure,' Clifford murmured through his beard.

'Like he really has cut loose,' Arthur said. 'Is that what's happening? – Ever heard of the *Tacuara*?'

'No,' Kennedy replied.

'They were running wild in South America, around 1960. Argentina to be exact. Recreating *Kristallnacht* every November. It was bad enough first time. 1938. What does it mean to copy it? What does that make you? How much has the hate grown? But were they copying – or just continuing?' Arthur lit another short cigarette.

'Vandalising businesses, beating Jews to death, cutting Swastikas in their backs, carving Swastikas in their breasts. When Eichmann was abducted by the Israelis, they went berserk. The Mossad boys didn't know what they were letting South American Jews in for. No fucking idea. Christ's sake. Were they pseudo-Nazis, or a second wave, or the ones who'd just slipped away? Who knows there weren't men from the *Feld Polizei* and *SD*, in the *Tacuara*? They spread like rancid butter. South America. Egypt. Syria. Palestine. Here as well; except they're never here. Hasn't ended. "Nothing disappears though all is rearranged. Lost are they who are unamazed!" Ever heard that before?' Kennedy said nothing.

'Who knows but they didn't drive out your wife's people?'

'But they weren't Jewish,' Kennedy said. Natalie must have gone into Barbara's origins during her and Arthur's 'bedtime' story. 'They left in 1982 anyway.'

Arthur stood to teach with gestures of his hands:

1938 to 1960 = 22
1960 to 1982 = 22
22x22 = 484
= half-H, H, half-H
= twice H
= *Heil Hitler.*

He sat. 'Mega at lecturing aren't I?'

Kennedy and Clifford grinned.

'Not that I'm talking about number magic,' Arthur Mountain explained. 'Just the pattern really. Why did your wife's family leave? Obviously they weren't doing too well down there. Maybe it was recent difficulties; maybe someone was settling an old score. Could have been they helped some Jews at one time – or they didn't toe the line when all the murdering was going on in the seventies.'

'I don't know,' Kennedy said.

'Why didn't you ask?'

'I don't like to press people. Not if I think they don't want to talk about something. But she was young anyway, you see.'

'Like to know people historically I do,' Arthur Mountain declared. 'Though I admit, it's easier with someone you don't know very well – or haven't met even. But that is how I like to know people.' Pulling his hat over his eyes, he asked to be excused for a while, leaving Kennedy in the company of Clifford. Shortly after, the countrywoman passed in front of them and through the pavilion gate.

Giving it a few minutes, so as not to sound too concerned, Kennedy asked Clifford if he supposed Arthur'd gone to fetch Johnny boy from his college. Clifford smiled at the thought. Arthur would never go for Johnny boy. Wasn't the big man's etiquette. Ah, Kennedy said, probably it wasn't either. No doubt Arthur'd have remembered some errand, or bit of business, Clifford suggested. But he'd be back. Kennedy explained that he'd been hoping to hear about these stoplines that sounded so important to Arthur. Did Clifford know much about that kind of thing? Clifford laughed and rolled a cigarette. You had Arthur with his wars, he told Kennedy after a while, and Natalie with her trains. Some pair! Gently he spat a little loose tobacco; his smoke curled into the breeze and broke. They observed the cricket, drank another can apiece.

'And are the stoplines to do with the wars?'

Clifford said so he gathered.

'But what are they up to the pair of them?' Kennedy asked boldly.

Clifford laughed. Many a time he'd asked himself. You could say they were both kind of tapped (or *twp*, to use Arthur's word). Yet he'd known many casualties in old days. Arthur and his lady made a lot more sense. For a while, Kennedy puzzled this. Why should Clifford be unable to answer his question, if Arthur and Natalie made sense? In his heart he knew.

'You must have heard that line,' Clifford said at last, '"Be careful how you interpret the world. That's how it is!" Yeah? Well that's how it is with these two!'

'But how did you meet?' Kennedy asked.

As if it were a kind of bell, Clifford pulled once at his beard. 'At a Black Auction in the Midlands. He was bidding for grenades, I was after Bengal diodes. Soon after, he came to visit. It was an early-summer evening. We sat in my shed with a bucket of beer smoking pipes. Arthur's looking at these little brown boxes of parts, like, "Tune me up, baby! We can roll time back with this shit! Be where they were when it was ending! Right among them!"' Clifford paused.

'Didn't know what the hell he was on about, Doc. But you know his eyes? So I ran it through. Rigged this signalling gear with a Clicky-Ba transistor and Arthur's fiddling and tapping away; technically hasn't a clue what he's doing, but he starts receiving. Like a séance. Chilling, man. Mind-blowing. He can see these Kraut units (357th Infantry or whatever), see the faces on the men like they're eye to eye. He can hear things too. Zhukov whistling before the Stalingrad encirclement. Sirens. .20mm cannon fire on engine louvres. And smell em. Phosphorus incendiaries on slate, pipe smoke in the War Cabinet, collaborators being tarred. It was a real show. Like old Beefheart and his players.

'I fancy he was jiving me about the electrics, Doc. What he was sensing, it's some kind of resonance he picks up on ... Strange.' Clifford fell silent.

'And the one you were looking for in that paper,' said Kennedy, 'who is it?'

Clifford looked at him and Kennedy wished he hadn't blurted that out since Clifford's eyes said he must answer now, and couldn't tell a lie.

'A rogue called Micky Voight.'

'A rogue?' replied Kennedy. Meant a rather delightful villain, did 'rogue', an incorrigible old rascal. Like Falstaff. That was meaning number one. Indeed, their chum Arthur was quite a rogue, was he not? ... It meant other things as well though. Someone who'd crossed over, or gone beyond all limits; someone who couldn't live with the rest of his kind. That was a rogue. Or in olden times, it meant a cutthroat, a man of great violence.

'Rogue will do,' Clifford said. His voice was as low as Arthur's a roar. 'Let's leave it at that, Dr Kennedy. Some call him the worst man there is. But let's leave it at rogue.'

The worst man there is. What could this mean? Kennedy went over possibilities ... 'So he's a football thug?'

'Oh he's been that,' Clifford advised him. 'Voight and his merry men used to wreak a lot of damage on the soccer scene. If they'd been through a town centre in the provinces or made a journey on the train, skulls'd be cracked, backs broken. Now and then there'd be a murder. But he's packed that in. – Wasn't his main thing anyway. It wasn't heavy enough for him. He's really streamlined operations now. He hangs around with a fat man and a woman called Heidi Walsh. She's got purple hair, this lady, and she's a journo …'

'Christ!' Kennedy said, 'she was over there!' He turned to look at the empty place to their left. 'That was her!'

'Very likely,' Clifford said. 'Be cool, Dr Kennedy. You'll get used to these things.'

Kennedy sat in silence. They were becoming familiar, these figures. Was he going their way, or they coming his? He rose and excused himself. When he returned to his seat, it was teatime. Sun fell on the pavilion from the west, and here was Arthur Mountain with a bag of pies.

23. 'Do you want to know?'

Heidi Walsh would no doubt be on the Web if she was a journalist, and Kennedy, he wasn't looking for her. These folk might be driven away by the search engine – that picture of Arthur Mountain and Clifford in a shed with antique wires and bits had impressed him greatly. Another thing: checking the name of the journalist (or rogue) would be a sign of distrust, as if his new friends were maybe taking him for a ride; which he knew in his heart could not be so – though whatever they were up to now preoccupied him.

At lunch with Cy in The Inventors' Arms, Kennedy thought suddenly of Uncle Toby and Corporal Trim, and their fantastic game. Frazer remembered the book well. Arranging Scotch egg, pie crust and parsley stalk, he demonstrated how the Uncle and Corp played at the War of Spanish Succession in the back garden, with make-believe artillery, fields of battle, named engagements and fortifications. Kennedy stood him another vase of organic pilsner, glad at heart.

For this suggested his friends weren't really up to anything; though at the same time the fantasy of Toby Shandy and the Corp was as real as they were, that salty knotted pair with their marvellous 'hobby horse'. Yes, as real as they were, the very making of them. To Kennedy, the idea that he'd fallen in among some people with a fantastic, twenty-first century hobby horse, was pretty attractive, not least because it meant all that talk of coming to the wars with Arthur was a game, without actual violence; and then because it meant that 'the worst man there is' was only the worst man for the game's duration, so that the violence he'd done in the provinces with his merry men (streamlined now to one fat man and the Heidi) was just make-believe violence for the game's sake, as Micky Voight was a make-believe character. You'd hope he was, really. And of course,

179

to call a character like Mr Voight 'the worst man there is' wasn't a historical or political judgement. Everyone could think of far worse men of the last century or this, living and dead, genocidal men who'd murdered millions. To call him the worst man was just to pretend that such a person existed, for the sake of the game.

Back in the office they chatted a while; then Kennedy went to call on Clifford.

Downstairs he saw no one, except the Estonian porter. At her desk she was solving a word wheel. The place was quiet as he passed through the main door and turned into the mews, where silence seemed to thicken. Alongside him in a gutter, a magpie hopped. For luck, Kennedy wished Mr Magpie good afternoon, and for equality, the same to Mrs M. Beneath his feet were bronze cobbles. Old stones, old path. At the far end stood a row of bushes.

An odd sort of growth. Behind the first row was a second, as if some kind of plantation was being gestured at – or even, Kennedy turned to look to either side, a maze, since the bushes really were thick and tall enough to form a pair of green walls, and a dirt-path ran between them. Yet at each end, the path, instead of turning, hit a blind wall. Getting through the second wall, he nearly lost an eye. Dark leaves sprung drops on his face and his lapels. Small wonder he'd never come across Clifford's office if this was the way! Miracle he ever got in to work. Why in hell's name should the university plant a copse back here? Anything for a sustainability grant. Cursing, he came at last to a wall on the far side.

At the end was an arch, covering the steps which Clifford described. Ascending, Kennedy entered a sunlit yard. The stillness was intense. As a kid, he watched a boy with a powerball, psychedelic swirls within the rubber, and the ball had a strange kind of 'off' or staggered bounce that made it hard to catch or follow. With similar motion, a recent thought reappeared ... What was never there, yet lasts longer than a man?

Kennedy crossed the yard. Beyond the wall at the end hung a motionless flag. Furtive and obscene, the stillness seemed to whisper. In the far corner he found an iron staircase. Clifford might be waiting for him. Descending was difficult, steps narrow and too close; the basement was a deep one. Out of the sun, the temperature dropped sharply.

At the bottom were the stone sheds Clifford mentioned. Squat, heavy, windowless, they seemed unlikely offices of the university. In the building to the left he knocked at a door, iron-hard, vinyl-laminated. No wonder they stored ammo down here. Veritable bunker. There was no answer. Kennedy was stepping back to examine a plate beside the door which might identify the building as university property but was in shadow, when a figure came from the side of the bunker to his right. The figure was holding something long, and dressed in a tight jacket, an old man apparently, hairless, old to be kitted out like that; one of those flying jackets with a sheen he wore. Popular among tough lads twenty years ago, light green or blue. Must be a colleague of Clifford's, walking Kennedy's way from the shadow. And by no means as old as apparent. The shaved fair head gave the impression of an old man, back there; but as he crossed the basement, he was younger, and fit, Kennedy's height but somehow springy, as if he could leap to the yard without using the stairs. The sun was behind him. A shaft had fallen in the basement, reflected at a surprise angle from a high window at the back of the Belvedere. He kept on coming this springy figure and his expression was if anything a little chummy, so to say, *What are you doing here, me old china plate, you of all people?* And when he spoke, there was a trace of music hall, looping, merry and snide:

'Do you want to know?'

Well Kennedy was about to answer that he was looking for Clifford, and would you have any idea if he was around this afternoon?, when he turned instead and began to run. Up the iron steps he went, heavy legged as a man in a dream, then across the yard in the gelified air. The question had not been an offer of assistance. The tool the figure carried was a long-blade screwdriver, raised for Kennedy to look at nice and close, point glinting in the sun.

24. Bitch metaphor and other surprises.

'Who d'you see at uni?'

In a flash of green Barbara entered from side door. Gave Kennedy a fresh fright, coming down his own hall like a thief.

Just Cy Frazer.

'What happened to your briefcase?'

He'd come home without it.

She laughed: 'What have you been up to? I'll have to check with Frazer ... one of these days!'

What about?

'La la!' She wagged her finger. 'Perhaps we didn't go in to work at all! Now where could we have been?' She sniffed him. 'With our Welsh friend? He's blushing!'

'Well I don't know what for!' Kennedy was well flustered. Obviously, he had been up to something, though not what she seemed to be intimating. What was she on to? Had she come in early to take him by surprise, softening him up with empty charges while the actual one lay in wait? In the dark night of his conscience, the references to Cy and his Welsh friend triangulated.

What had she been doing in the garden?

'Sunning myself! It's a lovely afternoon.'

Couldn't have been home long. That short-sleeved terracotta blouse and rather short black skirt, Kennedy thought he hadn't seen before. Who did women dress for when they went to work? He was curious about this (without wanting to read a thesis on it thank you – or anything by the columnists). Not for him anyway.

She'd just put on more perfume; like a butterfly, her mood floated in it. She was pouring him wine. Strange how much they were drinking of late. Welcome anyhow, because he'd come to see on his way home that the experience in the basement meant the game was real. Where had the technician's careful directions taken him? To the worst man there is, that's where.

'Why aren't you drinking your wine?' Barbara's tongue was a broad purple serpent. 'You want *un tentempié*?' She tuned the radio, got through Lil' Kim to the classical channel and smiled, tongue lolling in its cave.

Did they want him killed? Kennedy wasn't drinking his wine because he'd just seen his new friends as demons, leading him to his destruction – for amusement, or because it was their task. Those hooded boys who kept appearing ... here, Kennedy left the kitchen clearing his throat and went to the parlour to check the street for a shaven-headed figure, spring-heeled and actual. The afternoon was free of demons, hooded boys, worst men. Sun shone upon the walls.

'What's the matter?' cried Barbara. 'I wish you'd tell me if there's something wrong. Or something's on your mind. Please tell your wife! Is it something I've done?' She came over to look up at him. On his forehead she kissed him, soul squeezed into her lips, standing on her toes.

'No!' Kennedy was dismayed. 'Nothing you've done at all!' She mustn't be blaming herself, for Christ's sake. Nothing was her fault, nothing. Wasn't Arthur Mountain's either, Kennedy discovered as he held her, and the court who sat within shuffled, took turns to speak and examine the man who lodged them. Wasn't Arthur, or Clifford, who'd asked him to go prying in the basement behind the university. How dare he call them 'demons'? Should have waited for an invite before poking his nose in. That was it. Clifford had at no point said, 'Come and see me, man! Drop in anytime you're around!' Nothing of the sort. Softly he inhaled his wife's hair and perfume, flinching.

'What is it, honey?'

Say he'd left Clifford in the lurch. The rogue was prowling around down there with his screwdriver in search of the good old beatnik who lived on cider and tomatoes and wouldn't hurt a fly. Because Clifford knew all about him, and had been good enough to share the knowledge with Kennedy, an honour, since he had the respect of Arthur Mountain, did Clifford, as had been evident at The Parks.

And what did Kennedy do in Clifford's hour of need? Run off like a white-bellied rat, a cowardy custard, an early-to-bed man. 'Tchah!'

'*Qué pasa?*' Barbara pinched him in support. 'Tell me, honey! Why you made that sound?' Behind her a calendar appeared by the clock. He took too long to notice things she'd done around the house. It touched him she'd turned the page to April: ruddy cliffs, sea catching their colour. She put her trust in time, its cycles, the seasons, looking forward to what each might bring, hoping for the best, for herself, for both of them. If they'd had a bad month, not to worry, the next would be better! Touched him, not because it was childlike but because it was mature, human, optimistic by decision ... and he was still playing a kid's game.

'It's allergy,' Kennedy muttered, snout in her hair. Or they'd sent him to the basement as a test, like Sir Gawain. He'd failed. And the rogue with the screwdriver was a colleague of Clifford, who was observing the whole thing from some kind of spyhole in the shed of stone, Arthur in there no doubt as well guffawing. Which was why the 'worst man there is' hadn't chased Kennedy up the steps and across the yard: he was in the shed laughing with Clifford, not murdering him. If Kennedy'd introduced himself down there, there was no doubt what the punchline would have been, delivered in that looping voice. He was thorough with his evidence to the court within him, was Kennedy; kept back nothing that might possibly be to his disadvantage.

'Have you finished?' Barbara asked him in his chest. It was carnival red she was wearing.

'What with?'

'Thinking of the worst things you can.'

Kennedy disengaged himself to look down at her. Was there anyone who couldn't surprise him? 'How did you know I was?'

'Because,' Barbara pointed her finger significantly at his forehead, 'you are a brooder. A golden bitch in a basket of black puppies, that's you, Doc. They spend the day nipping you, but they are yours at least, your unkind black brood; and you, you are too busy with them ever to be truly unhappy!'

'Where's that from?' Kennedy was astonished.

'I thought you'd like it. So I practised!' And Barbara made to take her husband to bed.

Thirty-eight minutes later by the bedside clock, in the tone of one who's been attending to a nauseous or tearful pal, she asked again, 'Have you finished?' Kennedy, who'd in fact been enjoying himself with a surprise she'd introduced, was now considering her bitch metaphor and its provenance, when Barbara said, 'So I think you should really focus on your project again.'

'But what about the baby?'

'I've been selfish. Thinking about what I wanted without thinking of you.' She gave him her soul kiss on the forehead again, crouching as if he'd been stabbed in the street.

'But it's not just about you or me,' Kennedy protested. 'It's about both of us – together!'

'But when you came back from Swansea, you pretended you were going to be flexible with your project just for my sake. And now you've started imagining things and looking out of the window and it isn't well for you to lose focus because you're only thinking of me!'

This was awful to hear for Kennedy, who simply didn't deserve generosity on this scale, especially after the surprises (verbal and lewd) of the afternoon. He was trying to gather himself when she said,

'And you're drinking too!'

But she'd just poured him a large glass of wine – minute she saw him!

'But don't you see, *cariño*, it is much better for you to have wine at home where you can get on with your project and not be boozing with Welshmen! These trips you keep making – I'm sure you were hardly at uni at all today! Or the library. You aren't in trouble with the Old Bill are you, honey?' (Kennedy dug the way she picked up bits of slang like this from work; but indeed what the hell was he up to, involving himself with these dodgy characters – even if it was the vacation?)

Kennedy explained he'd just had lunch with Cy Frazer at lunchtime in The Inventors' Arms. Yes, Barbara said, in the pub at lunchtime then you come home looking like a ghost. She was helping him with his trousers and leading him to the table where he did his work and switching on his computer. *Venga!* Minutes later, she came back with a *tentempié* of ham and sherry for her scholar. By the way, the Radio 3 announcer said the piece just played was from Vaughan Williams' opera, *Sir John in Love*.

Falstaff everywhere! Kennedy was looking at a picture for inspiration, Welles and Jeanne Moreau. He kept it in a folder from years ago. The old knight and hooker were about to kiss. Barbara called from the hall. She was popping out. And here he saw what he hadn't seen before.

25. History shop.

Kennedy left the house the following day before Barbara, lips glossed a fleshy red, had time to declare her schedule. On the deck of a District Line carriage, his face pressed against a bolted sign, 'RFS Engineering: Hexthorpe'. At Earl's Court, he changed. The tube slid down an incline, rising into 'Triangle Sidings', and this space had the appearance of a playground by night; but where he alighted, the platform ended in a wall of earth. Tools and a trestle lay about, like an abandoned excavation.

Teenagers sat revising, consulting their phones. Bright windowed, the Reading and Reference Room was furnished with grand desks of dark wood, leather-topped. In tiny handwriting, an old African transcribed details of diseases, beside him a battered suitcase. Bending to a book of plants, an Englishman had customised his specs with carrier bags. Two girls whispered and giggled.

'What d'you actually want to know?' The words of the librarian grated and his name was Jonty Luff. Kennedy was now at the Information Desk, after fruitless examination of the *Encyclopaedia Britannica* and *OED* in a bay of books where he was watched by grinning teenagers. Jonty's face was pink, not unkind yet; but on a diet of school kids and loons, it was getting there; and Kennedy's promise to avoid technology had now been broken, since Jonty (after repeating Kennedy's discreet enquiry in air-scraping tones) was tapping 'stoplines' into Google.

Was Kennedy a cyclist?

Kennedy was not.

'Then it's military history.'

'Well where is the section?'

'There is no section. Why don't you just search it?'

Heart still beating, Kennedy was now on a bus bound for the West End. Recent minutes were a dream in which something surprising had occurred and passed. Either Jonty had shouted in Kennedy's face, or Kennedy had said a most insulting thing to Jont; possibly it was both – though which came first he could not remember. He might even have been escorted out of the building, down the stairs from the Reading Room and through the turnstile beside the Lending Desk. Certainly his departure had caused attention. His hand shook. Could he have called him a berk and told him he wasn't at all pleased to meet him? As the bus passed along Oxford Street, he stretched his legs beneath the seat in front.

With a tray of chips and curry sauce, Kennedy emerged from Dionysus on the corner of Charing Cross Road and made his way southward. The pavement was narrowed by hoardings that jutted into the road, squeezing and squirting the crowd. Kennedy regretted lacing his holiday snack with quite so much vinegar, curdling now with the sauce into a malevolent and staining posset. Crossing the road for leeway, he observed that the hoardings protected exploratory workings for the fabled 'Crossrail' project, which he'd been hearing about since he was a kid and someone said would take you all the way from Essex to Berkshire, transecting London. Berk. Berkshire Hunt. Cunt. Everything connects. He imagined himself in years to come, travelling on the new line to his mother and father; but as the project dawdled to completion, it became a visit of remembrance ...

There was a shop that sold military history down there on the left. Kennedy'd thought it to be a specialist store from the display of antique works in the window, but its main stock he now found to be remaindered. In the corner, at the end of a floor-to-ceiling shelf of books on armoured vehicles (and railway transport, for the unsoldierly customer), a staircase led down – evidently to a lower floor of the shop, since a grey-haired man came in from the street, passed Kennedy and descended. Kennedy was surprised by the material before him: handsome and glossy books devoted to single models of tank, T-34, Panzer Mk V ('Panther'), Churchill, Lees; books dedicated to single battles, theatres of conflict, types of rifle, grenades, specific submachine guns, though nothing on the 'Admin Box', in the defence of which, Kennedy noted, the Lees had proved its worth (in spite of being laughed at by everyone involved). His project, anyway, was to find out about the stoplines.

The handsome Frenchwoman at the till caught his eye and asked if she could help, but an enquiry about stoplines might cause embarrassment. She'd surely be no enthusiast, and he'd no sort of context to offer. He continued to look about him. Why was this stuff (the greater part of it concerned with the Second World War) published in such quantities, only to end up in a remainder shop? You wondered who was it written for, if no one was buying. Did the publishers not get the message? The grey-haired fella came up the stairs with an electric blue carrier and left the shop. Another followed.

Here was one about 'Kurt Knispel', Germany's greatest tank captain, who recorded 168 enemy kills before going up in flames when his King Tiger (a model which, of course, had a book to itself over there) was hit on the road from Wostitz, south-east of Prague, April 28th 1945. There was a photograph of Knispel with an ironic smile, several days' growth on his chin, greatcoat buttoned over vest. Perhaps the photo'd been taken minutes after an engagement ended and Knispel was trying to smarten himself up. What a face! For all the world, he looked like a mystic, a prophet or hectic artist, with his beard and shining, ironic eyes – not a tank killer. Barely older than most of Kennedy's students, yet he had killed 168 men; no – many more than that: tanks had crews of five or six; so perhaps he'd killed approaching 1,000 men, in his service in 503rd Heavy Tank Battalion. Serial killers, psychopaths, killed far far fewer than that to qualify. What did that make Knispel? A *megapath*? The text listed his decorations and honours. He accepted them with modesty, often allowing comrades to claim kills that were surely his own. Was this largesse, or shame? You'd hope it was shame, with a tint of irony. That wouldn't make it so bad, would it? … Yet was young Knispel, dead at twenty-three, really bad at all? Obviously, he was superlative – but superlatively what? How did the Wehrmacht's greatest tank killer compare with the worst there is? To have killed 1,000 men …

perhaps not worse than having killed just one, when you'd been made to go to war, in the worst of all wars; perhaps the worst man there is had nothing to do with quantity.

And this shop was certainly a place of quantity, for those who wanted their history with magnitude (soundtrack 'Mars'). Which wasn't history as your academic understood it. For the past never knew how bad it was; only we did, rousing it with our criticism from its drunken sleep – like, *D'you know how abusive you were last night?* But this dark place with its cheap shelving, was history's monumental store – history to stir the imagination, and heart, on the scale essential for drama; since on the authority of the ancients, tragedy has to be about something big. He was educated by his visit was Kennedy, more than educated; and though he'd still found nothing about the stoplines, he'd be back.

For these beautiful books, which you never saw reviewed in *LRB* or *TLS*, might be the fruit of a secret publishing agreement: displayed only here, so blokes could consult them in seclusion. Strange, but rather wonderful, that a period as vast in magnitude as World War Two was very nearly occult as a publishing area, when it came to books of this sort, thought Kennedy as he wandered out onto Charing Cross Road and bumped into Lydia Lightman. Lydia; and with her Dorothy Friend.

One of them laughed, the other laughed. Kennedy's momentum being towards his left as he came from the shop, he saw as well an orange sign that said, 'Adult Shop', and knew what they must think he'd been up to – precisely the same as the men who'd been descending to the lower floor; though with the added humiliation that Kennedy, empty handed here on the street, must seem as if he was too tight to buy any porn, a skinflint browsing sort of pervert with a photographic memory who stored up images to take home for a wank – unless he had a DVD stashed under his jacket. He knew what they must think with such certainty that the empathy expended in projecting their judgement left him utterly at their mercy, integrity shredded. In an effort to show there was nothing secreted in his jacket, he thrust himself forward a bit with hand on hip so as to spread the garment. They laughed on. If only he had bought something …

For there is a kind of man whose shamelessness and self-confidence conjure up integrity. That man would have known what to say, and – not giving a damn if they sussed what was in his carrier – taken the young women to that pub down there. Laughing with him in the sun over lager and chips, they'd not have bothered that he came to their home one autumn night; they'd be living in his spell.

But these two were not laughing with Kennedy, and he could no more join in than float away over traffic. Lydia Lightman had become less girl-like since their previous encounters, richer in the face from use of foundation, her hair sleeker. Dorothy, meanwhile, was now grinning in a manner that was almost affectedly wanton. On her T-shirt was a red and green design.

'We met your friend!' she was saying to him. Her eyes shone as black as vinyl used to.

'Which friend?' Kennedy said.

'Which friend!' repeated Lydia Lightman. She'd gained a rich girl's velvety stridence.

The two young women passed from under his eyes, northwards up Charing Cross Road as Kennedy unscrewed himself from the scene.

26. Murray the Hump. Honoured.

Homeward came golden bitch, thinking the worst he could. The encounter with the students was a disaster, irremediable. As for their having met his 'friend', speculation was cut short by the discovery in the hall of a letter bearing the stamp of the university.

Who'd bother to send a letter like this nowadays, in plain envelope of high-quality paper, name and address inscribed in severe black ink, unless it had been composed, or dictated, with particular attention? Such a letter intimated trouble, grave personal trouble. Only when matters were grave did the institution refrain from window envelope, Deskjet and HR database. In a way it was decorous (at least it would have been, were the trouble not Kennedy's). He needn't open it for the time being. What could it tell him that he didn't know, of the coils, the complications, in which he was crushed? So much for the Welshman's reassurances. 'Who can reckon my trouble?' Kennedy was saying to himself, as a man in an emblem book covered in plague sores, eyes raised heavenward, might hold at arm's length a creditor's note, when Barbara came in.

Kennedy tossed his letter to the back of his desk where it could blend with other papers, just before she found him. She'd been drinking, the brightness of her eyes being a sign that she'd had as much as she could take (not a great deal, admittedly), rather than one glass of wine with a client at lunch – which she normally washed down with a kilderkin of mineral water. Below the 'young countess' photograph of herself over Kennedy's desk, she came to rest. Her smile reminded him of something noticed recently – so recently, he could not name it. Later he recognised it as the grin that had caught his attention in the photograph of Kurt Knispel, mystical and hectic. Her face knew something it had not known in the photograph, though it was as if in her picture she had been setting off to find it and come back experienced: as a boy (or girl) soldier might return from battle knowing many times what they'd known in the morning. Perhaps what she knew was Kennedy's trouble, at last. Her lip gloss was still fleshy red. She'd been here when he left, seen the letter, steamed it. Maybe the police had been to visit, to speak with Dr Kennedy. The girls were laughing because they'd made a complaint. Stitched him up. It was what he deserved. Barbara had reglossed her lips after a 'revenge lunch' with her chum Melissa Butler (fabled to have driven over a policeman's foot). Under her photo, she looked older, more concentrated, a little evil.

To his surprise, she was on him now, and not primarily wanting to do harm. She really was quite tipsy; on her breath he could smell wine and something with a hot harsh scent, burning his ear which she was working at as if he were too thick for words and you had to go at him like this until the wax should melt.

Did he want to know about Murray the Hump? She bit his forehead. Did he know he suborned witnesses? He was Al Capone's right-hand man. Yes. No one hustled like the Hump was what Mr Capone said about him. It was a compliment when he said that, Barbara sighed, burning the eye of Kennedy, who was experimenting with her bum beneath a blue dress in which she looked kind of Greek. When Capone died Murray the Hump was No. 1 in Chicago. Llewellyn Morris Humphreys was his name. What was the matter? She'd now got Kennedy over near his reading chair. His name was Welsh. Murray the Hump was his tag. The Welsh got around. They got down to Argentina as well. Yes. There was a little town full of Welsh people, the Swansea of the *Cono Sur*, called Trevor. She got some of Kennedy's clothes off, who was in between thinking that he didn't know how lucky he was, that this may in fact be his last request, and that something was going on that he wasn't being told about – though not necessarily to his disadvantage (being an otherworldly fellow, did he really want the facts shoved in his face?). He'd suborn anyone to get his way, but if he gave you his word, he kept it. Break any man who crossed him ... she seemed to be reciting a lesson, but now she told Kennedy with a kind of fury that he had to mount her.

That was his word! Kept to himself like a Viagra stash. How the hell had she come upon it? First-degree connubial plagiarism … He'd have been ashamed for both of them – if only Barbara's dress wasn't now hanging off her right arm and shoulder like a statue of Apollo. Not down there! Onwards and upwards she drew him. Her *chocha* smelled of turpentine. He got a cuff on the head for noticing, which might have been meant as a stroke because she said sorry darling as he rose over her, a boy falling through a shop window …

'Why are you kissing like that? … Oh why don't you always do that?'

Kennedy, who might fairly have pointed out that he was kissing in his normal way, and always did do that (no innovator he), let it go. At the moment she didn't know herself, let alone him, customs turning to vapour. Let her bite. The screen of his computer had a mercuric tint in which he could keep an eye on himself and his wife, who'd ordered him to mount her. Where the hell had she been though? It was like a scryer's glass, that screen, figures surging and bending within. He wouldn't ask where. Rich as turpentine she smelled. If he asked, she might evaporate too.

Or if he should say that he loved her.

'We had a training day,' Barbara explained. It was teatime and Kennedy was ship's cook, the lady being a trifle unsteady still. 'That's how we heard of him.'

'Who?' Kennedy said; the eggs were at a gentle boil.

'Murray the Hump! They had an actor in to play him. Or one appeared anyway. It's a new initiative from Lord Goldsmith.' In her black pyjamas, she paused to drink Ribena. 'Law firms have to be alert to clients who may be planning to ride them. Especially the Entertainments Director, and her staff, because that's how they work their way in, *mañosamente*! They *inveigle*. So they got someone to take me for lunch; it was quite fun – he was telling me about Murray the Hump, but he was being him too!'

'Ah,' Kennedy said.

'He was the most corrupt man ever because he had everyone in his pocket – all the unions. They did what he said.' Above her was the calendar: those cliffs were ruddy as peaches. 'They had to yield. If he wanted to call a rail strike, he could make it last a season. Imagine the fuss if they did that here! He gave me far too much wine – the actor; not that he forced it on me but he ordered so much, I drank a glass from each bottle. I'm sure they were large glasses. He must have ordered four bottles. It was ridiculous. But this was how Murray the Hump was, darling. He hustled people and he bought them off – that's one thing, right? But on the other hand, he was the best friend you could have. 'I'll go out of my way to make a friend,' that was his saying. He'd always make a friend rather than an enemy – if it was up to him. And he was the most generous friend you could have. But if he made an enemy, he'd kill him if he had to!' She put down her glass for emphasis; the purple fluid shook and settled.

'But do you want to be friends with someone like that – *or* an enemy?' Kennedy wondered. 'Surely you wouldn't know where you were? It'd be bloody dangerous.'

'But that's the whole point of the training, idiot man! So we can be on the look-out for people like this who are so charming, right, and they could be a good friend – but they may also be dangerous, *muy peligroso*! And they can take you for all you've got. At least two law firms have collapsed because they've been ridden by lads like this!' Barbara shook her head. Kennedy was very diverted by the term 'lads', diverted from thinking through what was asking to be thought through (for the time being anyway). 'Because you can get at barristers and counsels through the law firms, and suborn them too!' Barbara continued, watching to see if Kennedy was impressed by the awfulness of this. 'Then where are we?'

'So it was a kind of role-playing?' Kennedy said.

'Yes. – Well, he just talked a lot really and told stories. So when Murray the Hump was being bugged, he'd pick up the phone and say, "Good morning to all my pals at the FBI! It's half nine in the morning and the sun's rising over Chicago. A great day for the race, gentlemen! Which race? The human race! I trust you gentlemen have not been cheating at cards again! So long for now." That sort of thing. He lived in the teeth of danger you see. He was so brave really.' Barbara's eyes were large. 'If he was being tailed, what did he do? He sent his own driver home for the day, got in the cop car and told them where to take him for lunch! He liked danger. Loved it!'

'Yes.' Kennedy drained the eggs behind her.

'And he so loved to talk. No one hustled like the Hump. No one talked like him!'

Kennedy turned to her, from a cloud of steam.

'So this character who took me to lunch, he could tell these stories so well, it was like being taken in twice over, or something – because the warning he was giving about these suborning lads, it was really fun to listen to. And you could see the danger of them. This was how clever it was. He was sort of being him, and warning against him. Because examples are always more educational. You know that from your students, *cariño*. I always thought so myself at college.'

'Was it a training day for the whole firm?' Kennedy wondered.

'No! It was *my* training day. We weren't all sitting there listening to him, monkey boy! It was tailored for me in my role in the firm. Everyone else will have a turn.' She was touching her ear, where she wore one of a pair of gold shells, then rushing out of the kitchen. 'Ah – it's here!' she called from Kennedy's study. 'Why haven't you opened this?' She returned with the letter from the university in her hand.

'I forgot.' In dismay, Kennedy took it from her.

'But you shouldn't forget. It may be something important.' With her hands on her hips she faced him, eyes unusually bright. She did want him to do well in his work; it was part of her love. So she looked up at him in her bare feet, like a child with a duff daddy. When would he become efficient, and everyone be happy? 'Perhaps it's about your project!'

'Yes,' Kennedy said. This was it then. It all ended in the kitchen, three eggs cooling in the pan. If only his wife could have some trouble of her own to match with his; but she was innocent, whatever she had done, in her life, this afternoon. Kennedy's soul was where the trouble was, and this letter had come to open it.

'*Venga!*' Barbara told him. 'They may have made you Senior Lecturer. We can celebrate!' The irony was heartbreaking. 'I'll open it if you're shy!' As she came to take it from him, Kennedy held her in pity; she wriggled out and made off with her letter. Let her have it; in the end, what harm can the truth do? He'd led a crummy, abject ...

'Oh ... It's just Jane Hall saying you don't need to attend the tribunal. She thanks you for your exemplary presence of mind and professionalism in this matter.' She handed it back to Kennedy, who read it to himself, doubt alternating with joy. The student in question, Ms L Lightman, had admitted fully to this and other assessment offences detected by Dr Kennedy, and was happy to abide by the university's system of mitigated penalties. These would now be worked out and imposed by the end-of-year Assessment Board, rendering unnecessary the Plagiarism Tribunal. There followed the thanks from Kennedy's Head of Department which Barbara just reported, with no sense of the happiness they brought her husband, since she had no sense of what he had been fearing. The illusion that this victory had been won by his own efforts, he allowed to subsist until somewhat later in the evening, exalting in his workroom as Barbara prepared herself for an early night.

By e-mail came a note of thanks from the Dean of Arts, commending Kennedy for his 'scrupulous attention to standards of assessment'. Well! And here, good God, was one incoming from Dorothy, to apologise if she had ever be a pain but it was only because the students thought Kennedy was cool and wanted to know his secret. She wished him the very best in his career.

Of course, he had Arthur Mountain to thank for easing his trouble. The truth of this had been at his shoulder, and when he thought of Barbara's new word, he knew the means. Everything had been made all right with the two young women because they'd been 'suborned'. *We met your friend.* Who else could that be? Had he threatened them? But they hardly looked as if they'd been threatened this afternoon. The opposite. They were utterly gleeful. So they'd been suborned with fun, not threats. *I'll go out of my way to make a friend.* Arthur must have got to them since Kennedy'd told of his trouble, which might account for his long absence in the afternoon at The Parks; though how exactly he'd tracked them down was another matter. It went with the mystery of why Arthur should wish to bring an entire institution into a posture of gratitude towards Kennedy.

The air in his study was thick with the scent of his and Barbara's earlier action. For an instant that prolonged itself as in the lighting of a flame, Kennedy fancied himself a sorcerer. He was in command of a powerful spirit that could appear in several forms, to do him favours ... and help itself.

27. Hamper & sword. Lecture for Plebs.

'I'll find the fucker if I have to turn the county over!' Arthur Mountain was hacking at tall ferns. Standing back, Kennedy followed.

'Wouldn't know it if it pissed in your eye!' In grey smock and straw sombrero, the Welshman turned to Kennedy, daring him to ask what he was looking for, like the county was to blame for being Kennedy's own. Breathing hard, Mountain hacked some more. As a matter of fact, Kennedy had a fair idea what his friend was alluding to.

The arrangements for this outing had unfolded as follows. At nine o'clock a card was delivered by hand. Hearing the clack of the letterbox, Kennedy hastened to the front room, where he caught sight of a hooded youth moving away past the wall with bowed back. Opening the envelope, Dr Kennedy found that he was invited to a picnic and if he was free this morning, please to make his way to a certain station in Essex, where his friends would collect him. He could hardly refuse. Besides, it was the last day of the vacation. He hovered by Barbara, who was in the kitchen examining texts, swore that she was running late, kissed him and vanished, leaving Kennedy to take a tube to Mile End, where he changed for the eastbound Central Line, plans for the day unannounced.

At a rural station, Arthur Mountain and Clifford were waiting by a gunmetal Mercedes. In today's costume, machete tucked in thick belt of brown leather, the Welshman struck Kennedy first as churl or beekeeper, hulking but uncanny; then he lit up and became a bandolero. Kennedy sat in the back, beside the unsheathed, dull-bladed sword. As they drove to the woods, Mountain asked where Kennedy's wife was. She'd been invited.

Here we go! Kennedy explained that there'd really been too little notice of the 'event' for her to take the day off work, and Arthur said what about spontaneity, so Kennedy pointed out that he'd not seen her name on the invitation anyway, and Arthur said crossly that Kennedy should have taken it for granted his wife was to come along too – if she actually existed, which he was beginning to doubt.

Had the Welshman really been helping himself where Barbara was concerned? This habit of referring to her as if he'd still to meet her – wasn't he too big a character to deceive like that? Suppose his interest was not carnal (not from experience, at any rate). Take today's outfit: could a man kitted out like that seriously be hoping to score? Granted, a woman in a certain mood might enjoy the connotations (TV Cornishman, Don Cossack, and so forth); there remained the question of what he was actually after.

Maybe nothing more than friendship. On the other hand, there was the Murray the Hump business. But it was beyond belief that Taras Bulba, sitting there broad-shouldered, had been employed by Barbara's firm for role-playing games with individual staff; unless the whole world was dreaming. Clifford parked on a dirt track. They left the car and entered the woods.

Arthur Mountain raised his machete above his right shoulder and in one movement flung it at the bole of a hornbeam, which it penetrated with a deep *shtuck*. The tree stood at the edge of a clearing, which they now entered, Arthur leaving the knife where it was, as a sign for Natalie, who, Kennedy was glad to hear, would be along. The Welshman sat by a smallish oak and Kennedy by him while Clifford squatted over the way.

'Natalie tells me,' Arthur said, 'that your wife's family went to South America to build railways.'

'Yes – well one branch of them were engineers, apparently. Not the Sicilians,' explained Kennedy, who'd surely specified nothing about railways.

'All the more chance they were Welsh then,' Arthur decreed. 'Not English like you told Natalie.'

'Ah,' Kennedy said, who felt the connubial hobby horse rearing above him.

'Entire railway system of the world was made from Welsh steel. Welsh steel, Welsh engineers – ask Natalie. Entire system. Welsh got down to the bottom of Argentina – and that's the end of the world that is: further south you've just got fowl. That's how far we extended our family like. Not in great numbers mind. Very few Welsh emigrated you see, Ken, compared with the Irish or Scots, or the English for that matter. Very few. But they made the most southerly railway in the world. They built chapels. They sung and told stories.

'Yes, the Welsh got there well before the Nazis.' Arthur Mountain waved his cigarette. 'Must have been a tinman among em. One night he had a skinful in Wind Street, woke on a coal-ship bound for Santiago. So he worked his passage, got off to look around. Maybe spent the night in a rum-shop, listening to a story told by a maroon. Maroon's got a fiend on his tail. Always looking round, lest fiend appear. Run 8,000 mile to escape him. Out in the alley, someone comes at the two of em with a marlin spike, so our man whacks him till he's finished moving. Can't get back on board. He won't see Swansea Bay again this life. East he goes, into Argentina. Comes to a town where they are working metal. He could advise them how to can their beef, without the cans corroding. They'd have to go prospecting for tin. He knew something of this. The language wasn't the same but they could understand each other – as men they could, and respect each other. The Welsh and the Spanish had this in common, Dr K, that they put community above class. The Welsh called it *gwerin*: the doctor, the miner, the tinman, the priest, all on first-name terms with each other. No fucking cap-doffing or "Sirring". With the Spanish, it was the *pueblo* – the people of a place, all on a level with each other. No "Señor" for this one and "Pepe" for that. They'd recognise this across the different languages: he was one of them, they were like him. What's Spanish for "He's killed a man"?'

'*Ha matado un hombre*,' Kennedy thought and said.

Arthur Mountain tried the words out. 'What about, "One day he'll kill again"?'

'*Un día, matará otra vez*, I think.'

201

Arthur Mountain tried the words, rolling the final syllable of *matará*. 'There you are. He'd have known what they were saying about him, not in English but in the language of his own country. The future tense's got more force, more promise in Spanish than it has in English. Same in Welsh. They have plenty in common, the Welsh, the Spanish.

'So he made his way there; he settled down; could even have prospered. Married into the *pueblo*. His blood entered the region. Maybe your wife is a cousin of mine.' Arthur Mountain hummed to himself.

His 'bampa' was a tinman, Kennedy thought. What did he mean by this romance? Was it a genuine yearning to find a relative, or even be reconciled with one, like in the late plays of Shakespeare? You could sleep with a cousin. He was disturbed that killing a man seemed to feature with some regularity in the Mountain family tree, though on the other hand if that was a made-up thing about a drunken tinman of the dynasty, it might just as well be an invention in the world of his strangely costumed friend.

'Well if you'd actually introduce us,' Arthur Mountain now declared, 'I could see if she was actually my relative. My kin. Dunno why you hold back on this, I don't. I'm not going to frighten her, for God's sake! You and me are pals aren't we?'

This was fair, obviously; though the word 'kin' was still elusive: was being a 'pal' the same thing, or was Kennedy's rank lower? Or was kin merely a matter of genetic relatedness (which wasn't what Arthur'd suggested on other occasions)? Anyway, Kennedy was about to apologise when Natalie entered the clearing in a green jumpsuit, carrying a large hamper. How had she got here? He went over to help her.

The hamper – Christ! What was in the bloody thing? – was so heavy, he nearly slipped a disk attempting to carry it one-handed. Natalie checked him then advanced towards her husband who was sitting by his tree smoking. As Kennedy struggled their way, Johnny boy passed him, carrying a slim brown leather satchel on a shoulder strap, and grinning. Natalie bent down to kiss Arthur. The light green suit made her look like some sort of jungle specialist, dropped in by a recon unit to advise troops on the ground, black hair catching in a shaft of sunlight.

'Is it heavy, Ken?' Arthur wondered, the former having arrived at his position with the hamper.

'Quite,' Kennedy said.

Light upon a branch-oh,
Hung Johnny boy his satchel-oh,
With a hey lillelu ...

'Know why?'

'No,' Kennedy said, who'd been thinking he ought to have brought some sort of contribution – a bottle of wine at least.

'Cos there's a table in there!' Arthur patted the hamper. 'And five chairs. And a fat waiter, with a face like a toad!'

'It's Pandora's Box!' Natalie said. 'Who's going to open it then?' She looked about her. At the front of her suit, the zip was down some way. The hamper, a traditional basket-work affair, was fastened by two brown leather straps.

'How did you get here?' Kennedy asked her. She'd noticed him staring. The Welshman wandered over to pull his sword from the hornbeam.

'Johnny boy brought me on his BMX Bandit.' She looked away from Kennedy like he wasn't in favour today. 'He gave me a croggy!' she laughed. 'Didn't you, lad?'

'Actually I drove Natalie all the way from London,' said Johnny boy, a little huffy; which was to Kennedy's liking.

'Where've you been this morning, Nat?' With his left hand, Arthur unbuckled the hamper.

'With a friend,' Natalie told him, in a manner which excluded all.

'Does your wife hold back on you?' Arthur Mountain enquired.

'No,' Kennedy said, loyally. 'Not as a rule – not as far as I know anyway.'

'Don't you keep an eye on her?'

'Not really,' Kennedy answered. 'I can't say I do.' They watched him.

'Look!' Arthur Mountain raised the lid. They moved closer, to see what was there. A good many English apples, a flat crate of tomatoes, a bottle of spirits, no wine (as far as Kennedy could see, though perhaps there was a second layer of things), six (at least) black cans, something long and elliptical wrapped in a fine white cloth, a bottle of Encona Original hot pepper sauce, a pot of mustard (English), a plastic tub of hardboiled eggs, some glassware.

'We'll have a drink first!' Arthur cried and began pouring the liquor, which was a particularly oily rum, into tumblers, then diluting it with careful measurements from a very small bottle of Evian that Natalie had on her. 'Spirits up!' Arthur declared, chewing on his. They sat drinking for a while on a tartan blanket, which had also appeared from the hamper. Clifford, who'd now come over, was privileged to drink cider from a black can. Kennedy, very thirsty, wouldn't have minded cider – or even a glass of water to begin with, rather than this.

'Come on, Dr K!' Arthur was now cajoling. 'Tell us about this project of yours, in the Plebs' League style! – Not the way you did it in Swansea!'

Were they there too?

'Tell or turn to dust. You're three quarters of the fucking way there already!'

Kennedy rose before them. So he'd been given another chance.

'Get your snake out and air it!' called Arthur Mountain. 'Like we know who! Have another before you start!' He thrust more rum Kennedy's way.

Tarry fire coated his oesophagus. An old voice was waiting down there …

'I saw something the other night and I hadn't seen it before. One day the Prince, his friend Poins and Falstaff were planning a robbery. Poins knew from a character called "Gadshill" (who was a 'setter') that some well-off travellers were going to be on the road in Kent the next morning. There was a good place for robbing on that road. The place was called Gad's Hill. See how Shakespeare confuses the issue? The man who sets the crime has the same name as the place. What's he up to?'

'Shakespeare you mean?'

'Yeah. Could have given the setter any name in the world. He chooses that. Anyway, when they get to the spot, Prince Hal and Poins slip off into the woods for a while – Poins has been calling the Prince his "good sweet honey lord", so you know their game. Falstaff, Gadshill, Bardolph and Peto (which means "fart") – they're left to rob the travellers. Falstaff's lying on the floor to hear their hoofbeats. He's raging at Poins, because he fancied his slot; he loves boys as well as whores.' Kennedy looked down at Arthur Mountain. 'He can't get up either. You should hear the stuff he comes out with when he's angry, this great chub stranded at the woods' edge.'

Johnny boy laughed and Arthur, he said something.

'So Falstaff and the other three, they commit the robbery, then Prince and Poins they come back out of the woods in disguise and they rob Falstaff and co. The others do a bunk, Falstaff stands and waves his sword then he's off too. Back at the Boar's Head, Falstaff's calling the Prince and Poins everything for ratting on the rest of them. How bravely he fought and against how many, well he tells the drinkers it was 100, 16, six or seven, 52 or 53, two, four, seven, 11 – before being surprised by three sinister knaves in Kendal green. He makes up numbers like a man pretending ferns are enemies. The Prince knows the facts. It took just two of them to make Falstaff run away. He also knows that Falstaff hacked his sword with his dagger to make it look like he'd been in a stiff fight; and told his crew to tickle their noses with stalks until they bled and then smear blood on their clothes, so they'd look as if they'd been fighting too.'

With his forefinger, the Welshman stroked the cutting edge of the machete. Blood began to stream across the blade in chevron. For a second he watched it, a man examining new livery.

'The Prince, he says to Falstaff, "Mark now how a plain tale shall put you down." What does *put down* mean, you plebs?'

'Humiliate! Snub!, you academic wunker!'

'Prove wrong, man.'

'Kill – like a pet with terminal illness, Doctor K.'

'Squash – as in Jack Cade's rebellion!'

'Good answers, pleb folk! When I spoke in Swansea, I used to think the Prince with his plain tale was like a scientist of facts. Here comes the facts, to chop off your head! Serves you right for making things up, boy, inventing people who weren't there. Inventing things you've done.'

Arthur Mountain sucked his teeth.

'But which of us doesn't do that? I might pretend I've killed a man when all I've done is whack some ferns with an old sword from an antique shop. Used to do it with my old man's ruler when I was a kid. Listen.

'You think of the Prince like that, it means the facts are a form of revenge. And revenge has a debt to what comes before. What comes before revenge is its cause or provocation. Obvious enough. So the plain tale doesn't fill an empty world with truth – anyone who's ever had a story corrected by one of these wankers who remembers how everything actually was but never opens his mouth till someone else starts telling it better, knows this.' Kennedy paused; there was a rattle of claps. 'The plain tale tries to knock down something bigger than itself.' Their eyes were on him.

'In the beginning was the Fable. That's where I'd got to till I met you all. In the beginning was the Fable. Then came revenge. Stories first, facts after. Think of the Greeks. Think of any human life. You get no facts for years. Then life starts to rot. You learn the distance of the moon, learn you're going to die.

'But the other night I saw something. This was what I saw. When the Prince says to Falstaff in the pub, after the robbery, "These lies are like their father that begets them, gross as a mountain, open, palpable" he isn't putting him down at all. He's bloody well admiring him. His lies are mountain-sized. How can a mountain deceive? Lies hide in holes. They don't go four miles up in the sky and say look at me! A mountain's the biggest thing you can see on earth. A mountain-sized lie is a fucking great lump of world. It's real, more real than real, it's grand illusion!'

At the edge of the clearing, a female blackbird bustled.

'What about three sinister knaves in Kendal green?' Arthur Mountain wanted to know. 'He said he fought hundreds but he ran from those three. What's that about, Doctor Kennedy? Grand illusion as well?'

Kennedy felt he should answer with care. He didn't care. The entire traffic of his veins was rum. 'He really saw them. Falstaff saw them all right. Shakespeare made sure of that … You're like a mountain.'

'I'm not "like" a fucking mountain. I am one!' Arthur Mountain showed Kennedy his machete, chevroned with darkening blood. 'And this isn't "like" a sword, or a fucking "antique". It'll take your lid off! So we can look for dried peas!'

'I'm the one supposed to have the sword,' Kennedy said calmly. 'Like Nun Nicholas had the girl with the hanger from Bilbao, to give anyone a tap if they asked a bourgeois question.'

'Who's bourgeois?' The Welshman handed Kennedy the sword. 'Answer with care!'

The sun was high in the sky. The Plebs' League audience would kick a lecturer's arse. Kennedy held his sword. He could cut their feet off. 'Everyone,' he said, 'who's bothered about their scale. Including you, when you worry about it. Shut up for a minute! I used to wonder where Falstaff's extra being was, his soul.

'I was sure it *was* there, because in Part 1 he tells his man Bardolph he's "fallen away". I'm as decayed as an old apple-john, is what he tells Bardolph. An apple-john was an old fruit, kept for winter eating. But he had to be something as well as being a funny man, to fall away *from*. Get me? The scholars have said this is all a joke too, self-parody. But I thought there had to be something beyond the joke, before it, behind it. The soul's private time if you like, as if the play was like a public interval and the character really got on with being when he was off-stage. I felt Shakespeare working on this ever so quietly. Listen. In Part 2, one waiter says to another, Never serve Sir John an apple-john. The Prince once compared him to one, and he's been sore ever since. Like Falstaff must have been remembering that episode when he was with Bardolph. It wasn't drama time Shakespeare was working in with all this apple gear; it was the time of memory, the dark matter of these plays. So character had a private memory. That's where the soul was. So I thought.

'But the other night, I saw the soul of Falstaff isn't concealed, isn't dark matter. Listen to me!' They were listening. He had a sword in his hand. 'The Prince calls him an old apple, he calls him a mountain. The mountain bears its soul, its secrets, traps, fatal ways, sublime possibilities upon itself, up front, for all to see, like the creases in an old man's flesh! *La montaña es también una manzana!*'

'Spanish that is!' Arthur Mountain was delighted. 'Very much like Welsh.' He began to applaud.

'Translate it then,' Johnny boy said, 'if you're so smart.'

'It means, "The mountain is amazing!"'

'No it doesn't. It means, "The mountain is also an apple."'

'What? You sure of that now, J boy?'

'Of course. I got Spanish A-grade.'

'Give me my fucking blade!' Arthur Mountain howled. Kennedy handed it over. 'You better have an explanation for this, squire!'

They could bury him here in these woods. No one would ever know. Who'd have thought it could end like this? Well, Kennedy said, with a kind of passionate tranquillity, 'An old apple is wrinkled and a mountain is.'

'I'm not called Arthur Apple, cunt! Get me?'

'Stop being such a bloody narcissist!' Kennedy advised him. 'I'm not talking about you. I'm talking about Sir John Falstaff. He's got soul. That's what I'm on about. In excelsis. It's all over him.'

'What about me?' Arthur Mountain objected. 'What have I got?'

'You've got green eyes, bwana.'

Arthur Mountain began to laugh: 'Mega! Come on down, out of the sun, Doc! Sit with us.' He clapped. They all clapped. Natalie came over with plasters, fixing his finger as he spoke: 'You didn't back down when I heckled. That's worthy of the Plebs' League, Ken! I'd like to see other modern academics hold their own at sword point when they are giving a lecture on these matters. You've given us the go-ahead. Tell our story we can now.'

'By the way,' Mountain shielded his mouth with one hand, 'I have got the biggest fucking wrinkle you've ever seen, butt! On my chest it is!' He raised his glass. 'Royal Navy ration was four parts water to one of rum.' Sun filled the clearing. 'My ratio's half and half. Gets a fellow talking! Let's have another. We can have our food then.'

The rum was Wood's Navy. On the bottle was a pale-blue label decorated with the head of a sailor, like the packets of cigarettes Arthur sometimes smoked.

'Johnny boy can take his grog,' Arthur said severely.

'You made me have it neat the first time,' Johnny boy scolded him.

'That's because you needed courage. – All right now, aren't you!'

'Suppose so.'

'Attaboy!' Arthur Mountain cried.

It did give you courage, Kennedy thought as Arthur poured out more, this time with mere splashes of water. What came over him just now? As for Johnny boy, what had he needed courage for? The time Arthur'd killed a man, was Johnny boy there, making notes in columns of three?

So Arthur unveiled the item from the fine white cloth, which was a large rather flat pasty, very large indeed, perhaps two foot in length, cutting it in four parts with his machete. Tossing Clifford several tomatoes, Arthur handed the pasty to the rest of them. Did Clifford *live* on tomatoes? The pasty was delicious, though the rum went so badly with it that Kennedy asked if he could maybe have a glass of water.

'Water or bumbo?' Arthur replied.

'What's bumbo?' Kennedy asked carefully.

'Kid's rum bumbo is. With nutmeg in it.'

'Just water thanks!' Kennedy reached out his tumbler, which Arthur filled rather stingily.

There was some talk of tripping on nutmeg and Browne's Mixture.

'What's in this pasty?' demanded Johnny boy, staring at a morsel of filling.

'Mixed wildlife,' Arthur Mountain told him.

'Delicious.'

'Made it with my own hands.'

'Liar!'

'I'll give you *liar*!' Arthur cried. 'Up at five this morning I was. Making pastry. Six fifteen, I had Tom poacher at my door with the filling.'

'Is any of this true, Natalie?'

'May as well be.'

Kennedy lay back in the sun, tarred rope linking cortex to gut. Natalie was a statue, fabled being in a place of great heat. She was Cleopatra, Arthur her Antony; Johnny boy and Kennedy, her melting attendants. Would it happen today, what they were all of them expecting? No one said it, but something was expected ... unless you turned expectation over, like a boy looking under a stone – and it was happening already.

An amazing languor took Kennedy. The heat of the woods was an effluvium, of his rum-heated soul – like the faun in the poem: did he make it with those nymphs, or dream he had? Were they ever there at all? Who was real anyway?

As if tracking a breeze to a rock-hole, he picked up Clifford, whistling softly over the way. 'Roll Em Pete': *You're so beautiful but you've got to die someday.* Characters were like a scent bottle. To meet them was to lift the stopper; to get to know them, never to put it back; then the scent, it spread around the world. Catch us now!

Arthur Mountain said something and Natalie asked what was it. Then he called out, 'Is he here today?', and took up something from the hamper.

Part III: Natalie's Tale

28. Doggers' last stand. Ian Brown.

As Arthur pelted the wood with eggs and apples, Clifford whistled a traditional air …

A bouncing man,
He came right out,
And up he zipped himself-oh.

You might think he'd been disturbed taking a leak, way he was calling Arthur cunt; but here came another in a West Ham shirt, leading by the hand a woman shouting wanker. Sword in hand Sir Arthur did advance, making to thrust, so they fled among the trees, those two men and their lady, and the Welshman returned to his company where they sat about the rug.

He appeared to have selected a dogging spot for the picnic. With one eye shut he regarded Kennedy, who was trying to form a picture of what might have been going on among the trees, then pulled new rum from the hamper so they could toast the action.

Was this what they'd been expecting to happen? Arthur chucking fruit at three swingers? But Natalie asked her husband if he'd finished, like teacher subduing the class clown; then clapped her hands and smiled, in a way to make Kennedy love her, and since everyone had been good, it was time for their story before they went home. Had Kennedy been good on the picnic? Maybe she meant they hadn't been good at all, and were going to hear a story to serve them right; but she wouldn't smile like that then, would she?

'Well there once was a lad called Ian Brown...'

He was born in the ancient Roman town of Doncaster, which meant 'the camp on the Don'. And there Ian Brown lived, until the time when he had to go away. Now Ian was a quiet lad and very pale, so that people would sometimes ask his mam if he was all right and they said to themselves that maybe Mrs Brown wasn't feeding him right. But Ian's mam gave him plenty for his tea. Friday night was his favourite. He got egg, chips and a grilled tomato, rhubarb and custard, a chocolate digestive in red foil and a cup of tea, and him and his sister watched the dinosaurs on TV. Nothing would bring the colour to his face though. Nothing. His mam made sure he played out with the other lads, and along to the fields he went for a knockabout. But that wouldn't bring the colour to his face either. So they had to settle for the fact he was white as paper. When they were in the fields, some of the other tykes called him 'Ghost'. Upset Mrs Brown did that; but Ian wasn't bothered. Maybe he liked it.

Well aside from his pale face, he was all right, Ian Brown. He didn't stand out, didn't really shine at anything, didn't make a fuss. In fact, you could positively say he didn't like attention: sticking in the background was what he liked. It suited him. But there was one habit he did have, though not everyone noticed it. Which was that he sometimes seemed to be looking at something else – something no one else had clocked, mainly because it wasn't there. Not that he made a big thing of this either. For the most part, he just carried on with what he'd been doing, but you could tell his eye were on summat else, that wasn't there for anyone else like ...

Kennedy sat to listen, as absorbed as a boy at the end of day in the appetising mellowness of chalk.

When he left school, he went to work on the railways, Ian Brown. A lot of lads ended up down the pits in those days, but Ian Brown chose the railways. Doncaster was important for the railways. Hands up if you knew it was the English, Welsh and Scottish HQ! When he started, Ian was a lineman. Balby Bridge to Marshgate Junction, that was his stretch of line, though sometimes he wandered north of the Junction. It was a grand job being a lineman when you were sixteen years old. You were your own boss. No one to keep an eye on you. All the older guys were sat in the shed smoking anyway, cracking on with the foreman. So the junior lineman, he could do what he liked. Suited Ian Brown down to the ground did that, because he liked looking at things, and as a lineman it was his job to keep his eyes open.

So he had to check for rubbish on the line, in case it caused a fire. Old newspapers, cartons, boxes, and there was a cable casing that could catch light and burn like a box of Zip. To Ian Brown it was like beach-combing was this. Amazing what people had thrown from trains that wasn't just rubbish: library tickets, letters they'd been sent, letters they were trying to write, dolls, rings, thrillers, bills – amazing. You could find out about people you had never laid eyes on, you could get an image of them. This was what he liked. You were never going to know these passengers, but when you found this stuff they were in front of you, dead bright they were; and so, he said, some of them stayed – though he wouldn't go into this. Not at first he wouldn't anyway. But he used to say, you had no need of books if you were a lineman. That was one of the things he said …

As a young man, Kennedy recalled himself. By the rug's edge, Natalie crouched to tell her story. She was wearing trainers today, of black nubuck, which accounted for a change in her figure. It was lower, fuller, feline. The trainers were by McQueen, each decorated with a little silver horn, or tear, on a tiny chain.

And as a lineman, Ian had to look out for vandalism. A lump of breeze block on the track could derail an express. Some of the delinquent lads weren't bothered if they caused a disaster. They'd bust open the power boxes and yank out the wires. Sometimes they hacked through the cables trackside. They left graffiti all over the shop. At the South Yorkshire Junction, there was a grey power cabinet where they'd sprayed,

WELCOME TO HELL

Ian Brown had a thing about that one.
He started getting into the graffiti, like he got into the jetsam –

that was what he called the articles thrown from the trains, that made him think of people they'd belonged to. So the graffiti, it was like the adverts you saw when you walked about the town – the adverts you didn't have any choice about looking at because they were plastered all over the place. Except the graffiti was like the adverts you'd see if you could write your own. If you could write your own, the adverts wouldn't have told you all the shit you had to buy, or drive or spread on your bread; if you could write your own, the adverts would have said, *WELCOME TO HELL.*

And from the graffiti, Ian Brown got to like the official signs as well. Things like,

GLUED BALLAST: DO NOT TAMP
METALLIC SHIELD BLOW-OUT CONTROLLER:
DEAD HAND ONLY
TRANSITION CURVE – QUARTER MILE RADIUS
PROCOR. BRT84075. NO NAKED LIGHTS
NOT TO BE LOOSE- OR HUMP-SHUNTED

Don't do this! Don't do that! Don't light a cig! Made him feel special, religious almost, down by the tracks – all those rules. The language was special too: not a lot of people knew about loose and hump-shunting, or the way to keep ballast in its right condition. Sometimes the signs glowed at you, they glowed through the drizzle. Not many lads looked forward to Monday morning like Ian Brown did ...

She must have known him to pick up all this stuff, thought Kennedy. Was she the sister he watched dinosaurs with? But since when did sisters share their brother's enthusiasm for railways? Sounded like she loved this stuff herself, way she recited, remembered, kneeling there. Could a woman like her be a trainspotter? Those containers she was timing; something Clifford said. She made it sound like poetry, modernist, avant-garde. There was a fella in a northern band came out with that sort of stuff, round the time she was telling of.

There were old fellas down by the tracks too. Dossers some of them, and winos; but there were straight guys as well, they felt more at home out there. Lived on nowt, nowt except tea – had no need of anything else. They didn't say much either, didn't bother you with advice, or the times they'd had. Officially, they were trespassing; but they were hardly noticeable, these old fellas. They had a word for the sidings: used to call them the 'lyes'. Ian Brown reckoned it was from them he got his habit, because these old fellas, they sometimes seemed as if they were looking at things he could not see, like there was a real busy scene going on in front of them, or an invisible film – just watching it quietly. Nothing surprised them. He reckoned if he'd got to know them, they could have brought a lot to light. But he would have had to get as old as they were first. That's what Ian reckoned; but his mam said he'd had that habit of looking at something that wasn't there before he went on the railways. Always had it, since he was a little lad. Maybe that's why it suited him as a lineman, at Marshgate Junction.

His favourite thing down there was an old waggon, on a long siding called Gainsborough Lye where grass came through the tracks. It was a dread object, this waggon, like a guard's van, but at the front between the buffers it had a plough-blade. There was a bit for standing on with a handrail, and under the handrail, this red and black piping came out and went back into the body just above the blade, like an elephant eating a bun. Friendly if you looked at it in a certain way, trunk in mouth. And outside the cab, you had an instrument like a ship's wheel, so you could imagine this waggon sailing the canals, or going down the Don to the seas on an adventure. Many a time, Ian Brown's stood by the long lye waiting to see a driver go on shift. But that waggon, it never moved – not when he was around. Just stood in the siding. And it was always dark in the cab, and the glass was all dusty and streaked over.

One day, Ian Brown saw one of the old fellas, 'Scotch Corner' they called him, looking up at the cab from the other side of the lye where it was overhung with trees, just standing there looking. So Ian starts thinking to himself, Who was the last bloke to stand in that cab? Does he ever come back to have a look at his waggon, pat it on the trunk, like? Did he put in his very last shift up there before he retired? How long did he work on the railways? What were his years? Does anyone round here remember him? Has his life gone into his waggon? How much does it know, that thing? What does it remember? An elephant never forgets. If you were to go up there, onto the footplate then into the cab, how would the world look through that window that's all dusty and streaked over? Would you see what you were used to? Or would the world be upside down, so what was real out here was the opposite up there – and vice versa?

It was called the SHARK was that waggon, Scotch Corner called out and told him. Its name was painted on the body once, but the paint had faded out. And Ian Brown, he dug it …

Why did one thing mean the world to one teenager, another to this young man? Waggon, film, old play. Kennedy looked to his left where Arthur Mountain lay, face covered by sombrero. Beside him Johnny boy took notes, as the guvnor murmured. The second rum bottle was half empty. And over the way sat Clifford, back propped against a bole.

29. Donny this is your last chance to run.

'When Ian Brown's seventeen, guess what? He starts courting!'

One weekend he went to Rotters with his mate Ray Chalice for someone's birthday, and that was where he met his young lady. He didn't act like a twat when he was with his mates, and he danced without making a fuss. His pale face looked great in a strobe. March 1980 was that, long long time ago. Could we all remember those days?

She was younger than him, Ian Brown's girlfriend, by three months, but she fancied herself more experienced, so she took him in hand, telling him what to wear, what to throw out, how to dye his hair, etc. And everything she told him to do, he went along with. Pissed her off at first. She didn't like a bloke who was a doormat. Wanted a bloke to stick up for himself, stand his ground. What she didn't see was he just weren't bothered. All the same to him if he wore straights or soulboy trousers. If she wanted him to get pointed shoes like she'd seen lads wearing at The Limit and the Warehouse, then he'd get some. He used to laugh. If it made so much difference to her they were wearing pointed shoes in Leeds, then he'd buy a pair. They'd get dead scuffed when he was walking up and down the lines, but he would get some. And with his hair dyed black and spiked – his natural colour being brown as the tea your mam gives you – and these shoes with points on, he reckoned he looked like a zombie, coming up the lines through the mist – a zombie or a gonk. But it was all the same to him …

Like Kennedy could have told Rebecca, when she tried to change his style; but he had to be himself.

Well in the same way he didn't care what he looked like, Ian Brown didn't seem to have ambition. Would have been a lineman till he was 65, if he had his way, mooching about looking at scraps and waggons with the winos. His girlfriend, she had other ideas. She was a junior secretary at GFS, which was a big engineering works that made railway parts, and underground stock. When she got wind there was a new PSB building at Doncaster, she encouraged him to apply for an apprenticeship.

'What was a PSB?' Kennedy asked.

'The PSB was the power-signalling box.'

It was the first in Britain, Donny's PSB. What it meant was that you wouldn't have to depend on wooden signs and beacon lights for directing trains anymore. With power signalling, you could switch trains and manoeuvre them all from one centre, and you could follow them, wherever they were, on this electronic diagram. So Ian Brown applied to become a power signalman. Made no odds to him whether he applied for an apprenticeship or not. It was the old fellas out on the tracks who had the real power, not blokes up in the signal box. When his girlfriend asked him, Why was that then?, he said because the fellas on the tracks had their own time; all the men in the box had was the timetable. She said yeah, well you had plenty of time if you were a bone-idle tramp – that was all you had. You didn't have a house, you didn't have money, you never had new clothes: all you had was time! Ian Brown, he laughed at that. He'd miss the graffiti and the messages, the old guys and the scraps, when he was in the PSB. Maybe he'd walk up and down the lines in his lunch break. He said that for a laugh; but it was the worst mistake of his girlfriend's life, forcing Ian Brown to take up that apprenticeship …

Kennedy averted his eyes. Arthur and Johnny boy were gone, Clifford too. He was alone with Natalie. Would they come back? Without them, he'd have trouble getting home. She came to sit closer, in the middle of the rug, face flushed from the heat and the rum. The story was for him now.

Ian Brown hadn't been much of a one for sport, but two of the lads he was apprenticed with were Rovers fans. They kept on at him to come to games with them. In the end he said OK. Wasn't a big deal. If it made them happy, he would come along to the next one. They were his workmates after all. Tried to make people happy, did Ian Brown. The next game was Lincoln City. It was a Saturday afternoon, end of October. He'd not been to Lincoln before. There'd been no reason to. What would you go to Lincoln for? Nowt there.

On the train that Saturday lunchtime, Ian and the lads from his work fell in with another bunch in Viking scarves and patches, 30 or so in number. Ian's mate Ray Chalice was among them. He was surprised to see Ian. They were talking about how Bremner was going to take them to the Third. Got on to Lincoln's supporters, what a mob they were, psychopathic – specially if you'd crossed their western border. They were down on fans from Yorkshire. Chip on their shoulder like a 2 by 4. Everyone knew where Yorkshire was, but no one had ever heard of them. So they made sure visiting fans never forgot them, specially Yorkies. Last season, the Blades took a real hiding. The train passed a bridge. One of the lads pointed out some graffiti:

DONNY – THIS IS YOUR LAST CHANCE TO RUN!

Stuck in Ian Brown's mind to the end of his days, did that graffiti. Then they could see the Cathedral above them, on a steep hill; and it was too late to run …

When she said so on the train was she rehearsing?

The way to the ground from Lincoln Central went round the backstreets. They were empty, though all the way, Ian Brown felt eyes on them. They were spooked, though they made it to the ground; but they went in the wrong end by mistake. This was where Lincoln's nutters stood. It was called the Clan.

The Donny lads didn't enjoy the game because the home fans kept turning round to stare at them. Didn't say much. Just turned and stared. They'd hid their scarves but couldn't do much about the patches. There was a goon in a white boiler suit, black bowler hat, Airwear. He stared a lot. Still, they were glad to get out of the Clan without being twatted. Maybe some of them were thinking Lincoln's fans weren't up to much at all. On that walk back through streets without a sign of life, maybe one or two of them were even fancying that they'd gone in and taken City's end. That'd be something to swank about on a Saturday night in Doncaster. But Ian Brown wasn't thinking of swanking about anything. All he would have wanted was to get back and see his girlfriend. Walking through those backstreets, the air was heavy-clear, like K-Y Gel, and very very still. Weren't normal air. It were air like in dreams. How much further did they have to go? So he asked himself, at every step.

They came out onto High Street. The streets were that crooked, they'd come back a different way from the one they went. At any rate they were on High Street now and Lincoln Central just over the way. Then as they were passing the Barbican, someone came down and stood in their road, fronting the lot of them. They were three-dozen strong, but on his own he fronted them. The air was still as when a frost's coming. The traffic sounded way off. But the horizon, it was red as a coal-grate; and the low sun bright in their eyes, as the man with the shaved head fronted them.

He was wearing a flying jacket; Ian couldn't see his face for the sun; all he could hear was the voice. He wasn't a northerner. Told them they would never make the station. His voice, it went up and down, like he was talking to kids at the pantomime: 'Well, well! You're only 20 yards off but you'll never make the station!'

Up and down went the voice; air as still as if they were all indoors, shut up with him. How could one Cockney hem in so many? They couldn't move. Thirty of them. Train at twenty-five past five, but they're hemmed in. Then he asked if they wanted to know and no one knew what he meant. Did they want to know?

He looked across the road, did the Cockney. There was a car park beside the station, and along the railings, end to end, Lincoln's waiting. Young men and old. Here were the eyes Ian felt when they arrived. Some in uniform of burgundy and denim, moustaches and streaked hair, stood with arms folded, top boys. And among them little lads with ancient faces, sucking on cigs and cruel already. And there were blokes old enough to be their dads. One of them had a fat padlock on a chain and another a hammer, and a third had something in a pillowcase that was lumpy and hard and he twisted the cloth to give it torque, and a fourth had a police-issue truncheon which glistened in the sun. And the goon in the *Clockwork Orange* costume was there; under the bowler he had pale-blue eyes and he munched on a pork pie.

Before them, the man with the shaved head was making signs to the car park army, signalling like a tic-tac man, hands moving faster and faster before their eyes, reminding Ian Brown of the St Leger, and home. Beneath his flying jacket he wore a *BRITISH MOVEMENT* T-shirt, and his hands moved fast as light and up and down went his voice like a terrible entertainer. They'd never make the station. Did they want to know?

'Do you want to know?'

And as the goon *sieg-heiled* to the Cockney, the massacre began.

Lincoln were so dedicated to hunting down the lads from Doncaster, they stopped the traffic on St Mary's Street. They were hunting them down three on one. Donny tried to make the station on an angle, but they had no chance. What chance did you have when there was one behind you, one in front, and one to your side, making sure you couldn't run? So they were kicking them under the wheels of cars, then the drivers joining in, giving out the treatment like Donny's causing the problem, screaming on the tarmac on St Mary's Street, all Lincoln putting the boot in, and girls with babies in pushchairs stopping to eat chips and look on, and whole families pointing, and a black-haired man raising the padlock above his head to bring the weight of it down on someone who had fallen, and the man with the hammer holding Ray Chalice against a van face forward while the man with the brick in a pillowcase went at him low down; and that was Ian's oldest mate. And it went faster and faster like on a roundabout when you're a kid and somebody's spinning it till you can only see one thing that keeps not being there, but it is there all the time. And some women were screaming but other bitches were laughing and throwing chips as the massacre went on and Lincoln hunted in packs of three. But for all their dedication to the hunt, no one seemed to notice Ian Brown.

The sun had gone down and the air was cold. He got a train home. What time, or how long the journey took, he didn't know. Could have been days. When he got back, everyone knew about the massacre. Ray Chalice was in hospital with neurological injuries. Another lad had been decapitated, under a truck. They looked at him to see if he had taken any shots. He was unmarked.

He was meant to be taking his girlfriend out that night for their first meal, but he went and sat in his room in the dark. His mam left a mug of tea outside for him, and sandwiches. The tea went cold. She left another mug. They could hear a noise in there, his mam, his dad, his sister. His mam went up again. The noise went on. Like tapping on the window. On and on. They shouted to him if he was all right. He told them to leave him be. Couldn't see anyone. He didn't come out of there till Monday morning. Monday morning he slipped out of the house and down to the tracks.

'Kennedy, you can't go yet!'

30. After the massacre.

'His girlfriend blamed herself. She'd been the one pushing him ...'

Natalie rose and went into the woods. Alone in the heat, Kennedy speculated; avoiding her face as she returned. Opening one of Clifford's black cans, she poured them cider.

So she blamed herself. It was her pushing him for promotion at work that led to him going to football. If she'd not started meddling, he'd never have set foot in Lincoln. He applied for promotion to please her. Went to football to please his new workmates. There it was. If she hadn't stuck her oar in, he'd have stayed on the lines and been happy.

It was terrible to see him now. Not that he blamed her. Wouldn't hear of it, that she was to blame. What got him was he'd come out of it scot-free. Hadn't taken a single shot. And everyone knew it. Hadn't even had his fucking eye blacked. People must be saying to themselves, 'How did Ian Brown survive the massacre? He's a jammy cunt is that one. Why didn't he step in and spar for the other lads? Why didn't he stick up for the lads under the trucks? Why didn't he stop them paralysing Ray Chalice with that brick in a pillowcase? – Because he did a fucking runner that's why! Yellow-bellied rat! Who knows but that he wasn't an inside man, tipping off that Lincoln mob which way they'd be coming back to the station?' That's what they'd be saying.

Ian Brown's girlfriend told him, no one was saying any such thing. And if they did, she would personally go round and crack them. He wouldn't listen. He knew what they were saying. He could hear them. If only he could have died there, instead of running off. He knew he wasn't up to much as a fighter, but if only he could have died. Anything rather than the guilt of coming back alive. On and on it went like this. All autumn. Into the winter. She told him he'd not done a runner anyway. He'd just been lucky, that was all. With his dyed hair and his pointed shoes, maybe they hadn't taken him as a football fan. The other lads didn't dress like that. But he said he'd run like he was in a dream. That heavy his legs were – but he ran. Well how could you argue with his 'dream' of running away? You can't argue with a dream …

Nothing disappears. All is rearranged. Kennedy, he could have shat himself right where he sat.

He'd moved out of his mam and dad's just before Christmas, had Ian. Wanted Christmas alone. Which broke his mam's heart. She was taking these food parcels for him. He wouldn't let her in – his own mother. She had to leave them on the landing outside the door of his flat. His girlfriend went round. Wouldn't answer the door to her either. Wouldn't see her anymore. Pretended he was out; but she knew he was standing behind the door in the dark. It was pitiable. At first it was. Then it started to scare her. What was he doing in there? His mates called. Then they stopped. It made her mad as well – but when she remembered the blame was hers, she forgot to be mad. What was going on in his mind? How on earth was he spending his days? What was going through him? Was he standing looking at something that wasn't there, like his mam said he did when he was small? Was there something he knew he was keeping to himself? She imagined his pale face in the dark. How long could he skulk for? It had been weeks now. He'd given up his job. He had given up everything. How could he live, the way he was? How could he exist?

At last his mam got in. She'd written him a letter to say he was killing her. There was nothing worse than doing nothing. Never showing yourself. Chronic skulking. So he let her in. Said sorry mam. Speaking in whispers. Pitiable to behold. He was so pale. Paler than ever. He'd only been eating the biscuits from his parcels, the biscuits and the instant meals, letting the decent stuff go off. And he couldn't open the tins – didn't like the sharp edge. His mam made him his favourite that night. The taste of the tea with the egg yolk, it brought his childhood back. A fine woman, Ian Brown's mam. She was a ward sister at the Infirmary.

She gave him the latest on Ray Chalice, the therapies he was having. Why didn't Ian take him out? They were best mates after all. So Ian Brown started pushing Ray round the park in his wheelchair. They'd go out from three to four, when the light was falling. What they talked about, God knows. Maybe they both said nowt, those afternoons in Underhill Park.

One thing led to another. Near the end of February, 25th it would have been, his girlfriend knocked on his door one evening on her way home from work, and he let her in. He was sat in the armchair smoking. He'd started smoking a lot of pot since the massacre. It looked like that was all he did, sit in this old dark-red armchair covered in ash. She got out her mirror and said for God's sake look at you! Covered in ash. He started laughing, to see himself in her mirror. Like an old demon. The colour of a winter sky. Like he'd spent the last two month shovelling asbestos. He said all that. He could still laugh. They both sat there laughing.

The following Monday he went back to work. He was through with the apprenticeship though; had to return to the lines. There or nothing. She didn't say a thing. Let him do what made him happy. Let him be. They were seeing each other again. Things were different though.

He'd gone off clubbing. Gave him the horrors, the thought of people dancing in flickering lights, other people standing round. So she took him to see a comic at her mum and dad's club. He could not wait to leave. Couldn't tolerate racist jokes anymore. So they went to an evening with a psychic called Rigel. Ian spent all night pissing himself, which was offensive to a lot of people who were asking about their loved ones. Admittedly, the fella was a charlatan, but people took him seriously about the spirit world, messages from their Gary and whatnot. They had to keep going outside for a cig, her and Ian. Anyone could do that, he kept saying. No need to come on like the *Ace of Wands*. No magic in it. She accepted what he said. He was boss now.

Another thing different was sex. He'd stop and say to her, 'You're having sex with a coward!' and his girlfriend would say no, she was having sex with a survivor. He'd laugh at that. Cowards and survivors were the same thing. Exactly the same. Couldn't slip a fag paper between them. He'd been reading about the concentration camps. So many of the Jews who survived the concentration camps of the Nazis had this terrible guilt, to the end of their days. Some of them, they just couldn't handle it. Committed suicide. To have survived was a sign of cowardice. If she could imagine him dead, he'd feel a lot better – more of a man like. He laughed and banged her womb. It brought tears to her eyes.

One night he took his girlfriend down to the lines, to walk by the tracks he worked on, holding her hand. When they'd been going for ten minutes, Ian saying nothing in the dark and her chattering her head off because she was dead nervous, they saw this orange glow. It was a little fire, trackside. She had a hell of a fright. At the fire, though it was so dark down there you couldn't tell him from the night, not until he moved and said something to Ian, there was a bloke squatting. It was Scotch Corner, the old fella from before the massacre.

He called Ian 'son'. It had moved while Ian was away. They'd brought it back now – either they had, or it just came by itself like. That was what he said.

Ian Brown led her on up the tracks. She kept stumbling – she was wearing high heels; but he was taking her to Gainsborough Lye. Dead set on that he was – and he was boss now. Suddenly he said they were there and banged something hard with his hand. It was the waggon he used to tell her about, the one he used to stare at when he was first on the lines. She was so nervous. Was it all right to go up there? He laughed and put out his hand to her. What was she scared of? It was just an old elephant! She followed him up onto the waggon. It was pitch black. With matches he lit the way for them. Took her round the cab on the wooden deck, round and round. Her heels made a hell of a noise on the planks. He told her don't worry. They weren't trespassing. How could they be? But she was freezing out there on the deck. It was like the temperature had dropped. Bitter. Her teeth were chattering. So he said let's go in, twisting the handle on the cab door. She was scared to follow, but it was so cold outside.

At first the dust was that strong she thought she'd choke to death.

It was terrible, the smell. The air seemed made of it, this black asphyxiating dust. No one could have been in that cab in years. It was like the dust had been waiting, brewing itself up for decades, stronger and stronger. Meanwhile, Ian was fiddling with his matches. He'd found an old lamp. It was dried out, but he found an old can of Esso Blue in this little cupboard with a sliding door and soon he had the lamp burning. It mixed with the dust, the smell of paraffin, like sniffing glue. The paraffin lamp was making their shadows move, on the wooden walls: black as spiders, the pair of them. She'd dropped acid a couple of times, Ian's girlfriend. It was getting her like the start of a trip.

He held her up against the wooden wall; he lifted up her skirt and started rubbing her. She was wearing fishnet tights. When was an elephant a shark? He asked her in her ear. She didn't know. He kept rubbing her. Was it when it was taking people to die? How many Jews had sex on the waggons to Poland? How many Jews had it off going East? Or, and he was grinning at her when he said it like someone trying to make you happy, was there a waggon that wouldn't collaborate with the Nazis? She didn't know what he was on. A waggon that went its own way! Slipped away from the death line and took the Jews with it so they could hide in the forest. She said how could a waggon slip off and go its own way? Didn't have a mind of its own. He grinned at her and said when it was the Shark, it could do things you wouldn't know. You didn't know what the Shark could do! And that was because you thought it was just a box of wood! But it could take them all on. All the cunts in black uniforms, and the Field Police and the cunts in bowler hats and the whole Third Reich, and the Barbican man, even him. The Shark could take them all on! And on and on he went till she was nearly screaming, up against the wall in that little cab with the lamp-light leaping and coiling ...

At the same time as Kennedy's life, this was happening; and he thought he'd been unhappy. He looked up from his shoes ... But the girlfriend and the mother – how in God's name was it for them?

31. Worse. Micky Voight.

'It gets worse now,' Natalie said, her tone a flat mixture of warning and promise, as Kennedy rejoined her in the clearing.

'Why are you telling me this, Natalie?' He'd been thinking of waggons and characters, as he pissed against a tree. Planks, paper, ink: common origin.

'Don't you want to know?' She squatted on the rug like a colonel in the field.

'Yes.' By now, how could he not want to? One might just as well emigrate to another land, make the effort to learn the language, find new friends, work, a place to live – then without cause, turn back for home. 'I do want to.'

'You really really want to?'

'Yes.'

'Do you promise you do?'

So he promised.

'You won't say you wish you hadn't wanted it, when you hear?'

'Of course not.'

'Well hold on tight.'

The trial came up of the men involved in the massacre in Lincoln. It was in the papers in the North. It got to Ian Brown did that, really got to him. Better never to have it mentioned again. Eight months on, he'd seemed to be getting over it. But now everyone was on about it again, like no one had ever had their head kicked in before on a visit to Lincoln.

It went through him, all the prattle in the papers, *Calendar*, *Look North*, the theories, the opinions, blah blah blah. *That October afternoon* ... they kept coming out with it. *That October afternoon in a sleepy cathedral city ... That October afternoon when innocence ended ... That October afternoon that ended in tragedy.*

Everyone had an opinion. You had the Bishop of Lincoln saying bootboys were a legacy of the permissive sixties and too often grew up in homes where they never knew the authority of a father figure. You had the Industrial Chaplain of the Diocese saying it was due to the Tories' economic policies which were consigning a generation of young men to the scrap-heap. You had womens' groups saying the Yorkshire Ripper had started off as a football hooligan before he became a truck driver. You had the British Legion saying a month on tinned rations at Wadi Zem Zem would sort out this long-haired bunch, and bring back the cat. You had a Professor of Social Psychology from the University of Nottingham who was an acknowledged expert on peer-group violence explaining that it was inappropriate to talk about evil as a motivation. And you had Alan Balan the Director of Tourism saying it might affect tourism. Everyone wanted a piece of it. None of them knew what it had been like. Not a single one of these twats with their professional opinions had a clue what it had been like *that October afternoon*, when the world was there and gone, there and gone as if you were on a roundabout; and the air was like K-Y; and bitches were throwing chips as your mates went down. And none of them knew what it was like to be a coward.

There were 21 teenagers and men, aged 16 to 39, up on charges of riot, violent disorder and GBH with intent. They were all local. Every one of them. There was nothing in the papers or any of the reports, nothing on the TV, about the Cockney with the close-shaved head who fronted up the lads from Donny outside the Barbican. All the addresses were local. The media never discussed the Cockney. Why would that be? He was the ringleader, the one who set the others on. He was the worst, the worst of the lot.

Ah, it screwed Ian up all over again, that the Cockney in the tight flying jacket and British Movement T-shirt was not in the dock at Lincoln Crown Court. Screwed him up that he'd looked in his face, eyes blinded by the sun, and heard his catch-phrases. *You'll never make the station*, that question he kept asking. Screwed him up he'd seen him tic-tacking, close as Natalie was to Kennedy on this rug they were sat on, signalling to the fat man with pale-blue eyes who was eating a pork pie and wearing a white boiler suit, like he was his Number 2. Screwed him up all over again. He'd been doing all right, in his own way, since he let his mam and his girlfriend back in and returned to the lines. But now it went from bad to worse. Because whereas he'd been fucked up about his own cowardice before, now he had a different kind of fear.

He started thinking the Cockney with the up-and-down voice was everywhere, did Ian. Couldn't settle, because he didn't know where he might appear. Kept thinking he was there, close at hand, wherever he was himself, watching his flat at night, waiting in the Gents', on the other end when he picked the phone up. Or he had a feeling he'd come across him as someone else, selling cans in the corner shop, checking his bus ticket. Then a terrible idea. What if the Cockney had got away scot-free because Ian Brown had? That'd be Ian's punishment, to be haunted by this demon with his tic-tac dance because he hadn't experienced the massacre the same way as the other lads, on either side. Just like Ian Brown hadn't been hit or battered at all, so the Cockney'd committed no actual assault. He'd just done a sort of dance with his hands flashing. Which meant they were made for each other.

His name was Micky Voight. Yes. Ian Brown told his girlfriend this while they were lying in bed together. Micky Voight.

How did he know?

Well he did know.

But it wasn't in the papers.

What had that got to do with it?

OK. He was the boss. It was Micky Voight.

That's right. Micky Voight. Say it.

Micky Voight.

And what was Micky?

She didn't know.

She did know!

She swore, she didn't.

Well lie back and look at the ceiling! He would show her what he was. Show her how he carried on. It were a right jest this one. Let it roll!

Well Micky Voight he led his men through many British towns. They followed a team from the capital, they sidelined with certain other firms; but wherever they went, pre-match, during and after, you got mayhem, ultra-violence. Had a special pocket in his flying jacket, did Mr Voight, and in this pocket he kept a sharpened screwdriver. And one day, the merry men took a train to Leicester, an ancient Roman city Micky Voight knew of old.

On account that last time he was there, an Indian kid was murdered in a phone box while some Cockneys stood laughing outside and one of them called, 'What's the code for Bombay, mate?' It was a fat man with pale-blue eyes who stabbed the Indian kid. Voight kept his special pocket zipped that day. The fat man wasn't a Cockney. He was from Suffolk. NF country was Suffolk.

She asked him how he knew all this stuff.

He said he'd made it up.

But he'd been reading an anti-fascist magazine. There was one over there on the arm of the red chair. She got out of bed and had a look. It was nothing like the *Sun* or *Mirror*, which were hooked on the Royal Wedding that summer. The Royal Wedding, what Botham was up to …

Oh Kennedy remembered that summer.

He had some brass neck did Voight, to be going back to Leicester. And the new season hadn't even started. It was weeks off. What were they up to, taking the train there when there was no football? The answer was a little East Midlands riot. If you were crafty, you could set the place on fire. Now you might be thinking it was an odd sort of project, these lads of the far-right wanting to burn an English town. But it wasn't them who were going to take the blame for it. Wasn't them who were going to do it either. They were craftier than those coons in Handsworth. All they had to do was wind up some of the local chaps and get a little ruck going. The wind up was easy. Simply sniff out one of those pubs where all the local chaps played pool and ask ever so politely at the bar if anyone knew the code for

Bombay. Unfortunately this particular question might be taken in the wrong spirit, and the local chaps would begin using their cues in a manner for which they certainly were not intended. Then what were Mr Voight and his little party to do? Allow their heads to be broken? Dear me no!

Why did he keep doing this voice? Ian Brown's girlfriend asked him that. It was giving her the creeps. Wasn't his own.

He said that was right. It was not his own. He was going into character.

Well it wasn't funny. She told him.

He said it wasn't meant to be funny.

Well she said he was saying it as if it was.

He told her she didn't get character. Didn't matter if you didn't like the way it sounded, or thought it weren't funny. What mattered was if you believed in it. That was all. The only thing. Did you believe?

But was he making this up, or wasn't he?

He laughed.

She looked at his anti-fascist mag again. It didn't have any of these details. So he was making it up. But he'd been fronted by the man he was talking about now outside the Barbican. That was a fact. Except no one else seemed to have witnessed him. So he was making it up? But the massacre had happened. That was a fact. It was in the papers, it was on *Look North*.

He just laughed.

She said OK. What mattered was if you believed. That was all.

So if the local chaps in Leicester began using their cues for a purpose they weren't intended for, Micky Voight's little party would unfortunately have to defend themselves employing reasonable force, as the law allowed, using only their fists and boots. And as they were a tool-handed little party, with veterans among them, the local chaps might soon find themselves calling for assistance. And when more local chaps arrived to give assistance, then would the Leicester Constabulary arrive as well, to investigate a reported disturbance among the local chaps of Melton Road, who'd smashed a pub and, now the police were here, were setting about burning one or two shops, a garage, a Black Maria, in their fury at being arrested for a righteous response to extreme provocation by some white men, strangers to the area, who'd come in from outside, to taunt them about a race crime that occurred the year before last, and had now slipped away so that the police wouldn't believe they had been there at all though one of the white men had been standing chatting to a fucking copper who was smiling at him, while he did his hands like Ted Rogers, 3-2-1.

So this was how you got a riot going, and once the place was smouldering, you could draft in some more lads from the South to help not put it out. And as the fire grew, patriots would arrive from far and wide to see for themselves how it was that 'local chaps' were treating an English town, and do their best to reclaim the streets from these pandies on behalf of its original locals, who were frankly there long before the Romans came and the Danes came, not to mention Johnny Vindaloo, and the police hurrying this way and that with things hitting them, half-bricks, petrol bombs, tins of Rajah chilli powder, all confused about their duty, and then a couple of majors or colonels from the Fusiliers or Staffs, or 2 Para, they would intervene with half a dozen machine-gun platoons so as to clear up any confusion over duty and let everyone know where they stood. Namely, on Day 2 of the Third English Civil War.

Now that was Voight's plan. But the train, it didn't stop at Leicester that day. It was scheduled to, but did not. And for why was that?

Because there was an Inspector on board who was keeping an eye on the merry men in Coach H. When they were pretending to have a pleasant talk with the trolley man and asking him if he enjoyed his work and shyly he said he did, the Inspector noted the way the conversation concluded: 'Well why don't you let a fucking white man do the job, Mohammed?' He noted the talk of stabbings and cut throats. Noted the lines of amphetamine being sniffed off tables. And he pretended not to notice when they tried to burn his uniform trousers with their cigarettes, but he said to himself, 'I am going to take you cunts round and roundabout.'

He knew some tricks, did this Inspector. One time he was coming down the East Coast main line when he saw something on the A1(308) and he put the train into reverse. It was a Range Rover heading north that had his attention. The Inspector's at one of the train doors with a megaphone ordering the vehicle to pull over onto the hard shoulder and give up. The Range Rover maintains its speed. The train's reversing at 90 mile per hour on the up-line towards Morpeth. At Seahouses the Inspector produces a Very pistol and he says this is your last warning. Stop or I fire. He's got a thing about that Range Rover has the Inspector. Before he can aim, the vehicle's rammed the central barrier and mounted the embankment on the right and escaped onto the beach. However, there's a disused coastal mine a bit further up, and the Inspector shifts his Intercity Express off the main line and onto a freightline that runs in and out of the mine, and from there he takes the train down a standard gauge track used for running coal waggons up and down to some workings by the beach, so when the Range Rover comes over the sand, no doubt thinking it's got away safe, this fucking 125 is waiting for it like a dragon!

Ian Brown's girlfriend said that didn't sound very clever. What if he ran into a train that was coming behind him when he was pulling these stunts? And killed all his passengers. Hey? What was more, it was bloody silly to imagine you could make trains go wherever you fancied.

He laughed at her. He laughed and laughed. It wasn't as silly as she thought. Quite possible in fact.

Bailey taught them so when they were in the PSB, Ian and the other apprentices – Bailey was their guvnor. He'd shown Ian their section of the network on the VDU, which was where the trains were operated and kept on time. But there was a hell of a lot of track, sidings, lyes, freight and industrial, and also privatised and heritage, that never showed up on the electronic diagram because it wasn't operationally relevant. One day, Bailey, he got a British Rail atlas from his locker and opened it on the bench. It was amazing to see. All the extra track that wasn't marked on the network, like little hairs or nerves, coming off the main lines, coming off the branches. Made your eyes swim to look at it. And here and there were blown-up diagrams with numbers and letters and different-coloured inks keyed to the little lines to show where the track and sidings were as dense as a forest, where you could make a train disappear. It were easy. Right off the main line into one of these lyes. Easy. That was why it was such a responsible job being a signalman, because you had all this power in your hands, power over other people's lives. The *Standard Timetable* was only half the story. There was a lot more track than the 'Bible' knew about. But you had to use that power responsibly. When he thought about it, he was glad his girlfriend made him apply to be a signalman, was Ian Brown. Wouldn't have met Gaffer Bailey otherwise, with his atlas of spells.

Well on the day that Micky Voight was returning to Leicester to organise a race riot, the Inspector had phoned Doncaster's PSB and instructed Bailey and the apprentices to use the full capacity of the network. He had some authority this Inspector. So the train didn't stop at Leicester, didn't terminate at Sheffield either. The Inspector took it north-west, and across the border.

First stop, Carstairs. Buildings on a low fenced mound, cottages like they were cut from coal; no sign of life. The merry men sat tight. Fence rang in the wind. What else were they to do? Get out and kick off? Trash the place? There was no one to fight with, no one to hate. Nowt moving but the wind. This Inspector had something on them. From the vestibule they heard him shout, 'Split it there, Cally! Take the good people on to Edinburgh!' There were a couple of bangs. The rest of the train rolled east and H was on its way.

As the sun set, they slowed. The merry men beheld a sign in the dying rays, and the sign was marked *LAW JUNCTION.* Then the Inspector had the apprentices at Donny put Coach H on a reversing spur. The rear power car moved off south, and the Inspector called up the Shark, so as to shunt H to sidings east of Motherwell. They went in over a hump like the Big Dipper and the Inspector was riding on the Shark. He was having some fun up there with the air-horn, amplifying his voice: 'Two dozen English heroes! By express!' Just beyond was a marshalling yard; the sky glowed with hot lights of a steel plant.

A Scotchman called out, 'OK, boss! Cut em loose!' Now let's see how these cunts handled it, outside their jurisdiction.

They filed out of Coach H and they lined up on a wooden platform made of trestles, a kind of scaffold. They'd lost initiative. They'd lost their will. Around them were engine sheds and generators, swart engineers, linemen. And these men, they were gathering round to see what had appeared in their manor. A couple of them fired up welding guns, to examine the English heroes. You can cut a man in two with a welding gun. The English heroes stood there paralysed, all of them except Voight. Someone shouted, 'Give us a joke!' In white acetylene light, they tried to tell a joke. They could remember only one: 'What is the code for Bombay, mate?' The Scotsmen scratched their heads and said come again! Like, *What is the code for bumboy? That whit these cunts are saying?* So they told the English heroes to repeat the joke, in case it was their accents were making it disunderstandable. So the English, they repeated their joke: 'What's the code for Bombay, mate?' 'What is the code for Bombay, mate' 'What's the code for Bombay?' And the Scotchmen shaking their heads, like, *Where is the colon on this bumboy? Cannae be whit these cunts are saying!* And on and on they made them say it, till their voices were turning to wax in their ears and throats and Voight's merry men were like little lads who've forgotten their turn at an adult do and all eyes upon them, and one or two wetting themselves for fear or shame, piss dripping through the scaffold, maybe wishing they could hide behind their mams' legs like they did before they were wicked, if there'd been such a time. But only Voight wouldn't tell a joke.

Then these Scotchmen, they made them skip along the scaffold in narrow ellipse, like,

Boys and girls come out to play,
The moon doth shine as bright as day!

And they skipped because they did not know what could happen to them in this jurisdiction where their lordship of violence could get no purchase ...

God this was cruel as anything Kennedy had heard. Terrible how cruelty spread, wide as the air. Was this how it got worse?

'Skip for your lives you wee bastards!' called a voice from the crowd and the Scotchmen roared as the English cunts skipped round

238

and roundabout in their long narrow circuit; for these were mayhem merchants and masters of cruelty, but they must skip for their lives now, breeks all mawkit and beshitten, before the watchers whose eyes were bright, in the blackened masks of their faces. But one Englishman, he would not skip.

Not a pace. Just stood at the scaffold's end arms folded, looking down on the scene. He had some contempt did that one. Now either the Scotsmen couldn't see him, or they chose to ignore him and carry on humiliating the others. Because what could you do with him? Who can answer that?

So what if you could pull him down from his place on the scaffold where he shook his shaved head smiling, at the terror of his crew and the taunting of black-faced engineers; pull him down and lynch him from the gantry over the way; or drag him to a derelict siding where long pale grass grew through tracks, and have the Govan boys kick his brains loose; or quarter him with a welding gun with 3000 degree flame – so what? So what if you could? It would not finish off his contempt. You could terminate him, but not terminate his attitude. That was the issue here. Unorthodox methods were required for the elimination of Micky Voight. Because of his contempt, because he didn't fear for his life. How do you break a man who doesn't fear for his life – and holds nothing dear? How do you exorcise his cold smile, his voice of an evil entertainer? How the hell do you rid *yourself* of him, once you've got rid *of* him?

He was still around them. Perhaps he'd even set on the massacre in Lincoln to eliminate apprentice signalmen. Perhaps this bad spirit was that strategic. Then he would never let up till all the signalmen were finished.

Ian Brown's girlfriend said don't talk like that – it gives me the creeps. He laughed his head off, lying beside her. Could she see him on the ceiling?

32. Interlude.

'So that was how it started getting worse,' Natalie declared.

Kennedy looked at his shoes. Something ratty about them. *Started*! So much to ask. The fate of the 'merry men' concerned him. Sent back to England, where they learned to love? Voight's sidekick with pale-blue eyes, where was he that day? Questions about who was, and was not. For a man who'd just given a lecture on the priority of fiction to fact, Kennedy was mighty agitated by the desire to know which of these people he was hearing about was, in the manner commonly accepted, real.

'What d'you think of it so far?' Natalie lit a cigarette, eyes dark as night. 'D'you wish I hadn't told you?'

'You asked me if I wanted to know,' Kennedy said, troubled by her look.

'And?'

'I did, Natalie.'

'In the North, when we say "want", it can mean "need". Like, "He wants shooting for that," doesn't mean he wants to be shot. It means he needs it, whether he wants it or not. Or if you said someone wanted a good shag, means they need one to sort them out, whether or not they've thought of it themselves.'

'Yes,' Kennedy said.

'So did you want it, or need it?'

Did he want to hear about a life unlike his own that reminded him of himself? Or need it?

Natalie began to unlace her trainers.

'We all need the truth.'

'How do you know it was true?'

'When we're impressed by a narrative even though the content is so,' Kennedy paused, 'terrifying, and malevolent and desolate, then it must be because we feel we're getting the truth.'

'Do you say things like that to your students?'

'I suppose I do.'

'What are you afraid of?' Natalie'd got her trainers off.

'Micky Voight.' Having looked upon him.

'It was Ian Brown was scared of him, not thee. Bothered about summat else you are. You're changing the subject. I asked you what you thought of it so far. You haven't said.'

'Well I keep thinking of the beginning. Before the massacre. When Ian Brown was a lineman, when he first got the job after school, he was digging all these old fellas who hung about the tracks at Doncaster and saw things he couldn't. The one called "Scotch Corner" – he had a big influence on him. Isn't it because of him Ian Brown got into the "Shark"? But didn't you tell me he used to invent characters – or imagine them – from the jetsam that was thrown from passing trains? Letters and bills and things. So he could see things too – of his own accord, I mean.

'And even before then, didn't you say' – she'd pulled her socks off now and was considering her feet, nails painted a dark violet – 'that when he was small, even then, he used to have a habit of looking at something no one else was aware of?' No answer. 'So maybe,' Kennedy continued, 'Voight was there from the beginning – or early on anyway: he was already seeing him when he was small. Maybe he'd been seeing him all his life!

'What I mean is – did Ian Brown make everything up? Or did you make him up? Are you the beginning, Natalie? Are you the source?' He heard the German, *Quelle*, from another conversation.

'What the hell are you?' Natalie called, her face hard.

'I'm sorry.' Had he gone too far?

'You're a good lad,' Natalie decided, 'that's what you are. You have been listening!'

'But of course I have!'

'Gold star for Kennedy! Then he shall have a reward!'

'Oh that's OK,' Kennedy protested.

'Who's best at stories?'

241

'You are!' said good lad. Across the rug, they faced each other.

'So you don't believe what you've heard?'

'I think I do,' Kennedy said. 'Really.'

'Why d'you believe it if it was a story?'

'I think it was a true one.'

'You'll believe owt you will. I've been watching you. When are you going to grow up?'

While Kennedy was preparing his answer, Natalie cried, 'I'm toasting in this!', rose, and unzipped her jumpsuit, which she now removed totally. While she sat back on the rug, Kennedy kept his eyes on his shoes. Round her ankle, she wore a platinum chain. She was a creamy-bodied woman, paler than Barbara, though her skin ... ah, was Kennedy dismayed! She'd known his thoughts from the beginning. What the hell to do?

'Aren't you hot?' she asked gaily.

'No,' said Kennedy, torrid as a log – and icy with alarm. 'Not too bad really.'

'Come and sunbathe!' She lay back. 'Take it easy! Don't be afraid – I'm not a student!' She laughed. 'We can make-believe we're at the bay. Or a palace. Or pretend the sky's the ceiling and look at monsters!'

On guard! The creamy mass of her just there, in black and violet underwear that seemed to sparkle in the burning air, was a torment like Moreau's Salomé. Don't even think about it, Kennedy!

Among a bank of ferns, a creature stirred.

'When are you going to grow up, cock?' she called.

'I don't know,' Kennedy said, not to be provoked.

'D'you believe in me? Do I exist for you?' She raised her left foot towards him, as if she was a dancer and he an expert. Jesus Christ. Suppose she were a nymph he'd dreamed, a northern nymph, then he was safe: phantasmal temptation. She lit a B&H. She was all too real. He could smell liquorice off her, blackberries.

'Yes,' Kennedy said. 'Of course you do.'

'What proof have you got?'

'I don't need it.'

'You think I'm here, three foot from you?'

'Yes.' She'd taken his arm once. He'd heard her heels on the pavement. Did she want him to go over? Lick her pants like a dog? Or was she testing? And he knew with terror, but also a kind of firmness, that if he touched her, sank into her, then his encounter in the university basement would be confirmed and that was Voight down there and the screwdriver could do real harm; whereas if he held his ground, a demonic reality should remain in the offing.

Contraries melted. He was being taught a grown-up lesson by these new friends; he was being confirmed. His project was a kid's game … right all along. The whole affair was a story with living characters and narrators, a spreading pattern on an opening fan. And Micky Voight was painted on the leaves, as Kennedy himself was – and Natalie over there. But who then was the author? Whose hand upon it?

'D'you know about the sorcerer's apprentice, Natalie?'

'Tell me! Is it a nice story?'

Kennedy looked at the sky, to tip her from his gaze. 'One day, an old sorcerer goes out on a trip. His apprentice says, "Thank God he's left the house for once! Now I can have a go at his spells!" He was meant to be bringing water in from the brook, but he magics a broom to do his chores. So the broom, it trots down to the brook and it brings a pail of water. "This is rare magic!" says the apprentice. "Go fetch another!" And the broom fetches another, and another, and another, till all the vessels in the house are full of fresh water.'

'What was the apprentice doing?' Natalie enquired.

'Oh he was just sitting back enjoying himself.'

'Was he cracking one out? That's what young lads do in their leisure time isn't it?'

Kennedy held his face to the sky. 'He can't control the magic; the broom won't stop bringing pails. So the apprentice, he takes an axe to it, but it won't die. One broom turns into two. He takes his axe to them. Two becomes four. They start to divide of their own accord. Soon there's an army of the bloody things running to the brook with pails. They flood the sorcerer's house. The apprentice, he cries in despair,

Die ich rief die Geister,
Werd ich nun nicht los!'

'Whooo! What does that mean?'

'It means,' Kennedy said proudly, '"These spirits I've called up, I can't get rid of them!" Luckily, the sorcerer comes home from his trip and commands the brooms to cool it. Order is restored.'

'What's the moral?'

Kennedy said nothing.

Natalie lay so he could see her ribs and the movement of her heart (he fiercely wished she would not smoke so much), enjoying the sun. Then she asked if he was watching over her with all his soul, and when he promised he was, she said are you ready for more?

33. Edinburgh. Marc Stone. The bam.

'What possessed Ian Brown to leave for Edinburgh, no one knew.'

He didn't let on he was going. Snow was thick on the ground, hard ridges of it, coloured like a smoker's fingers. It had been falling for three weeks. On the morning of 27th December, he just slipped out of the house and left. His mam caught him on the stairs but there was no holding him. So she gave him fifty quid and two packets of cigs and begged him to keep in touch. He didn't tell his girlfriend a thing. She went to his flat that evening with a new jumper for him, because he'd promised he would see her there. Promised. The flat was empty – he wasn't hiding this time. So she went round to his mam's. Mrs Brown was distraught, for all that she was a tough woman. They'd had a party at the house, Boxing Day, and he stayed over. He'd drunk a lot and made jokes nobody really got though they laughed along anyway; people weren't at ease with him. But he didn't seem any worse than he'd been since the trial; maybe someone'd said something that got to him. His girlfriend was gutted. Should have gone to the party herself to keep an eye on him, but she was with her folks. Now he'd walked away in the snow ...

We could have formed a club, thought Kennedy.

He'd only been wearing his denim jacket when he left, God help him. At the beginning of January, it fell again for two weeks. She kept looking at the weather reports in the newspapers. Scotland was one of the worst places. Minus 27 up there, and Ian only in his denim jacket. It broke her heart to think of.

After a couple of weeks, he wrote to explain he'd gone to Edinburgh in the Shark. She was nearly physically sick when she read that. Had his mind gone completely? Or was it one of his jokes? In the letter he said that if she checked Gainsborough Lye, she'd probably find the Shark hadn't been there for a few weeks. So she went along the lines at night with a little bike lamp. She got in through a hole in the fence near the Bridge, that he'd showed her once. The snow was still hard; under her Wellingtons it cracked like glass. She was so frightened the night-shift would catch her trespassing, but she was set on getting to the Lye. However when she was half way up the line, a dog came at her. It was black against the snow, but in the light of her lamp its eyes were flashing blue. Horrible heavy dog. She turned and legged it, slithering all over. If it got her she'd be savaged. Robin Cousins couldn't have run on that stuff. She dropped her lamp and the only light was from the snow itself; then slipped and twisted her ankle. That was it, she was dead. But the dog wasn't behind her at all. Must have been on a chain.

Maybe as a lineman, they'd given him a ride on the Shark: he got free rail travel anyway. It had that big blade. Maybe BR'd used it as a snowplough on the main line to Edinburgh and they let him go up front in the cab with the engineer, or whatever. Maybe that was all he meant. He wasn't tapped after all. Except there was something else he'd written.

Which was that the reason he'd gone to Edinburgh was he wanted to go in the opposite direction to Voight's train. Because when the Inspector split that train at Carstairs, Voight and his merry men went one way, but the coaches with all the good people went to Edinburgh. So he had come to Edinburgh to hang out with the good people. His girlfriend wondered what the hell was up with the good people of Doncaster? But she had no right really. Wasn't she to blame for his trouble, and letting him believe his own stories?

At the end of January he wrote again. Thought he'd met someone who'd been on the train. Met him in a bar. He was sure he'd been on that train, this new friend of his. Positive. It was a great place for bars by the way, was Edinburgh. They had 24-hour opening. So this new friend of his was going to look after him. They weren't to worry about him in Donny. He wasn't on his tod. He'd found a flat and signed on. And this new friend of his, Marc his name was – he spelled it with a 'c' – this new friend was going to introduce him to some like-minded people. He was chuffed with this was Ian, because the one thing about South Yorkshire was that he'd not really had people on his own wavelength – not people his own age, at any rate. But here he was going to be introduced to plenty of people who were on his wavelength. He didn't want her to worry about him. And let her tell his mam not to worry. He was going to be all right. There were more lads up here with dyed hair and pointed shoes like his.

Well his girlfriend was in bits to hear she'd never been on his wavelength. They were meant to be in love, for Christ's sake. If that wasn't on a wavelength, what was? She'd listened to his bastard yarns enough had she not? As for him getting his hair dyed and his look, who'd persuaded him to do that? And she was worried sick about these 'like-minded people' his new friend was going to introduce him to. Worried sick. What would they do to him? She was starting to go mental herself. In March, she got the sack. She'd been drinking too much and coming in late. Then she screwed up some orders. That was her finished at GFR. It meant so much to her at one time, that job. If she hadn't let her ambition run away with her, she'd still be in it; and Ian Brown would still be there with her. His mam took redundancy from the NHS. They gave her a three-grand severance cheque. The girlfriend couldn't bear to speak to her now, on account she'd caused her Ian's trouble in the first place. And she was so ashamed about getting the sack.

There was a third letter from Ian. Marc had indeed introduced him to some like-minded people, and these people had introduced him to some others. It was ace to have a few pints with all these new friends. They were all of them trying to help him find anyone who'd been on the good train. They reckoned they had relatives who had, some of them did, or mates. They were going to bring them along to meet Ian. He felt he could trust them, these new friends. They always stood him a pint. Luckily, he had enough brass to get them one back – all of them. His mam was sending him fifty quid a week from her severance. When you added what she was sending to his giro and his housing benefit, he was minting it, though Marc had taken him aside and said be careful of one or two of these new friends because he wasn't sure he could vouch for them and call him a cynic but he had a feeling they might be sponging for drinks – and if there was one thing Marc Stone detested it was a sponge. That was the kind of mate Marc was.

Then there was no word from him for two weeks and they were well into February. Another week passed. Still no word.

She wrote to him. She was coming up to Edinburgh the following weekend. He didn't reply, so she rang. Someone answered – it must have been one of his flatmates, though he hadn't mentioned any – and said he'd pass the message on. Ian's girlfriend said could she possibly speak to him herself please? The flatmate went off to see. He came back and said Ian had a stomach bug at the moment. He was in the toilet. But that'd be fine for her to come up Saturday. He'd look forward to seeing her. They both would! And that was that.

Well it wasn't as she'd have wanted, but she had to see him. She was that worried about what was going on up there. He sounded far too pleased with life. Wasn't him at all. She bought some new things and had her hair done. She'd not been to Edinburgh before. When she arrived at Waverley the following Saturday it was like a gale was blowing inside the station. Place was screaming.

Her train had come in on Platform 13; just over the way was a ramp that led up to the city, and along it were black taxis. She was hoping he'd be there to meet her – she had his address in case. There was no sight of him, so she was walking towards the ramp when someone shouted. In the wall across the way you had an arch, inset in the brickwork. A man in a cream raincoat and boots like a German officer, stood there smoking. Hair slicked back, eyes bright as a bird's. He was smiling and calling her name.

He was Marc. Marc Stone. Maybe Ian had mentioned him in his letters home? She said yes he had once or twice, and Marc Stone, he made a face and said he hoped all she'd heard hadn't been bad like, and he sucked on his cigarette like that and threw it on the floor where he stubbed it out with his boot. Because he knew Ian wrote to her religiously and she might have thought that Marc Stone was leading her man astray or keeping him out late at nights ... But what was this? She had not been receiving her man's letters? Had only three from him since he came up here? Marc Stone stared at his fingers. It was a good 10 weeks Ian had been here, approximately – arrived

December 27th and now was March 5th. Sixty-nine days anyway. She was impressed he could remember exactly. Must have been true what Ian had said about him being a good mate. Well Marc knew for a fact that Ian wrote a couple of letters or cards per week, bulletins like – as well as setting aside Sunday afternoons for writing long letters to his fiancée. Because he had often said that to Marc, when they met and Marc asked him what he'd been doing the day. Indeed, Ian had been keeping to himself a bit recently, so you might think he'd been writing even more letters. Marc looked down when he said this, and she wondered if he was sad because Ian'd started cold-shouldering him or hiding, in the way he had. She asked if Marc wasn't Ian's flatmate, and Marc looked surprised and said he wished he had been. Wished he had.

Believe it or not, and tell him if it wasn't his business, Marc had made a point when he was seeing more of Ian, had made a point of suggesting that Ian wrote *fewer* letters and actually tried to visit his fiancée, or invited her up. And if you were to ask him why he'd stuck his oar in like that, Marc Stone would tell you that letters were no substitute for human contact. They needed to see each other, Ian and his lassie, and letters were not a substitute. For God's sake, he was but two point two five hours on the train from her. Let them visit before spring was terminated like. All very well using the January snows as a reason not to travel; but the thaw had come and gone. In Princes Street Gardens, the tulips were out. And Marc Stone, he raised his face in the wind like a bird.

Well Ian's girlfriend was overjoyed to learn that Ian referred to her as his 'fiancée'! You can imagine. First she'd heard of this – but she was delighted. Delighted that he had a special way of talking about her when he was so unromantic in his letters. Meant he really loved her. They were on a wavelength after all! She was so happy too that he'd found a friend who really cared about him – about them both in fact! Only she didn't have time to be happy because she was panicking. What had happened to the rest of the letters, if he'd been writing at least three times a week? How could all the rest have gone missing? There must have been about two dozen she'd never had! Marc Stone raised his face like a tired bird and he sighed. With his hair slicked back and his tired face on, raincoat belted tight, he was Humphrey Bogart. He took out a 10 pack of B&H, lit one, put the pack away, pulled it out again and offered her a smoke. Could they sit down a minute? There was a bench just over there.

Well, she wanted to get in a black taxi and go and see Ian immediately. Her heart was thumping. Something bad was going on. But Marc Stone took her by the arm and led her to the bench.

This was what he had been worrying about. Exactly this – though not only this. And he blamed himself. Entirely. Not but that Ian Brown hadn't been begging Marc Stone to introduce him to more and more like-minded people. But it was time for the truth. He couldn't keep it from her. Some weeks ago there'd been a big fella who turned up in Edinburgh, a Welshman – or if there were any believers left around this godforsaken hole, they'd say the Deevil disguised as such, because he'd been making their lives hell to be honest with her.

Now this Welshman had appeared a couple of days after Ian, to the best of Marc's memory, or at least he'd clocked him then in Cafe Royal, the day before Hogmanay, which was the first time he set eyes on Ian, shivering like (and Marc had offered him his own pullover, not as a loan but a gift), Cafe Royal being Edinburgh's finest tavern, just over the way there (Marc pointing up the ramp and scooping his right hand). He was positive now the Welshman had been there, keeping in the background like, but up to something, trying to make pals by the looks of him, and pumping out a lot of noise, being one of your psychos who don't play it quiet but the opposite like as a sort of disguise. And if she thought he was jumping the gun, listen on.

So the following night, Marc's called round on Ian in his new digs so as to take him for something to eat, socialise a wee bit, get to know him. And as it happens they end up in Mathers on Broughton Street. You could have sworn they'd been followed because they have scarce kissed their pints before your green-eyed Taff appears down the bar, bamming it about railways and acting like he owns the place, and everyone sucking up to him for that he's ane sizeable cunt.

If she'd excuse his language – and Marc hoped she didn't think he spent all his time in bars either, though he'd be a hypocrite to conceal the fact he was himself a bit too fond maybe of the public houses of the 'Northern Metropolis' – yet only in the way that some ladies were a little too fond of shopping; and if the results were as terrific as in her case, who was to say there was anything wrong with that?

Howbeit, couple of nights later, Marc's taken Ian to Kushi's Lothian for a pakiora, a bowl of gravy and a chump chop thinking our boy was looking awful peellie-wally, and you could swear bully-huff was in the booth behind them. Like you could hear him but couldnae see him. What a volume on the fucker, putting on some poor bastard he's got with him on the history of Swansea and World War II, trying to persuade him of Christ knows what Nazi plans and making the whole fucking thing up as he gaes along in a way to put an honest man off his scran, and totally upset our boy Ian's appetite with all this sham-shite like *they're back again and they haven't ever been away either*! And so it goes on. Every place Marc takes his new friend along to, the Welshman's either there already or turning up five minutes later like he's glued to the pair of them.

Wasnae not long but lampit contrived to introduce himself to Ian Brown behind the back of Marc. One afternoon in the Cowgate this was. Now the point here was that Marc Stone had been taking the measure of his new friend since he arrived. That's what friendship meant to Marc. And if he picked up on the fact that a person'd had some tragedy in his past, then it was his duty as a friend to listen to that person's experience of what had happened to them – and then, only then, and not before, to try and help them forget all about it. Therefore, Marc had had some talks with Ian, at Ian's own pace, about this massacre in Lincoln. And he'd heard, eventually, all about this character with shaved head and loop-de-loop voice who'd been the numero uno, the ringleader. So he'd told Ian some of his own experiences of violence, being beaten by his father, being beaten at his school, more often than not for telling the truth – he couldn't help that; and no one to stick up for him. And he told Ian how he just pretended it had never happened, by sheer force of will. And he felt he'd succeeded – and Marc Stone might not have achieved much in life, but here was something he felt he could be proud of – he did feel he had succeeded in persuading Ian Brown that your man with the shaved head and flying jacket was no more than a bogle. And if his fiancée could have seen the improvement in her man afterwards, she'd have been more inclined to believe all Marc was telling her than she looked at that very moment.

Howbeit, they're sitting by the fire in Bannermans Bar the two of them, Ian and your green-eyed hump, when Marc comes in and the Welshman asking Ian his trouble because he can see he's got some and doing himself no good keeping it back, pretending it never happened, because a man should pass his trouble round like a rugby ball and no good sitting on it because if you don't play the game, you got nothing coming, and no team mates to look out for you. Then getting Ian to go over the fucking massacre *for the twentieth time*! Making him say 'Micky Voight' and write it on a beer mat and Ian getting paler and paler, asking this detail and that like he's genuinely interested in Ian's life, then humming to himself and making up a thing or two to surprise Ian with, and Ian now white as your ghost of Xmas Never, as if Taff's talking anything but pure bully-huff shite in order to wind him up, like Taff himself has seen this roll-about cunt with pale-blue eyes who hangs around with Micky Voight and he was eating a pie the time Taff saw him too believe it or not – as if pie-eating was one of the most *esoteric* activities of the entire human race, and by the way has Ian encountered the public-school lassie with purple hair? Net result of which is Ian starts drinking more and more to keep his nerve, then Taff loading on this horrorshow about Swansea and the Third Reich and 'stoplines', whatever the fuck they may be (something he's made up on his way to the boozer no doubt), and the war hasn't ended yet, and your Baghdad-Berlin-Bury St Edmunds Axis (another bam he made up on his way along the Cowgate), and God knows what, till he's got Ian real spooked and sitting there head in his hands then laughing like a maniac (in a way horrible for Marc to witness) treating Taff like a fucking god and asking him if he knows what Voight and the pieman done in Leicester by the phone box. And all this shite just to soften Ian up.

Because there are two or three black-and-tan facts obvious to any citizen watching the performance. Uno: your bam-ruffian has a thirst on him the like of which no one has beheld, even in this capital of the gae-down. Duo: he has turned up here with not a penny to his name. Truo: he has swiftly made himself well aware of the fact that Ian's ma is sending him a cheque every week.

Well before you could take your next breath, old green-eyes – a two-forty carat cunt if ever – he's started telling Ian he has a better cure for Ian's fear than eighty-shilling and Famous Grouse, a cure deluxe. And he's taken Ian away and got him on H …

Couldn't she see he was a liar? All along, lying to her.

When she heard this, Natalie started crying in these great gulps and shaking and Marc, he put his arm round her and hid his face in his hands. He was gulping himself. It was all his fault; he should have been keeping an eye on Ian Brown – it was his duty; if only the Welshman hadn't been too quick for him – too quick for anyone, spieling so an honest punter could never get a word in edgeways. But Natalie said no, wasn't his fault. It was all down to her that Ian was in this fix; she'd do anything to get him out of it.

And it was some fix. Marc Stone could not lie to her. Since the Taff had gone and fetched Ian some H on tick one day when he was short, because Ian's cheque from his ma wasn't expected till next day. (It seemed the Taff had become postmaster general where Ian's mail was concerned, which explained of course why Natalie'd received nothing from her man.) But the letter from Ian's ma did not come the next day, so the Welshman gets them a wee bag to tide him over and of course Ian is too out of it to get his cheque cashed when it does arrive, so they're into the beginning of the next week and the dealer of a sudden gets heavy and applies Ordinance One Nine-Nine, which is that for every day you don't pay up, you owe another 99% of what you owed in the first place. Now Ian had been allowed a day's worth of drugs on tick, all well and good; but the understanding was he paid promptly the next day when his cheque came in – which he had failed to do, and counting from the fact that he'd been supplied on Wednesday and now it was Monday, he owed the original sum plus 396%. But the original sum being £15, that gave a grand total of £74.50, which was more than your man had to his name, since his ma was in the custom of sending him £50 at a time.

She asked Marc how he knew all this – she was so grateful to him for telling the truth, even if it was so terrible – and Marc Stone said the Taff couldn't keep his mouth shut. Wherever he went, he bragged how he was ripping Ian off. All this got back to Marc, who still had a few spies left thanks. He grinned at her like a bird that's been battling a storm. She asked, what about Ian's benefits? Marc Stone looked tired and shook his head. The Welshman had been helping himself to those, as his 'consultation fee'.

Now she might be wondering how Ian's dealer could enforce Ordinance One Nine-Nine, and the answer to this was that he had the Light Brigade at his disposal – as anyone with a microgram of savvy knew, provided they hadn't come up here from Swanseashire thinking they were the Big Noise. If only Ian had checked with his friend Marc first, he'd have told him not to touch Dick Dealer with a barge-pole (and given him a fucking good talking to about heroin while he was at it, for that was an evil evil drug). But there you were. If you did not cough up pronto, Dick Dealer had the Light Brigade on you without compunction. Minute you stepped out the front door of your tenement onto the street, you were like to have your face slashed – or if the debt had got real big, no less than an arm would do or sirloin even. There were a number of one-armed junkies and flatbums wandering around the place courtesy of Dick Dealer's Light Brigade. Pitiful to see them.

Well of course, the Welsh hump now is telling Ian not to panic because he is the man to broker a deal with Dick Dealer, and off he goes leaving Ian twitching in fear and no doubt reliving that violence he was witness to in the cathedral town of Lincoln. Back comes the Taff with the deal, swanking like Neville Chamberlain. 'Peace in our time!' or some such shite. And this is how it goes. For £500, Dick Dealer will declare an amnesty and call off the Light Brigade. Provided the money is on the table the day after tomorrow. So here's what. Let Ian dictate a letter to his ma –his hand's shaking too much to do the writing, so let Taff be penman – and let Taff nip out and buy a stamp and post it, and go and brag in the Tap of Lauriston on the way over a clutch of pints, leaving Ian a soupçon of skag as a treasure hunt, hidden in a thimble with the Queen Mother's head on.

Well you could see what was afoot here; the whole world could

– excepting poor Ian Brown. Cos this Welsh fiend had scratched a deal with Dick Dealer to milk Ian dry. They were going to halve it on the amnesty fee, £250 each – and who knew but that the Taff hadn't written more than a monkey on the letter he penned to Mrs Brown, say £600 or even £650, so that he can rip off not just her son but also the son of Mrs Dealer of Glenrothes, Fife. And of course in all the excitement and joy of being spared his arm, Ian's let Taff let him forget to stump up for a certain wee bag, a debt now mercifully compounded to the amnesty figure. Consequence? The Welshman has to write another letter to Mrs Brown of Doncaster, asking for a little more money to 'pay some bills', aka, 'pouring oil on the troubled offshore waters of Island Dealer.' And after a few short weeks of this, her redundancy money is used up. Finito. By which time, the Taff has moved himself into Ian's flat (rent free), thinking to himself that although the Bank of Yorkshire has run out of credit, here's a tidy drum to use as his HQ.

Well by now, Natalie – oh, could Kennedy imagine how she felt sitting on the bench in the wind listening to this? She was in *hell*. It was like listening to the things about the concentration camps Ian used to tell her. The cruelty of it, the deviousness, it was hellish. The Welshman was a devil. And she felt worse than ever because she'd not called on Ian's mam for weeks. And all that time Mrs Brown being bled dry.

Kennedy, who'd been listening to this tale with mounting fear, doubts he dare not utter and obvious questions, was almost poisoned with shame about his recent defence of lying. He asked Natalie why she had finally named herself as Ian Brown's girlfriend.

'I try and tell myself as if it's about someone else than me. I've been over it so many times. I'm getting better. Used to name myself much sooner than that. I'm sorry, Kennedy.' She raised herself and kissed him on the cheek.

'Don't be sorry!' Kennedy said. 'Please. It made me less scared to know it was you. But what happened then?'

'Well I was hysterical. I was screaming at him to let me go and see Ian. But Marc said the Welshman kept guard over the flat. What's more, now he was pally with Dick, Dick had put the Light Brigade at his disposal. You probably think Dick Dealer's a really daft name, Dr K, but I couldn't think straight. Marc Stone said he'd been round himself, twice, to try and get Ian out of there and into a safe place. Been round that very afternoon. But the Welshman gave him a ten-count to sling his hook – that or get himself lopped. He took me to a B&B by the Meadows. Stayed with me till I stopped shaking. Then he left me there.'

Part IV: Secretarial Version

34. The original Arthur Mountain. Check the vision.

'If the stopline was here, we could get it on! He'd have to show and we could get it on!' Arthur Mountain told them, waving his machete. With Johnny boy marching behind him and Clifford languidly in file, he'd entered the clearing.

'He's cut down acres with that sword of his,' Johnny boy said, examining Natalie and Kennedy, hands on hips, 'and he's found nothing.' The insinuation that Kennedy hadn't been pulling his weight, brought him round unkindly from Natalie's tale. After all, the three of them sneaked off into the woods without asking him to help, did they not? And you could bet Johnny boy, with his customary well-bathed glow, had not been exerting himself like Arthur and Clifford, who were grubbier than before. Could she have finished? There was much that Kennedy wished still to know. Did she see Ian Brown again? And this green-eyed Taff whose rep was once so foul – what persuaded her to marry him?

'Natalie will get heatstroke if she's not careful!' Johnny boy added, as Arthur made a tour of the space, chopping air.

'The sun's going down,' Natalie said, stretching back on the rug. Kennedy was grateful for this frank motion. Above her black and violet pants, her stomach tautened.

'You should watch your mole,' Johnny boy persisted. Her pants were sleek, and neat and gorgeous; Kennedy hadn't been anywhere near them.

'I do,' Natalie advised him.

'Kennedy should wear a top-hat,' Johnny boy said, 'like in the French painting where the lady's bare buff. Or maybe not.'

'Oh fuck off!' Natalie murmured. 'What's the matter with you?'

Eyeing Natalie, Arthur joined them in his smock, hat tilted

back, machete tucked in belt. He wasn't half grubby: aside from the marks of earth he bore, there were one or two stains, his expression a mixture of bashfulness and audacity, like a boy returned from an escapade. Meanwhile Johnny boy had been to a bush on the edge of the clearing, pulled from under it his satchel and returned. So as he opened one of his notebooks, inscribed in three columns, they sat in expectation of a new account, and Arthur produced a third bottle of Woods 100, rising to open it by sabrage, splashing the ground in libation before pouring for the crew.

'We're going to keep to the middle column,' Johnny boy said, 'because that's where it's at and we've all had enough of him going on about things and trying to be funny, which is basically what you get in columns one and three. Middle column is the life of the foreman, and Dr Kennedy will understand that before we hear what happened when Arthur came to Edinburgh and encountered the Lord of Lies, we have to go back to the beginning.' Johnny boy looked Kennedy's way, so that for the first time, Kennedy felt a warmth pass between them and wondered, as he drank the black rum which he'd begun to enjoy, if Johnny boy had been preparing his notebooks and keeping his accounts with Kennedy himself in mind. 'We have to study the early life of the foreman,' Johnny boy continued, 'because as Aristotle says, "To understand a phenomenon, it is necessary to study its origin and its development."'

'You have never heard me describe myself as a "phenomenon",' Arthur advised him, looking over at Kennedy.

'I so detest it when you butt in!'

'Come by here for a *cwtch*!' Arthur Mountain patted his knee.

'Not on your Nelly in that smock! I just want to do my job and get on with my own life – what's left of it.' The secretary glanced again at Kennedy.

'For God's sake cool it!' Natalie told Arthur. 'Dr K will be thinking you're ashamed of your career. Go for it, Johnny!'

'Check the schoolboy.' Arthur Mountain was big, and he was original. One time in the late seventies, he and his pal Ravi Williams were watching Glamorgan versus Lancashire. A drizzling afternoon at St Helen's. Out of the beer tent came a man singing, 'Hi ho fucking sambo!' *Sine mora fiat justitia!* Arthur Mountain put his fist down that fucker's throat and kicked his bollocks into orbit; for he was ashamed to be a Welshman himself when he heard such language. It wouldn't let him be what he was, you see, tainted his status, when the breath of another was so poisoned. All over Britain, the National Front and the far right were mobilising at this time, and we like to think of this as Arthur Mountain's original political action. While the man searched the mud for his incisors, another group who'd been watching bought Arthur and Ravi a pint of Double Dragon each. We also like to think of this as the foreman's first demonstration in practice of the ancient ideas of *sarhad* and *braint*, which you might have had heard about in The Inventors' Arms one night, Dr Kennedy. The acknowledgement of kinship (*braint*) being the response of the other men (pints bought for Arthur and his Indo-Cambrian pal), which acknowledgement validated Arthur's forceful response to the offence (*sarhad*). It might be added that there was in those days no specific law against the use of such terms as 'sambo', so the reparation for the offence against Ravi Williams could have proceeded only by means of an ancient Welsh idea which the foreman revitalised that August afternoon. There's original! Yet within days of the event, Justice Kingsley was announcing legislation against behaviour or language likely to incite racial hatred. Who knows but that it wasn't the action of Arthur Mountain on this occasion that determined the law of the land? *Fortiter in re, suaviter in modo!*

Later, the two pals and their kin by the beer tent saw something wonderful: Malcom Nash of Glamorgan going for 34 in an over ...

'Bloody hell!' Kennedy cried. 'Is that true? He once got hit for 36 – by Garry Sobers. Which was a world record. Really?'

Indeed this was true. Very same ground as well. They'd had an idea Dr Kennedy would enjoy that, as a connoisseur of cricketing mysteries.

'But what a fantastic coincidence! That it happened to him twice – in the same place. Poor Nash!'

Don't be surprised to learn that Arthur Mountain was also watching when it happened the first time. A seven-year-old boy with his Bamps, August '68. The only man living who has seen an aggregate of 70 from two first-class overs. Lost be they who are unamazed!

Kennedy was amazed. It was lovely to hear this, after the terrible tension of Natalie's tale.

Strength. Originality. Curiosity. As it says on the tin. Arthur Mountain was foreman for curiosity too, and what stimulated his curiosity above all as a young man was the Fall of Swansea. Time had been, the town was prosperous as Bath or Brighton and the centre of British metal-working: copper, tin, iron, steel. Ben Evans' store was the Harrods of the West. Swansea looked like Knightsbridge back then, when the world was furnished with Welsh steel, from Russia and India to the United States, and the ships left Swansea Bay for Bilbao and Cape Horn, exporting coal from the valleys, tinplate and pig iron, bringing in copper ore, bully beef, nitrate, the Jacks singing shanties like 'Thirty Fathom Fran', 'Crossing the Line' and 'Bumbo 'pon Me Keel', while the Anglo-Persian pipeline carried oil into the Queen's Dock, and from there to the world's first refinery ...

'That bit sounds like a fucking leaflet from the tourist board,' Arthur grumbled, 'or Sunday night TV. Hasn't got the tone at all. Either that, or you've been peeping at the Internet, which I told you you mustn't do ever!'

'They're your words you great fool!'

'Well you're meant to improve them, shitkin. You weren't sent to Jesus College to come out with this pap about Harrods and bully beef. Dullest thing I ever heard. What's Dr K going to think?'

'It's fine!' Kennedy reassured them. 'It's extremely interesting. I'm learning something here.'

'Well he gets it all from a brochure!' Johnny boy cried. 'He won't let me look at *Wiki* or *Jane'sCranes* but *he's* always poring over a brochure with a woman in a big hat baking Welshcakes on the cover is Arthur, down on the carpet with his enormous arse in the air getting in people's way and blocking the light, selecting snippets to show off with.'

'I'll give you you little fucker!' Arthur roared. 'That's not how I've learned what I know. Making the whole fucking thing up you are. Give me that notebook immediately! Sit on my knee and speak of California!'

Time was, industrial men and politicians and academics, spoke of South Wales as California Mark II. This was in the 1890s and no chimaera either, because no region of Europe experienced net immigration in those years, not a single one, except Swansea, Cardiff, the Valleys. Check Ireland, England, Scotland, Italy, Denmark, Spain – people couldn't get out fast enough. And where did they go? They all of them went to the USA, or South Wales. Nowhere else on God's earth. No wonder Professor Jevons called it a second California. They were predicting a population of 20 million in *Cardiff*, and they had cause. Imagine that. Four times the size of London. So what had gone wrong?

If you were Arthur's age, you had no illusions the place was anything but a fucking dump. When you walked down Swansea High Street, you caught the spleen before you'd done twenty yards, a dragging grey despondency, fat men and women in daps, shuffling, smoking Embassy, spirit broken. Did not resemble Knightsbridge down by Castle Gardens nowadays. On Oxford Street, the council made a pedestrian precinct, so it looked like no one could afford a set of wheels or all the oil had run out, and men who should have been in work hung around by a concrete plant holder outside BHS or in the doorway of Woolworths smoking. In the four big docks, there was no water, no ships. His Bampa took him down to watch them shut. The old man knew the King's Dock well; it was where the tinplate had been loaded. Oil, tin, coal, copper, steel: plants and pits were long shut, lately shut or shutting soon, labour force liquidated. This was the Fall of Swansea.

And you could rehearse the stats like any Marxist history man, talk about economics till you were blue in the arse, but analysis of industrial decline in West Britain because of cheap foreign coal, ore grades and pay ratios, aluminium cans, or twenty-year cycles, did not represent what was wrong here in particular; just rationalised it – like advising a man with depression that everyone has to die someday. Economics had no feel for the character of a place. You needed something else for that, a different way of talking.

Arthur's Bampa introduced him to The Brooklands. They sat in the corner with Jack Morgan. A cop car or fire engine passed on Oxford Street. Set the old men talking.

At Llandarcy, the Luftwaffe set the oil tanks ablaze with high explosive and phosphorus; they dropped anti-personnel mines with time-delay fuses to discourage the firemen and civil defence, who were doing their bloody best to put out a 2000F fire without using water. Half of them were young women with sand buckets who volunteered when the men's fingers started coming off like wax. Jack's sister Nancy was there. Nancy's pal had her leg blown off at the knee, fighting the blaze.

Bamps told how Jack Morgan climbed into a burning house, brought out Mrs Manship on his shoulder. Sat at the mirror on an antique chair she was, trying to button her coat. She tried to make Mr Morgan go back for the chair. 'Bugger the heirloom!' That's what he told her. Ah, the Blitz did for old Swansea. The men supped to the memory, smoked their short cigs and coughed. 'Watch your legs, mun!' they said to Arthur. At 17, there was plenty of him, in The Brooklands or Swansea Jack.

February '41, it was night after night. Nazis wanted to smash us in the west before the Russian invasion. Blew up thirteen thousand houses. Boy, the stink! Whiffed like kippers, dung, rotten cheese. In your nostrils for weeks. When you come out from under the stairs or the Anderson, Swansea looked like a slag heap, or mountain pass. Some sailors got locked down at The Cuba, North Dock. It was a three-day blackout. When they'd drunk it dry they went up the attic and smashed a skylight. They had hold of a Gatling gun believe it or not because the landlord's old man was a Boer War vet who collected such things. They made some scrimshaw ammo, because bullets were rationed – which was bloody dull considering there was a war on; but they were very handy these sailors and they were firing this piece through the skylight along with a Very pistol, and they hit a Heinkel and brought it down. Swarming round Weaver's like flies they were. They wanted to starve Swansea out.

Arthur asked the old men about Weaver's. It was the flour mill that fed the town.

At Fairwood Common, you had girls manning two-pounders. They shot the *Luftwaffe* to fuck. Never came again. Last raid that was. Feb '43. Didn't dare come back after that one. Three of the girls were killed by shrapnel. Only volunteered the week before. They were on one and ten a day – which was 9p in today's money. Girls didn't get as much as blokes. Nine pence to man a flak gun, and lay down your life. Norma Jones, and Norma Lewis, and who was the third? The old men clicked their fingers to remember. *Numquam domandi*, that was the motto of the RAF group in Swansea: 'Never dominated'.

And in such talk, Arthur Mountain found the character of his town.

One evening early spring, the three of them were leaving The Swansea Jack. Behind his hand, Mr Morgan told Arthur, 'You should ask Bamps about the stopline.' But the old man wasn't telling …

Where were his mum and dad? His Bamps took him round the docks, to the cricket, the pub. Where were they when all this was going on?

In the autumn, however, Bampa was taken sick. There wasn't much to do for him except morphine and tea, drop of rum if he could keep it down. His lungs were the texture of heavy crude. He said a lot to Arthur on his daily visits, while the young man cut oranges for him to suck in quarters when the nausea abated. Told him about the 10th Cwmbwrla Home Guard, in which he was enlisted, the men he trained beside for civil defence, and a small detachment, taken from the regular unit for 'ops'; which got him onto the West Glamorgan Stopline.

He made Arthur swear not to let on: the WGS wasn't for everyone to know about. Mr Churchill feared the Nazis would invade Britain from the south, which was why it was designed. The WGS had positions, but was mobile and had to be. The men and women who manned it were a sort of shadow force. That was the secret of the WGS. He'd known a number of them, but sworn on his mam's grave not to utter names; and kept the promise, because breaking it would turn the stopline into a monument. Wasn't official see: if you said names, you'd be making statues out of shadows. In any event, if Britain had been invaded, these shadows would have pestered, obstructed and above all, killed by any means the enemy, with bricks, fists, elbows, cricket bats, bread knives, farming implements, poacher's traps, nooses, firearms stored or issued, shotguns, Webley .38s, the odd Sten and No. 76 grenades. And if Britain had fallen, they would have continued. That was the idea. Chronic resistance. What year were we in?

1980, Bamps.

Well if Britain had fallen, they would still be resisting, the shadows of the West Glamorgan Stopline! The old man coughed and Arthur held his broad red hand.

'I could crack a man's neck with one blow, Arthur.' From his fist he made a hammer. Coughing like a demon was behind his eyes, he gave the foreman one position.

The following weekend, Arthur Mountain made a visit. Taking the No. 14 from the Quadrant, he alighted in a village at the top of a valley. An autumn afternoon it was, still, sunlight unbroken. In the west, the sky was reddening ...

That day for all of them. Brown, Mountain, Kennedy.

He came down through a churchyard; headstones were so old you'd need Braille to read them. Solitary place it was, air bright; time seemed to gel; the door of St Teilo's was open; he felt the church might pull itself up and follow him, felt he was watched yet could be anywhere. Today was no longer the edge of time. Strange feeling: brought him out in a sweat like committing a dare.

'You ever felt anything like that, Ken?' Arthur Mountain said.

'I think so.'

Beyond the church was a dry ford. Mountain crossed and made his way uphill. At the top of the lane, camouflaged by brambles that still bore fruit, an anti-tank block glowed. He saw it manned by a figure with a cocoa tin, two wires protruding. There was a deep crack and boom and a red cliff trembled. As thunder follows flash that heats the air, it magnified his vision. A half-track was stopped by a home-made bomb; men in field grey and black rolled out burning.

Down the lane came the figure unto Arthur. They checked the

dead and gathered small arms in a sack, to share among kin, and poor folk in daps. When the enemy reappeared, Arthur Mountain was going to hit them hard, on a stopline designated No. 45 (position variable).

'Check the vision.' That was young Arthur's perspective on character. History and place were of the essence; and like all young men's visions, it was ideal to a fault, and quite fantastic. But it had the power to originate a story you could live by, if you were flexible about plot – and 'reality'.

Postscript. That explosive crack heard by the foreman on the lane bisected by the West Glamorgan Stopline was not imaginary only. The source was Barlands Quarry, which lay north of the lane. They blasted on a Saturday in those days. So his Bampa told him.

35. The North Shore Finance Company.

Over the way a crow moved, in scholarly promenade. Johnny boy
shut the book. 'What d'you think then?' Arthur Mountain wanted
to know.

'Where to start!' Kennedy said. 'It's all so – '

'Start with the vision, mun!' Arthur urged him. '"VS45" we call
it. Is it original?'

'The way you were having the vision, then heard blasting from the
quarry,' Kennedy shook his head in astonishment, 'that's original.'

'Why?'

'Because it's like you were prompting the world.'

'How?'

'The vision caused a real bang. The bang became part of it.'

Arthur Mountain hummed and sucked his teeth: 'Do you think
it's sound though?'

'In what sense?'

'Politically.'

While Kennedy was organising his answer, Arthur Mountain
said, 'Does it make me a fascist to believe in war?' Kennedy seemed
to feel his breath, words formed of rum and smoke. 'C'mon, Doc!
Give us your verdict in the Plebs' League manner. Have the sword!'

Kennedy stood with the sword. Over the way, Clifford winked.

'Some philosophers make a distinction between civil association
and enterprise association. Civil association is a form of society in
which individuals are free to follow their interests – within the law.
Whereas enterprise association is an arrangement of individuals, a
collective arrangement, with a common purpose – such as fighting
a war. One's a peacetime association, the other's for war or crisis.'

'What sort of theory is this, Doc?'

'It's basically a Liberal theory.'

'Excellent!' Arthur Mountain raised his glass.

'Hold on a minute, Lloyd George!' Kennedy said. 'Your vision was of an enterprise association, but you had it in peacetime.'

'Meaning?'

'Well that's not so liberal.'

'Absolutely! It's statist,' Johnny boy said. 'I've told him he's a fascist till my teeth ache.'

'Who's asking you?' Arthur Mountain affected to punish the secretary with his foot, and spat. 'Chop my foot off if I'm a fascist. I sharpened that thing this morning. Go on!'

Concentrating, Kennedy said, 'Statism doesn't necessarily make you a fascist. Don't forget that socialists favour collective planning. It's a characteristic of rationalist politics as well as fascism.' He paused.

'You don't believe in the state anyway. You believe in your town. And its character.'

'So it is sound, the vision?' Arthur Mountain insisted.

'What's important is that it was necessary,' Kennedy told him.

'Why's that?'

'If you can't come up with your own vision, you'll get dragged into someone else's.' Kennedy swished the sword.

Arthur Mountain laughed, they all did.

'By the way, what are "daps"?'

'What we calls plimsolls, mun!'

Through broken shell, the crow pecked at an egg.

'Check the young man in his first position.' Towards the end of 1980, Mountain became clerk at the North Shore Finance Company, which was, among other things – many other things, if truth be told – a cheque-cashing agency, for punters who didn't have a bank account, or people who needed cash fast. Of course, not everyone who needs cash fast is either honest or lacking a bank account, so that an agency handing over money to the value written in words and figures once the cheque is endorsed with the name of the person who's just passed it to the bloke across the desk, has to make sure quickly that it isn't a bent postman, a villain who's tortured a straight postman, a teenager who's got hold of granny's cheque-book, a new friend who's looking after the cheques your mam sends to help you out when you've left home, or some other form of psychopathic hobbledehoy, who's standing there with the gold bells flashing across their eyes like a one-armed bandit on the jackpot. Arthur Mountain was just the man for this. With his green-glass stare, Arthur Mountain could make cheats babble and run, like a hellhound was on their tail. He could sus a fraud in the woodpile the way he flushed out those doggers with his apple-johns ...

Kennedy was aware of them sidelong, checking his face.

Or if it was a resolute villain, a hardened hobbledehoy, Arthur Mountain would talk to them until they showed themselves, which was a trick of his. Years later, the government passed the Cheques Act (1992), which made endorsed cheques much more difficult to cash, an instance of statute replacing human practice, and not for the better. Surely it was preferable to rely on the wit of the individual in the management of transactions, than have the state impose regulation? (It's a matter of legend that the foreman's opinion was sought from Whitehall when the act was at committee stage, but no time for that!) At any rate, the cheque situation at the time we're concerned with gave Mountain the opportunity both to protect the integrity of the North Shore Finance Company, and train himself in techniques of character analysis and unmasking.

We could say a bit more about the NSFC, and will, because it was a lot more than an unorthodox bank, and may be the last institution of its kind in Wales. One of the models for it was the counter-community of Arthur Horner in the Rhondda. Horner was a miners' leader and after the Fed was busted in the General Strike, he turned a place called Mardy into a communist village – but not on Soviet lines. Welsh life went on in Mardy: you could have a pint or a sing song or play rugby; you could go and see a bit of music hall or variety on Saturday night; you could even attend the Conservative Club to play billiards or chat. But the spirit was genuinely communist. If you'd injured yourself in your work, everyone chipped in to look after you. The dead were buried under the red flag; Methodist and Catholic funerals were repealed. Being Welsh wasn't being part of

Britain in Mardy: it was being part of the international fraternity – or just as true to say sisterhood, since the women led the way in militancy. You'd get teenagers, no more than 13 or 14 years of age, going off to check things out for themselves. Wouldn't hear from them for months. How about that for independence from the bourgeois family? Like fuck the 'school run'! When they came back to Mardy they brought gossip, from Kiev or Volgograd. A lot of the young people from Arthur Horner's counter-community, they went to fight the fascists in 1936: Spain and Wales was one place to them, *pueblo*, international community.

So, for example, a taxi service was run from the North Shore Finance Company, and the controllers were miners; maybe they'd lost their jobs, or their lungs were packing in. They didn't want to live on benefits. They wanted to work. So that job was reserved for them. There was a lab there too, which was the adjunct of a brewery where the North Shore made its own bitter and mild, the latter being an outstanding morning-after bevvy. In the lab, a chemist was experimenting with isotopes of tin, for use in whelk-friendly marine paint. If that sounds whimsical, it's fucking hard luck cos it was for real. He could have had his pick of university jobs, but he preferred to undertake his research in the North Shore, nice and quiet. He'd been spoken of as a Nobel candidate. This was the God's honest truth. Swansea offered abundant supplies of scrap tin for his work. Dr Price his name was. There was also a *cegin* where you could eat bloody well for 30p, and a crèche. The crèche was open to all infants and toddlers; it was particularly favoured by the dancers upstairs. And there was a little theatre, where anyone with a good idea and a cast could put a play on, or just get up and talk about something they thought others might like to hear about, either for laughs or instruction. And there was the Nun Nicholas Room, which was a library and study area.

Here we had the second model for the NSFC, which of course was the Plebs' League, and all the other workers' institutes in the 1920s, where you could get a university-quality education, provided you had the patience to set your arse down on a hard chair twice a week for a three- or four-hour stretch in philosophy, history, politics, mathematics, physics, and Popular Front materials. Because these working-men's institutes had three quarter of a million books between them, as many as the college libraries of Oxford and Cambridge.

Well after a morning's work, the foreman might take himself off to the Nun Nicholas Room of the NSFC, where he followed up things he was curious about and made some pretty deep study into mediaeval Welsh legal concepts and the history of the Welsh kings, and wondered about the connection between these things and the modern world. He read too of the tradition of unorthodoxy, which took him back and forth between the Gnostics of the early Christian centuries and our own time. And he read at length about the Second World War, which was the event of events in the modern world, its great and evil drama.

No doubt his own vision had something to do with this, but he had the uncanniest feeling, there in the Nun Nicholas Room, that the war refused to leave the stage, and in fact had knocked down the walls of the theatre, not to let the world in, but to allow the play to spread, at the same time multiplying its cast, and reproducing its politics, strategies, values, battles and characters, with a demonic subtlety. Unless it was subtlety's opposite, and the multiplication and reproduction, the spread, constituted a lurid cartoonisation of the drama. Was it subtilisation, or a matter of kitsch, to find the losing side thriving all over the globe? What d'you say? South America, North Africa, Middle East, there they were. Had the Third Reich sophisticated its operations beyond the conventional-military and genocidal, or merely turned itself into a universal Ahriman-cum-Big Bad Wolf?

When Arthur found that top Nazis, for example the resourceful Otto Skorzeny, who'd bewildered the Americans with black ops in the Ardennes, December 1944 – when he found Skorzeny had chummed up with the Egyptian Presidents in the 1950s, and helped Nasser and then Sadat with the most excellent military advice; when he found that Otto Remer, loyal defender of Berlin after the failed generals' plot against the Fuehrer in July 1944, was hanging out in Cairo around 1953 with the Mufti of Jerusalem (who'd raised a Muslim SS Regiment to fight against the allies, on the understanding that Adolf Eichmann kept the Jews well away from their homeland), and filling the Ministry of Information with Nazi pals who taught the locals one or two lessons in practical anti-Semitism, along *Kristallnacht* lines; when he found that wanted mass murderers like Oskar von Dirlewanger and Eugen Eichberger, who'd walked in blood in Poland and Ukraine, and Gestapo torturers and ballistics specialists, had trained the commandos of Yasser Arafat, later of the PLO, beloved by lefties and actresses and loons in chess-board scarves, to make war on Israel, which commandos Nasser then glorified with the name *Fedayeen* – when he found out this sort of thing, Arthur Mountain wondered who had lost; and whether it had finished at all, because the racialist core of National Socialism wasn't beaten and it was not reduced. So he began to see the war everywhere.

'Check the traveller.' One day Arthur Mountain went to Spain, then down to Patagonia, to look around and see if he could spot cousins. He also visited certain battlefields. It took some effort to get a look at the Kursk salient, for this was well pre-Perestroika, but an old woman in Prokhorovka, who'd actually served as an armourer in a T–34 in the terrible battle around the village, when 1,400 Soviet and German tanks of the Steppe Front and Fourth Panzer Army joined battle in an area the size of Hyde Park, took a liking to his green eyes and decided he might be obliged (he spent a day or two turning the soil in her beetroot patch first while she watched him in her apron). So she got her nephew to take him up there on a tractor, to conceal the fact he was a visitor. On the journey, Andrzej told Arthur about the thunderstorm that had marked the end of the tank battle in the village (the Germans' last attempt to cut off the salient from the south west), when raindrops the size of pears hissed on the hulls, and the corpses of the crews, and for two days the sky flashed as if in imitation of man and the *Prokhorovskoe poboische*. At Kursk, Arthur beheld the remains of the most colossal stopline in history, concentric rings of tank spikes and dragon's teeth, stretching back for 100 miles into the Russian positions, in an area the size of Wales. Beneath his feet, the black earth crunched or bruised the sole, from rusting shells and shrapnel, fired from 10,000 Russian artillery pieces. The Third Reich was stopped here. Arthur Mountain went back and gave a talk on what he'd seen in the little theatre of the North Shore Finance Company.

They made a tape of it for him to take up to Fat Parry's '24' that evening. This was an all-nighter (and all-dayer) at the top of the building, and very select, though open to all. No contradiction here. If you could make your way to Fat Parry's, you were in. But the stairwells and corridors were as narrow as in dreams, so the only way to approach the 24 was in the manner of Greek dancers, you and whichever pals you happened to have with you, stretched out sideways, hands raised; many punters turned back before they reached the top.

Fat Parry was drinking rum and supervising a dancer called Barbara D. There was a burlesque show in the 24 around this time as part of the Sunday Social …

At the name, Kennedy's heart rolled.

Yeah. She was a top dancer, Barbara Diaz, got guys going like you never saw. Maybe it was her interpretations. The family arrived in Merthyr about 1903, from the north of Spain. 'Come and sit by Fats!' said the gaffer and they inserted the cassette of Arthur's talk about the Kursk stopline and sat to listen the three of them. Then Barbara D put 'Oh Yeah' on Fat's turntable, scratching and repeating the H-Bomb blast at the track's beginning till they all got the mood, and she rose and danced to the rainstorm percussion. Almost had Fats himself on the good foot.

He'd been lodged in the 24 since 1977 Fats had, around which time the corridors became impractical for him. Ever a portly man, he once kept a pub in Neath. On Spring Bank Holiday '72, a Hell's Angel stuck a sheath knife in Fat Parry's belly. Vibrating, it lodged there till Fats twanged it, pulled it out, cast it to the floor and said, 'Should have used a fucking harpoon, mun!' Then picked up a chair and cracked the Angel's skull with it. That chair he still sat upon; brought it with him when he opened the 24. His throne it was, a good oaken chair. Maybe it was the one Jack Morgan left in the blazing bedroom forty years before. It survived a phosphorus incendiary, it could endure Fat Parry's tonnage. He had a kitchen and WC there in his club, all the facilities, and you know if he was out of anything, Arthur Mountain reeled it up to him in a basket from the street, because there was a handy pulley system on the top floor of the NSFC, which was an old warehouse. He was a dad to Arthur Mountain, Fat Parry was, now his Bamps was gone.

So this is our portrait of the foreman as a young man. He had entered the political realm in a most practical manner that afternoon by the beer tent at St Helen's. He'd got hold of his own peculiar sense of history from the older men, and he could see under the surface of people. Then he'd backed up his peculiar sense of history with some deep and specialised reading in the library of an unorthodox institution. And he'd gone on his travels to broaden, or maybe *deepen* was the word – to deepen his historical sense. There may have been a lot missing, no denying that. But he could scrap, he was curious, and he saw things his own way. Which was why the world accorded with his visions, whereas anyone with a broader education than Arthur's would no doubt be trained to think that coincidences are explainable by statistics, people by sociology, psychology, semiotics; and that beings are what they are, not secretly something, or someone, else …

Though Kennedy did not think that.

Put the case as follows. A fat man and another man, and a young woman, standing on the street outside the North Shore Finance Company, they won't seem to anyone with a broader education than Arthur's unusual, on a December morning, 25 years ago. The young woman's fashionable, in the style of the time. The fat man has pale-blue eyes, and the other has a grown-out Number 1 crop, and an up-and-down voice, and they might be right wing, though the woman writes features on a glossy mag that's anti-Thatcher and is definitely to the left – but if you look at them like that, then they are only what they are, and as they are. For fat men and suedeheads walk most British towns, and many young women have hair that colour, and they have friends of all sorts, since it's an 'eclectic' business being young. Skinheads, and punks, and posh girls, and futurists and Gooners and Antpeople, and rudeboys, and gays, and Mods, and gays who dress as skinheads, and soulboys, and psychowilliams, and Teds old and new, and Sloanes and New Romantics and Headhunters – they're in and out of the melting pot, 'reinventing' themselves like billy-oh, experimenting with affiliations and stances, radical, individual, tribal, extreme. So these three are typical for 1980s Britain, if you look at them in a broad and liberally-educated manner – in which character has been swallowed by social semiology, or journalism, and perfectly digested.

For instance, that talk of starting a riot in Swansea for the young woman's mag to write an anti-Thatcher article on with lovely glossy pictures, that's just the way they talk in this year of riots, the jargon of a little party from across the border looking down their noses at Swansea, *comme il faut*. And their laughter – well, everyone mocks the Welsh. That's how people are at this time. You could do a graph or pie chart about the jokes they tell, and relate it to the width of their trousers, or the way they dance. You could make recordings on a field mic. The imitations of the mockers will sound like Indo-Pakistanis; or to be accurate, the mockers will sound the same when they do the Welsh voice as when they do a Pakistani grocer or an Indian GP. Listen: *duh-duh duh-duh duh-duh*. Sociologically, this would suggest minimal perceived difference between these racial groups.

So on this winter day, these three could be imitating Indo-Pakistanis or the Welsh, in permutations. For example, one might be doing a Welsh voice, two a Paki voice. Then they'll swap: *What's the code for Bombay, mate?* in a Welsh accent, then *What's the code for Pontypool?* in an Asian accent. *You'll never make the station!* Duh-duh duh-duh duh-duh! Then Arthur Mountain comes out the main door of the North Shore Finance Company and onto Wind Street, and he sees and hears them under the aspect of today ... but he knew their secret character, knew their history. Nothing disappears, though all is rearranged. Boo!

So they watched him, the young woman with aubergine hair, the bloated man with the pale-blue eyes and the Cockney in the green USAF flying jacket, gotten from a surplus store in Bury St Edmunds on a visit to bloat man and the squires of East Anglia. They'd have seen a green-eyed man with hair thick as the snout in a pack of Golden Virginia. His shoulders were broad in his black suit jacket as he came to them across the pavement.

'Good morrow!' said he to the folk on the kerb. 'Can I get you some lunch? We've got a very fine *cegin* in the North Shore!' And there he stood with his hands at his side, but his right foot was at the corner of a rectangle behind his left, heel raised, and he was ever so slightly crouched; his stance was good.

The Cockney laughed and in his up-and-down voice said they had had some lunch. In England. As if lunch did not exist in Swansea.

'Well you could do with some more by now,' Arthur Mountain said. 'Cos England's a long way off from here. You may start feeling weak before you go home, particularly in this weather. And your friend there, he looks as if he enjoys his food, if he doesn't mind my saying so.'

The young woman with aubergine hair turned her head to one of her colleagues, and then the other, then back to the first, in a kind of wonder. And the Cockney smiled as if the Welshman wasn't getting it. But the pale-eyed man wasn't smiling.

'I think the Taff wants to know, boss,' said the pale-eyed man.

'I fucking know already,' Arthur Mountain told him.

The Cockney smiled even more, and put his hand inside his flying jacket to feel for something in his pocket, but the girl with hair dyed purple and whitened face, and little pumps on her feet, she said, 'We can't just have it here! It's so lacking in style just to have it here!' She spoke such perfect English. 'There'll be all these fat proles going up and down and gawping, if we have it here. I wanted some cool people in it. And I need the photographer anyway. This is just recon!'

'As you please,' the Cockney said, and replacing what he had in his inside pocket, he looked at his wrist as if to tell the time – although he wore no watch. 'It can wait for later, Heidi. The Taff can wait.' He smiled at the door of the North Shore as if Arthur Mountain had never appeared and the three of them had been debating whether or not to go in, and thought they wouldn't actually. And so strong was his contempt that for the once in his life, Arthur Mountain did not know where he stood, as the three walked away down Wind Street.

The afternoon of that day, Arthur Mountain spent in the 24, discussing his humiliation with Fat Parry and Fats told him this and he told him that and he advised him. In The Swansea Jack that evening, Aubrey Evans, who worked in the Quadrant car park, mentioned a Cockney with a crew cut who'd caught his attention. Said something to the couple he was with about going to Doncaster to top a signalman. Funny way he had of putting it – like he was singing an old song. Then the three of them drove off in a Range Rover.

As Arthur Mountain made his way north, snow began to cover the country.

36. What's in a name? Low-power Light Brigade.

When he hit Doncaster, the snow was two foot deep. He found a hole in the fence by the railway tracks. Trains had stopped running for the weather. A little fire was burning down the line. An old man sat on a box by the fire, and Arthur Mountain squatted there and listened. A riddling cove he was, giving little away, but the foreman was well used to these *dynion hen*. A dog howled. Someone else was out there in the snow, keeping from sight. Then the old fella remembered the pale lad who worked on the signals for a while and said he reckoned he'd be heading to the end of the line before the year was out. Came down this way with a lassie once, to look at the Lye. Came down the other evening as well, to say goodbye.

With this information, Arthur Mountain was reconnoitring eastern Scotland by the third week in December. On Christmas Day he came to Edinburgh.

The first thing to do was find the signalman, the latter being the *casus belli*. We wonder if you could imagine Arthur's being tied to him as Britain to Poland in 1939, by a treaty that swore to defend him if attacked? Granted, the circumstances of hostility were not yet evident; but once he found him, the Cockney, fat man and Heidi would show up, in compliance with VS45.

The Cafe Royal was the bar for newcomers to visit. Here Arthur Mountain made his presence felt. Near the end of the month, he witnessed another young fellow introduced to a table in the corner and welcomed in such a way, you might think him a hero or a star; but this young man was no hero, no star. He was pale and wore a denim jacket, and he looked all about him, maybe for somewhere to run, until the table pulled him in. And after they'd made a fuss of him and bought him a drink and another drink, he took on an eager expression. The foreman was there the next night, for he could see what was going down in that corner.

This time, he kept his eye on the pale youth's sponsor, a fellow with bright eyes and his hair slicked back after the fashion of the 1940s, who patted this fellow and winked at that one and whispered to a lassie like he was pretending to tell a secret when everyone could see, there on the bench of leather that curved about the table below the tiled murals of Sir Walter Scott and Sir Humphry Davy. Then the pale youth came up to the bar to get a round and a big round it was. Arthur Mountain could hear he was a Yorkshireman as he counted the lagers, the pints of heavy and large nips. Here was his man. In the corner, the fellow with bright eyes had his jumper up over his head pretending to be a spook and all the company was rolling and making with the hands like the wheels of a train in the days of steam. The barman wished they lot in the corner'd fuck off back to Mathers.

To Mathers in the west end went Arthur Mountain, the night before Hogmanay. There he fell in with a weathered callant by the name of Mungo Haigh. Master Haigh told him where he could obtain work, a bonded warehouse in Leith having need of a clerk. He told him who the bright-eyed man was as well. From Arthur's description, it sounded much like a rude boy of Haigh's acquaintance, and this man about town Master Haigh named as if smiling through toothache. It was the Mathers in the east where he hung out. Across the city were two pubs of that name.

So New Year's Eve found Arthur Mountain in Mathers of Broughton Street, and into the bar came the pale youth and the bright-eyed impresario. Now Arthur was settled with some boys talking politics and the Celtic issue came up, so to say, how far did Margaret Thatcher represent the Scots or the Welsh? So the foreman, he makes out they're having a quiz and he calls out who can tell me where the Labour Party came into being? Pint on! Two pints! Someone says give us a clue, my man, so Arthur says the clue's on the railways. And with the pale youth in tow, up comes bright eyes with his patter.

For Paleface has been looking to meet like-minded people has he not? Bingo! Here is a like-minded person, if ever there was! Our pal here at the bar. A 24-carat Celt too by the sounds of him! Stone's the name, Marc Stone, Marc with a 'c' as in canny, clit and Christian! Introducing Ian Brown. Ian Brown, come on down! You know all about the railways. Where did the Labour Party come into being, hey?

Now Christian Stone is extremely eager, Arthur notes, to scoop the free pints – so eager that he'll have something sharp to say to Mr Brown, if Mr Brown fail to answer the prize question, or even pinch him in an unfriendly manner when they're alone together, for all his blarney and bonhomie. And indeed, Mr Brown does not know about the ASRS and the nascent Labour Party on the Taff Valley Railway, 1901, nothing at all, which has Mr Stone grinning hard like a shot man, in his belted cream raincoat; but Arthur Mountain's so glad to have found the South Yorkshire signalman that he buys pints all round to celebrate anyway and Mr Stone is cock-a-hoop, no doubt thinking that it is his charm that has obtained buckshee drink for him and his sidekick; and Arthur lets him think that, for he does not want Ian Brown to know why he has drawn Ian Brown his way: the tyke appears such a bag of nerves, the information would sore distress him. Strange way he has of looking about him.

At midnight they went up to the Tron where there was a big crowd, and Ian Brown, he watched the revellers as if they were all of them missing something. One more thing to note of this meeting. When Marc Stone was occupied with some young ladies as they came down the Royal Mile, Ian Brown says to Arthur, 'Are you one of the good people?'

They met a couple more times, the three of them, Arthur discerning that Stone was a watchful and jealous friend who had no desire to share Ian Brown with him, but was unwilling to look a gift horse in the mouth, for Arthur Mountain was keeping them all well provided with beer and whisky. Why Stone should have latched onto a quiet and frightened lad like Brown was a puzzle, until a night when Arthur was dining in Kushi's Lothian Restaurant with Mungo Haigh. The pakora were, famously, the size of grenades, which had the foreman speaking of military matters, loudly since he'd heard Stone and Ian Brown sit down in the high-backed booth behind them. This was an invitation for Mr Stone to come round and say hello, which that gentleman desisted from doing, confirming something about his amiability. And when Arthur went off noisy to the toilet, he passed a note to Master Haigh to listen what the boys in the booth behind were talking about. Well what they were talking about was Ian Brown's money, his mam, his benefits. Mungo tapped his nose, and Arthur now felt it was imperative to speak to Ian Brown on his own. The wish to help him was growing.

He managed this soon after, on a Saturday afternoon when Stone was out shoplifting, having gone round to call for Brown (Stone had been unable to prevent exchange of addresses at an earlier meeting, without showing his colours – or cutting off the beer supply). He found him trying to write a letter. His hand shook. Beside him lay a half eaten biscuit. Arthur took him for a baked potato and a couple of pints. With a drink, Brown regained a semblance of nerve. Arthur now asked what the hell was the matter with him.

Well they then had more palaver about the 'good people', and Arthur Mountain said frankly that if Mr Ian Brown had come to Edinburgh looking for good people, whoever the fuck they were, he might just have come to the wrong place, and that A Mountain himself wasn't a particularly good person, and made no effort to conceal the fact either. But anyway, what was it Ian was running from? Could he tell a not particularly good person that, please? So Ian Brown told Arthur Mountain all about the Lincoln massacre, and when he spoke of the Cockney with the shaved head and up-and-down voice, and then of the trial, the foreman knew that the latter must have been heading to Doncaster to murder a witness, viz, the young man now sitting beside him in the Cowgate. Then Ian Brown uttered the Cockney's name, and the name was Micky Voight. And Arthur asked how Ian knew this if it had never been reported, the skinhead's name, and Ian said that many knew it but no one else said it, except Scotch Corner.

And who might that be?

Scotch was a hedge-scholar. He knew the Inspector who split the train at Carstairs when the good people went off to Edinburgh.

OK said the foreman. But who was this Inspector?

Oh he was a top man. He looked after the good people, and he had a special way of dealing with the bad, did the Inspector. But even he – he couldn't figure what to do with Voight. Ian Brown sat with his head in his hands. In a while, he looked up. Arthur Mountain was still there.

But how had Scotch Corner known Micky Voight's name? This was the question. Was it told him by your Inspector?

No.

Ah.

No. What happened was this. One day Ian Brown took his anti-fascist mag up the line to drink tea with Scotch, and he scratched the name on a broken base plate with an old nail. Scotch could hear from the scratching what the name was. He recognised the name. Knew that name of old, did Scotch Corner.

And where did the name occur in the anti-fascist mag?

Nowhere.

So how did Ian Brown know the Cockney with the funny voice was called Micky Voight, if he didn't mind explaining?

Scotch, he must have been dictating it while Ian scratched, though he never said owt till Ian was finished scratching. Ian Brown held his head and shook, till Arthur administered a large Grouse and said, Not to sweat it. He believed Ian Brown. And what was in a name anyway?

'We've been worried about this for a long time, Ken!' Arthur called out now. 'This names palaver. It can make the whole thing seem a sham – know what I mean? Like there's nothing there in the first place.'

'It's the same question as my own,' Kennedy said with a full heart, 'except I've always known the names. Because they're written down. The characters were the problem for me. I know they exist, but some people think they're only names. It's like your problem in reverse … but I don't think it really matters. It doesn't matter at all, as long as we believe. Once we believe, being and names are superficial: how many forms does God have? And how many names are there for Satan?'

'You can see why we've needed you, Doc!' Arthur declared. 'J boy, pray continue!'

So Ian Brown, that afternoon late January down in the stone-floored cellars of Bannermans, said to Arthur with ghastly joy, 'Have you seen him as well, mate?' Arthur Mountain said he had. Seen his pals as well. A fat man with pale-blue eyes and a posh girl.

'That's him too! The blue-eyed one!' cried Ian Brown. 'The droog. The pieman!' And when he asked what Voight had said, Arthur replied that Voight said he was going to kill the pair of them. Then Ian Brown smiled and declared that Micky Voight wouldn't come for him up here, because Marc Stone had promised he wouldn't, as long as Ian did what Marc said. So Arthur was about to tell Ian Brown that he had better start doing what Arthur Mountain said from now on since Micky Voight was on his way north, when Ian's attention was drawn to the low window onto the Cowgate, through which Marc Stone was grinning with bright eyes. Then Stone came in waving his nicking holdall, to show he'd flogged all the books he'd pinched that day, except for one, a book of trains and barry pictures of waggons of all kinds, which he'd kept for Ian as a present like. And if Ian'd come round to Marc's flat now to get his present, then they'd be back down to treat Arthur Mountain to a few drinks for a change, within the half hour. So up gets Ian and away with Christian Stone.

Which was the last that Arthur saw of the pale tyke for quite a while, for it was now that Stone began to introduce him to the benefits of H, as a much superior means to beer and whisky of taking your mind off the notion that a merry Cockney was coming for you, in the company of a fat man with pale-blue eyes.

Mungo was Arthur Mountain's main man over the next weeks. Stone had warned him that 'Gear' Haigh was haywire, especially when whacked on the solvent he delivered as a salesman for *Lady Macbeth's Stain Eliminators*. Arthur took this as a tribute, surmising that Stone must have found Master Haigh not easy to rip off, corrupt or manipulate.

Presently, Mungo advised Arthur that Stone had moved in with Ian, and was supplying him and frightening him, supplying enough to keep the fear at bay, then frightening him sufficient to stimulate demand. It was likely he was using the 'Dick Dealer' stunt to rip Ian off as well, which was an old one with greenhorn junkies round these parts. So the foreman asked how that stunt worked, and Master Haigh explained that it relied on a phantom dealer with a phantom cavalry outfit that would come along and lop a hand off, a bum unit, or an arm, if there were any payment difficulties, which there inevitably were since the double D was based on shark rates, if Arthur kenned? But Stone, who fancied himself a bit of a film director if only he'd had the chance and hung around with arty types at Festival Time, Stone had his own version of the phantom cavalry, which he called the 'Light Brigade', though it was just the one boy, a schemey riding a pushbike up and down the street outside Ian Brown's flat at exactly the few times of day when Stone let him look out of his own window, and waving a cutlass as he went. In truth, the Light Brigade was just a pal of Stone's called Blaney who worked in the bakery off Lochend Road, who was in hock to Stone for cocaine, which Stone'd shown him how to turn into a super-high by cooking it up with a raising agent that was in abundant supply at MacBlane's place of work, this novel derivative certainly keeping Blaney well-wired for cavalry work – not but that the MacBlanes weren't genetic headcases, the older brother being a frequent lodger at HMP Saughton.

So this was the jam Ian Brown was in, all February of 1982; and the English still had not turned up as the weeks went by. But the day came when Mungo Haigh called Arthur to report that he just saw Stone entering Waverley Station as he drove past, so Arthur went round to release Ian Brown from house arrest in his and Stone's drum on London Road. Brown was very reluctant to come with him, and stared down onto the street white-faced, not knowing who to trust, because Stone had given him a number of chats about Arthur Mountain being not one of the good people, so Arthur made something up to get him shifted, which was that Marc Stone had gone off to meet Micky Voight and bring him to see Ian, then Ian said he wanted to see his mam and his girlfriend before he died so could Arthur take him? Could Arthur take him in the Shark, so he could say sorry? Arthur Mountain told Ian he didn't know what the fuck he was on about, and would he care to leave with him now like a man, and less of the dying talk too if he didn't mind? But Ian had no shoes because Marc Stone had swapped them for a pack of cigarettes one night when they were tense, so Arthur said he'd have to leave like that and he'd get him a pair of daps once they were up in town. Then he packed Ian's things for him in a Scotmid bag and took him out of there …

Beneath Kennedy's eyes, Natalie rolled on her side, left hand on her face, flank gleaming in the falling light. This was not going to end all right, was it?

At the junction of London Road and Easter Road where they were standing with Ian in his socks like a little lad, looking for a taxi, Ian pulled Arthur's arm and said there was the Light Brigade! And coming up behind them on the cobbles, bearing a cutlass at shoulder height in his right hand, mounted on a pushbike with cow horn handles, was Blaney. Well Arthur Mountain knew a cutlass was a naval weapon, not a cavalry sword, suited for hacking and close chopping in the confines of a ship's deck. The proper sword for the cavalry was your sabre, a longer-bladed weapon to cut down an infantryman below you or strike at an hussar or lancer wheeling past. He knew too did the foreman, from his time spent in the Nun Nicholas Room, that an uphill cavalry charge is a tactical error – and the gradient on Easter Road was hard going for a cyclist using only one arm. This conferred two advantages upon Arthur and his pale lieutenant. The first was that the Light Brigade had to get in close to make his weapon effective. The second was that his momentum was limited by the exertion of energy on his uphill ride.

Thus, in order to acquire hacking momentum, Blaney would have to cycle further up on the cobbled road, turn and then come back down at them, fast now, but with the cutlass in the wrong hand. Either that, or dismount and fight there and then. As the Light Brigade slowed in deliberation, Arthur Mountain had his long coat off, threw it over the rider's head and with a roundhouse kick sent Blaney, off balance, onto the cobbles on his left side, the pushbike on top of him, jumping with his full weight on the crossbar and frame till Blaney was groaning no more.

Then Arthur Mountain, he got Ian Brown away from there and took him to his own flat in Tollcross, just over from the theatre. As

Arthur wiped the blood from his shoes, Ian Brown tried to tell him that it wasn't a real cutlass Blaney'd been carrying; but Ian Brown could not tell real things from pretend ones. Ken?

37. 'Reasonable force'. Stone's jurisdiction. What was said in the guest house.

So that was when he killed a man, the grubby swain now holding hands with Natalie. What was the law on this? But hadn't all Kennedy heard made it just, even if he did trample him to death? Though when you remembered that a young man called Blaney had left his job at the bakery to cycle up a hill and wave a cutlass, and thought of the buns and soft rolls he might have been making on his last shift, it seemed – perhaps not less just, but terribly sad, because his mother might have been proud her boy had a job in a bakery, a job he evidently held down although this character Stone turned him on to crack cocaine. Now there was truly a foul being. Clifford said Micky Voight was the 'worst man there is', but surely Stone ran him close? And Stone was flesh and blood, an all-too-solid man of the world, whereas the status of Voight did appear to be intractably phantasmal ... so long as you didn't reckon your own experience into the story.

Well, Mountain did have this thing about war not being over, and in war justice differs from its manifestation in peace, when it comes to necessary killing; though wasn't this also the gangster's justification, the violent individual arrogating the authority that legitimises state violence? But surely Arthur Mountain had used reasonable force in dealing with Stone's cavalry, if the phrase could have any meaning – though under inspection, 'reasonable force' seemed a pretty stupid conjunction of ideas anyway. In what sense could stamping on a baker with a sword ever be said to be *rational*, even if the baker were equipped to chop your arm off? Wasn't it an act of primal will to stamp on him till his organs were crushed beneath the frame of his bike, rather than the behaviour of a reasonable man? Indeed, any modern reasonable man would in the circumstances probably allow the killer baker to mutilate him, rather than retaliate by trampling him to death. This was our sign of rationality, a willingness to die or be severely harmed when the alternative was to respond with primitive vigour. No wonder he asked if he was a fascist! But how was Kennedy going to respond if, or when, it came down to it, as he felt soon it would? Rationally, or the other way?

'Natalie's tale and Arthur's life converge here,' Johnny boy was telling Kennedy, with a nod at that couple. 'But the next bit isn't first-hand.'

'That's cool,' Kennedy assured him.

'Aren't you bothered if it's true?' Johnny boy asked him. Arthur Mountain hummed. 'D'you think I've done all this,' Johnny boy waved his latest buff notebook at Kennedy, 'just to amuse him and his friends?'

'A story can be true without witnesses to the facts,' Kennedy said evenly.

'Oh tra la la!' cried Johnny boy. 'Don't tell me you're just another post-modern smartarse!'

'I hope not.'

'So how can it be true?'

'By making you believe in it,' Kennedy explained. He'd underestimated the young man. Real skill and care in channelling Mountain's wild nature had been there all the time, alongside his salon manner. 'And there's nothing post-modern about that. It goes all the way back.'

'D'you think none of this happened, Ken?' Arthur Mountain urged him. 'All this we've told you?'

'You've made me believe it,' Kennedy told him. 'The three of you.'

'But do you think it happened?'

'That's not the issue, once you start believing. Once you start believing, you're in a different world. You aren't concerned with facts or happening – they aren't your primary concern. Maybe never have been. It's the meaning you're after. Like catching fish,' Kennedy went on, surprising himself: 'once you have them in your net – you aren't bothered whether they existed this morning or last week.' He saw fish quick and shining, their world returning without them.

'And does that go all the way back, Dr K?'

'Folk were sitting in a wood telling a story,' Kennedy said, 'from the beginning. History, science, the news – they all came later.'

'You're absolutely right!' Arthur shouted. 'This is why we've chosen you, Ken. You see the whole thing. You've got a primordial streak. Come by here and let me kiss you!'

'Behave yourself for Christ's sake!' Natalie said. 'Johnny boy's not finished.'

Now that day when Marc Stone went down to Waverley Station and Arthur sprung Ian Brown from the drum, Stone had gone to intercept Natalie, because he obviously did not want her to discover her boyfriend in the state to which he'd reduced him; nor did he want her taking his cash cow back to England. That was why he went down; but you'll remember that Arthur told Ian Brown that Stone had gone to meet Micky Voight and bring him to see Ian, which was a white lie to get Ian out of the drum? Well the irony was that later that day, Stone did indeed hook up with Voight and his crew.

In the meantime, Stone had deposited Natalie at the guest house on the Meadows, gone back to the drum, found that his bosom mate Ian had been abducted and that his cavalryman had been murdered on Easter Road. Late afternoon, Stone was in Cafe Royal complaining about these mishaps, and imputing full responsibility to Mr Meshuga, Arthur Mountain. His interlocutor was Mungo Haigh, whom Stone had called earlier to discuss the possibility of some discount spunk solvent for a massage parlour known to Stone, with which fluid these premises did tend to get maculated …

'Ugh!' Natalie said. 'You should be ashamed of yourself, young man. What a disgusting thing to put!'

'Arthur dictated it!' Johnny boy cried. 'Don't blame me!'

'You didn't have to go along with it! You've got a degree! I hate that stuff.'

'I never said put that word for word!' hissed Arthur Mountain.

'I wasn't there with Marco and Mungo. — It's him trying to sound Latin! — I'll fucking give you *maculated*!'

The row continued briefly, Johnny boy looking to Kennedy for support. The young man seemed to be blushing.

Anyway (like it or not) Stone's intention seemed to have been to show a new friend of his around the parlour aforementioned, with a view to some work experience, but he was so sore about the abduction and the murder that this was all Mungo heard about, Stone being quite unaware that Master Haigh was Arthur's friend more than his own, which served Stone right for taking the piss out of that callant by referring to him in company as a 'Keith Richards glove puppet' for the partiality to gear and commercial solvent that had made him look about 54.

Well Stone had been complaining to Mungo for a while when a posh English bird with purple hair came over and asked if she could look at the copy of the style mag that Stone had liberated from McColl's on his way — the one he had on the bar there. At the table she'd risen from, two men sat, a smiling man with a Number 3, and a man who wasn't smiling with pale-blue eyes. Now Mungo wasn't sure, but he thought he could remember Stone chatting to the young woman at the Festival the year before, coming on like Captain Culture. At Mungo the young woman looked like a princess going on her first walk from the palace and setting eyes on a frog, or wog. Then she starts reading the style mag and ignoring the fact Stone's patted the barstool beside him for her to sit upon, and you can see Stone's chewing his face like he does when things aren't going the way he wants with his bitches, and she looks up at the two men sitting over there and says, 'Here I am!', so over they come, one of them smiling and the other one not. Then she shows them something about inner-city riots in the style mag, which she's written herself, and Stone's nebbing at it with the two men, the fat one eating a pink crab-stick and sticking an elbow in Mungo's snitch as if to say, 'Fuck off, pal! You're not wanted here.'

Then they're asking Stone if Stone happens to know of a chap from Yorkshire who's come up this way lately, railway wallah, signalman or some such, for they really want to see him again, very badly actually, and Stone looks like the kind of gentleman who has his finger on the pulse. Stone, humming to himself, wondering what he can get out of this like, says he thinks he may know who it is they're after but what would their particular interest be? So the smiling man says that this railway wallah has been taking names in vain, for which there is a penalty, and the princess with purple hair says in her naughty way that the penalty is having your head cut off! Then the smiling man says this is Stone's jurisdiction by the looks of it, so it's up to him to produce railway wallah and the fat man with pale-blue eyes turns round and stares at Mungo and says, 'Is this coon still here?' Then he tells Stone to make Mungo go away before he cracks his skull like an egg and sucks out the filling, which is what Stone does as it's his jurisdiction, and they all laugh as the callant slings his hook; and makes his way hot-faced to Tollcross, to tell his real pals what he has just heard.

And what you had here was Stone in the role of gauleiter. As the Nazis conferred the title of Governor General of Poland on Hans Frank, filling a small man with love of cruelty and power, so that meeting in Cafe Royal made Stone a figure in the war that had not ended. This was Arthur's view as he heard Mungo out; then he began to plan their next move on S45 (northern vector). He had to tie Ian Brown's new daps for him, the lad's hands were shaking so bad.

Meantime, Governor General Stone had returned to the guest house on The Meadows with an update for Natalie. He gave her the bad news first, sitting on the bed smoking one of her B&H. She was in the chair by the dressing table with her coat on still. The bad news was that three English psychos had turned up asking for Ian Brown's head, literally like – they'd stop at no less. This was all linked it would seem with that massacre their man Ian had been witness to, which he'd blabbed too much about for a certain character's liking (though who could blame Ian for that? – Marc would no doubt have done the same thing, and named names – it was only human). But this character, well he was exactly the way Ian had described him in his talks with Marc – and Marc did now regret trying to persuade Ian Brown that this character was no more than a bogle or worricow, and *disbelieving* him, because then he could have taken measures to protect Ian from this psycho with the voice that went up and down like Mr Variety. And a serious headcase he was too, from what Marc had gathered just now, no mere right-wing hooligan such as you might find ten a penny at a Hearts home game, but an ex-marine. Indeed, the reason he'd taken so long getting up to Edinburgh after Ian Brown was that the Draft Board was on his tail because apparently (and this was top secret) there was a wop war planned in the South Atlantic for later in the spring, so this character'd been forced to make smoke and hug the dirt the last month or two. But now he was here. And he was no bogle. Indeed, Marc was not ashamed to admit that this ane and his pals had put the wind up Marc Stone himself, who did not frighten easy. That was the bad news. And it was pretty bad. Here, Stone came over and tried to comfort Natalie, who did not wish to be comforted, only to hear the good news, so Stone sat on the bed again and said wait until she heard this and maybe she'd change her opinion of Marc Stone.

It had not been easy, he'd taken a risk, but the life of his friend Ian, and the love Natalie had for him, was worth the risk Marc had taken with his own when he proposed to the English that they accept the head of the Welshman in place of Ian's. Natalie said, well, how had he sorted that out? It did seem to her poetic justice, since as Marc had been telling her at the station, it was the Welshman who'd been leading Ian into ruin and ripping him off, hadn't it? But how had the English agreed to it?

Well, when Marc had mentioned that it was difficult to set hands on Ian Brown for the reason that he'd been taken over by a green-eyed traitor from Swansea, the Cockney with the up-and-down voice said oh ho!, like he smelled a rat or the description rung a bell or whatever, then the fat man said, 'Sounds like a Taff we've come across!', and the posh bird said she hadn't liked that person one bit when he kept trying to make them come in his council flat for lunch, and he needed to be taken down a peg in her view. She was an educated piece by the way, Oxbridge University. So Marc advises them that to his certain knowledge, the Welshman had been promising to help Ian Brown get even with Sir Cockney and his associates, and making some big kind of political issue out of it, and

World War II all over again, or some such shite, and totally turning the boy's head with his theories and his threats and his promises what he'd do to the English folk. And they murmur to themselves in camera for a minute (at Marc's suggestion), and the Cockney laughs and the posh lassie from the University of Oxbridge is telling them some secret, then they ask Marc in again and say, Well, it's your jurisdiction. You organise the punishment. But make sure you bring us the Taff's head. It's got to be a head, Tyke or Taff. Failure is not an option. Fail, and the fat man with pale-blue eyes will be entering you for the wheelchair Commonwealth Games. So there it was. And Stone told the English that'd be fine. Leave it to him.

Then at last, Natalie knew he was a liar because the way he said 'fine' reminded her of a voice, which was the voice of the flatmate who'd told her Ian had a stomach bug when she rang his flat to say she was coming up, but it would be fine. It was Stone who was the flatmate, not this Welshman – which was obviously how he'd known to be at Waverley to meet her off her train that lunchtime. And she believed in nothing again, except that she must see Ian; and except that she now believed everything, because the things Ian used to talk about when they lay in bed after the massacre and walked along the lines, those things seemed to be true. And the good news was that the man grinning at her like a bird on the bed over there and unbelting his cream raincoat, was going to cut off the head of a man who was not Ian Brown.

'How did you get through this and survive to be like you are?' Kennedy asked her.

38. The Battle of Waverley (1982).

'People get through wars. Millions of them do. Why shouldn't I have? Go on, Johnny.'

Well Natalie wanted to challenge Stone there in the guest house, about the lies he'd told, wanted to make him understand what he was. She couldn't though, because she was depending on Stone's achievements as executioner to see her love again; so she had to play along, asking herself exactly how a bright-eyed twat with his trousers tucked in his boots like Hansel the Hun was going to set about cutting a Welshman's head off, all by himself. But it turned out that Stone had recruited a militia.

For it happened that the older Blaney was just this day out of jail, and older Blaney was mad to hear what had befallen his brother in the afternoon. Here, Stone paused to explain to Natalie that (tireless in his attention to the wellbeing of Ian Brown, and sick at heart to think what the H was doing to his body) he had sent round his trusted pal Joe MacBlane, a lovelier fellow than whom you could not hope to meet, with a parcel of cobs and sandwiches, and a bun or two, just for Ian to get some solid food inside of him for the love of God. Joe worked at the bakery down there in Lochend, and in the goodness of his heart had cycled up in his lunch hour while Marc was down at the station waiting on Natalie. Known Joey MacBlane since infants school, had Marc. Here, Marc bit his lip and looked at the rug and the floor a while. Well, Joey he had pleaded with the Welshman to let him come up to Ian with the food, which provoked mortal fury in yon green-eyed fiend. Next thing, he's down on the street, knocked wee Joe off his pushbike and stamped on him till Joe was but a puddle of jam and bone.

Well here was Joe's brother out the jail, drinking at Jimmy Clabb's in Fountainbridge, on Marc Stone's best information, so Marc had dropped in on his way back to Natalie and suggested a collaboration. Which had been neither easy nor safe for Marc Stone, since Billy MacBlane, swearing revenge on the slag who'd just murdered the family angel, was in a spirit to kill the messenger as well, and Marc had had to endure several kicks (rolling up his trouser leg as evidence, where aubergine bruises were gathering). But it was done.

Sir William MacBlane was sworn to get in a train of boys from Glenrothes this very night, another from Methil, a third fae Bathgate, along with a dozen of the best Gorgie fanatics, and spread the leprous skin of this Welsh slag around the town till every wall and monument was pasted with it. Well let it happen at Waverley Station was Marc's counsel, where your force is most concentrated (the spreading can wait till we've got the head). You bring the boys in Sir William, and I will lead the enemy into the trap. Which was where Marc required the help of Natalie, since he hadn't quite worked out how to get the Welshman to the killing ground. Here, Stone fell forward some way, head in hands. He was tired. So tired. Tired of all this. And if he failed, not only the English but Billy MacBlane and his boys would be requiring explanation, for it was Stone's jurisdiction.

Things can get worse when you thought you were at the worst, as it says in *The Old Tragedy of King Lear* ...

'That right, Doc?' Arthur Mountain enquired.

'Yes,' Kennedy said.

... because just when Natalie thinks she's going to see Ian again, Stone's involving her in murder. And from her point of view, it's not even revenge, since she knows full well that Stone's been lying high, wide and hard about this Welshman. What is she to do? Who can advise her? What would you do? Any of you?

There in that basement room in the guest house off the Meadows, with the green light coming in from the links, she knew that all she could do was follow her heart, and take responsibility, like her heart was an infant sovereign, and she its protector.

So she told Stone that he should ring Ian's flat and tell the Welshman that she was at the station with a big cheque for Ian from his mam, but it was no good the Welshman coming on his own to collect it because she would not identify herself unless Ian was with him. Now when she made that proposal, she must have been playing on Marc Stone's tale of the Welshman who would not let Ian out of his sight. And this vexed Stone, who sat there chewing his face, because the truth they both knew was that it wasn't the Welshman who was after Ian Brown's money, though Stone did not know that she knew; and he had to be wondering how he would get the Welshman to the station without demurring from Natalie's plan, which was so consistent with all he had told her this March day – and what if Ian just turned up alone?

But what indeed was she proposing? If Ian turned up alone, wouldn't he just cop it instead? She must have been hoping that MacBlane and the Cockney'd be so mad at being cheated of the Welshman, they'd do Stone instead, allowing her to get away with Ian. It was a chance. Can you think of anything better? One thing she knew, they would take Ian Brown over her dead body.

And Stone, he chewed his face and wouldn't look at Natalie until he smiled and his eyes shone like a bird on the sill, and he seemed to have had a brainwave, and slapped his thigh as if he'd been missing something. Then he went out into the hall of the guest house where was a payphone, closed the door and made a call.

'What it was that Stone had missed then remembered, that's something we haven't filled in,' Johnny boy told Kennedy.

Heart in throat, Kennedy nodded.

Well when Arthur got the message from Stone (obviously, Stone had rung Arthur's flat, Ian no longer being in the drum), what he heard Stone to say was that he was tired of all this fucking about and he knew when he was beat. He'd been keeping Brown here against his will when the boy'd obviously come to Edinburgh for a New Year break, no more than that, and now was the time to bring it to an end. The boy's lassie was waiting for him at Waverley Station, to take him back to Yorkshire like. There was a train at half seven. Marc would be there himself, because he had something to say to them about what he had done, and how his intentions had never been anything but good when he tried to introduce Ian to some like-minded people and help him forget his terrible past, but his own rotten childhood (here Arthur heard Stone's voice to tremble) had made him an abuser (here Stone's voice went low), an abuser, when his intention was to help. He wished to apologise to Ian and his lassie. He wished to apologise to Arthur himself, as a pal he was now likely to lose. And of course, he knew that Arthur probably did not trust him. Why should he? Well Ian's lassie had given this password, to show it was all kosher. The password was *Shark*. OK, boss?

Now Arthur Mountain readily saw the whole thing was a trap. Please recall, he'd given enough psychopathic hobbledehoys the bum rush in the North Shore Finance Co to know when he was being put on by a gauleiter who wished to deliver Ian Brown to his death. So he asked Marc Stone to get Natalie on the phone for a sec if he'd be so kind, but here Stone's change ran out.

There was no holding Ian Brown. He'd heard Natalie discussed on the phone and he'd heard the password. He'd been locked down and banged up enough in recent months. He had to make the station. This was all he would say. Had to make the station. This time Donny wasn't running. And Arthur Mountain knew it was a trap, but he would not let Ian go alone to face the English Front in his new daps, down to 98lb, skin and grief, God help him. They were in this together.

They drank a bottle of Woods on the way down, passing it between the three of them, cos Mungo Haigh was up for it as well, and damned if he was going to spend the rest of his puff flogging lotions for *Lady Mac's Stain Eliminators*. At the top of The Mound, Playfair Steps to their left, Arthur whistled 'Men of Harlech' and Mungo Haigh, he smiled for love of what lay ahead of them, whatever the hell it might be while Ian coughed sufficient to make himself rattle. Mountain's was a ragamuffin army, if ever there was. The wind dropped in the city, and Ian Brown said, 'That's how it was the other time! The air stood still!', and they descended The Mound, turned left for the station and came down the ramp, Arthur Mountain holding Ian's hand. A woman cried out and began to run towards them. Taped music was playing over the concourse. The wind that bothered the station had let up. The music was Acker Bilk. Over the way stood Marc Stone. From somewhere he'd obtained an officer's cap, field grey with a dark peak, under which his bright eyes claimed this as his day. The dark-haired woman came on and Ian Brown was trying to free his hand from Arthur's and croaking to her. In the still air, the clarinet played sweet. The dark-haired woman was yelling something at Arthur. He had to run. That's what she was saying. *Run for Christ's sake! Go on you daft bastard! It's your last chance!* But Arthur Mountain laughed, and would not run. He was so pleased to see Ian Brown reunited with his girlfriend, he stayed where he was, toasting them with the last of the navy rum.

At length, Arthur looked behind him, as Stone seemed to wish he would, and all down the ramp were Billy MacBlane's boys, the Gorgie crew this must have been, one or two gurning with hatred, ready for the off. Meanwhile, on the short platform left of the ramp, a local train had just arrived, to which Stone was trying to draw MacBlane's attention, but MacBlane was marshalling the boys on the ramp, and shouting for the Welsh slag to come aheid. Catching Stone point at the incoming train, the boys on the ramp, out of their skulls on Tennants and vodka and not heeding Sir William, rushed round and found a bundle of their rivals from Bathgate disgorging from the rear carriage. A same-side skirmish was the outcome, which reduced the forces allocated for the main target, who was standing on the concourse with his arms folded laughing his head off, calling to Stone if he was auditioning for *On the Buses*, and beside him, Natalie embraced our Ian like a child.

'This ane!' Stone was screaming. 'C'mon MacBlane! This cunt here!', as the boys from Gorgie and the Bathgate boys knocked shite from each other o'er the jazzman's clarinet and passers-by stared or looked around. Then among the crowd, outside the concourse newsagent, Arthur Mountain saw the girl with purple hair, and the fat man with pale-blue eyes, watching like a photo from history, but the Cockney in the light-green flying jacket who stood a little in front of them was signing or conjuring with his hands, as if to make a dove appear from the air. Ian Brown shouted to him, voice rattling, then steadier,

'I made the station this time!'

The Cockney laughed and called, 'But you brought him to the slaughter!' Stone was trying now to make the Cockney notice him in his Nazi's cap, with scoops of his arm, as MacBlane sallied forth with eight or nine boys he'd plucked from the clamjamfray, and a dozen troops who'd just detrained fresh from Methil. On they came towards Arthur, Ian, Natalie and Mungo Haigh, spiked up on vodka and amphetamine, and Arthur knevelled a couple with crosses and jabs but they were swarming about him, so he took the rum bottle off of Mungo and smashed the neck in the face of a red-haired messan in a leather bomber jacket who told him he was gonna die today, and over the way Marc Stone was screaming in triumph at his orchestration because Arthur Mountain was over-run though Natalie'd taken off her right shoe and trepanned a tattooed and bare-chested nyaff with the heel who was down now on the floor blood-blinded. Then Sir William MacBlane, he battered his way through his ane boys and Mungo Haigh tried to protect his chief with a kick like he'd seen one time in *Enter the Dragon* which made scant impression upon Sir William who was dropping Arthur Mountain with a sports sock filled with ballast that we reckon he must have picked up from the tracks while he was waiting.

'This is for ma brother!' roared Sir Will and as King Arthur sunk to the floor, he said, 'You've got me square then, bud!' So Governor-General Stone begged Sir William to desist from further battering and pulled out of his roomy trews a cutlass wrapped in newspaper which he drew from its temporary scabbard, face sweating and you thought he was close to heaving, when a woman's voice said in perfect English, 'Oh for God's sake, it doesn't have to be literal! You really don't know what you're doing, do you?' and Stone withdrew, sword at his side.

Then the Cockney in the light-green flying jacket, he squatted over Arthur Mountain, something long in his hand.

39. Dénouement.

Johnny boy closed his notebook, then he, Arthur Mountain and Natalie walked towards the woods. At the edge of the clearing they paused, and in the dusk Kennedy could see Natalie dressing. She placed her arm around Arthur and they went away.

'Like the three bears!' Clifford said. Beyond the rug lay the hamper, lid raised. Clifford rolled a cigarette and came to sit by Kennedy.

'What happened to Ian Brown?' Kennedy asked.

'Ah – Natalie got them all out of there, man!' Clifford laughed. 'Ian Brown was looking for the Shark, but they ended up on the 20.00 southbound. Ian she sent home to his mam; Natalie proceeded west with Arthur, on a relief train. He was at death's door. His skull was split, you know, and he was mutilated. She it was who'd drawn him into the trap. She felt responsible.'

'Yes,' Kennedy said. They were alive and together, Arthur and Natalie; yet Ian Brown – had the pair of them betrayed him? Or was he not meant to be happy, that pale youth who'd sometimes reminded him of his own life? Could he have turned out OK?

'It was bloody smart of her to find the train she got Arthur back on. Wasn't timetabled,' Clifford murmured. 'He wouldn't go to a hospital. "Take me to the North Shore!" He's saying this again and again. "That's where I want to die!" In the end, she told him to shut the fuck up. How in God's name they got him up to Fat Parry's, we'll never know. You heard how narrow those passages are. At any rate, they managed it. They made up a bed for him, and that chemist on the premises synthesised some methadone. There she watched over him.'

'And that was 24 years ago?' Clifford nodded. 'But what have they done since?' Kennedy asked, feeling brought up short, as if the text had run out in a book he'd been reading, leaving a thickness of blank pages.

'Well, bringing up Johnny boy for one thing!' Clifford laughed.

'What! He's their son?'

'Sure,' Clifford said easily. 'He was born late November that year.'

Should Kennedy have seen this? He replayed scenes between the three of them ... 'But Arthur – Arthur said his dad was a cheese maker. I'm positive.'

'Probably told you that to amuse you, Doc! When he's mad at Johnny boy, he tends to invent silly fathers. Maybe he thought it'd ring a bell.'

Like one of Falstaff's jokes. So much they said had rung a bell. And now, thought Kennedy sadly, the story seemed to be at an end. Yet these characters who'd become his friends, lived so vividly and violently, had produced a living character of their own, running the gamut of existence – while Kennedy had not. For his part he'd existed so pallidly, he could hardly ask what they'd been doing for 24 years.

Let the fish slip back into the sea.

They'd chosen him to listen though. Arthur said so. And they'd heard about his trouble. He'd had a story, after a fashion.

Clifford was waiting to answer another question, rolling a cigarette, so Kennedy said, 'Why does Arthur still talk about the stoplines, after all these years?'

'He wants a square go with Voight. When he finds Stopline 45, he knows Voight will show up again. Has to.'

'But it was in Edinburgh. Johnny boy told us.'

Clifford smiled. 'The position was always variable. His present thinking is that No. 45 starts in these woods here, tracking south east across the county. Passes through the station where your mother lives.'

'That's why I saw him there. Mothers' Day. He was hanging round on the rolling stock.' Perhaps the story wasn't over.

'Probs,' Clifford said. 'Though he might have been killing a couple of birds with one stone. When they got married, he promised Natalie a Shark as a wedding present. She's been hankering for one.'

'Right,' Kennedy said.

'Like Richard Burton bought Liz Taylor her own jet, Natalie asked for a Shark. Fraction of the price.'

'Yes,' Kennedy said.

'Natalie, she'd heard I think there was a Shark in the siding at your mother's station.'

'Was it the original one?'

'Couldn't say, Doc. She travels about looking for them. Round the network.'

'Yes.' You could almost see the whole thing as the enthusiasms of a couple, such as might be prominent in the local church, in an English town; though even there they would retain their distinction.

'Who's the woman with purple hair, though?' Kennedy asked.

'And she's getting older, like the rest of us,' mused Clifford. 'Heidi is getting older.'

'But who is she?'

'Her old man's an East Anglian squire; her mother was a German hippie.'

As Kennedy pondered this, Clifford said, 'Did Arthur tell you about the 3 BT? Berlin-Baghdad-Bury St Edmunds triangle?'

Here was another tangle. It kept the story going.

'Yeah,' continued Clifford, 'a dark business that one. Very dark. *Darkissimo*. It was a supply line of chemicals to the Arabs for anti-Israel deployment. There's a farm in Suffolk that was a camouflaged plant. The fat man was the security gaffer there. Stopped people turning up to buy eggs. It's near her old man's land. Voight used to come up there on visits. It was big NF territory. He and the fat man were Front officers. They left for the British Movement. Then they got into C18. They don't stand still.'

'So she's a neo-Nazi?'

'Heidi Walsh? Not she! Check her website. Heidi is most ironic about extremism.'

This of course was news to Kennedy, who'd never searched the names. 'She takes irony a long way, does she not, hanging round with people like Voight and the fat man?'

'I guess so, Dr K.'

'I saw her in the pavilion at Oxford,' Kennedy said. 'The day I met you.'

'I know. She's an Oxford graduate. As a young lady, she won a prize: student journalist of the year. Distinguished herself with some droll reviews of the Edinburgh Festival around 1980, then she started reporting on the riots, from a youth point of view. No doubt it was round that time she first encountered Micky Voight. They hang out to this day.'

'She's still a journalist?'

'Indeed!' Clifford laughed. 'One of your columnists – don't you read the papers, Doc?'

'I try and avoid them,' Kennedy said. 'But what's her interest really? What does she see in him?'

'That he's the worst man there is?' Clifford suggested. 'Journalists like superlatives!'

Kennedy recalled the descriptions of Voight. Such a cold manifestation of evil, a strange sort of skill in his manner, as if the world were only a stage and he came on from elsewhere. No wonder Heidi hung out with him. Kennedy shuddered. He had the attraction of the otherworldly; there are foul beings among them, as well as saints, and they too have their zest …

Unless it was the media where evil had found its home, and not the other way round. For every time you did read a paper, you were bullied by opinions, orthodoxy, recommendations, lists, provocation, cliché; threatened with the most violent dedication to the present: all of it meant, none of it meant, the whole of it a sham that assumed total authority over our being, our thoughts and hearts. But wasn't this the subtilisation of frank tyranny? So that Nazis now hung out with journalists because they'd realised that the journalist was a sort of *überfrau*, compared with the Nazi whose violence was so crude as to appal our civilisation. If cruelty was your way, let journalism be your vocation, irony your tune.

'They go around in a 4x4,' Clifford said now, 'a one-car cavalcade. Arthur's been trying to blow them up. They were down in Swansea on a recon lately. He torched the hotel they'd been staying in. Penalty for collaboration. Fixed the tank on their vehicle too, with a little piece of sodium. An old Provo trick! They were on farmland near Cardiff when it went off. Voight's canny though, ex-services. He could hear something amiss with the tank. Got them out of there just in time.'

Would have been the burned-out vehicle Kennedy saw from the train. Who were the three checking it? The black 4x4 that cruised them at Stamford Bridge when Arthur threw the padlock, must have been a replacement. But why could these two sides not get at each other? There seemed to be a great deal of circling and reconnoitring, particularly if this had been going on for a quarter century. Was it a game after all, like Uncle Toby and Corporal Trim's garden war? Or would the discovery of Stopline 45 settle everything?

'What happened to Marc Stone?' Kennedy asked.

'God knows. He's probably still ripping people off.'

'I came to look for you at the university, the day after the cricket. Bumped into Voight instead.'

'Sorry, man. I was helping Arthur with something that afternoon.' Clifford felt about him in the grass for his rolling tin. 'Did he say anything to you?' he asked Kennedy at last.

'He asked me if I wanted to know.'

'Yeah,' Clifford said, emitting smoke. 'D'you know what a "know" is?'

'The noun?'

'Yeah.'

'I can't say I do.'

'Means an image of a living person, a phantom image.'

'Ah!' Kennedy said, surprised. He heard Voight's accent: *D'you wanna know?*

Two crows flew up to an oak. Clifford rose and lifted the hamper.

Part V: To the Wars

40. Success.

January 24th 2007. On a night of wild gales, their first child was born. Kennedy noted visitors comparing the lad's face and Barbara's. Well at least his eyes weren't green ... though Kennedy might not have minded being usurped, so long as it kept a trace of the foreman in his arms, filling his ear with little blasts of genius.

The picnic was their last meeting. No more of those hooded youths, bearing invitations. For a while, Kennedy haunted The Inventors' Arms, but Mountain never again showed up. Why indeed should he? The story was over; Kennedy'd heard it out that afternoon in Epping Forest. So he'd not have objected altogether to holding a tiny Arthur. From a website, he discovered green eyes could take 18 months to appear. Now and then, the infant watched him like the Welshman that first time in the Gents'; quietly, Kennedy repeated his barbarous greeting.

Considering paternity, why was it that Johnny boy had not reminded him of Arthur? As fine-boned in the face as his mother Natalie, that young man, with her blue-black eyes; his dad he bore no sign of. Could Natalie have conceived him with Ian Brown whom she'd loved so bravely, on that last train south? The d.o.b mentioned by Clifford made it possible. A snake stirred in Kennedy's breast. Going by that date, it could have been in the guest house with Marc Stone, who may have forced her, or tricked her, or perhaps she'd done it with him in order to gain some advantage; for it was out of the question that she should desire the bright-eyed liar. Terrible image, the two of them in that room with the greenish light. Had Arthur Mountain entertained this? Kennedy recalled his words on free love and, as Barbara looked on, he jiggled his son.

Thinking back to their arrangement, the presence of this creature must indicate the termination of Kennedy's project. Kennedy was cool with that: he did feel he had come to the end of something, even if it wasn't quite clear whether the issue he'd been absorbed in had been solved, or grown out of. The whole thing was fading now, though after Arthur and his band took their leave, his ideas had glowed a while longer.

So in the fierce summer of 2006, Kennedy actually got down to a proposal of the Falstaff book. The words appeared of their own accord; as he sat light-hearted in his workroom, Barbara brought him rum (he was tippling more than he used to). The proposal having been sent to an academic press, he left the university mail room rubbing his hands, glad to be shot of the bastard.

Months passed. On the occasion of their son's five-week birthday, Kennedy received a reader's report. Recalling words of Arthur Mountain, he worked up a fine contempt about academic publishing as he ripped it open. He was in the office at the time. Cy Frazer came to look over his shoulder. This called for a drink, and he wasn't hearing no! The press was willing to consider contracting Kennedy to write his book, since it was evidently so attuned to the recent resurgence of theoretical interest in character, and indeed appeared to offer a significant extension of current work in the field. Kennedy, Cy and Hannah went to the Belvedere Hotel to drink champagne. Barbara made the baby congratulate him; phoned her friends with the news.

One thing after another. The following day, they took Master Kennedy for his first trip to the West End, visited John Lewis to order a fridge and drank coffee in the sun in St Christopher's Place. Returning, Kennedy found urgent messages from Hester Pygg, beseeching him if it was at all possible to speak at 'Character Now', on the first of April.

★

He knew his paper by heart, so bought a miniature and drank to old friends. Did Natalie take his name when they married? Look out for containers. Rain slapped the carriage window in grey curtains. Kept faith with Ian Brown, though she ended up with Arthur. Would he see her again? The trolley man passed; he bought more rum. Silver drops shivered and raced. He examined them, one pair, another. Pals. Arthur and Natalie. Barbara, me! Was he losing his mind? All right with Kennedy. At Port Talbot, he watched for orange fire; rain crossed the window in massed waves.

An audience of 80 or more heard what Kennedy'd discovered in the last year; their faces bright, nearly child-like. As he concluded, the chair caught him in her white smile. Thankfully there was time for questions.

Someone dug the connection he was making between character, environment and institution. How had he hit on that?

All he'd meant was that the fear that takes us to church, we may lose on the mountain – nothing more than that really.

They murmured.

Then a woman who was sitting where that woman in the tweed cap was last year, she asked if his commitment to character embarrassed Kennedy professionally because she thought it was damned courageous; so Kennedy laughed and said that when a 'presumptuous and unruly Welshman' (to paraphrase one of Shakespeare's sources) had you at sword point in a forest and threatened you with extreme violence if you failed to explain without academic jargon why Falstaff was like a wrinkled apple, that took some courage; but since no one had a sword with them today, as far as he could see, she shouldn't overestimate his bravery.

They smiled, and nodded.

So an American in a shirt and tie asked a hard question about the social dimension of Kennedy's project and Kennedy said sir, we are all of us plebs, and characters our mistresses, and masters.

Someone laughed, and someone else did, and another asked where she could find some characters, so Kennedy said, 'This town's as good a place as any.'

At the Cefn Bryn reception, the American hovered by Kennedy and called *him* sir, and a gathering of people waited to ask extra questions beneath the framed photo of Badfinger, and the less academic the answers he gave, the more they were impressed, so they passed him their cards, or put his e-mail on their phones, and what was he doing that evening? He would come along to the Bodega?

In his heart, Kennedy wished to go and stand by the sea, to hear that voice rise from the little boat, or wander the city till he found his friend. But went along to the Bodega.

Which lay at the bottom of Wind Street. A young woman from Warwick in a beautiful raincoat walked eagerly beside Kennedy, apprising him of her own research. She so loved the way he'd said this town was as good place as any to find characters. What had he meant exactly? He paused at a large notice whose bottom edge was fluttering in the sea breeze. The young woman looked on with interest, as Kennedy studied it. Fastened to the door of a building, the notice advised that the North Shore Finance Company had been struck off the register held by Companies House and dissolved.

Trading ceased from March 31st 2007.

'Are you OK?' the young woman was asking Kennedy. 'Have I said something wrong? What is it?'

41. S45. Fuzzy Felts.

You could have climbed to Fat Parry's like a dancing Greek, sat up there with the foreman. Between the last of March and first of April, he took his leave; remoter now than the stars, the other side of the wind ... Women's voices called Kennedy back to the A12. Could they stop for flowers? Mama wanted trifle sponges. They were visiting Kennedy's family, with Barbara's mother and the baby.

How much character did this creature contain? Like primitives at a fire, they gathered round. Barbara's dress was the colour of Jane Avril's, or the orange bar on the flag of New York, button-fronted. She whispered to Kennedy's old man: there was something else to toast. When his sister'd re-filled their glasses with cava, they heard the full tale of Kennedy's achievements. Barbara told it well.

The old man was stuck in the recliner with his grandson, so after lunch Kennedy set off alone. Leaving he looked in at the window; Barbara mouthed, Goodbye! Did she know he'd pollute the child one day? Words, numbers, knots, hours – it wouldn't stand a chance.

Roads with the names of English poets led through the estate. When he passed the first field by the lane, rapeseed glowed through gaps in the hedge. The air was still, rather thick for the season, yellow light blotting the covering cloud. Thinking himself back to the beginning, he sensed another just beyond ...

'Come with me to the stopline!'

'Is it you?'

'Course it is!' Arthur Mountain called back, and coughed. 'There's a hole in the hedge by here look! Come through, butty!'

So Kennedy went through the hedge and there he was in his leather overcoat, shaking hands, embracing, Kennedy all choked up, a little lad who can't explain what the matter is, sniffing old smoke off the black hide.

'There, there!' Arthur Mountain coughed again. Hands on knees, he controlled his breathing, blowing like a trumpeter.

'Are you ill?' asked Kennedy, ashamed of weeping.

'Hold on,' panted the Welshman. 'Hold on a minute, mun!' Presently he stood straight. 'I've had this fucking emphysema.' Reaching inside his coat, he produced a pump of grey plastic from which he removed the lid, then inhaled loudly two or three times. 'That's better. Natalie got me this. What a woman! Latest steroids. Like a new man I am with this gear!', and he threw the inhaler into the hedge.

'But don't you want it?' cried Kennedy. 'You're sick. You mustn't throw it away!'

'I'll give you sick!' Arthur Mountain lit an untipped cigarette which he seemed to smoke halfway down in one puff till its tip glowed red in the still air. 'Didn't have you down as a decadent, Ken, but I fear that's what you've become, harping on the other fellow's illness.'

'Let me keep it for you!' Kennedy hurried to pick the object from the hedge, placing it in his pocket.

'Well I won't need it again. Come on, Doc.' They began to walk down the side of the yellow field. 'How's your wife, by the way? You never introduced me in the end. With you this afternoon is she?'

'She's at my mother's. With the baby. We've got a son now.'

'Ah. Congratulations!'

'Where's Natalie today?' Kennedy asked politely.

'She can't be here, Ken.' Ahead of them, the spire of the church came into view.

'What about Johnny boy?'

'Who?'

'Johnny boy.'

Your secretary. Your son.

'Do you remember him?' Here, Mountain drew a white plastic box from his pocket, fitted it with a tube into which he blew with force, then asked Kennedy to read the figure to which his breath had raised a little green arrow. He'd scored over 500. 'Attaboy!' the Welshman cried. '80 it was, before I took my inhaler.'

Kennedy, who now had the feeling of talking to an old man, said, 'Of course I do.'

'He's not well either,' Arthur replied. They were approaching the end of the field. 'Johnny bach.'

'What's the matter?'

'Down with it, he is. I suppose his mam's looking after him. It's bad some days.'

'Down with what?'

'Voight got to him.' The hedge was much lower here, and a 4x4 driven at high speed passed them, turning right past the church then continuing up the sloping footpath across the field where Kennedy'd imagined other times. 'Voight's running wild now. That's cool. The tide'll turn. Like late '42.'

'Can't you tell the police?' Kennedy asked, wondering about Voight's effect upon the young man.

'From all we talked about in our time together, I'd have thought you'd recognise the futility of that question, Doctor Kennedy.'

'Sorry,' Kennedy said, grateful that Arthur seemed to be in possession of his memory again. They crossed the hedge at the field's bottom and back onto the road.

'When a war's on, you don't tell the fucking cops, do you? Outside their jurisdiction it is. Well outside. Don't forget, I've killed a man myself.'

They passed the church and at the kissing-gate which led onto the footpath, Kennedy said, 'I wish I could have seen Natalie again!'

'Saw quite enough of her when she took her clothes off in the woods, didn't you?'

Kennedy cleared his throat: 'She was just sun-bathing.'

'Didn't you fancy a jump, mun?' Arthur came to a stop to wink at him.

'She wasn't my wife,' said Kennedy truthfully.

'Wouldn't have stopped most blokes.'

'Maybe not.'

'You're an uncommon fellow, Ken! Always thought so,' Arthur

Mountain decreed. 'You just wanted to see Natalie again out of friendship?'

'Yes. I thought she was a character.'

'You'll never see her like again either.'

'Why not? Where is she? Where's she gone? You said she was looking after Johnny boy.'

'She's probably taken him out for an Easter egg. Unless they've gone to Yorkshire.'

Dismayed by this vagueness, for all that it seemed plausible, Kennedy said, 'Why should she go up there?'

Arthur cleared his throat loudly: 'To look in the railway museum. Her and Ian Brown's mam go fishing sometimes. Pals.'

'But won't she come back?'

'Not today, mun.'

'But she's your wife!' Kennedy was close to despair. 'Why don't you know where she is?'

'Well when I asked you once if you kept an eye on your wife,' Arthur Mountain said, with an air of respect, 'you told us all you didn't. So I don't either. Learned from you, Ken.'

'But you're not supposed to learn from me! I'm a failure,' Kennedy explained ardently.

They passed through the gate.

'You thought to yourself once, quietly like, that I can't love,' Arthur said. 'I know everything you've thought, Dr K. But I loved Natalie, and I loved her the best I could because I owed her my life. I loved her the best I could because I knew we were at war together. And in war, you don't expect people to make it to their natural span. Don't expect it yourself, either.'

'What!' exclaimed Kennedy in panic. 'You said she was taking Johnny boy for Easter eggs! Just now you said that, or fishing with Ian Brown's mother. Now you're saying she's dead!' He gripped Mountain by the lapels then began to beat his big face, weeping: 'Why are you just saying anything? Why are you speaking like this? Why don't you care anymore?'

The Welshman let himself be punched a while, then pushed Kennedy off who stood gulping beside the sloping field. 'Here!'

Mountain produced a bottle of Woods from inside his coat. 'Lucky it isn't broken, mun! Have a drink of this. Just firing you up with that speech I was, Ken. Glad to see you've got it in you. Proud of you. You've got love in you, you've got guts.'

Kennedy swallowed the brown-black liquor, burning. Never in his life had he struck a man. A flock of dark birds rose like beaten dust from the wood at the top of the field. Wiping blood from his lip, Arthur Mountain watched them.

'Tell me something else about her,' Kennedy said.

'As a matter of fact, I'm expecting her. Be along any minute, Natalie could. If she's found the Shark. Her and J boy. Along by there through the flowers then up the path. They'll be glad to see you. Give you a ride. Like that?'

'Brilliant!'

Then Arthur put his hand on Kennedy's heart. 'You've proved yourself now. Proved yourself to me. Are you sure you want to come on? There'll be no disgrace if you turn back, Kennedy. You've got the kid to think of.' They had another belt of rum.

'I'm coming with you,' Kennedy said. 'To the wars.'

'Want me to hold your hand?'

'No.' Kennedy moved on up the path beside his friend till they were abreast of the wood, and the next field dipped broadly away beneath them. Among the trees flashed bluebells, like fairies were pranking, and below in the field was the white stony surface that had shone at Kennedy, then disappeared from sight as he moved along the track. The field was now sown with a stubbly crop, allowing the structure to emerge fully. It was a squat little house.

'Pill-box, that is,' Arthur said. 'Stopline 45: position identified. Knew it'd cross these parts.' Winking at Kennedy, the Welshman raised his hands in his coat of black, chanting the words from the Tower of the Ecliptic.

'We can get it on here,' Arthur Mountain decided. 'That wood,' they were now descending the field, 'will make an admirable killing ground. You can take a man out with a bluebell, couple of sharpened twigs!' The ground was uneven, dipping. 'So the farmhouse, right, that's their forward HQ.' He indicated the building at the bottom of the field, where timber was stacked beside the path as it passed under a gate and into a field beyond, and a George Cross hung from a post.

Beyond the gate was parked the black 4x4.

The exterior of the pill-box was scratched and graffitied. Kennedy would have liked to check for inscriptions but Arthur took him inside, where it was littered with cigarette ends and condoms. Here they drank more rum and Kennedy smoked one of Arthur's untipped cigarettes. The place smelled lightly of piss. Together they looked through the slit. 'Imagine them coming up the field now,' Arthur instructed. 'Can you see them? Hear them laughing? It's a gas being an invader. Like being a rapist. Already been through your mam's house. Imagine em with Barbara and the kid! Can you hear them yet? They've occupied southern Essex. What are we going to do with them, butty?'

'Do we have a weapon?' Kennedy wished for a machine gun with a curved mag, to fire through the slit at the laughing men.

'That's a Bren Gun, that is!' Arthur whispered. 'Nice one. Let's have it by here, you fire, I'll steady the stock!' They enjoyed the action for a while, picking off Germans in 5-round bursts, till above their whispering, they heard voices, and Arthur Mountain and Kennedy went out to look.

On a mound covered in scrubby grass sat the Cockney in the light-green flying jacket; beside him was the purple-haired woman, and she called, 'See who's here! The Hallelujah Man! He thinks we've all got souls!'

'This fucking plum?' the Cockney enquired. 'Why's he hanging around?'

'This is Dr Kennedy.'

'Is he sorting you a lung transplant, boyo?'

'We don't say "boyo" in Swansea,' Arthur said. He breathed a while through his nose, lips pursed. 'We say "butt". And he's a PhD, not a medic.'

'Where's his diploma?' the Cockney said, turning to Kennedy. 'Adolf Hitler locked you lot up in your own briefcases!' He looked sick as well, but he ground out the words successfully, cancerous vaudeville man.

Arthur Mountain took off his coat, handing it to Kennedy, then raised his shirt. 'Here's what this gentleman did to me at Waverley. 25 years I've lived with it. Still burns.' On his chest, Kennedy beheld the red cross with bent arms. 'All this time I've waited for him.'

'You haven't exactly been building your strength for the encounter, Taff,' the Cockney said. In a soiled tweed cap, the woman seemed older now than when Kennedy had seen her at the cricket, looking from Arthur to the farm down there.

'I've been running myself down on purpose. Give a scrut like you a fighting chance.'

'Hey–ho!' the Cockney said. Crooking his right leg, he drew from inside his jacket a long screwdriver, end sharpened. 'D'you wanna know?'

'That's the *Tacuara*,' Arthur said to Kennedy. 'Remember? Give me my coat, butty.' Kennedy passed Arthur's heavy leather coat back, and the latter took from it the empty rum bottle, which he broke end first against the pill-box. These must be their weapons; but the Cockney was thin, wasted, and Arthur's lungs were finished. Like old men now, both of them. The woman watched, hardly noticing Kennedy, then looked again toward the farm. At the roots, her hair was rusty grey. Surely she was no older than Kennedy – none of them was. Had these characters aged differently? Kennedy found himself in a strange state of terror and liveliness, as if modelling his own dream. Now the woman's face was animated with recognition. Looking at them again, she grinned like she was coming. Up the slope from the farm, a heavy figure was making his way, and on a thick lead he had a black bull terrier, surging, straining. He wore a white boiler suit.

'Well he hasn't been stinting himself at the luncheon table,' Arthur said. 'Look at him! Wunker can hardly walk. He's getting a tow from his dog!'

'He'll cut you a fresh arsehole!', the Cockney sung. 'Redecorate your guts.' In all they said, these figures were frightening and exact, while Kennedy still had not spoken; yet they scarcely moved. He was intent upon the scene on which they were somehow embossed, Fuzzy Felts, still, vivid things. But here came this dreadful stout figure whose pale eyes stood out from his chalky face, up the field behind his dog. When he arrived would it go off? With his screwdriver Voight squatted where he was; watching Kennedy greenly, Arthur held his jagged club: motionless the pair of them. On drove the fat man, hard by now, and Kennedy's wife and child a mile away. Should he see them again? There was whistling from the wood.

A figure emerged in a dark pullover, penetrating the stillness with 'Yankee Doodle Dandy', and over his shoulder he carried what looked like a crucifix as used in church ornamentation. But when he brought the object to waist height, it was a well-polished crossbow.

'Hey Cliff!' laughed Arthur Mountain. 'Over by here, mun! We're outnumbered! – Tell him what to do, Ken! Tell us what to do! Tell us all! Let's get it on!'

I don't know you! Don't know any of you! Kennedy whispered, and he tried to make his way to the track, where the sign said, 'It is an offence to drive on a footpath or public bridleway. Road Traffic Act 1988, Section 34.' But the figures were beginning to dance about him, and you know, it was like his feet were tied.

Acknowledgements

With half a dozen publishing houses like Route, Britain would see a literary renaissance. Thank you to Ian Daley and Isabel Galán for all they have given this book.

And thank you to these people for reading, inspiration and good cheer: Min Wild; Paul Bernhardt; Andrew Caink; David Cunningham; Gwen Davies; Saul Frampton; Monica Germanà; Nick Groom; Roy Harper; Paul Hendon; Seki P. Lynch; William ('Scotch Corner') MacRae; Annalisa McNamara; Ben McKay; Sas Mays; Jack Morgan; John Moser; Dave Nath; Paul Nath; Tony Nayager; A.T. Short; Steve Sims; Jack Sims; Louise Sylvester; Lorna Tracy; Alexandra Warwick; Leigh Wilson; Anne Witchard; Jessica Woollard.

Also: John Aubrey; Ian Brown; J.W. Goethe; Nigel Jenkins; William Shakespeare; Edmund Spenser; Paul Valéry; Kendall Walton; Orson Welles; Gwyn A. Williams; W.B. Yeats.

Michael Nath was brought up in South Wales and Lincolnshire. He is a senior lecturer in English at the University of Westminster. His major teaching and research interests are in Creative Writing and Modernism, as well as in Shakespearean Drama. His first novel, *La Rochelle*, was shortlisted for the James Tait Black Memorial Prize for Fiction.